DARK ANGEL

DARK ANGEL

WICKED ANGELS
BOOK ONE

LILITH DARVILLE

eBook ISBN: 978-1-998127-30-6
Paperback ISBN: 978-1-998127-33-7

Cover Design by Atra Luna Design (www.atraluna.de)
Editing by Kay Springsteen, Word Whisperer Literary Editing
(kayspringsteen.wordpress.com/word-whisperer-literary-editing/)

SOCAN: The song is Hearts Not Here. Red Dirt Skinners. From the Album Bear With Us (2021). Lyrics used with permission.

FRIEND & FAMILY ALERT

Hello Cherished Readers!

Once again, I've been accused of romanticizing abuse because my heroines don't always respond the way people expect abuse victims to react. Some say I don't know what I'm talking about, but I'll leave that debate aside. What I do know is that, as a survivor of emotional, physical, and sexual abuse who found healing through the wholehearted love of my Hubster, I represent one type of survivor—the thriver. There's a whole subset of us who choose to heal and break the cycle of abuse with determination and courage. These are the individuals I write about, and these are the stories I tell in the hope that they will reach those living in the midst of abuse, showing them that there is a glimmer of hope, that abuse can be overcome.

I've met well-meaning folks who offered various pieces of advice, including "sucking it up" and accepting abusive situations. But in my darkest times, it was romance novels that solidified my belief in the possibility of wholehearted, healthy love. Fairytales do come true—I am living proof. After enduring years of abuse, including an incident involving a drunken boyfriend that landed me in the hospital, I was drowning in despair, believing there was no way out. And then, Hubster walked in, the lead singer of a band I'd followed in high school but hadn't seen for months, with another bandmate.

"What are you doing here?" I asked in shock at the sight of these two gorgeous men, whom I barely knew, appearing at my hospital bed. They were members of a rock band who lived together on a farm, pursuing their dream of creating music.

At that time, he wasn't my Hubster, just a much older, incredibly handsome, and out-of-my-league rock singer. I was the teenage "loud" fan who had a bit of a love-hate relationship with him. High school ended, and I moved to the city, where I ended up with a man who turned out to be a deeply troubled alcoholic with a violent temper.

Hubster insisted on hearing all the "sordid" details and didn't stop pressing until he was satisfied he'd heard the whole story. Then he declared, "You're coming to live at the farm to recover."

His bandmate and I raised objections, but Hubster had a single-minded determination when he felt "the right thing" needed to be done. With a bit of arrogance mixed in, his response to objections was, "I'm the lead singer. This is what I want." And because he rarely asked for anything and was known for doing the right thing, all objections were silenced, some might say. That marked the start of our rather unusual and reverse romance (note, I said reverse romance, not reverse harem romance... hahaha). He not only encouraged me to embrace my strength as a woman and ignore criticism about my "manly" behavior, he insisted on it. We truly had a love story for the ages, and that love helped us both heal from childhood trauma. For me, he differed from one of the strongest heroes in romance novels in one way only: he wasn't a billionaire. He said that was my job. 😜

So yes, I write heroines and heroes who are strong, resilient, sometimes aggressive, and occasionally abrasive. Yes, I write characters who don't conform to societal norms. Because let me share a little secret, folks—most of us who break the cycle of abuse do so because we refuse to accept the norms that protect and, in some cases, encourage abuse in our society. I do it in the hope that, like me, there's someone out there who will read my stories about redemption and healing through love (yes, with some steamy bits thrown in) and hold onto that kernel of hope that will give them the resilience to survive, knowing there are better days ahead.

Keep reading and feeding your hopes, dreams, and fantasies! ❤️‍🔥

PS: For those who wish to join me on the quest for wholehearted living and loving, I highly recommend *I Thought It Was Just Me* by Brené Brown. It's a life changer!

1

JADEN

"Get that look off your face, or you're going to fuck this up, Jaden. Keep your macho testosterone bull-shit tucked away in your back pocket." Sasha, my childhood friend and partner in this madness pauses, punching my arm while piercing me with her steely eyes. "And do not kill anyone. We're here for one rescue, that's all."

I let my eyes wash over the dilapidated building where an air of abandonment masks the horror within its walls. Celestial magic hums through me with powers that never get old. I pull the power closer to me. Fuck off. I've got this. I pivot my head, mouth ready to spew my venom on her. Sasha gives me the hand and my mouth snaps shut. She's right. We've been following a trail of trafficker crumbs leading to the pimp, Viper, who runs the Ontario stable. The plan is to extract one crucial victim, a linchpin in our strategy. While my instincts scream to rescue them all, focusing on this specific target aligns with our meticulously crafted operation, Pandemonium Eruptus, designed to dismantle The Game from within.

Sasha straightens her broad shoulders and heads for

the desolate warehouse. Our shared determination and a pit bull approach brought us to this terrible place—a human slave stable—where women are sold to the highest bidder: men with enough money to satisfy their twisted depravity. We will rescue another innocent life. Is that what they call kidnapping these days?

Viper's making a public spectacle of this Vic and if she's been close enough to rattle his chains, she's been close enough to learn valuable intel about his trafficking operation. Intel I intend to gain . . . before damage turns to absolute ruin. One more step toward finding and killing the leaders of The Game, the national sex trafficking ring responsible for killing my fiancée.

Wind whistles through the warped sheet metal siding. I tug the collar of my leather jacket hardening my heart against the emotional pain we're about to witness as chill fall air chases the late afternoon sun. Shutters hang askew, flapping in the wind. Broken glass grinds under our feet as we make our way through the litter and detritus. The gleaming, solid steel door looks incongruous in the desolate terrain of the industrial graveyard.

I square my shoulders, preparing for the callous inhumanity we'll find within and ignore the niggling warning raising my heightened intuition. I can't shake the feeling that something's about to change my life and there's not a fucking thing I can do about it. "We have a special mission for one of your rescues. We task you with protecting her at all costs." The angel of death's words, long forgotten, choose this inconvenient moment to drop by for a visit. At all costs?

I am a killer. The celestials call me a warrior angel, but whatever the title, I destroy those who prey on the weak and defenseless. Mind games are my weapon of torture, although I favor my magic knives to deliver the killing blow. Truth be told, it's the mind games that give me juice. I rob scum of their identity and their precious assets until they wish they were dead.

I give payback to the most deserving by planting their dirty little secrets where they will do the most damage. Like dropping sexually explicit text messages to the unsuspecting wife of some rich bastard whose assets are in her name, exposing his true nature. But others need to be erased . . . period. Some might say I've lost my moral imperative. They would be wrong. I believe I've found it. I have zero tolerance for the pond scum who prey on innocent women and children. Make them suffer. Deal the killing blow . . . Walk away.

A blink is all it took for me to lose my goddamn mind and embark on this desperate path. A path where one misstep leads to certain death, where there is no room for emotion. All for the love of a woman . . . or so I told myself. My Savannah, who they took from me. My Savannah, who died in my arms. My Savannah, whose memory is inexorably linked to my soul. Something I will never forgive or forget. At least that's what I tell myself because that way, I don't have to face the demons that consume me—I couldn't save her, and I can't save myself.

Reckless with rage and single-minded obsession, I'd set about to make the fuckers who'd made Savannah suffer pay. No risk was too great. As long as I kept killing, I didn't have to think. On my own private vigilante quest, I'd taken foolish chances while I hunted down and erased her killers, almost getting myself killed in the process. On the brink of death, something miraculous happened. The angel of death appeared with a mission and the gift of magical powers. In exchange, I agreed to join a team of humans and supernaturals bringing retribution to predators who escape justice in the Earth realm.

Now, with the blessing of the celestials, I hunt men like Viper and make them pay for their sins. Most, I don't kill. That would be too easy. I make them suffer. Panic will do in the best of them. In most cases, they do me the favor of offing themselves. In the meantime, we rescued and reha-bilitated the victims who weren't already broken and lost. Only time would tell which camp our latest rescue falls into.

After talking our way past the muscle and brainless security at the door, Sasha and I stand in a damp basement room with crumbling cement walls. Small barred windows are set high on the walls, well out of reach. Exposed wiring snakes around damp rusted pipes. Dark stains that look a lot like blood decorate one corner. We find Whippo, the dirt bag snitch we've bribed, and let him know we've come to collect the goods. After the requisite whining on his side and threats on ours, he leads us into the pit where people considered human waste are held for their next owner.

Several bunk beds that have seen much better days line the walls. Women in various stages of undress and despair sit on several of them. The sharp tang of excrement, old blood, and rabid fear attacks my empathic senses. My new gift. My curse. Struggling not to gag, I have to stop myself from cringing as the long tendrils of their desperation try to encircle me. Sasha steps aside, her green eyes scanning the room.

Whippo locks the door behind us. I steel myself against the flinch as the lock slips home. Let me out. I push the thought from my mind and stop myself from punching Whippo as he leads us to a stack of rags lying on the floor next to a molding, bug-infested mattress on a lower bunk in the corner. A small still hand sticks out from under the pile of rags, yet nervous energy vibrates from it like the voltage from a power grid. Electromagnetic current arcs toward me and slams into my heart. It takes every neuron in my body not to react. In this world, any show of emotion is a sign of weakness.

"Get up. Kneel." The stupid bastard kicks the bundle of rags on the floor, eliciting a pain-filled grunt. Despite appearances, whoever lays there is on the alert, ready to spring and flee at any moment.

"Don't. Do. That." I clench my fists so hard I almost break the skin. *Keep your cool, Jaden.*

"Don't tell me my job, man," Whippo snarls back.

A slim brown finger shoots up from the rags. "You'll get your piece of me tonight and not before, you fucking asshole. Wasn't last night enough for you? Greedy bastard." The rage in the husky voice matches the solid defiance of the extended middle finger.

Whippo grasps a rag-doll girl and hoists her into the air. She glares at him through smeared glasses with eyes dark as a midnight sky. Her matted curls frame a face battered by hardship, yet filled with resistance. As she swings from his grip, desperately searching for the floor, she slaps Whippo's arm with surprising strength.

"Get your goddamn hands off me!" she snarls, her voice ripped with defiance. Her words, though tinged with bravado, tremble with a hint of vulnerability. I catch her eyes once more, and within those dark pools, I glimpse something akin to hope—fragile, nearly extinguished, but not quite dead. Something that speaks to the darkness in my soul.

My insides combust with a blend of unwanted emotions—anger, curiosity, and another sensation I can't quite put my finger on. These feelings shoot through me like electricity, yet something about this filthy, dirty, defiant yet delicate little thing I'm assigned to protect draws me in.

Whippo pulls his arm back. I catch it mid-swing and let the stinging vibration run up my arm. The man has muscle and might be a formidable match if we have to go nose to nose.

Whippo's head swivels toward me. "What the fuck, man?"

"I'll take it from here." I lock eyes with him while he debates whether he can take me. I almost hope he'll try; I'm spoiling for a fight. I narrow my eyes at Whippo, letting my disgust wash over him like a tidal wave. "Get out of our way. We've paid your price, now you'll do as we say." The venom in my voice leaves no room for argument, and he lets her go while releasing a foul stench of fear.

My gaze locks with hers and a surge of energy crackles through my fractured soul. Swollen lids barely conceal the spark of intelligence and curiosity behind her rage-filled eyes. She masks a deeper layer of uncertainty and longing beneath her bravado, then just as quickly it slips away and the light in her orbs fades. Still, she never looks away, even shifting her glasses up on her nose with her index finger. Sasha tenses beside me, ready to pounce and protect me. I subtly unfurl my fingers, signaling her to stay still. Sasha stills.

"Don't know about this," Whippo's nasal voice makes me flex my fist. Now, he decides to have doubts? "Viper going to be goddamned nitro about this. He has plans for little Miss Destiny here. Five hundred bucks ain't worth getting killed for. We'd better call this off." Whippo's whining reminds me of a large, annoying insect. In this world, everyone can be bought, and he's just told me his fee. I sigh and hand him five hundreds. "Better now?"

Whippo grabs the bills and releases Destiny. She stumbles to her knees. He wiggles his fingers for another bill. I clamp my teeth and hand over another hundred.

"How old is this kid, anyway? What plans? You never said anything about plans." I spin bullshit as I take a step toward Whippo, getting up close and personal.

Something just doesn't smell right and maybe he knows more than I give him credit for. Our intel confirmed Viper intends to make an example of this particular victim at one of his infamous pimp circle parties. However, there isn't usually violence at a slave stable, at least nothing beyond the usual slaps, pinches, and the occasional earlobe twist. They like to keep the goods in working order—the better they look, the more money they fetch. Finding a victim with such obvious injuries is highly unusual.

Within these grim, putrefying walls, the menace breathes, a cruel beast lurking in the shadows, ready to strike at the slightest provocation. Whippo, the embodiment of this menace, snivels and stammers, his reptilian eyes darting about, sniffing out the prospect of treachery or money.

"Plans?" Whippo's voice cracks, and he swallows hard, his Adam's apple bobbing. "That ain't none of my business. She's fourteen, maybe. But Viper wants her for something special. Something big's coming down, and this kid's a part of it." His eyes gleam with avarice. He chews on his bottom lip, his mind calculating risks and rewards.

I can feel the weight of Sasha's gaze, a burning intensity that speaks to the shared purpose that has led us down this harrowing path. Her presence resonates with a silent, steadfast support. This world, the monstrous reality we've immersed ourselves in, is a cancerous growth on the soul of humanity. Yet we persist, driven by an unyielding mission to obliterate the disease, one festering sore at a time.

Sasha steps forward and runs her finger down Whippo's arm. "Can we go now, sugah. You gonna get me in trouble with the man. I need to clean her up and get her all pretty. She's got to make us some money." Sasha shimmies up against him, grabs his sack and squeezes, making sure he has no second thoughts. "Oh my, you really are a big boy."

Whippo startles. and his eyes dart to me. I give my don't-give-a-fuck shrug.

Sasha steps even closer and murmurs, "Want to take me for a test run?" She squeezes his junk harder.

I suppress a smile as Whippo struggles to find his bravado. He doesn't seem to notice Sasha backing him to the door. I bury the internal eye roll and hunker down, keeping my gaze fastened on the ragged woman kneeling at my feet. She tugs the moth-eaten blanket, quickly covering an orange tube top, a short pink skirt and ripped fishnet stockings. An outfit so dreadful it can't be a mistake. Between the fresh bruises dotting her skin like cans of paint thrown on canvas, her skin is the most beautiful shade of caramel. I lock eyes with hers and am rewarded with a jet stream of pure hatred before she lowers her eyes. But I swear I saw a flash of connection, of recognition. What the fuck is wrong with you, Jaden?

"We've got work to do." I turn to Whippo and give him my most forbidding "get lost" look. "Thanks, man."

I breathe a sigh of relief as Whippo leaves the room. We must get Destiny out of this place. Now. I look at Sasha, and she gives a slight nod. Ten years of hanging together twenty-four-seven means we rarely need words to convey our thoughts.

The VIC, Destiny, scrambles to her feet, pride etched in every line of her face. "I'm not going anywhere with you unless you tell me who you are and why I should trust you."

"We're here to help," I reply, the words feeling foreign on my tongue. "We're getting you out of this nightmare. But we need your cooperation."

"Help?" she scoffs, her voice tinged with skepticism, yet her eyes betray a longing to believe. "What's in it for you?"

I step closer, close enough to smell the stench of her captivity, to see the spark that refuses to die. "Justice," I say softly. Her eyes widen at the word, a flicker of understanding passing between us.

Sasha steps forward and firmly grabs Destiny's chin. "We're not going to hurt you."

Destiny jerks her head away and glares in return. Her muscles tense, ready to spring. Great.

"Are we going to do this the easy way or the hard way?" Sasha reaches out a hand. Destiny slaps it away. "Have it your way."

Sasha grips a pressure point near Destiny's neck. "Nighty night, sweetheart," she whispers. Destiny struggles. Sasha holds firm . . . eight, nine, ten. When Destiny slumps to the floor, Sasha picks her up and sweeps out of the room.

I follow a few beats behind ensuring they get safely out of the building. One slip, one show of weakness, and I will lose my foothold in this cesspool. And that could mean the difference between life and death.

2

DESTINY

I thought I knew all there was to know about pain. A universe of suffering encapsulated in the battered vessel of my body, but it turns out I don't. Every fucking cell within me howls, a symphony of torment. It's my just desserts, my self-made requiem for opening my goddamned big mouth and back-talking Viper. Words escape like wild horses, unchecked and reckless. Then, insanity entwined with rage, I slapped him.

The tactile memory of his assault lingers, as if his fingers are still there, violating my very existence. I kept telling him to fuck off—silently, a scream trapped within a cage of fear. Once, it slipped out, an "Oops" in the midst of horror.

He hurled me against the unforgiving wall, a dance of cruelty and lust. My reflex was primal—I spat, I slapped, I resisted. Time splintered as he slammed my head, a staccato rhythm of brutality I lost count of, sometimes losing consciousness and perhaps a part of myself. He added kicks, an encore to my suffering. The constant pain that has marked my small frame whispers the haunting melody of violation.

I lie now, feigning sleep, clothed in rags and invisibility, until Whippo's kick jars me. An irritation, a reminder of the world's injustice. My middle finger's response is an involuntary rebellion, a tiny spark of defiance in the darkness.

Then, another figure appears, enormous and wreathed in an aura of danger, a tornado of dread and power. His presence ignites a sensation within me, a tremor of fear and anticipation. My eyes meet his, and for a fleeting moment, I see compassion in his wolf-like gaze. A flicker of humanity before the mask of the predator falls back into place.

He stops Whippo from striking, a surprising act of kindness that leaves me stunned and momentarily speechless. No one has ever stood up for me, no one has ever seen me, but he does. In his deep tan eyes, a blend of races and histories, I glimpse the angel of my dreams, a tantalizing mirage of salvation and desire.

But dreams die, and hope is a dangerous illusion. I can't trust him, can't allow myself to be ensnared by false promises. My past screams a cautionary tale, a bitter lesson I've learned time and time again. I choose to hate him, even as a part of me longs to believe.

Whippo stammers, his false bravado crumbling before the mountain of muscle in front of him. I almost smile, almost forget the impending nightmare of the party where my body will be a plaything, where my very soul will be flayed and torn.

The man and his towering companion approach, and the battle within me ignites anew. They won't take me without a fight; they won't separate me from my sister. Even as darkness descends, my mind sharpens, ready to confront the storm.

The woman's pinch is a sharp reminder of reality, a sting that propels me into action. My muscles tense, ready to strike, to defy, to survive as her grip tightens. The world narrows, and I am a creature of instinct and fury, a wild thing cornered but unbroken. Darkness descends, but my spirit blazes, a beacon in the night.

I startle awake, a wave of panic sweeping over me like a sudden storm, every sense instantly sharpened, alive. My pulse isn't just racing; it's relentless, savage drumming, a furious echo of my disquiet. Where am I? Where is Summer? My eyes remain shut, my body poised on the precipice of flight. That's always been my fatal flaw—leaping without looking, plunging headlong into chaos. Usually, it's just words that betray me, but oh, how life loves to remind me of my overconfidence.

A strange golden light sears behind my eyes, pulling me back to that moment with him—the monster, the kidnapper. Bronze eyes that whispered secrets and unknown promises. Those eyes haunt me now, distracting me from the urgent reality . . . while at the same time bringing me a sense of belonging or peace. As if he's the one I'm meant to be with. I shake my head at my fanciful thoughts. Love? A fantasy I'm never destined to find. A cruel joke played by Fate. My slave name, Destiny, is a bitter reminder, a taunt. Now is not the time for dreams or regrets. Now is the time to save my very life.

I lie motionless, forcing my heart to slow its wild dance. Panic clouds judgment, and clear thinking is my only weapon. I find solace in the wisdom of books, those faithful companions. With a mental tug, I wrestle my anxiety into submission, sending a silent plea into the universe—keep Summer safe. Not that I believe in gods or prayers. The pious sicken me, especially those who wield faith like a weapon. But caution is my ally in this dark moment.

A pang of agony washes over me, a sudden deluge of fears and regrets, memories and nightmares. I let the pain flood in, filling me with the terror that they may kill Summer before I can save her. Sharp needles of self-pity sew threads around my wounded heart. None of this is our fault. The injustice of it claws at my soul, but there are no tears. There is only resolve. It's up to me to save us. I stand alone.

My self-reflection is cut short as I take stock of my situation. The rags I'm clothed in cling to my body like a grim reminder of my reality. I've been kidnapped, not rescued by Prince Charming. At least my dignity remains untouched, though I can't help but cringe at my own scent. A bath, once a simple pleasure, has become a desperate need. But fatigue overwhelms me and I slip back into the abyss.

I awaken, nestled warmly in a bed that whispers of luxury and bears the faint, calming scent of lavender. The shabby warehouse, those lifeless motels that have been the dismal backdrop to my existence these last weeks, feel distant. My terror ebbs, melting into the pool of anxiety that never leaves my side. Surely if they were going to hurt me, they would have done it by now. Wishful thinking! The very fabric of my being strains, listens, reaching out to the unseen, touching only white noise, bird song, and the caress of leaves in the wind.

Curiosity, that ever-present companion of mine, nudges

my fear aside just enough to allow my eyes to open—a mere sliver—and I explore the room without moving my head. The world's a blur, yet it's enough to detect any shift in the air, any sign of presence. No one. The room breathes emptiness. Gingerly, I push up on my elbows, and the silence greets me still. Huh... highly peculiar behavior for a pimp. Yet, I sense the watchful eyes of my captors, hiding in shadows.

Where the hell are my glasses? My eyes' trusted allies, gone, leaving me vulnerable. My heart drums a rhythm of warning, but I'm anchored, unwilling to move until I'm sure I'm not dancing at the edge of a precipice.

My other senses surge forth, warriors on high alert, searching for that sound, that presence. But the house hums its own song, mingling with nature's chorus. I close my eyes, diving into myself.

Like a storm unleashed, my mind hurtles into hyperdrive. I cloak myself in anger, letting it eclipse the intense fear threatening to devour me. Fear of the past, the betrayals, the monsters that walk in human form. Pure, untamed rage floods my veins, fuels me, becomes my fortress.

The memories loom, specters in the dark. My stepfather, a vermin of a man, trading Summer and me for gambling debts. His face flashes before me, twisted and greedy, and I'm filled with a revulsion that tastes like bile. I would die before letting them own me. But not Summer. Sweet, fragile Summer, surrendering her soul, piece by piece, until all that remained was a shell, a mannequin's vacant stare. My heart aches with the memory, a wound that never heals.

Summer's essence drifts in my mind, a fragile thread that connects us. My intuition, my hidden gift, reaches out to her. The world once scorned it, labeled me mad, but it's my compass, my secret strength. All I find now is murky fog, but it tells me she breathes still.

A quick glance around, a touch to my own skin—no new injuries, just the map of my survival etched in scars and bruises. Did they drug me? Kidnap me? Ransom me? My mind spins, but I shake the thoughts away. This room, this moment, is my reality. I must face it, explore it, understand it. Everything else is mere shadows and whispers, echoing in the chambers of the unknown.

The lavish surroundings tell me I'm in the den of the very wealthy. The contemporary design, minimalistic elegance, no photos—it's a world foreign to me yet oddly fascinating. It's a fantasy, yet my intuition tells me there's something more, something special about my captor. A sizzle, a connection, something unspoken and mysterious that tugs at the edges of my consciousness. But for now, it remains a puzzle, a secret waiting to be unraveled.

Men forcing me brings me back to reality. Most of the girls said their minds left their bodies, that they didn't feel or remember anything. Not I. The drugs couldn't drown out the visceral memories of the stinking, sweating bodies, their movements a grotesque dance that still lingers in the corners of my mind. No matter how hard I strained to detach, to drift into oblivion, I remained tethered. Bound to the reality, even as the drugs kept me dull-witted and numb. Viper, his very name a snake's hiss, had one of his vile henchmen glued to me, shadowing every move. A sudden flare of indignation erupts within me: What have we ever done to deserve this? I quell the surge, banishing it down the dark path of self-pity. Later. There will be time enough for that later.

Summer. Her name is a balm, a flicker of warmth in the icy void. I turn inward, reaching for that delicate thread where I touch her soul with my intuition, my so-called "spidey sense." It's a secret I've guarded fiercely, ever since the day I confided in an aunt only to watch the word of my "psychosis" spread through our fractured family like wildfire. I sigh, a weary exhalation, and refocus. When I tune in, all I find is murky fog, a nebulous sensation that tells me she's alive. But it's a whisper, faint and distant, and my heart aches with the longing to know more.

Another quick glance around the room, a cursory survey that reveals no immediate danger. My eyes drift down, examining my own form. No new injuries, except for the bruise blooming where that blond fiend pinched me. My lips tighten at the thought. Should our paths cross again, she'll feel the bite of my words. My stature may be small, but my tongue wields a sharpness that can slice through the toughest armor.

The taste of dust coats my mouth, dry and gritty, and a band of pressure tightens around my head—a testament to whatever they used to render me unconscious. My body bears the marks of my survival, the physical toll that life has extracted, each scar and bruise a chapter in a story written in flesh and blood. Questions churn, relentless. Why the drugs? Why the kidnapping? Ransom? A bitter laugh escapes me. Viper won't rest until he finds me, his darkness a black hole from which there is no escape. Am I merely bait? I shake the thought away. Now is not the time for speculation, for shadows and echoes. This is my reality, stark and demanding. Deal with it.

"Justice." His faint word whispers through my mind.

The room around me, with its minimalist elegance and contemporary design, offers a surreal contrast to my turbulent thoughts. That these people are loaded is evident, yet it's all surface, an opulent facade that can't quite hide the underlying tension. My intuition stirs again, a sizzle, a connection I can't quite place. . . disturbing yet intriguing. The man who brought me here, my captor, is not what he seems. Something more lurks beneath the surface, a mystery that beckons, tantalizing and elusive. I don't know where I am, but I know I'm on the brink of something profound, a dance at the edge of understanding. But for now, it remains a question without an answer, a song without words.

A groan claws at my throat, but I stifle it, swinging my legs over the side of the bed as a throb of pain pulses in my head. It's a dance of agony, an intimate embrace with suffering . . . and it's not the kind of dance I like. My head swims, a whirlpool of confusion and nausea. I rest a minute, forearms on my skinny little thighs, gulping air like a fish out of water. When the sickness passes, I raise my head, feeling the weight of exhaustion draped over my shoulders. The luxurious bed is a siren, teasing me with the promise of oblivion. But no time for that now—I've got to get my ass in gear and get my shit together.

My glasses. Please let them be— My silent prayer cuts off, a symphony of relief, as I find them on the minimalist bedside table and slide them on. The world sharpens, new lenses bringing life into focus. Sweet. They fixed them. My smile withers quickly as realization blooms. How long was I out? Is this some cruel illusion? Those magnetic eyes sear into my mind, leaving a sizzle of connection, of belonging. Will I see him again?

Hate surges, a violent tide, as I take in the luxury surrounding me. Surprise and curiosity momentarily blanket my fear, and I flop back, moaning as my sore torso meets the queen-size bed with its artfully dropped ceiling, forming a modern canopy—an eight-foot embrace. To my left, a window stretches like a glimpse into another world, twelve or fifteen feet from floor to ceiling. A view of a vast body of water lies before me, like a great lake, its surface a mirror to my confusion. The sun is aloft; the world outside has moved on without me.

Where the hell am I? How long have I been here? If my screaming need for fluid is any indication, it's been at least a couple of days.

The room is an echoing chasm of opulence. Midway across, a dividing wall houses a glassed-in gas fireplace, a beacon of contemporary design. A round wood table, surrounded by inviting chairs, sits on the other side, a large vase of lilacs at its center as does a pitcher of water and a pretty glass. It's a stage set for comfort, yet the luxury only twists the knife of anxiety. The whispers of other girls haunt me, tales of wealthy men who bought and broke them. Viper's venomous words about my appeal slither through my mind. "Daddy kink is big business," he'd say. My youthful appearance is no blessing here.

I rise, heart hammering a desperate rhythm, waiting for the next wave of horror to wash over me. A lesson learned in the dark corners of life: joy is a prelude to pain. I stand stock-still, holding my breath, my senses sharpening, reaching for any sign I'm not alone. No Viper... I'd sense him. His brutality would be a storm, tearing the place apart. He's nowhere, and yet his shadow lingers. Nothing subtle about that man.

Pain and tension stretch through my body as I roam the room, examining my luxurious prison. Everything is ultra-modern every single thing looks more expensive than anything I'll ever be able to afford. I don't know a lot about decorating, but everything speaks of extravagance. The door's unlocked, a silent invitation. But I know better. An unlocked door in a rich guy's mansion doesn't mean freedom—it whispers of surveillance, of unseen eyes watching.

A knock rattles the silence, and I freeze. Memories of Viper's cruel regimen rush to the forefront, but I push them away, straightening my back. I won't bow, not again. My new captors will learn I'm no meek prey. *Yeah right.*

A second knock, impatient. "For Christ's sake, Destiny, would you open the goddamned door?" That voice, edged with irritation—it's her.

Destiny. A name that tastes like ash. My pulse quickens as I summon my courage, testing the waters. "Leave me alone."

"Oh, for God's sake." A crash, and she's inside, a loaded tray in hand. She's all sharp angles, her eyes like weapons. I sink to the floor, feeling her scrutiny, a judgment passed without words. "Get up off the goddamned floor."

I stay put, a stubborn ember refusing to be snuffed.

Her disdain is clear. "Fine, stay there for all I care. Your brunch is on the table. Eat. Looks like you haven't had a good meal in months." At the press of a button, the windows shade, turning opaque. Smart glass. Fascinating and terrifying, all at once.

Her words continue, clipped and brisk, telling me about clothes, meals, the new reality I've been thrust into. But I can't help it; I need to know more. "What's your name? Where am I? Why am I here? You can't hold me against my will, you know."

Silence.

Then, chillingly calm: "Are you talking to me?"

That voice is like ice, cutting through me. Damn, I messed up, pushed when I should've been careful. The weight of what's really going on starts to sink in. I've seen some stuff, but this is something else, hidden behind all the fancy crap and pretty things. It's not just money; there's something else going on here.

The answers to my questions? They're just hanging there, like some unspoken dare. Who's this ice queen glaring at me? What's with this place that feels more like a gilded cage? And those eyes, staring into me like they know something I don't—what's up with that? It's all a tangled mess, and I'm right in the middle of it.

I'm stuck in this maze of riches and secrets, and finding my way out feels like grasping at straws in a pitch-black room. But there's something else poking at my brain. A connection, a vibe or something, and I can't shake it—it's there, hanging around like a ghost.

I give a nod, but my eyes are still on some invisible dirt on the floor.

She laughs, that husky sound she's got. "Name's Sasha Byrne. My bad, I should've told you that sooner. Jaden Stone's the one who got you out of that mess. You're in his crib now. Why? Good question. And hey, you can hit the road whenever you want. But for now, get up."

Here we go. I brace myself, pulling in a sharp breath, waiting for the beating to hit. I get to my feet, but my eyes are locked on some spot that doesn't really exist.

Sasha's there, right in front of me, and I'm trying my hardest not to back away. I hate pain, yeah, but what I hate more is looking weak. Her hand shows up in my sight, and I can't help but twitch a bit. She grabs my right hand, and her fingers, strong and warm, wrap around mine.

She's looking for a handshake? I awkwardly grab her hand back, and she gives it a firm squeeze, yanking me up.

"That wasn't so bad, huh? Now spill, what's your name?"

Time to play dumb. "Destiny," I mumble, keeping my head down but stealing glances at her from the corner of my eye.

Sasha's standing there, towering over me like some fierce warrior chick, even though she's probably only about five-eight without those massive heels. Slim, blonde, blue-eyed, and rocking those jeans and leather jacket like they're a second skin. She's seriously fit and gorgeous, and I can't help but hate her a bit. But also, I kind of want to be as badass as her. And is she with Jaden? Jealousy slams into me before I can think about it, but then she's turning away.

With an elegant shrug, she says, "Okay, we're here if you need to chat. Your call. You're safe. I'm outta here for a few, but Jaden's around if you need something. Just chill and get better."

Leaving me here? With him? Alone? Panic jumps in my throat, but I'm not sure why I'd think Sasha's less dangerous. I can't think about that right now, though.

"Where am I, really?" I shoot back. "How do I know it's safe here?" Her answer might help me figure out this whole twisted puzzle. Maybe.

3
JADEN

The room is dim, lit only by the pale glow of the monitors. Each screen is another eye, another layer of control, but since she's arrived, they're all trained on Destiny. I broke my own rules bringing her here, to my private space. I could've taken her to Harmony Hills, a fortress of a rehab center, but I didn't. *She matters.* That thought is an itch in the back of my mind, a contradiction to everything I've known and believed. So is the strange current streaming through me since the moment our eyes met.

Love and all that romantic nonsense have been dead to me since I was a teenager. I've used the appeal of victims to bait traps for predators, sure, but never have I let any of them breach my personal walls. So, what the hell is so different about her? Why do I feel compelled to be with her?

I lead a regimented life; that's how I like it. Sasha, Steve —they're the exceptions to my rule of keeping everyone at arm's length. My life is a pattern: work, eat, sleep. For physical needs, there are Masquerade Clubs, brief dalliances

that hold my attention for a time. It's clear-cut, uncompli-
cated—temporary, always.

Nighttime is for the hunt, for taking down human filth.
Daytime, that's for my security firm. I've got a knack for
cybersecurity—a gift amplified by some not-so-natural
abilities—and both the government and corporations pay
me well for it. Opportunities are everywhere, more than I
need, more than I can handle.

But here I sit, watching her instead of tackling pressing
contracts. *She matters.* There it is again—that unsettling
thought. She stirs something in me, something I've locked
away deep inside since my teens. Since.... I slam the door to
that past shut in my mind. I force myself to look away, to
refocus.

After they killed Savannah, something else inside of me
ruptured. Life now holds one purpose and one purpose
only: find and kill the men responsible for the rape and
murder of my fiancée. *Men who rape innocent children.*

In the aftermath of her brutal end, that crack irrevocably altered who I was. In the weeks following her death,
my focus narrowed. The doctor in me retreated, replaced by
a man hell-bent on retribution. Each day became a hunt,
each name crossed off the list a grim milestone. My path
was dark and blood-soaked, a precipitous slide that nearly
cost me everything, until celestial forces intervened. An
offer from the Tribunal—redemption for service—pulled
me back from the edge, transforming me from mere mortal
to something more. An avenger with a heavenly edge.

Now, the hunt is different, but the mission remains the
same. The bloodlust has been replaced by a different kind
of warfare, one that unfolds in the shadows of the digital
world. We find these human stains and, with surgical precision, dismantle their lives. Financial ruin, social isolation—

it's a long, drawn-out unraveling that leaves them with nothing. In this line of work, erasing someone's digital footprint is far more brutal than any physical act of violence. The slow exquisite mind fuck I've perfected makes them suffer in a way no physical torture can.

In this relentless pursuit, a quest that's washed away whatever innocence I once clung to, I find myself mired in "The Game." It's a dark underside to southwestern Ontario's polished exterior. The notion of "The True North, strong and free," feels like a farce when you're wading through this filth. Canada may boast a lot of good, but its evils are cavernous.

Sasha, my partner in this, relishes the more brutal aspects of our work. Her penchant for sadism is, in a way, its own weapon. Yet it's rarely necessary. When we strip these criminals of their financial and personal identity, they usually self-destruct, crumbling under the weight of their sudden irrelevance. A poetic sort of justice.

The object of our current focus is a woman, a twist that neither shocks nor deters me. Together with Sasha and our covert team, we've navigated the maze of this operation, tearing through its layers until one name surfaces again and again: Viper. He's the linchpin, and his downfall will be the domino that triggers the rest. Word on the Net says he's pissed, which is good. Emotion clouds judgment, a weakness I intend to exploit.

Is this what I live for? It's a jarring thought that disrupts the focused stream of my mission. No, this isn't living; it's survival. It's walking a fine line between an ambiguous moral code and a form of justice only the desperate could rationalize. But desperate or not, it's the line I walk, each step carefully measured, each decision a testament to the man I've become.

I lean closer to the screen, zeroing in on Destiny's every move. She's hard to read—taking her sweet time like she's looking for something specific. A mix of curiosity, fear, and some weird x-factor whizzes through the link we've got, as if her brain's flipping through a bunch of options. It's disconcerting, to say the least. It triggers something deep in me, a feeling I can't remember having for a long time. But hey, I'm a pro at pushing away emotions. The way she moves reminds me of my cat—elegant but always on edge. That unsettling feeling in my gut kicks up again. I quickly lock it up and turn back to Destiny's image on the screen.

No hits on facial recognition, just an old Facebook account. So, she's a mystery. How did she even end up in this situation? She doesn't look naive, and she definitely doesn't look like an easy target.

I grab my hair and tip my head back, staring at the ceiling. Why the hell should I care? She's an informant, maybe even bait, and that's it. My usual concern for women in her situation is pretty straightforward: help them get the resources they need to move on. But the first time our eyes locked? That moment's burned into my brain. It wasn't just irritation at this assignment. It was something more. I saw the child she's never had the chance to be, hidden behind walls she built for self-preservation. And something else struck me deeper, as if she sees me on a cellular level. Again, I acknowledge it's unsettling. I find myself wanting more— her thoughts, her trust, her everything, given freely. I smack my forehead, trying to shake off these thoughts that are way out of character for me. *Get your act together, Jaden.*

Pulling myself back to the task at hand, I'm still puzzled by Destiny. She doesn't act like the women I've dealt with in similar situations. She hugged herself for a while after Sasha left then attacked her food as if she hadn't eaten in days. Her slow movements suggest she's in pain—cracked ribs, probably. But from what I can tell, no broken bones, just a lot of bruises and cuts.

She's a wildcard, not fitting any molds, and that makes her interesting. And, for reasons I don't fully understand yet, increasingly hard to ignore.

Her movements trace a captivating ballet across the monitor, a dance somewhere between grace and vigilance. Suddenly, the unbidden fantasy of Destiny in a gym—her body pressed against the mat, sweaty and defiant—surfaces. What kind of boxer would she turn out to be? Would she play the mind games I revel in? Float like a butterfly, sting when least expected. No knockout is planned for her, not now. The image of her, small and vulnerable under me, makes me go rock hard. A drawn-out sigh escapes as I make a subtle adjustment to my junk, tearing my eyes away to answer a slew of emails. The woman needs time to adjust, I rationalize, but one eye keeps straying back to the screen. You're dodging, a quiet voice accuses. No, I vehemently deny, I'm not.

Instead of taking the well-trodden path—the one where Destiny would be safely delivered to the rehab facility sponsored by our black-ops funds—I veer off in a different direction. I bring her into my personal space, a domain hitherto untouched by the chaos I combat. The finances to set her up with a year's rent and a job aren't an issue. The ill-gotten gains we recover from the human traffickers more than pays for the recovery, treatment and of the Harmony Hills Treatment facility. But money isn't an issue as I've amassed enough, not through my own business sense—I have none—but thanks to Sasha and Steve who steer the ship. The minutiae? That's for the accountant.

I catch myself. What's so different this time that she's here, in my sanctuary? I almost sigh but catch it, turning again to the monitor. There's something about her that gnaws at me, like a pebble stuck in my shoe.

Her next move captures me entirely. I'm riveted as she combs through every nook and cranny of the suite. I pretend not to care, yet I'm glued to her every action. She paces, stops, and seemingly debates whether to open that door and step into the corridor. Instead, she leaves it closed and folds into herself.

What is she searching for? Bugs? I discard the thought. She's not from a world where hidden cameras are a given. And yet, her fingers trace every object as though reading Braille, gleaning stories from inanimate things. She pivots, eyes scanning her environment one last time, and then her gaze pauses ... as if she's looking through the lens, straight into my core.

In that fleeting exchange, something perilous stirs within me—a tremor in the fortress I've built around my emotions. It's as if not just the digital screen but years of meticulously constructed defenses lie between us. Yet, her eyes seem to recognize something in me that I've long denied. This is the impasse, a tantalizing blend of allure and vulnerability I never wanted to confront. I'm caught in the gravity of an unspoken question: What's the next move in this mysterious game we're unwillingly cast into?

My attention is cemented to the screen, grappling with a reality that's stubbornly testing my technological invincibility. She found them, every hidden eye, as if she could sense the gaze that follows her. Her disappearance into the bathroom leaves a void, an absence that stirs an uncomfortable feeling in my gut until she reemerges with a gaze so piercing, it nearly fractures the lens.

Faces don't lie, at least not to me. I've honed a skill, a craft that's become my shield in a world rife with illusion. And there it is—a fleeting crack in her armor, a slight contraction of brow, a tautening of her lips shrouding a core of pure, undiluted fear.

She stands swathed in a Turkish towel that all but engulfs her, leveling her gaze at the camera, at me. Our eyes lock in a silent duel, time elongating like taffy pulled taut. What is she looking for? What chasms of my psyche is she probing? I shake off the disquieting thought; that's terrain better left unexplored.

A sigh escapes her lips, a releasing of pent-up tension, as she sheds the towel and slowly submerges into the water. The steam rises, tendrils beckoning like the fingers of temptation. My body rebels, a surge of unwanted desire rippling through me. I muzzle the urge, framing it as sterile observation. But my inner voice scoffs, disdainful of the lie.

She scrubs at her bruises like she's trying to wash away more than just dirt, wincing but not letting up. It's as if she's ridding herself of filth that goes way beyond just getting clean. As her hands roam to her torso, my gaze tightens. The canvas of her skin is marred, a gruesome tapestry of her recent past. My scrutiny narrows on her breast, where a grotesque bruise defiles her left areola. A tempest churns within me—retribution looms on the horizon.

This is more than mere observation; it's a plunge into a chaotic pool of conflicting sensations and unsolicited yearnings. As I sit here, the boundaries blur—between protector and intruder, between control and frailty. It's a precipice that threatens to consume me, prompting a soul-searching reckoning about the precarious tightrope I'm walking. And it's an epiphany that startles, compelling me to ponder the fragile line that separates power from vulnerability.

Destiny's bathing ritual comes to an end as she settles into the water. Her sigh is like the soft murmur of a distant brook. My junk does a back flip, but I stamp it out, almost wincing at the effort.

The bathroom window offers a crafted view of a tranquil Japanese garden, flanked by sentinel trees. It's enchanted many—like Sasha and Steve. But Destiny hardly glances its way. Instead, she methodically explores the lineup of grooming products on the marble counter. It's a meticulous act that I can't help but appreciate, sort of mirroring my own habits. A bit OCD, maybe?

She picks a bottle of unscented lotion and applies it with focused intent. Every movement screams of a decision, of a plan coming to life.

Destiny moves to the dressing room. Contrary to my weirdly baseless expectations of her choosing something delicate, she opts for athletic wear that breathes a resilient aura. I need to check myself; my assumptions are getting ahead of me.

Now that she's clean and clothed, she doesn't scout the area for escape routes as I half-expected. Instead, she sits down in an easy chair and looks straight into the camera—into me—as if asking, "What's the next move?" She's an intriguing bundle of contrasts: sometimes elegant, sometimes twitchy, but now perfectly still. We're in a visual standoff.

I can't shake this weird feeling in my gut—like I'm connected to her on a level that's more than just basic instinct. She shouldn't know I'm watching, but she gives a compelling performance of someone who does. It throws me off, leaves me unsettled. She's a mix of everything unpredictable and fascinating, a challenge to my senses and thoughts. I'm on the edge, a thin line between clarity and an unsettling ambiguity.

I break the gaze first, a quiet thank you to whatever force governs luck that she can't see my internal struggle. *Or can she?* Hands go through my hair in frustration. What was I thinking, bringing her here? Enough stalling, Jaden. I can only glean so much from a screen; real intuition needs proximity. I hit the intercom button.

"Meet me in the hallway."

She surveys the intercom and pushes the button. "Why?" Her voice is laced with caution but tinged with challenge. She seems to brace herself, shoulders squaring like she's armoring up.

I stay silent.

"Alright."

I leave the security of my combination high-tech lair, medical clinic and safe room and head for the elevator sighing heavily as I always do when I have to leave the shelter of my cave. It's a mix of necessity and reluctance that gets me every time I have to step out of my sanctuary. The elevator ride up gives me time to detach from a space that's more than just walls and tech—it's a piece of me. As I head down the hall leading to the bedrooms and near her, her eyes size me up. A complex evaluation, as if she's peering into my inner soul.

"Follow me."

She obeys, but the silent barbs she shoots into my back are almost evident as she walks quietly behind me. We enter the *pièce de résistance* of my space, the solarium. She gasps audibly and moves toward the glass.

"Oh wow, this is incredible. You live here? Up on a

mountain? Never met anyone who lived so high up. Aren't you—"

I cut her off. "You sure have a lot to say, don't you?" I almost question her newfound interest in my home but stop myself. Can't let her know I've been watching. "How I live isn't your concern."

Her body tenses, and she shoots me a glance that might as well be a vocal 'How Rude,' then lowers her gaze. "I apologize."

Regaining composure, I opt for a more measured tone. "Destiny—"

She moves so quickly that she's in front of me before I even realize it. "Let's get to it."

And there we are, the two of us suspended in this charged space. The atmosphere is dense with unspoken words and tensions, an unseen but deeply felt layer that distances, yet strangely connects us. She fiddles with my zipper. I grab her wrists and push her away. "Get the fuck off me." Reflexive contempt drips from my tone and expression before I can stop it.

Her body shrinks into itself, forming a protective shell as she rubs her wrists. Goddammit.

"What are you doing? This isn't what I had in mind." *Don't touch me.* I layer disdain over my vicious tone.

"I'm trying to give you a hand job." Her gaze anchors to the floor. "Viper says guys want blow or hand jobs, and if I give them one, they won't hurt me. I'd rather stick with the hand job." Her fingers dig into her thighs, skin stretching thin over her knuckles. It's a miracle her nails don't rupture the fabric. But some strange thread in this connection we seem to have tells me she's scared to death. Tells me she refused to do blow jobs. So why now? So, she could take control of her situation. I recognize the signs but knowing me has to be on *my* terms.

"And maybe if I do this, you'll let me go." Her words resonate in the depths of my mind. This is a new facet of my celestial abilities, unanticipated but indisputable—the emotions behind her thoughts are reaching me directly.

"Enough. Stand up." My voice is harsher than I intend and an unusual brew of emotions bubbles within me. Her contradictory actions defy my previous experiences with victims. I sense her internal rebellion even as she stoops to such humiliation.

"Don't belittle yourself like a whore." I pivot, my frustrations simmering. A disquieting discomfort seeps into my being, a gnawing energy that I can't ignore—I instinctively know it's coming from her, yet it pulls at me like a magnet. She's plucked a cord deep within me.

The air around us tingles with her rising ire as she inhales sharply and chases after me. "Wait just a minute! Don't you dare speak to me that way. Take that back. I am nobody's whore!"

I whirl around, bracing for verbal battle. But the defiance in her posture, tinged with vulnerability, blunts my wrath. I feel a strange, emerging urge to shield her. Swiftly recognizing the danger of such sentiment, I quash it with practiced skill.

"If I'm not here to have sex, then what in God's name do you want?" Her words are sharp, each accentuated by her finger prodding into my solar plexus. The emotional energy behind her touch sears through my armor, mingling discomfort with newfound understanding.

Holding back a wince, I clasp her wrists in one hand, gently this time, drawing on my celestial reservoir to neutralize the charged atmosphere. Leading her to an armchair framed by a grandiose fireplace, I take a beat, letting us both catch our bearings. This room's always been my go-to spot when I need a break from the real world—solid stone walls and majestic views through those massive windows.

I was hoping Destiny would feel the same sense of peace. But judging by her outburst, it's clear she's not the type to calm down easily. As I let go of her hands, she frowns and pulls back. She walks over to the armchair and sits, crossing her arms and legs like she's building a fortress around herself. She's on edge, no question about it. Her eyes dart around the room, revealing layers of unease and suspicion.

"Let's start over. I'm Jaden Stone. I work in cybersecurity, and right now, I'm here to protect you." I sound as reassuring as I can. I walk over to her and extend my hand, half-expecting her not to take it.

As I get closer, a mix of emotions plays out on her face —fear, anger, disbelief . . . and hope? I can feel them too, thanks to whatever strange connection we've got. She's wary, I can see that. But after a moment, she unfolds her legs, stands up, and takes my hand. Her grip is strong, stronger than I expected. "So, if you don't want a hand job, what do you want?"

Her directness takes me by surprise. She's sizing me up, and I can't blame her. There's a lot I'm not saying, and she knows it. It makes me wonder what it would be like if we could trust each other, really trust each other. But right now, that's a big "if."

"Because I don't. Need I elaborate?" My voice carries a layer of challenge, mingling with a newfound respect for her straightforwardness. There's an unspoken understanding between us, like we're two pieces of the same puzzle. Yet, my guarded instincts keep me from diving too deep, too fast into this uncharted territory, even though there's this compelling pull I can't ignore when I'm near her. I'm at odds with myself, torn between this urge to let her in and maintaining the walls I've built over the years. As I look into her piercing gaze, I'm left with an uneasy yet intriguing sensation that this could be the start of something transformative for both of us.

"All men want their needs satisfied. It's in their DNA." She makes this declaration as if she's written the book on male motives.

A stifled chuckle tries to escape me. We're still holding hands. It's as if letting go would mean more than just physical separation. I release her hand as if it were a burning ember.

"Well, not this one," I retort. "Your name?"

"I'm Des—"

I don't say a word, but my eyes convey the unspoken command.

With a sigh, she relents. "I'm Rayne Turner. I'm nobody, and apparently, now I'm your slave."

Her voice is so melodramatic that I can't hold back. For the first time in three years, I laugh—unrestrained, uninhibited. It's a sound I had almost forgotten, and it surprises even me. The absurdity of the situation washes over me like a cleansing tide. Yet, in that laughter, something shifts. A piece falls into place; one that I didn't know was missing. And I can't shake the feeling that my life—and hers—will never be the same.

4
RAYNE

He laughs, and something about it chips away at the weight I've been carrying on my shoulders. What's his deal, anyway? One minute I feel like prey, the next I'm feeling foolish for even trying to rattle him. But there's something about him—something that makes me want to know more. I threw myself at him and he didn't bite, and that pisses me off. Who turns down a come-on like that? I bet if I was blond and blue-eyed he'd probably already be coming. But some part deep inside knows better, knows this man doesn't give himself easily. His eyes dig into me, like he knows what I'm thinking, and it only makes me want to know what's locked up behind that tough exterior even more. It's frustrating as hell. Is he gay or something? Nah, there's too much sexual tension in the air for that.

Look at him—T-shirt and jeans, work boots half-laced. He looks like he stepped out of a movie or something. Sure, he's got that bad-boy vibe down to a science, but there's more—like he's hurting but won't admit it. Cocky, but it feels like there's a reason he's built these walls.

And God, those scars on his face—they make him real,

not some poser. He's got that wolfish thing going on; the way he watches me makes me want to run and come closer at the same time. Those curls, man, they're just begging for my fingers. And don't get me started on the body—he's built, but not like a gym rat who's overcompensating for something.

I know I should back off, keep my guard up, but something's pulling me in. My brain's flashing warning signs, but there's this weird connection I can't ignore. It's messed up. I'm both drawn to him and want to push him away, and that's what scares the shit out of me.

A bulge in the front of his pants tells me he's either huge or getting hard because of my stare. Humor sparkles in his eyes when our gazes meet again. The twisted thought of me across his lap sends a wild shiver through my body, igniting a fire deep in my belly. A warmth I've never felt before pulses between my legs. My ears flush as I imagine my bare bottom quivering beneath his punishing hand. How can I even consider something so perverted? Especially with a man who just kidnapped me. Is there something in me I refuse to accept?

Sex? It's always been a double-edged sword for me. It's not about intimacy or connection; it's a power play, a battlefield strewn with landmines from my past. Each one's left a mark, cut me deep. Yet I can't let go of my certainty that it can be something good, something special with the right person. So, when this man—his smoldering stare inexplicably warming the cold recesses of my heart—looks at me, I'm thrown. A stupid flicker of hope ignites, daring me to dream that fairytales aren't just for little girls with untouched lives.

Yeah, this guy screams "creep"—no lie there. But some defiant part of me, maybe the one that's taken too many blows, tells me to stick around. His gaze is different; it's as if he's peeling back layers of me no one's dared to touch. My pulse races, not from fear but from some foreign kind of excitement. Is it the lingering effects of Viper's last punch? Because the heat rising in me is disturbingly new, and my gut's telling me he's watching me from more corners than one.

When our eyes lock this time, it's like fucking fireworks. Bronze skies at twilight—that's what I see. And there are those rare occasions when he lets down his guard, when he winks; he grins. And goddamn, my knees turn to Jell-O, and there's this electric warmth spreading like wildfire between my thighs.

He's onto me. I can see it in that arrogant half-smile of his.

He turns away, sauntering over to the window like he owns the horizon. My eyes narrow as I take in his sculpted back. Is he the game-changer, or am I just running on fumes of desperation? How can I know he won't be just another chapter in my ongoing tragedy? Should I feign weakness or not? That's always been my card, but this man, he's got a penetrating gaze, like he's seeing the real me and won't accept anything less.

And damn, as much as I've grown numb to physical allure, I find myself soaking in the sight of him—every defined muscle and curve. A warmth I can't name kindles inside me. Usually, big guys set off every alarm, but this one, he makes me want something I can't put my finger on.

Caught in my stare, he swivels, his eyebrows arching like he's just deciphered a complex equation. I avert my eyes, donning a mask of indifference. "Well?" He sounds as disoriented as I feel.

So he wants a trade-off—a quid pro quo of sorts, as if

secrets are currency we can barter with. He thinks I'll crack first, spill my guts to appease him. Typical. But he hasn't fully read the room yet. I'm not as easy to break as he assumes.

He reclines on the couch, folding his elbows on his knees and lacing his fingers together. Dynamic energy and focus exude from every pore of his body. An artful stillness engulfs him as he holds my stare captive. "Your move."

"What do you mean my move? You. Stole. Me. Presumably to be one of your nobody sluts you can fuck whenever you want." My fire mingles with a sliver of fragility, sharpening the edge of my voice.

The thread of humor vanishes and my brooding captor returns. "I didn't steal you, I rescued you. Big difference. And all of my sluts, as you call them, are somebodies. I don't do the nobody thing. Unlike your previous acquaintances, I don't fuck anyone who isn't willing. What about me makes you think I'm a predator?" His eyes bore into mine — a predator assessing its prey.

My stomach churns at the thought of him with someone else. Panic claws at my throat when he demands an answer. I shake my head mutely, unable to even utter a word. He leans closer, and anger flashes in his eyes like flames dancing in the dark.

"Lots of people have sex slaves. It's a huge business." The words tumble out of my mouth before I can stop them. "And you rescued me for a reason. I wasn't born yesterday."

The scrutiny he gives me is unbearable as his gaze rakes over my body, making me squirm under his penetrating stare.

"Look, I'm not interested in you sexually, okay?" His fingers run through his golden-brown hair in frustration.

"It's my job to protect you and find out what you know about Viper's operation."

The pit in my stomach deepens, carved out by his words. He doesn't desire me. There's a flicker of relief, but it's quick to evaporate, leaving behind a sediment of shame.

"Alright, what do you want to know about Viper?" The sting to my pride flips my inner switch, or maybe it's the harsh slap of my current reality. Screw worrying about if he's into me; I should be figuring out how to use him to get out of this mess.

Viper—the name crawls up my spine like frostbite, resurrecting memories I've worked so hard to suppress. My mind should be a laser, zeroed in on finding my sister, Summer. Instead, I'm snagged on Jaden's words: "I'm not interested in you sexually." My gut contradicts him. Every time Jaden hovers near, this weird energy pulses through me. A primal alert system I can't ignore, although I'm not sure I want to

"Why aren't you into me?" I challenge, my voice edged with even more steel. I feel the hot tension rise, our gazes lock like grappling hooks. It's a struggle not to bridge the scant inches between us and explore the texture of his stubble.

Jaden hesitates, his eyes a storm of emotions, before muttering, "Look, Rayne, let's just trade info. I'll start if you agree to follow suit."

Sly fucker, evading my question like that. I gauge him, wondering how many layers I dare peel back. Screw it; curiosity's got its hooks in me.

"You first, big guy. Start talking."

He leans into the couch, exhaling a slow breath, like he's stepping into a familiar pair of boots. "Fair deal. I want to know about Viper. He's at the top of a food chain we're trying to dismantle. His info is so coded it's like he's a ghost. You've been close to him, and from what I can see, you don't miss much. So, we need your help." His piercing gaze lets me know this isn't just an ordinary request.

We, not I. For reasons I refuse to examine in my fucked up mind, I wish *he* needed my help.

"What's in it for me?" Good sense kicks in and reminds me what dire straits I'm in. ES took everything from me when he sold me into slavery, and now I don't even have an ID on me. I need money to take care of Summer.

My breath catches as I take Jaden in, those bronze eyes piercing me like a sharpened blade. His face is unreadable, but inside his head I feel emotions rolling around like wildfire.

"That depends on what you have to offer." He throws the words at me like a challenge.

A wicked grin spreads over my face before I can stop it. "You mean besides a hand job?"

Something about poking at Jaden relaxes me, and I'm determined to figure out why. The wacky humor slips out before I can think twice, and for some reason that makes him squirm.

His frown tells me he knows exactly what's going through my mind, yet he still asks the question. "I mean, what skills do you have?" He leaves the words "if any" unspoken but they echo between us regardless. A trickle of disappointment oozes through that strange connection I have to him.

"Lighten up. It was a joke."

He looks at me as if it's anything but and says nothing.

I sigh dramatically and add an eye roll for good measure. "Look, I'll tell you what little I know about Viper, but first I need to know how I got here. You said you rescued me. How did you find out about me?"

A sly smile flickers on his lips, and a weird heat unravels me layer by layer, as if my skin can't hold what I'm feeling. I can't ignore this magnetic pull, a subconscious whisper that this guy's more dangerous to me than anyone I've ever met. I shouldn't trust him. But goddamn it, when I see that I've made him smile, something rebellious flutters in my gut.

"I'll answer your last question, but you're not going to believe me." His intense eyes hook onto mine.

I inhale sharply. "Try me."

"A tribunal of celestials sent me." His words hang heavy in the air, like a gauntlet thrown. "One of them was the angel of death, I think."

My grin carves a defiant curve across my lips. "What, like Joe Black?" My usual caustic humor laced with an edge of disbelief bubbles from me.

The air hums, its vibrations caught in a taut wire of tension strung between us, making everything feel like a high-stakes game of poker. Neither of us is ready to show our hands, yet we're both glaring at the chips on the table. The invisible thing between us lingers, thickening the air like some forbidden incense. He squirms under the weight of my gaze, and that small quiver in his demeanor—God, it fascinates me.

This time, Jaden rolls with my humor, unsettling in its own right. "Same concept, except Joe Black is confined to the screen. Now it's my turn. Tell me about how you came to be part of Viper's stable." His abrupt pivot catches me off guard—a skill of his I should probably get used to.

"Oh, the blame for that lands solidly on ES's shoulders. ES stands for Evil Stepfather." My next words aim to deflect him, to make him chase after a distraction. "Could I maybe use your computer and phone?"

His eyes, those scrutinizing eyes, trap me. His eyebrow rises like a gauntlet thrown. A silent, 'Try harder, Rayne.'

"First, let's stick to ES." His relentless pursuit mirrors the indomitable focus I recognize in myself. No half-measures, no evasions.

I tilt my head, recalibrating. "Got any pot?" I'm not an open book, and although being around this guy makes me want to spill my guts, I'll be damned if I let him read me cover to cover without some herbal armor.

"Oil or leaf?"

"Both?" My voice skitters upward, an inadvertent slip revealing my eagerness.

He exits without a word, reappearing minutes later holding a metal box—a pothead's treasure trove. He leans in to show me his selection, and my pulse quickens, not from the offerings, but because of his closeness. My senses saturate in the scent of him: cleanliness overlaying an earthy, masculine base. A universe away from the olfactory offense most men are.

"Thanks," I manage, and hate myself a little for the struggle it takes to spit out one simple word of gratitude. He's my rescuer, right? And yet, I can't shake the niggling thoughts of what he can offer me. What I can wring out of him. As if he's the one who should be grateful.

His impatience rustles the air, tugging on those yet-to-be-defined strings within me. "So, you're going to tell me about how you got involved in The Game." He uses the code name for the Viper's trafficking ring.

I pull a slow drag from the vaporizer, letting the aromatic haze dilute the storm in my mind. The raw edges of my thoughts smooth out, malleable yet still guarded. How much do I dare share? The guy's like a predator eyeing his prey, a stuffed toy in jaws ready to tear it apart. But I'm no stuffed toy. And he's about to find out how many layers I've got.

Taking a huge breath, I relive the horror of that night and swallow down tears I've never been able to shed. "ES sold my little sister and me to some guy he owed big time. That guy sold us to Viper. Viper kept us drugged while shipping us around from motel to motel—until we eventually forgot who we were and what day it was. Summer was a virgin, but ES hadn't spared me his abuse. I was the oldest and not his biological kid, so he convinced himself that fucking me was his right."

I'm jumping all over the place but I need to tell the story in my own way—life's never given me the courtesy of a straight line. Jaden says nothing but something inside that connection between us pushes me to continue.

"When he crawled into bed with me one night, holding me down while he pumped away all the while telling me how much I wanted it, something inside of me snapped. In the morning, I held a butcher knife to his throat and threatened to kill him if he ever touched me or Summer again. This led to months of abuse, probably lighting the fuse that led to him selling us."

Inhale. The smoke burns a path down my throat, a brief fire that both numbs and awakens. Exhale. My eyes stay locked with Jaden's. He's a goddamn mystery, this man—those eyes, like dark tunnels leading to something I can't quite grasp, won't quite let me look away.

Jaden's legs are crossed at the ankles, a study in casual poise, but something about the way he holds his gaze mesmerizes me. It's as if he's dissecting my words, looking for more than just the tale. "You think I should've done the world a favor and offed ES, don't you?"

Sucking the vapor deeper into my lungs, I let it cloud my mind just enough to dull the edge of my emotions. Then I focus on the smoky exhale, each particle carrying away fragments of my composure. "Let's talk about Summer instead." There's a heaviness in my words, a sediment of sorrow settling in the corners of my mind. "She had her own ways of coping. Her drug of choice? Cocaine." I fight to keep the tremor out of my voice, as if saying it aloud could make it all too real again. Another pull from the vaporizer steadies my shaking hands, at least for now.

Jaden's voice slides into the fringes of my thoughts, velvet over gravel. "And how did *you* cope?" That sympathy in his gaze cuts through me. I don't need his pity.

I rip another drag from the vaporizer, let the burn etch away the disgust I feel for his unspoken compassion. "The drugs? They tried, sure. But it didn't work. Call it a genetic defect or cosmic bad luck. Drugs don't work on me the way they do on most people." My hands rise in a half-surrender, half-defiance as my eyes nail him with a challenge. "Your turn."

He leans in, elbows on knees, every line of his body like a chord of suspense, resonating in the space between us. He's like an unsung melody, a pending storm. The tension builds; I can almost hear the notes forming, feel the charged air on my skin. And yet, he stays silent, his eyes locked onto mine—a duel where the first to look away concedes. But neither of us is willing to yield, not yet.

And so, we sit in that dense, almost distinct silence, two souls stubbornly circling the truth, each daring the other to dive first. . .

5

JADEN

Rayne sinks into the couch, a look of detachment clouding her features. An unease coils in my gut, leaving me to wonder if it's a reaction to the drugs she's taken. My thoughts dart to darker places, seething at the thought of her stepfather or anyone else causing her pain. The swell of emotion puts me on edge, challenging my self-control. Just then, her voice slices through my turmoil.

"What do you know about Viper?"

I keep my reply curt, my frustration barely masked. "Not enough. That's why I need you."

Her fingers work a knot in her shoulder as she gazes out the window. It takes every shred of willpower not to close the distance between us, to offer her protection or solace. I'm usually a vault—steel walls and a lock without a key. Emotions? Kept in check, out of sight. But when it comes to Rayne, my usual defenses are failing.

"How long have you been hunting him?" Her voice carries a touch of impatience.

"Six weeks."

Her probing questions are a distraction, shifting my

focus from the mission—protecting her at all costs. She doesn't get it, can't see past the surface. Not that she should. Trust is a long game, and I need to be patient.

Rayne shifts, hands cradling her stomach. Sharp stabbing pain shoots through me . . . but it's not mine. Closing the gap between us takes an eternity of seconds. My fingers touch her pulse, and her soft whimper confirms my suspicions.

"What's wrong?" I can't keep the worry out of my voice. Her pulse is off, uneven, and it sets alarm bells ringing in my head. I crouch beside her, an unwanted flashback of Savannah flooding my mind. I can't go through that again.

"Where does it hurt?" I can't pin down the cause of her distress, and it gnaws at me. "I can't help unless I examine you."

Her body tenses, a hiss slipping past her lips. Whatever's wrong, she's not letting on. My powers should've picked up on this. Should have warned me she's not okay. But I didn't want to push, didn't want to scare her off. What a fine line to walk—between intrusion and concern. I can't help but think of the scars that the world has likely etched on her, scars I can't see but feel, as if they resonate with some hidden part of me.

Rayne shoots me a suspicious gaze before curling over in pain once more. "Okay, go ahead." She finally relents.

With utmost care, I lift her, cradling her weight as gently as possible, and settle her onto the couch. Her chest rises and falls with each labored breath, unshed tears shimmering in her eyes. Biting back my fear, I ease under her shirt, my touch tender as I press against her abdomen and back. My fingers cautiously reach her right kidney, and a grimace of pain crosses her face, but she remains stoic.

"How bad is the pain on—"

"A scale of one to ten. I know the drill," she interrupts, her voice strained yet determined. "Nine." She draws her legs closer to her stomach, hissing through her teeth. "Don't worry. It will pass soon."

Her stoicism both astounds and concerns me. I wish I could ease her suffering entirely, to take away the anguish etched into her features. The intensity of her pain tugs at my very being, awakening a fierce battle within. My instincts urge me to shield her, to protect her from all harm, but I must remain restrained, mindful of the fragile trust we're beginning to build.

In this moment, the depth of my internal struggle tells me I'm fucked. It is my sworn duty to complete this mission, to keep things strictly business, yet the growing connection I feel for Rayne threatens to undermine my resolve. As much as I long to dive deep into my inner fortress, I must set aside my own conflicting emotions. Lives hang in the balance—Rayne's and her sister's.

As my fingers graze Rayne's legs, I'm surprised by the underlying strength of her toned muscles. Her dedication to taking care of herself is evident in their sculpted and defined form. With gentle pressure, I guide her legs to extend then start a full-body assessment, silently noting the possibility of a cracked rib and a myriad of both fresh and old bruises marring her skin. The scars bear witness to the vile scum who preyed upon her vulnerability. I struggle to maintain composure, a tightness gripping my face as I witness the physical remnants of her abuse.

"We really should get you x-rayed. Any blood in your urine?"

"I'm not sure that's any of your goddamned business." *Hostile much, Rayne.*

Meeting her gaze with unwavering determination, I

draw upon my rusty medical skills. "Rayne, I'm a doctor. Let me help."

The venom in her eyes gradually fades, replaced by a cautious relaxation that allows me to continue my examination. There are no broken bones, but countless lumps, bumps, and scars mar her skin. Channeling the healing touch bestowed upon me by the gods, I allow a small amount of celestial energy to flow through my hands, accelerating the natural healing process. It should ease her distress without alerting her to my otherworldly gifts. Gently, I readjust her shirt and settle back on the couch, observing as the pain dissipates from her expression.

The moment our hands touch, it's like a jolt of electricity zaps through me. She pulls back quickly, clearly thrown off. At the same time, something else washes over me—an urgent need to protect her and not because I've been ordered to. Too much is happening too fast for me to process. Who could inflict this kind of pain on someone like her? Why do I care so much? I find myself fighting a surge of desire, something I've got no business feeling for a myriad of reasons. I reach out to check her pulse at her neck, feeling the undeniable warmth flood me. No, I can't afford to go down that road. I pull back.

"How are you feeling now?" My voice is steady, even though standing this close to her, feeling her heat, is like standing next to a space heater.

Her scent fills the air—a rare orchid's sweet and musky aroma, mingled with the freshness of earth—all instantly recognizable.

"Better," she says. Her eyes, a mix of brown with black flecks, are hard to read, like she's wrestling with something big. She's a fighter, no doubt, but there's this vulnerability that's just as evident and handcuffs me to her.

"How did you do that?" She looks at me, her eyes searching.

"Do what?" I keep my voice flat, playing it cool while I try to get a handle on what I'm feeling.

Her expression changes, tightening. "You know what I mean. I felt different after you touched me." Her voice has a challenging tone, like she's daring me to lie.

I step away, buying some time while I roll a joint from my stash. I can feel her eyes on me, watching, sizing me up maybe.

"If you want something, just ask," I finally say, fighting back a sudden surge of anger I didn't see coming.

"I'd be a lot better with more of whatever you just did," she snaps back. But there's something else there, beneath her words—a layer I can't quite identify but want to understand.

I can't help but feel curious, despite the emotional guardrails I've put up. "Why did Viper beat you so badly?" I change course, pushing the victim envelope more than I should. Fighting the growing attraction.

In my mind, the warning lights flicker on. Love's a raw deal, always has been. It promises heaven and delivers hell. She might be an mystery, but no one will make me gamble with those odds again. My scars, some you can see, some you can't, stand as cautionary tales.

"As I said. . . ." Her words trail off on a sigh as she exhales smoke into the night air.

I stand my ground, all too aware of the pull between us. But I won't go down that rabbit hole, not now, not ever. I keep my eyes on her, a mix of caution and captivation filling my thoughts.

She finally relents, exhaling another puff of smoke as if banishing a demon. "Look, I told him I won't kneel. He tried to make me, failed, and now he's making me an example. That's it."

I lean in slightly, feeling a spark of adrenaline as she talks. "But what's his endgame? What makes you so special to him? You can't be the first victim to defy him." The unsaid tension is heavy, thickening the air between us.

"I did it in front of his thugs. More than once." Shame and pride blend with resolve and hidden dread before her voice goes flat. "I'll never belong to anyone. This time, if I don't bend, he'll kill me. Simple as that." Her words hang in the space between us, a whispered ultimatum that neither of us can ignore.

"When did your stepfather first rape you?" My hands fist into balls as I ask the painful question; the silent room a stark contrast to my thundering heart.

She doesn't answer right away, but when she finally speaks up there is an edge of anger to her voice. "Don't call him that. He lost the right to be my father when he raped me at fourteen."

Empathy surges within me, an unwanted guest breaching the gates I've meticulously fortified over the years. I see her, standing resilient despite the weight of her past, a quality I find myself unwillingly admiring. I bury this fleeting emotion deep inside, a reminder of the emotional exile I've chosen. No one can map the territory of my heart—it's a place too perilous, scarred by traumas and fears I dare not confront.

A strange sensation coils around my heart, as if daring me to acknowledge it. It exhilarates and terrifies me in equal measure.

"Did he . . . did he live?" I'm startled by my own question, unscripted and revealing. She fixes her gaze on me, pondering, perhaps searching for an answer in my own eyes. Then, she laughs—a real laugh that resonates in the hidden alcoves of my hardened heart. Tears stream down her face, an unsettling mix of joy and pain that cut through me. I hand her a box of tissues, a meager offering to the hurricane of her emotions.

"You're funny." She breathes out a concoction of surprise and delight. She grips my humor as if it's her life-line, and that pulls another reluctant smile to my lips.

"Thanks, I needed a good laugh. I didn't kill him, though God knows I wanted to. I threatened him, told him I'd kill him if he ever touched me again. I wish I had done more. Maybe then..." Her voice trails into silence, swallowed by the ghosts of her past.

She locks eyes with me, her gaze unwavering yet void of desperation. "I need to find my sister. Will you help me?"

Her question hovers in the air, heavy with unspoken promises and concealed dangers. On its face, her request appears straightforward. But I sense an undercurrent, a hidden peril that threatens to pull me under. Despite the magnetic pull of her vulnerability, I recall a vow I never put to words: I will not succumb to the chaos of love, especially not with her—a storm with the power to shatter my defenses. Love is a gamble, a pathway to devastation. It's a price I won't pay, not even for her. For a second, I wonder what prompted all this thought about love but know better than to ignore my instincts.

She studies me, her eyes a blend of wonder and something darker—anticipation, perhaps. Her expression says she expects rejection, both of her plea and of herself. There's a raw intensity emanating from her, and I almost grin in recognition.

"Yes, we'll find your sister and we'll bring her back. That simple." The words escape me before I can rein them in.

Commitment—a foreign, choking concept. I've just entangled my fate in a web I swore never to be caught in.

Hope flares in her eyes, betraying her earlier words. "They'll find us and kill us. You can't escape them, especially after abducting me like that. Viper won't let it go."

Suppressing a grin, I choose my words carefully. "I excel at what I do, and I have a feeling you're not as defenseless as you let on. We pool our resources, we'll find your sister." Why am I doing this? Aside from Sasha, I've never had a partner in anything.

She gnaws on her lower lip, mulling over my proposition. "You said I'm free to go. Maybe I should just leave." Her posture stiffens, her resolve crystalizing through whatever strange connection is forming between us—a connection I never asked for, never wanted.

"If that's your decision," I keep my tone devoid of emotion, heading toward my lab. The ache that pierces me at the thought of her leaving, I ignore. I've had enough of these celestial games. It's time to return to what matters—my work. She either contributes or she doesn't. Either way, I have things to do.

She takes her leave, traversing the garden, heading for the gate. On the monitors, I watch her walking steadily, shooting occasional glances over her shoulder. Then, a vibration syncs through my control panel, silently signaling a breach in my security. Rayne bends over, clutching her arm. A large man approaches, swiftly injecting her. Within a celestial nanosecond, I'm there, closing the gap. One quick stab to the heart and the intruder falls, lifeless. Lifting her into my arms, I rush her back to the house. I'll deal with the others later. My medical instincts momentarily trump my need for vengeance.

Stopping just inside the door, I hold her tight. "I've got you," I take her pulse. "What's going on with your arm?"

"It burns where they injected me," she squirms, her voice descending to a near whisper. "I've been drugged. Again."

"What injection?"

"Vaccination," she groans and her head drops heavy on my chest.

Another alarm buzzes on my wristband, raising my hackles. Another breach—now what? But I'm already in motion. Rayne takes precedence over any intruders.

"The bastards implanted a tracking device." I hoist her and move swiftly toward my lab. This changes everything. I should have checked for a tracker. There's no time to lose.

6

RAYNE

Pain gnaws at me like a starving beast as the drug kicks in. Jaden's hauling ass through the solarium, down corridors, through the library and down the elevator. My veins are on fire, every cell in my body screaming for relief. It's like I'm swimming through razor blades. I try to clutch onto the heat radiating from Jaden's chest—anything to anchor myself to reality—but it's like trying to hold onto a bolt of lightning. Viper may torture my flesh, but my mind? That's mine. Always will be.

The cave engulfs us, a dark fortress that's beginning to feel less like a prison and more like a twisted sanctuary. Jaden drops me onto a gurney in a makeshift infirmary. The pain? Relentless. Like a drill sergeant hell-bent on breaking me.

His hands are iron clamps around my biceps, steadying, grounding. "Rayne, keep still. I need to get this chip out. We're safe—for now."

His voice, clinical and detached, clashes with the warmth that courses through me every time his skin grazes mine. Makes me question my own sanity. What's this tingle of care, of protection? Am I really starting to lose it like ES warned? I don't even like this guy yet every time I'm near him, I'm crushing on him. I groan out something—hell if I know what.

He takes my garbled sound as consent, loading a syringe. "Local anesthetic. Probably won't kill you combined with whatever shit they gave you. But this will hurt. Keep still."

Before I can warn him that sedatives do jack for me— just wind my thoughts up tighter—he jabs the needle into my shoulder multiple times. My eyes slam shut. Maybe it's a nod or just a twitch, but he gets the message.

Gloves snap. His grip returns to my arm. "Incision time. Don't move."

Teeth grinding, eyes stinging, but I'm stone-still. I might be in hell, but I won't give him a reason to doubt me. Gives me something else to chew on, anyway.

Finally, the cold creeps in, numbing the area. I exhale, forcing my body to unclench just a bit against the gurney's unforgiving surface. He grabs some freakish tool—looks like tweezers mated with tongs—and digs into my shoulder. But his eyes? They're not on me, they're fixed on some screen showing my insides. Real comforting.

There's a focused tension in his face, then a tight smile. "Got it."

And just like that, a weight I didn't know I was carrying lifts. Not fully, but enough for me to glimpse what relief could feel like.

"That's so cool." The throbbing in my arm subsides, its once violent screams fading into murmurs. Is it the drug he gave me? No, stop, pull your head out of that dark hole, Rayne. Why do I assume the worst of every damn person who crosses my path? Because I've learned not to trust anyone, least of all someone who looks like this man.

Across the room, Jaden drops the patch into a small cylinder. It's like watching a spider tuck away its prey, setting it into this tech-infused web he calls a lab. The cylinder slides into a tunnel, vanishing into the bowels of whatever masterpiece of engineering this place is.

"Need a top-up for the pain?" Jaden's voice is a melody that's at odds with the sterile backdrop of medical equipment. I shake my head. No, I don't think so. It's hard to tell as my senses dance to the lullaby of his words. What I want is whatever he did earlier that made the horrid pain so much better.

Here I am, plunged into the guts of a real-life Batcave with a stranger—a compelling, yet clearly dangerous, stranger. He just killed a guy for fucks sake, and all I can think is 'good riddance' to the fucker. And instead of guarding my vulnerable state, I'm drenched in the sweetness of his voice, in the closeness of his touch. Am I that desperate for a modicum of warmth? Evidently, yes.

His needle bites into my flesh, yet each prick is paradoxically soothing. It's not just the numbing agent; it's the fact that he, in this chaos, remains a constant. His hands work deftly, each stitch a testament to a strange mix of brutality and care. And hell, why am I hung up on studying his every move when I should be watching my own back?

You're losing it, Rayne. This guy's cut into me, drugged me, and I'm under some kind of spell, his rhythm, his everything. Dangerous doesn't even cover it—he's a ticking bomb and I handed him the detonator. And what for? To get a good look at his ass? Seriously? This weird link we've got messes with my head, blurring how risky he is. But deep down, I know the only damage he could do is to my heart—if I give him the chance. "That drone of his is off on a long trip," he says. How reassuringly vague. The drugs tear down my shields and the bitch in me comes out to play.

"So, where the hell are we?" A voice in the back of my head murmurs that I should give a damn, but right now, everything's hazy.

"We're in my lab." He finishes up the stitches, starts wrapping my arm. A lab that feels like it could be either my coffin or some twisted sanctuary. God, even I want to roll my eyes at myself. *Melodramatic much, Rayne?*

Then his hand lightly brushes my back, and damn if that doesn't send fire down my spine. "You okay?"

I shake my head, not letting my eyes meet his. Because the only pain that's real right now is the one I'm inflicting on myself—the walls I've built up cracking under the weight of something I can't even name yet.

"Rayne." With that one word, his tone changes from sunlight to storm cloud. I swat his hand away.

"Okay, okay, you got me. It sucks. Isn't the second day always a bitch, anyway? But I'm solid." My heart's pounding like a drum solo, but whether it's the meds or him messing with my head, who knows?

Jaden prods my kidney just enough to make me double over. "As I suspected. Let's assess the extent of the damage."

"Great." I let him lift my shirt. He absorbs the full spectacle—bruises, cuts, all of it. No doubt pity drips from him as he takes it all in . . . I refuse to look at him. I won't let myself break, not because of physical pain or anyone's judgment.

"Shall we continue the examination?" He steps back, hands folded, waiting to pounce.

I roll my eyes and shed the pants. Undies are non-negotiable. His expression darkens, like storm clouds rolling in as he surveys the damage. "You need an x-ray."

"I told you, I'm fine."

"Indeed." His voice drips with so much sarcasm you could bottle it. "You didn't answer my question about blood in your urine."

I flick my hand dismissively mustering up more bravado than I feel. "Look, there's a little blood. Not the end of the world. Are we done here?"

Without another word, he guides me to an adjoining chamber with an x-ray machine. The scan is swift. Then he points. "As you can see, your rib is fractured. I presume it's painful to breathe."

Hell yeah, it is, but I refuse to admit it.

He raises his eyebrow as if calling me on my stubbornness but says, "Your rib needs to be stabilized with tape."

He snips off several lengths of KT Tape and waits for me to give the go-ahead. Despite the temptation to refuse just to prove I can, common sense takes over. I relent, removing my shirt to give him better access but can't stop myself from covering my small boobs with my arms. The room goes quiet except for the sound of tape unspooling and securing flesh to flesh.

"Monitor your kidney. Any changes, particularly increased blood, you need to inform me."

The taping's done, and he starts cleaning up. Mindful of my ribs, I fight the urge to lunge for my clothes.

As I struggle to get my shirt on, I take a closer look around. "So, what's the deal with this place? It's like Batman's hideout. Is there a Batmobile in the garage or something?" Yeah, it's a dumb question, but I'll do anything to direct his attention from my half-naked body.

Jaden's rare grin warms me in a way I don't want to admit. It's like a Chinook wind that creeps in, slowly melting the self-imposed glaciers surrounding my insides. "I call my safe room the Hole, but if you want to talk Batman trivia, I'm game." And suddenly Mr. Hyde retreats, leaving Dr. Jekyll to morph into an animated Prince Charming. "The original Batmobile was a 1939 Cadillac. The series used a Lincoln Futura. The Tim Burton movies used a Chevy Impala chassis."

"Yeah? Well, the Tumbler says 'fuck your chassis.' It's its own beast, more tank than car," I shoot back. "And I think I'll stick to calling it your Batcave."

He chuckles, his chest puffing out with a tangible sense of pride. "Uh-huh, but it can't beat my Bugatti Chiron."

I don't even know what a Bugatti Chiron is, but I'm already pulling up a mental note to Google it later. "You some kind of car junkie then? Because you're totally a Batman geek."

"Nah, cars are cool, but my real love is knives and dragons," he says.

Putting on my T-shirt turns into a circus act of discomfort. He tosses one of his own shirts my way, as if offering some sort of truce. I hold up my hand, halting him. *I got this, thanks.* The freezing cold from earlier still clings to my skin, but as I stretch to pull the shirt over my head, a surge of pain lances through my shoulder like a live wire.

Shit. I muster the strength to descend from the gurney, each muscle movement shooting new flames of agony through my frame. I brace my good arm against the bed, consciously avoiding yanking the stitches right out of my damn skin.

"Easy, you'll make a full recovery. Just give it time."

Jaden's voice washes over me, his touch brief yet unsettling as his fingers graze the nape of my neck.

Fuck. My synapses sizzle, like I've been given a shot of something divine. Part of me wants to dive deeper into why this troubled man has such an effect on me. But there's a cacophony of other voices in my head—what about Summer, what about Viper—and I shove them into the mental closet where I keep all my other inconvenient truths, locking it up tight.

"Why the hell do you know so much about medical stuff? What's your story, Jaden? And what's Viper got that you want so bad?"

His demeanor shifts, his face going from approachable to a frozen mask in a millisecond. I trail him into a room plastered with monitors. A rush of air escapes him as his eyes scan the screens. I peek over his shoulder. On display is a real-time manhunt—Viper's goons, room by room.

"As long as we're holed up, might as well get comfortable." His voice carries a finality that halts further questions.

He strides out, not even a backward glance. I hesitate for a nanosecond before chasing after him.

"Wait. They won't find us here?"

"No."

Not a talker, are we? "Explain."

"It's a safe room," he curtly replies, "make yourself at home. I'll be back."

His words hang heavy, an irrevocable full stop, as the elevator doors slide shut, trapping me in the ambiguity of his world.

7

JADEN

I creep through the darkness, my feet crushing the pavement in silence. The compound hangs thickly with an eerie quiet, punctured only by the occasional cricket's chirp or a rustling leaf. I've been waiting for Viper's enforcers since leaving Rayne in that safe room, and I can sense them drawing near. *Rayne, my little dragon.* I shake my head as thoughts jumble through my mind. I can think about what the fuck's going on with her or avoid the topic all together once I've made sure she's safe. Right now, that's all that matters.

I slip my cell from my pocket and text Sasha.

Me:Pest invasion. Clean-up in aisle four.

I press send and make sure the phone's silenced. By the time I've handled Viper's goons, Sasha will be here with our special ops clean-up team. As I slink through the shadows, their presence presses against me—tangible in the night air. I stop, steadying myself for what lies ahead, gathering strength to deliver justice.

I summon my Brazilian jujitsu training, allowing my body to move in unison with my mind. My breathing is slow and steady, the chorus of crickets and birds a tranquil backdrop to my trance. I heighten my senses, letting my angelic perception open itself to the presence of three enforcers. I can sense their malice, their cruelty, their maleficent dismissal of life and humanity.

I creep up on the first enforcer, a man. My dark clothes help me blend in with the evening shadows. The closer I get, the more of his vile crimes against the vulnerable flood my celestial perception until I become a killing machine. Some small part of rationale quells the blood-thirsty demon wanting to make him suffer as he has so many young girls and boys. I don't have time to prolong the pain right now.

I reach out to my celestial gifts for strength and skill as I conjure an obsidian blade into my hand then drop into a crouch behind the human trafficker. Summoning my magic, I hurl myself toward his back like a missile, calling on all my speed. He barely has time to turn around with terror in his eyes before the blade sinks into the flesh below his clavicle. His body drops silently into the waiting arms of the soft grass.

The second is a woman, her scent reminiscent of strong coffee. The creases in her face are not from age, but experience. Her body is poised for the fight, and for a split second I think about letting her go. Killing women goes against my values, as I understand the pain and suffering that most of them have experienced that turned them from human to depraved.

But before I can make up my mind, she launches an attack—a feint followed by a violent kick aimed at my head. Instinctively, I step forward and wrap both arms around her thighs, lifting them off the ground and destabilizing her balance. She's quick and agile but I've faced tougher adversaries before. Anger wells up within me as visions of how she's abused young boys overtake me and eliminate any rational thought. She deserves to answer for all of her crimes.

I deliver a precise and powerful drive forward, taking the perp to the ground and maintaining control as she fights back with a wild ferocity. I transition into a dominant position and take the killing stroke, this time slicing her carotid artery.

Suddenly, I sense someone else in the air—the third enforcer. With extreme care, I creep closer until I make out the imposing figure of a tall man clad in an impeccably tailored dark suit. His features are sharp and chiseled, his hair jet black, and his eyes intense and piercing. I can feel an underlying evil emanating from him along with something else that sends a chill down my spine: this man is the leader, here to take Rayne away for interrogation by some of the most sadistic methods imaginable.

A booming voice echoes through the darkness. "Where is the girl?" I freeze on the spot and clench my fists, sending ripples down all five inches of my shimmering celestial dagger. "Tell us where she is, and no one will be hurt." The threat in his tone is as unmistakable as the sadistic violence rolls from him in waves.

When you hear something like this there's only one answer: it's time to deliver justice. The promise I gave her when we met. Rayne won't be threatened by these savages, not while I'm alive.

I inch closer as the enforcer's vile essence grows more potent with every breath I take. My muscles tense as I ready myself for battle. In one fluid motion, I draw out my dagger and lunge forward. They will fall just as they entered—mortals who won't survive the day—and justice will be served.

As consciousness drains from the man's eyes, I raise my arm again to deliver another blow, but a sharp jolt shoots up my forearm and draws me back to reality. "Enough, Jaden", Sasha's gravelly yet commanding voice rings clear in the battlefield strewn with bodies. "We need one of them alive."

With a curt nod, I wipe the bloody blade on the grass and stand. I quickly scan the area, my eyes locking onto a fourth enforcer—a dangerous individual radiating power and menace. With a surge of adrenaline, I take off toward him, channeling my angelic essence to bolster my strength for what's to come. The memories of innocent victims flash in my mind, fueling a primal fury that burns deep within.

I lunge for him, my heart pounding in anticipation. Our collision sends tremors through his muscled frame, and I feel the perverse energy of his soul through my heightened senses. Revulsion and anger mix in a potent cocktail within me.

As I hiss my question, my voice holds a cold edge that cuts through the night air, "Why are you here? What do you want?" I'm ready to unleash the justice that these vile individuals deserve. The gray veil descends over my psyche, a celestial gift that allows me to exact retribution without hesitation, at least for now.

Gratitude fills me for this power that sets my heart strangely at ease with tormenting him. I know there will be consequences when my human morality and conscience return, but for now, I embrace the fury that drives me.

He scowls at me, fear and hatred swimming in his eyes

as he realizes he's met his match. "Viper sent us, beautiful. You stole his property, and we're here to get it back."

The reference to my looks as "beautiful" sets me off. The demons within me ignite and nothing matters but suppressing the anguish of my own past.

When I come to, I find myself in one of the specially designed interrogation rooms in the PE Operations Centre, my back against the wall. Sasha, my anchor in the storm, is by my side. " We've got what we need, Jaden. We know where Summer is."

The location the enforcer gave us was a desolate, abandoned warehouse at the outskirts of town. It was a typical spot for an organized crime boss to hold one of the women from his dreadful stable. As we speed toward our destination in my Aston Martin DBS, Sasha's concern for me is evident.

"Jaden, you can't keep losing it like that." Her voice is casual yet firm. "I get it, man, the anger, the pain, it's all part of what we do. But you need to get your feelings under control, or it's gonna get you killed one day."

I grip the steering wheel, my jaw clenching. "Mind your own damn business, Sasha," I snap, my emotions simmering beneath the surface.

But Sasha doesn't back down; she's always been the kind of friend who cares enough to push. "I'm not trying to be a pain in the ass, but you know I worry about you. We all do. You can't carry the weight of the world on your shoulders like this. It's eating you alive."

My grip tightens on the wheel as I try to contain the storm within me. "I said back off, alright?" My voice is tinged with frustration. "I'm working on it, okay? I know I've got a damn problem, and I'm trying to deal with it."

Sasha doesn't let up, her concern shining through her eyes. "You're not alone in this, Jaden. But you don't want to talk, I get it. So, let's talk about Destiny instead."

I shoot her a sharp look, my defenses still up. "Her name is Rayne, and I said drop it, Sasha," I reply, my voice low and harsh. Not a tone I generally curse her with.

She gives me a determined look, undeterred by my harsh words. "Fine, this isn't a good time. Let me know when you're ready to talk." She turns away, and we retreat into our individual solitary places as we prepare for the rescue ahead.

The purring of the sleek black Aston Martin fills the air as I accelerate toward the desolate, abandoned warehouse. My emotions are a tempest inside, but I can't afford to let them consume me now. We pull up to the warehouse, and I feel a surge of adrenaline coursing through my veins.

Inside, we find her—Summer. Although her skin tone is much lighter than Rayne's, the resemblance is unmistakable. My heart clenches as I see her innocent, limp body, and a surge of fury crashes down upon me. I know what those bastards have done to her, and my anger boils like a cauldron of hellfire.

With ruthless precision, we take down Viper's goons, and I scoop Summer into my arms, cradling her like a fragile angel. She's alive, but barely. Healing energy flows through me, accelerating the healing of her physical wounds, but my powers can't penetrate the emotional void that was once this vibrant girl. Thankfully, her vitals stabilize. I glance at Sasha, my jaw clenched tightly, and we leave that wretched place.

The drive to Harmony Hills Treatment Centre is a blur

of desperation and worry. I can't shake the feeling that something is amiss; that time is slipping through my fingers like grains of sand. I don't know why I'm drawn to Rayne, why her presence lingers in my thoughts, but there's an undeniable pull—an inexplicable connection that I can't ignore.

The car hums beneath me, a mechanical lullaby that can't drown out the buzz of my thoughts. We're in a race against time to get Summer to the treatment center, but it's Rayne who keeps drifting into my mind. She's got a hold on me, some kind of magnetism I can't shake. The pull I feel toward her goes beyond physical—it's like she silences my inner chaos. Just met her, and already, there's this bond? Celestial intervention? Ridiculous. I took this assignment to protect her, so there's no reason for the gods to spellbind us. We pull up to Harmony Hills. The sterile smell of the place hits me with memories I'd rather ignore as I hand Summer over to the professionals. They know how to handle this type of damage; I don't. I catch glimpses of her past traumas, little snapshots that can't even compare to what Rayne must have gone through. I can't shake the image of her, haunted yet intense, and it's unsettling how much I find myself wanting to protect her.

Stepping back, I force myself to breathe. Now isn't the time for my own issues. But thinking of Rayne, her gaze that seems to cut through all my defenses, lights a fuse on emotions I don't want to deal with.

The farther we get from her, the more restless I become. My past is a constant weight, always there, always pulling me down. But with Rayne, there are moments where it all seems to fade away. That scares the hell out of me.

My thoughts are a damn mess as we head back. On one hand, I want to shut down, to avoid all this emotional turbulence. On the other, I feel a pull to be near Rayne, like she's some kind of lifeline. I've got to get my head back in the game; this isn't the time to come unraveled.

I suspect Rayne's darkness is more like a Roman shield wall instead of the very dark hole where I exist. Knock down one of her shields and she'll come charging out, a blaze of light.

I make a silent vow that comes out of nowhere. I've got to make peace with the wreckage. But for now, it's Rayne who's at the forefront of my mind. As much as it pisses me off to admit it, she might just be what I need—a glimmer of light when all I've known is darkness. And as much as it terrifies me, I can't shake the feeling that she could be my way out.

8

RAYNE

Nausea consumes me for several minutes that seem like an eternity before my system starts to adjust to the drug coursing through my veins. It's not as if I haven't been here before. The drug is probably Viper's favorite cocktail of Rohypnol and cocaine. He didn't give a shit how sick the drug made me, as long as the johns could spread my legs. On the upside, it saved me from a host of distasteful blow jobs . . . vomit will do that.

When I can open my eyes without the room spinning, I'm looking at one big-ass security monitor that I hadn't noticed before. The screen is divided into about ten different windows, displaying the perimeter of a large, beautiful home in what looks like real-time surveillance. I watch a lot of comic book movies, and I feel like I'm watching a scene from one of them playing out before me.

I spot a remote nearby. Grabbing it should be simple, but with my stomach doing flip-flops, nothing's a given. Breathe in, breathe out. My hand hovers, then snatches it up. No new wave of nausea hits. Small victories.

The screen zooms, and I'm watching a view of a

corner of the house where the waning sunlight casts shadows over much of the grounds. Then, something moves, shadow to flesh. Jaden. A shimmer surrounds him. Hallucination, got to be. The drugs playing tricks on me. But I can't look away. He downs the guy. Permanently. A nausea of a different kind claws at me. The first kill was in self-defense; this one most definitely isn't. *Deep breaths, Rayne.*

What did I just witness? My brain's a cyclone, but I can't dismiss what's right in front of me. The brutal, unfathomable truth: Jaden just went all-in for my sake. Why? What's his angle?

This man's not a puzzle, he's a maze. He's all hard edges and darkness, sure, but there are these slivers of vulnerability, windows into something tortured and too damn familiar. A connection I can't shake.

I've spent years building walls, damn high ones, but this man, in mere moments, threatens to tear them down. Goddammit. Why can't I expel him from my thoughts? Is it just lust? No, it can't be that simple. Jaden's not simple. He's a storm cloud with a silver lining I can't quite place, but for the first time in a long while, that lining looks a lot like hope.

My body aches, my mind's a whirlwind of emotions, but there's no denying what I saw. That's part of my curse —once I see something, I can't unsee it. Jaden, this dangerous man, just risked everything to save me. How is that even possible? Why would he do it? I can't wrap my head around the idea of someone, anyone, going to such lengths for me.

But then again, there's something different about Jaden. He exudes power and darkness, but I've glimpsed moments of vulnerability in his eyes—flashes of torment that mirror my own. It's as if we share a connection, a bond forged in the depths of our darkest secrets.

I don't know what it is about him that pulls me in, why I can't get him out of my mind. I'm terrified of the intensity of my emotions when it comes to him. I've always been cautious, kept my walls high and my heart protected, but with Jaden, it's as if all my defenses crumble with a single glance.

Maybe it's just lust. I want to hate him for what he does, for the darkness surrounding him, but I can't deny how he makes me feel alive like I'm more than just a victim of my past. He ignites something in me, a flicker of hope in the shadows of despair.

As I slump against the cold gurney, I wrestle with the chaos in my head—Jaden, the drugs, this sense of being tethered to him. Fucking hell, my brain's a mess. My eyelids turn to lead, and finally, I let sleep claim me.

It's unclear how much time has bled away when I jolt awake. I still feel like shit, my body fighting against the remnants of whatever's been pumped into me. I shake my head, trying to air out the cobwebs to reel in the string of events.

And yet, it's Jaden's face that's stuck in my head. The way he tore into those guys, his eyes like twin embers of a burning fire. He's a mysterious riddle, and for some goddamn reason, I can't shake the feeling that he's as fucked up as I am . . . despite appearances.

The logical part of me screams that this is a red flag. Danger. But fuck it, something about him reels me in like a magnet. He's a puzzle I want to solve, a maze I'm tempted to wander.

I should be on my guard. This pull, this spark between us—it's like playing with fire. I don't even like the guy, and he's the enemy. Yet, here I am, wondering if he's got a way out of my mental mess. Hell, even the absurd notion of love flickers at the edges of my thoughts.

"No one will ever love you. You're a waste of space." ES's voice pierces through my jumbled thoughts. I'm torn between the dregs of the drugs still in my system and the torrent of emotions threatening to drown me. About Summer. About the whole fucked-up reality I'm in. And through the haze, Jaden's kill hangs heavy—raising more questions than answers.

As sleep creeps up on me again, that unsettling thought refuses to fade: Jaden killed someone. For *me*. Is he my savior or just another twisted turn on this fucked-up path I'm on? One thing's for sure, our lives are knotted together now, whether by fate or some fucked-up design. And as I drift off, one thought rattles in my head like a damn echo: *he killed for me. For me.*

Jolted awake, the warmth on my arm yanks me back to here and now. Where the hell am I? Memory floods back as I recognize the couch in Jaden's Batcave. The couch is like lying on a cloud—if clouds were made of kickass leather. It's dark and mysterious in here, kinda sexy but also kind of "watch your back."

I snap my focus back and there's Jaden, this huge guy just hovering over me. His eyes are like an X-ray, but now there's this new layer, almost like he's eyeing a prize. *What're you thinking, Jaden?*

Okay, Rayne, reel it in. Don't show him the tornado of crap swirling in your head. He can't know how much he's messing with me. That's locked up tight inside.

"You're shivering," he says, and the concern lining those works triggers a massive flight response. I spring off the too-comfortable couch, then almost double over from the pain. Shit. With a slow exhale, I straighten, refusing to show weakness. I've had my share of crappy guys in my life; I'm not lining up for more. Especially not from a guy who's killed for me. Could kill *me*. God, I can't even unpack that shit right now.

He stays put, looking like he can't decide if I'm insane or just unpredictable. I've got him on his toes, good. He's still a wildcard to me, and handing out my trust? Not on today's menu.

"I'm fine," I snap, keeping the words short and sharp as I put some distance between us. Like drawing a line in the sand.

He throws me for another look—almost hurt, not angry. "What did you think I was going to do to you?" His voice is cold as ice and twice as cutting.

Whoa there. Nobody ever gives a damn about how I feel. "Nothing." I avoid his eyes like they're traps. "Just lost myself for a sec."

Then comes this heavy pause, like he's seeing stuff in me I didn't think was showing. "Rayne, one rule. Don't lie to me. You can say you don't want to talk. Say it's none of my business. But don't lie."

His words hit a raw nerve, can't help but make it quiver. "I thought you'd hit me. It's a learned response." My voice carries the shakiness I fail to hide.

Now the air's thick between us, like we're wrapped up in some complex puzzle neither of us can just walk away from. There's this electricity, this tie that's more confusing and tangled than this freaky room . . . or us.

He looks relieved, like he was afraid of something. "I'll

take that as an apology. That's a natural reaction." His voice sounds weary. "You have my word. I will never intentionally hurt you. I repeat—you have my word. Now, I need to take a look at that shoulder." He walks away, heading into the other room.

The problem is, I believe him despite every logical brain cell giving me several hundred thousand reasons not to trust him. I sit back on the couch, my mind spinning with conflicting emotions. Part of me wants to trust him and believe that he won't hurt me like others. But another part of me fears getting close to someone again and letting my guard down. But there's something pulling me toward him, something I can't explain. It's like we're connected in some weird way, like he understands me in a way no one else does. And I can't help but shake the sense he's hurting too, if he's trying to keep his own demons at bay. My gut also screams that he's way more damaged than I am, but that's simply not logical.

I follow him to the infirmary, and he's all business, tending to my wounded shoulder with skill and care. But I can't ignore the intensity in his gaze, the way he looks at me like he's trying to figure me out. I get another shot of this strange connection between us, like we're two lost souls drawn together by some unseen force.

It's downright strange for me to be this aware, this captivated by a man. I rarely find real people attractive—there's that small crush I had in high school and my undeniable obsession with Chris Hemsworth. Yet, with this guy right beside me, touching my skin, Chris might as well be Steve Buscemi. And unlike any other man I've met, he's not trying to hit on me. I've mistaken idle curiosity for desire. In fact, I'm getting the distinct feeling that he's not even remotely interested, that I'm just another body in the healthcare meat market. That should make me very happy but instead it pisses me off.

But the longer I spend with him, the more I want to know about him and the darkness surrounding him. I swallow down a sigh as my rational mind tries to talk some sense to me. I'm scared of what I might find. This guy just may have more baggage than I do. I'm scared of getting too close, of letting someone in. Because even the nice guys are only nice until they try to bang me. But at the same time, I can't deny the pull toward him, the way he makes me feel seen and understood.

But he's not like the other guys, not even Tom, the only guy I've ever had a relationship with. I'd adored Tom at first. He'd been nice to me and told me he loved me. He'd even moved in with me for a while. But he'd turned out to be a fucked-up drunk still in love with the wife he neglected to tell me about and I'd kicked his ass out. ES took great pleasure gloating to me, over and over, just like he had in my teens, that Tom's deceit was the best someone like me deserved.

Maybe Jaden is no different. Maybe I'm looking at the world through the Pollyanna glasses everyone accuses me of wearing. Absently, more out of habit than anything, I finger my glasses up the bridge of my nose as I inhale his scent. My senses come alive, and I'm hit with a whirlwind of scents mingling around him. It's like nothing I've ever experienced before. His unique musk envelops me, a subtle blend of strength and allure that's both enticing and intimidating.

But there's more to it—a mysterious undercurrent that I can't quite place. A faint whiff of something almost earthy, a woodsy note that reminds me of lying in a hammock in the woods, with a hint of spice, like the smell of a fresh cup of coffee. His smell is so complex, and yet so familiar, like he is. Like it's part of me.

Yet, beneath the inviting aroma, there's a faint undertone of danger—a sensation of static electricity lingering in the air. It's the scent of someone who has walked through fire, carrying the weight of his past with him, like a storm on the horizon that hasn't fully unleashed its power.

The mixture is intoxicating and unsettling, drawing me in and pushing me away simultaneously. I can't help but be drawn to it, to him, despite the warning signals that flash in my mind. Jaden's smell is a contradiction—a captivating puzzle that entices and warns, leaving me curious and cautious all at once.

As he finishes tending to my shoulder, I find myself drawn to him, wanting to comfort him, to take away whatever pain he's carrying inside. But I don't know how, and I'm scared of what I might uncover if I dig too deep. All I can do is offer him a small smile, a silent promise that I'll be there for him, just like he's been there for me . . . so far. And maybe, just maybe, together we can find a way to heal each other's wounds and find the light in the darkness. Clearly, I've lost my mind. I just hope and pray that this isn't another case of my eternal optimism that's going to turn around and bite me in the ass.

He tidies up the infirmary in that OCD way of every doctor I've ever seen, with precise and methodical movements. I watch him without saying a word, feeling a mix of frustration and fascination. He doesn't look at me, but his intense aura still lingers in the room, pulling me in like a moth to a flame.

"I don't do needy, and I don't do clingy." Out of fucking nowhere he makes this announcement while he braces his hands on the edge of the gurney as he frowns down at it.

His words sting, a not-so-subtle warning to keep my distance. But beneath the tough exterior, I sense his internal battle, a desire to push me away and a longing to keep me close.

He heaves a deep sigh, and without another word, he turns and marches his tight ass into the other room, leaving me with a swirl of emotions. I don't know what to make of him, and the way he alternates between hot and cold is enough to drive anyone crazy.

"What the fuck is that supposed to mean?" Frustration surges through me as I yell after his retreating back. And what the fuck difference does it make to me anyway what he does? I plan to stay just long enough to find out where Summer is, and then I'm out of here. There's no place for a connection between us in my life. I'll be gone like a gust of wind.

But even as I tell myself this, part of me can't deny my magnetic pull toward him. It's like I'm caught in a dark web, unable to break free. As much as he wants to push me away, the strange link between us tells me that he wants me to stay just as badly. His conflict mirrors my own, and like me, there's more to this man than meets the eye. I can't shake the feeling that I need to find out more.

With a heavy sigh, I put my weighty thoughts aside for now. The priority is finding Summer and getting the hell out of here. But as I leave the infirmary and step back into the main room, I can't help but feel that my life has taken a dangerous turn. Jaden may be a storm of darkness, but there's a glimmer of something else hidden beneath the surface, something I can't quite put my finger on.

As I try to figure out my next move, uncertainty gnaws at me, and I know that nothing in my life will ever be the same again. The puzzling man with the tight ass has drawn me into his world of shadows, and there's no escaping it now. But this bond between us, this tangible pull of sensations and emotions, keeps growing stronger; right now, it's screaming that he needs someone. Hell, I don't want that responsibility... or maybe, deep down, I do? My heart's thudding against my chest, tangled in fear and curiosity about the road ahead.

9
JADEN

My emotions are a raging tempest, relentlessly tearing at my soul. The aftermath of the killing left me battered, physically and emotionally. My angelic powers have been pushed to the limit, and now, I'm left feeling drained and vulnerable. It's like walking on a tightrope, trying to balance the vigilante seeking justice with the desperate need to care for myself.

Rayne's presence is a double-edged sword, the embodiment of both comfort and fear. Ever since I met her two days ago, I've been fighting to shut out her energy, her emotions. They keep hammering at my defenses, but I can't let myself get consumed by them. My powers are tied to my emotions, and I know that letting her in would replenish me, but the risk is too great.

Yet I can't shake the feeling that there's something very special about her. If I didn't know better, I'd swear she's been casting a spell over me. But that's simply not possible. She's a mortal and they don't have superpowers despite what the comic book franchises would have us believe. I know because the celestials told me when they made me an avenging angel. Maybe this is their way of telling me I have no fucking choice in the matter of protecting Rayne. And none of that answers the larger questions rolling around inside of my psyche—why am I here on this earth? What is my purpose? Who am I? Questions that fuck me up every minute of every day.

Fuck. As usual, nothing in my fucking head makes sense. And something about Rayne threatens my darkness. The memories of my past haunt me like malevolent ghosts, threatening to shatter the fragile peace I've built around my heart. For the first time ever, I want to share my pain . . . with Rayne, to let her in, but the vulnerability terrifies me. Even the thought of cracking open that cesspool a hair makes every last cell in my body scream. Too bad this new gift for healing doesn't extend to obliterating the mental anguish that is my life. But my angelic powers, my greatest strength, are also my biggest weakness. I can't heal myself and the more I use them, the more I need them replenished.

Strangely, I can't completely shut Rayne's presence out, no matter how deep into the abyss I go. It's as if a tiny filament of her light radiates in the background, letting me know that when I'm ready, she'll make it safe for me to come out and play. No matter how feisty she appears, I sense a calmness deep within her that soothes me. But there's also her tenacity that leaves no doubt she'll try to break through my walls like a hound on a scent, another reason I can't let her too close. The ache in my head intensifies, a blinding headache washing over me, as my mind tries to drown out the thoughts and memories I can't bear to face. I clutch my temples, trying to blot out the darkness, but it claws at me relentlessly.

The physician in me knows I need rest, to recharge my depleted powers, but the vigilante inside pushes me to keep going, to keep fighting for justice. To obliterate Viper from this planet for what he's done to Rayne and Summer. It's a constant battle, tearing at my soul with every heartbeat.

You're losing it, Jaden. I know it, but I can't do a fucking thing about it but retreat to my fortress of solitude, the fortress of self-imposed isolation with impenetrable walls where I escape. Impenetrable until now because try as I might, I can't shut out the thread of light coming from Rayne. It's as if in the midst of my turmoil, she remains a beacon of light, a soothing balm to my fractured spirit.

Hurt because of my withdrawal radiates from her like heat waves on a scorching summer day, and a wash of guilt gnaws at me like a relentless predator. I want to be the one to mend her wounds, but I'm too afraid of inflicting deeper scars—whether on myself or her remains an open question.

The TV flickers with mindless images, the background noise filling the racket in my mind. It's a pathetic attempt to numb the pain, to escape the demons clawing at my memories. But they persist, haunting me like a never-ending nightmare.

For the first time in forever, I want, no *crave*, a woman's body. Because that's all that this can be, sex. Because I don't do love. I can't do love. And caring leads to love. The thought surfaces, unbidden: *Maybe you can be friends.* I'm not sure where it stems from, and I take a beat to consider it. Even Rayne's friendship is a gift I'm unworthy of, a treasure that threatens to slip through my fingers like sand. I can't give her the friendship she deserves when I'm grappling with the darkness of my past. How can I know her fully when I'm still running from my own demons? And besides, she thinks I'm the enemy.

As the night stretches on, my internal battle rages,

tearing at the fabric of my being while I absentmindedly channel surf.

"Better eat." Rayne's tone has that firm edge, the kind that brooks no argument, as she sets a plate on my lap. I feel this little spark of defiance from her through our connection, as if she's silently daring me to call her out for taking the reins. Truth be told, I'm too drained to push back. Plus, there's a part of me that appreciates her stepping in, like she just knows I need her right now.

Little dragon. Like the mythical creatures, she's already proving to be curious, playful, and stubborn. But it's her innocence and vulnerability that call out to my soul. Two things she's hiding well from the rest of the world, but I see. Because like me, she's built a wall, but hers looks more like a Roman shield wall and mine is a replica of Gollum's cave. Dark, damp, and no visitors allowed.

I've made the walls I've built around my heart seem insurmountable, yet Rayne's presence makes me long to tear them down. She seems to see past the scars on my soul, and that terrifies me even more. But it also makes me want to be better, to confront my past and find a way to heal. Fuck!

I can't deal with all of this. So for now, I retreat into my cave, seeking solace in the silence of the night and mindless sex. Except tonight, I don't have the energy or desire to seek out some random woman at the Masquerade Club. I want this woman tonight, which is precisely why I won't have her. Never mind that she's damaged goods . . . and so much better than I am and doesn't deserve me. I know I'm hurting Rayne with my withdrawal, and that knowledge gnaws at my conscience. But I can't allow myself to care about her baggage, not right now. Not when I can't even face my own inner demons.

I lean back on the loveseat, shifting aimlessly through channels. The low volume bleeds into my subconscious like an insidious lullaby. I stumble upon some tolerable porn and decide to stay for the night's entertainment. My hand replaces my dead lover as my most reliable source of pleasure after Savannah. I close my eyes and let my imagination wander, thinking of Rayne's lips on me, her ass taking every inch of my length with each thrust. It has been too long since I felt a woman's touch, awakening emotions I have long tried to bury—emotions that terrify me.

My eyes fly open at a quiet choking sound. Rayne stands, leaning against the archway leading from the hall. I groan inside as she stares, her mouth agape. Concern turns to curiosity on her face as she watches me, my lounge pants resting low on my hips and a small towel across my belly. I keep my head on the back of the recliner as I stroke my cock, turning my gaze back to the screen. Pretending she's not there. Despite the low volume, there's no mistaking the moaning and sucking sounds issuing from the TV. I wait for her to leave. She stays . . . a presence I can't ignore.

I whisper, "Watch with me," despite the voice in my head warning me not to.

My heart thrums as she stays motionless, undecided. Anxiety and anticipation whirl through me in heated waves, both hers and mine. Will this enflame her further? I have no idea how much experience she has. *Jaden, get a grip.* This is a woman who was sex-trafficked so of course she can handle it. But still, I sit there watching her from the corner of my eye, suspended in a moment of uncertainty. Should I stop or continue?

After several long moments of pregnant pause, she sits on the recliner, hovering on the edge of the seat next to me, her eyes glued to the screen in equal parts revulsion and curiosity. Like she longs to watch me pleasure myself but won't let herself admit it. Something the voyeur in me recognizes. She's close enough that I can feel her heat radiating off her skin, yet too far for me to touch her without effort.

"Do what you want." I try to hide the desire leaking from my voice and fail miserably. Her head snaps up so quickly it's almost comical, beautiful chestnut irises darkening with desire.

"What do you mean?"

I swivel my head toward her, our eyes connecting like magnets.

"Take whatever pleasure you want from this experience." *Show me who you are.*

Her lips are a deep, alluring brown and part slightly as she pauses in surprise; it's clear that no one has considered her enjoyment before and she is unsure how to respond.

Little Dragon, I'll show you just how good it could be if you'd only let go. I'll make you scream.. . .

She curls her legs up under her, turning my way. Not enough to seem too eager but enough for me to notice. She clasps and unclasps her hands, while I secretly smile. Our growing bond tells me she's desperate to touch me, despite all her claims of hating sex. My gaze drops to my dick where I slide my thumb around the head, tracing the precum around the glans. Her eyes are glued to my hand as she licks her lips again. Goosebumps rise on my skin as I imagine those full lips engulfing my cock. I grow harder, balls clenching tight, begging to come undone beneath her watchful eye.

I grip hard and stroke fast. It's a motion I've done a million times before, yet something about her watching me stimulates me even more, and soon enough heated jets of cum shoot onto the towel across my belly. I smother any sound that wants to escape from my mouth, not wanting to do anything that might spook her. Refusing to let her see she's affected me. As the tremors fade away, I glance at her out of the corner of my eye. Her breathing is heavy yet shallow, as if she's struggling to keep it even.

"You act like this is the first time you've seen someone masturbate." I watch her startle in surprise.

I lock eyes with her, shadowed by yearning. Uncertainty gnaws at me, teetering on the edge of whatever comes next. Never have I allowed anyone such an intimate glimpse—not even Savannah. But Rayne stands apart, a blend of vulnerability and raw sensuality that fuels my desire even more.

As I sit here, the air thick with tension, she goes stiff, her eyes narrowing like she's zeroing in on a target. "Don't you dare judge me," she fires back. Her words hit something raw in me—my deep-seated fear of judgment, a vulnerability I didn't think I'd ever have to confront again.

Her anger has an unexpected effect, sharpening my arousal but also making me cautious. I've spent years not giving a damn about anyone else's opinion. After losing Savannah, it was just me against a world I'd grown to resent. But right now, in this moment with Rayne, something's changed.

"I'm not judging you." I contain my own rising frustration. If she's going to make everything a battle, we don't stand a chance—not even as friends. "I'm saying stop following society's script and figure out what you actually want. Especially when it comes to your own desires."

I ditch the towel, adjust myself, and hold back the lecture right on the tip of my tongue. While I figure out why I give a damn, I wait for her to say something, some final remark to close this volatile chapter between us. But once again, she throws me off.

"You're probably right," she says, turning her attention back to the TV. But I can feel it—the question still hanging between us, amping up the tension, doing similar things to my cock.

And then a thought breaks through, uninvited but not unwelcome. Could we find something neither of us has experienced before? Great sex, but without the scars and baggage. It's a dangerous idea that threatens to pry open compartments of myself I've sealed shut. But sitting here, watching her, it's a possibility that I can't easily dismiss. And for the first time in a long while, I wonder if I should even try to.

10

RAYNE

I don't even know what the hell I'm doing, going back to Jaden's den after delivering that pizza. His rejection stings, but there's something about those low moans from the TV that reel me in. *Curiosity killed the cat.* Screw it, I won't overthink this. I'm tired of playing it safe and trying to be logical. So, I quietly tiptoe toward the doorway, my curiosity and desire battling for control. And when I finally see what's inside, it's like . . . no way, it can't be.

The storm outside matches the turmoil in my heart as I'm pulled in, unable to resist the wild and chaotic attraction he stirs within me. Un-fucking believable. Caught in the act. *He's masturbating.* My heart rate kicks up as I stay glued to the doorway, watching in fascination and horror. He notices me with a whisper: "Watch with me."

I should turn and run. But instead, I slowly saunter over and perch on the sofa beside him. Watching this porn together should be wrong, but I blame the drugs as his desire washes over me. Could it be true? Does he really want me for me, not because of some curiosity about dark meat?

"Do what you want." His voice commands my attention. He wants me to take pleasure from this experience, to show him who I am. My heart thuds as I force myself to meet his gaze—dark and mysterious, calling out to something deep inside me. Seems as if I'm just as perverted as he is.

"Take whatever pleasure you want from this experience." His voice is soft seductive, but the message he sends through our connection shouts, *"Show me who you are."*

Nobody's ever given a shit about who I am and I'm burning with curiosity, so I sit and watch. My breath catches as I watch Jaden stroke himself with ferocious intensity. His tapered fingers move over his length in strong, steady strokes, kneading it like firm dough between thumb and forefingers. His body tightens under my gaze, a barely audible groan of pleasure erupting from his lips as he spills onto the cloth laid out on his stomach. My body tightens in return and heat floods through my lower regions. Longing to taste that essence and feel its warmth on my tongue courses through me. That's a first. I don't do blowjobs, but I can't tear my gaze away from his softening cock, so it's a moment before I notice his golden-hued eyes studying me intently. My cheeks heat at the scrutiny.

"You act like this is the first time you've seen someone masturbate." His beautiful tenor voice is low and seductive, pulling me to him. Making me want to comply.

I open my mouth to reply when his words register fully. My whole body tenses up, my instincts on high alert, but damn it, I can't lie. The words spill out, raw and honest, before I even have a chance to think. It's like my soul won't let me hold back, even though my mind is screaming for me to shut up. "Don't you dare judge me. I told you it's the first time I've watched. It's the first time I've done most things."

"I'm not judging you." Jaden's fires back at me, clearly pissed. Sitting there with his cock still hanging out and his cum all over the towel. The cock and cum my eyes are locked on,

"I'm saying stop following society's script and figure out what you actually want. Especially when it comes to your own desires." The tension radiating from him as he puts himself together should alarm me, but it has quite the opposite effect. Because he's right, if people are really doing the kind of shit we're watching on TV, there's been a lot missing from the romance novels I've read.

"You're probably right," I begrudgingly admit. More out of embarrassment than shame. What twenty-five-year-old doesn't know about sex these days? Those of us trying to survive.

He arches an eyebrow, and for a moment, I catch a glimpse of a secret amusement in his eyes before he shifts his attention back to the television. A nauseating blonde is on the screen, blowing one of the men, and I can't help but wonder what he finds appealing about watching fake sex. But I know better than to ask, especially with his moody nature.

Once, in my life before Viper, I stumbled across an erotic movie filmed abroad—in Bombay, perhaps, or some other city of exotic beauty. The women were stunning, the men beautiful. The acting was passable—it was enough to take me away from reality and indulge in heated fantasies. In my memory, I can still see their oiled bodies intertwined between silken sheets and sultry curtains as they moved together like one harmonious creature. There was no explicit nudity, yet every subtlety had been amplified to teasing intensity. Even now it provokes a stirring deep within me. Now, smut like that is worth watching.

In this silence between us, a subtle air of smug right-eousness surrounds him, as if he's stumbled upon some hidden purpose, and I'm somehow at the center of it. His curiosity sends shivers down my spine. It's as if he's trying to figure me out, peering into the depths of my soul with those piercing eyes.

I sit there, my heart racing, feeling the weight of his gaze on me even though he's seemingly engrossed in the TV. There's something about him that both intrigues and frightens me. I've never met someone like him before, someone who can make me feel so exposed and vulnerable without even saying a word.

As much as I want to know what's going on in his mind, I'm also afraid of what I might find. He's a man of secrets, and I can sense that he guards them fiercely. He's built a fortress around his heart, and I'm not sure if I'll ever be allowed inside.

So, I sit in silence, my own thoughts swirling like a storm. Our connection is both undeniable and unnerving. Will he ever let me in, or will he always keep me at arm's length, a distant spectator in his life?

For now, I have no choice but to watch, wait, and navigate this complex dance we're in. And as I steal glances at him, I'm certain he's watching me just as closely, as if trying to decipher how to decode me.

Suddenly his hand reaches over and grabs mine, drawing it up to hover over his groin. Heat radiates through me, and my heart pounds wildly in my chest. Now he wants a hand job? But he just came! He looks into my eyes, and I swear I can see all the way to his soul in that moment.

My heart races faster as Jaden leans closer. His breath swirls around me, a dark caress that sparks every nerve ending in my body. I can't focus on anything but him and the strange connection between us. I'm trying to look sophisticated as if I'm in control of the situation . . . and failing miserably. All I can do is fight the urge to surrender to this burning desire inside of me.

The muted TV screen flickers to life, the blonde beneath the man in a passionate embrace snatching my attention back to the screen . . . while my hand stays locked about an inch above tenting lounge pants. I can't tear my eyes away as my heart pounds against my chest. I've never been this turned on, ever. The strong yearnings in me beg for something that both terrifies and fascinates me—sex. It brings nothing but pain, but with Jaden . . . maybe it won't hurt. Maybe with him, I could feel something more than fear at his touch. I let my hand drop onto his crotch. *What the fuck do I do now?*

Jaden's eyes meet mine, filling me with a sudden burning desire that overtakes all other thoughts. Only a whisper of command escapes his lips. "Take off your panties." His words roar through me like rippling thunder and the heat between us makes it hard to breathe. His hand slides farther up my thigh, and the promise of all the wicked things he could teach me hangs heavy in the air, an unspoken temptation between us, daring us to cross the line. There's no sound except that of our breathing.

His movements are deliberate, each touch like a slow burn, igniting a fire within me that I can't ignore. I wait for the dead feeling to come . . . that numbness that always washes over me when men touch me. Except, this time it doesn't. His fingers trace delicate patterns along my skin, awakening sensations I'd never known before. It should terrify me, but instead, it's like a forbidden thrill that I can't resist. My mind swims in a storm of conflicting emotions, but the intensity of his touch drowns out everything else. I can't deny it any longer—I want him, body and soul, and the fear that courses through me is exhilarating.

In this moment of darkness and desire, I see the vulnerability in his eyes, a glimpse of the man beneath the extremely rude exterior. I know I should be cautious, for the secrets he keeps and the pain he hides, but the pull between us is magnetic.

He's giving me a choice, a chance to walk away if I want to, but I can't bring myself to take it. I want to explore this connection, to delve into the depths of this unspoken desire. I trust my instincts and heart; they're telling me to stay right now. I try to deny it, yet my traitorous thighs fall apart as if they have a will of their own, and with trembling fingers, I obey him and wriggle out of my panties.

His fingertips brush my hip as he guides me back, teasing me with what could be if I give in. His gaze sears through me as his thoughts become clear through our strange connection—I can feel them exploring every inch of my body, making me desperate for his touch.

He gazes down at me with a heat that burns my skin, and shame washes through me. What he must think of me splayed out in front of him like a wanton slut.

"None of that," he whispers in my ear, his breath warm on my neck. My body tenses, anticipation coursing through me. Again, he barely moves, yet I am thrown off balance, reacting as if pushed back. His magnetism is a force in the room that threatens to consume me, and I collapse against the couch, my legs spread wide. His hand travels slowly up my thigh, and my pulse quickens. A wave of desire crashes over me as his fingers dip between my legs, tracing circles around the swollen wetness between my thighs before sliding down and teasingly circling my clit.

A moan escapes my lips, and I can feel his intense satisfaction at my surrender, but I'm already lost in the delicious sensations consuming my body. His fingers deftly explore every inch of my girlie bits, pushing deeper with each thrust until I'm coiled tightly—too tightly—on the edge of ecstasy.

"Let go." He breathes it in my ear. His fingers circle before applying just a little bit more pressure. I let out a long moan, tense, on the edge. Anxiety seeps in. I try hard not to pant—I concentrate every ounce of energy on it.

He kneels over me, grabs my curls, and yanks my face to his. He isn't rough, but he's insistent. My eyes fly open. His gaze drills into mine. "Stop thinking." Low, insistent, commanding. He lets my head drop back, and I collapse against the cushions. After a few seconds of intense staring, he seems satisfied and resumes where he's left off. I let myself look for just a few seconds. He is glorious. Greek God glorious. I always liked the Greeks better than—

Jaden plunges three fingers deep into me, and waves of pleasure and pain jolt through me. My clit pulses in time with the rhythm his other hand sets as he caresses it. I bite my lip to stave off the scream that threatens to escape me. My body rebels against this invasion, trying to push him away. But the warmth of his touch seeps through me like honey, melting away all resistance. I moan long and low as I rock against him, meeting each thrust with one of my own. He moves his fingers like they are performing some kind of ancient magic, weaving patterns of pleasure inside me that threaten to break any semblance of control I have left. Every move pushes me closer to the edge. . .

I can't let myself think about what I want. So I lie there, suspended, like a steam engine without a vent, waiting to explode. His hands roughly yank at my shirt and pull it up to reveal my hardened nipples begging for attention. He grasps one between his lips, sucking hard until I'm on the brink of screaming out as pleasure and agony mix. My every nerve is pulling me closer and closer to the hidden abyss I yearn for—but just can't reach. So I do what the girls at the warehouse taught me to do and make appropriate moaning noises faking an orgasm.

I almost sob as he withdraws his fingers. I want more. He sits beside me while I recover . . . not touching, but not withdrawn either. I get my breath back and try not to let the confusing chorus of my thoughts ruin the sensations coursing through my body.

Several minutes later, Jaden gets all businesslike. He pulls me up and points me toward the bedroom. "Get some sleep," he says. "We'll be leaving first thing."

Wide-eyed from confusion, I stumble from the room. What does this mean? Did I just . . . sell myself? The thought makes my insides coil tight with shame, but at the same time a shiver runs up through my core as I recall his touch. How can something feel so wrong and yet so good? What will happen now? Will he throw me out after what happened?

But no matter how much guilt I feel—a tiny smile lingers in my heart as warmth floods between my legs whenever I think about him. I try to deny it, but I want more.

11

JADEN

The bitter aroma of freshly brewed coffee permeates the air, a scathing reminder of my lapse in judgment. As I pour the liquid into my cup, it's not just the steam that rises; it's the untold complexities of my involvement with Rayne. A part of me detests the implications—she's someone I swore to protect, not exploit. But a more self-serving part revels in the euphoria of last night. A euphoria too familiar, too inviting.

Stepping into the shower, I let the warm droplets cascade over my skin, each one a memory of her touch. As alluring as a dream you want to go back to, even when waking life calls. No. I shake my head, banishing the thought. Last night was an escape, a hiatus from my internal strife. For the first time since—I wince and push past the threatening anguish—in ages, I felt almost tranquil.

And then, as if mocking my fleeting sense of peace, the recurring nightmare intruded. *"Don't be such a wuss."* This time, however, it retreated when I sought refuge in the recesses of my mind. What unholy game is my psyche playing? The phantoms I had wrestled into submission have resurfaced, and their haunting is intimately linked to Rayne. Her soul reverberates with my own suppressed emotions—shame, desire, and an unsettling curiosity—intermingled with a self-contempt that I can't quite grasp. For some absurd reason, she matters.

Why, then, this magnetic pull towards her? Soulmates and destiny are notions for romantics and fools. Yet she possesses a haunting allure, unsettling the fortress of emotional detachment I've meticulously erected.

Then a flicker of a thought breaks through. Maybe my perspective has been myopic. Rayne survived her trials not defeated but defiant, unbroken despite the horrors she endured. *Unlike me.* Another thought I push away. She's not just a survivor; she's a warrior, a kindred spirit fighting her demons. And that strength, that resilience, intrigues me in a way I hadn't expected.

Could I be the mirror that reflects her intrinsic worth back to her? Not romantically—God knows I'm not the man to offer that—but as someone who recognizes the exceptional nature of her spirit. She's not just a potential lover; she's an asset, a future cornerstone of our operation with her eye for minutiae. I can offer her sanctuary, a place for her resilience to thrive, while she offers an invaluable skill set to our mission.

So, I suppress the urge to dissect my burgeoning plan into its finer details. Those can be elaborated upon later. The focus now is on the near future: she stays. She'll stand beside me, her unbroken spirit complementing our collective purpose, as we bring Viper's empire to its knees. And for a moment, despite my deeply ingrained skepticism towards emotional entanglements, that prospect seems disturbingly comforting.

As Rayne enters the kitchen, a subtle tension coils around me, binding the air with its weight. Her tousled curls cascade around her face, an artful mess that beckons and warns in equal measure. In this moment of silence, our future teeters on a precipice. If she reverts to the possessiveness that's all too familiar with other women I've been involved with, then the vestiges of potential between us will evaporate. But there's a gut feeling—a sensation that she defies my assumptions in every aspect that resonates with me.

Pretending to be engrossed in my coffee cup, I observe her from the corner of my eye. She moves with a deliberate grace, fetching a tea bag and hot water. Her actions are neither hurried nor hesitant, but purposeful. And when she finally stands, clutching her mug as a protective shield, she maintains a distance that echoes my own guarded demeanor. A silent nod of approval echoes in my mind.

"Morning." Her voice is like a gentle sunrise—soft, warm, and slightly hesitant.

"Morning." The word catches in my throat as I wait for her to ask for something I can't give. Yet, the aura she emanates is not one of possessiveness but an uncanny echo of my own caution and intrigue.

Her brow furrows, a response no doubt to the guarded undertones in my voice. As if she senses the boundaries I've fortified around myself. I brace for the typical sentimental rhetoric that usually comes after a sexual encounter.

"So, when do we leave?" She eyes me while sipping her tea. Her question shocks the shit out of me and sends a ripple through my expectations. This little dragon avoids the familiar terrain of emotional attachment and opts for the practical. Once again, that foreign yet comforting feeling pulses through me, a testament to her uniqueness.

"As soon as you're ready." I surprise myself with my easy acceptance. Honestly—and I'm always brutally honest with myself—I'm already strategizing ways to maneuver the conversation to avoid the emotional minefield, whether it's real or just in my head. How can I make it work with her in my life? I pause, then ask, "Why didn't you press me about your sister last night?"

Her eyes fixate on me, piercing through her glasses, which she adjusts—her physical tell. It's as if she's probing the thick walls I've erected, searching for an entry point. She won't find one, not today. I may be magnetically drawn to her, but the barriers I've built are fortified by years of self-preservation.

She sighs and shakes her head, clearly grappling with her feelings and how to articulate them. Her demeanor has no pressure or entitlement, and I find that oddly reassuring.

When she finally replies, her voice tinges with a vulnerability she can't fully cloak. "You said she was safe, and you clearly needed time." She pauses again, then heaves a sigh. "And so did I."

Her agreement hang in the air, adding new dimensions to our intricate dance. She may be calculating her steps and measuring the distance, but her focus is unwavering. And it's trained squarely on me.

"I had to take a step back." A mix of determination and vulnerability threads through her voice. "Last night was intense. I needed a moment, some space to process. And I think you understand that, maybe more than anyone else."

"Taking a step back was essential." A mix of determination and vulnerability threads through her voice. "Last night was overwhelming, and I needed room to breathe. I get the sense you understand that feeling all too well."

Her words reverberate through me, binding my

emotions to hers in a momentary but potent link. It's a foreign experience, acknowledging selfishness without recrimination. She's right; we're both trying to keep our pieces intact. I hold my tongue as I reach for the bread, the hum of the toaster a convenient distraction from the complicated emotions welling within me. It's been a very long time since I had someone to care for. *Since Savannah.*

She finally looks up, eyes fixed on mine as if seeking a response I'm not ready to give. "Our mom's a paranoid schizophrenic." Her words trail in the air like smoke. "So, crazy is in the blood."

My medical training kicks in involuntarily. "Catatonia isn't genetically predetermined; it's a psychological state."

As she stares back at me, an unspoken understanding passes between us, an acknowledgment that mental health is a complex terrain, often misconstrued.

"Guess I'll be staying with Summer now." Her voice is flat with resignation, and the abrupt change in topic jolts me. "I'm sure they have people who can help me find us a place to live."

Fear flashes through me. *Don't leave.* "Why the hell would you do that? You're staying with me. Razor wants you on the task force. You need time. We both do." I punch my voice with the command I use as a Dom and thank the gods that it keeps my voice from wavering. I don't thank her for not touching me, for recognizing that might have broken me even if a part of me longs for it. I slide two pieces of buttered toast across the table. "Eat."

She contemplates her tea for a moment before taking another sip. "I'm not hungry, thanks."

My eyes narrow, irritation and concern rising in tandem. "Eat something." The command in my voice is hard to miss. "Being stubborn won't help if you're on the verge of collapse."

Her eyes lock onto mine, a defiant blaze flickering within. "Thanks for the concern, but I don't need a babysitter, Captain Control."

"Stubborn woman!" Frustration and unspoken admiration infuse my words. "Your body needs fuel to heal. Strength doesn't come from starvation."

For a moment, my rough exterior softens as I recognize her prickly barbs for what they are . . . Self-protection. I place some jam in front of her. "Eat. It's not up for debate."

Her gaze locks with mine, a fleeting game of mental chess unfolding in her irises. Ultimately, she decides it's a battle not worth fighting today. "Thank you, kind sir. Would you happen to have any orange marmalade?"

Her feigned politeness triggers my short fuse, igniting an emotional tinderbox I've been trying to contain. With barely repressed force, I reach into the fridge and place a jar of orange marmalade on the table. "A few things you should know about me. I don't do fake. Either show me who you really are or don't show me anything at all." While I've got a full head of steam on, I continue, my voice tinged with a biting cold, "And, I don't do love."

Her eyes morph, the soft brown toughening into something resembling steel. "Well then, Captain Control, here's my response to that bullshit. First, I have no interest in love. It's merely a tool for manipulation. Second, my politeness is not a sign of being fake; it's a courtesy, one your upbringing apparently overlooked. But I'll remember for next time that instead of saying thank you, I should say fuck you, asshole. When I say I don't want to eat, I mean just that. Now, take me to my sister." She slams her mug on the table and marches toward the elevator, stopping midway and turning back to face me. "Oh, and if I were being polite, I'd have said please, but you've pissed me right off. I said take me to my sister." Turning back toward the elevator, she mutters something that comes through our link loud and clear. "Sick of people thinking the worst of me."

And just like that, she takes the wind out of my sails and kicks my ass leaving me utterly disarmed by her verbal onslaught. Strangely, I find myself savoring the sting of it. She halts at the elevator and pivots, arching an eyebrow. "Well?"

My retinas do their biometric dance with the elevator scanner, and I sense her irritation shifting into intense curiosity. "Super cool, Batman. How did you do that? With your eyes?"

I keep my emotions under lock and key, masking the unfamiliar thrill her curiosity elicits. "It's a security measure, nothing more."

A complex silence unfolds as I acknowledge, if only to myself, that Rayne poses a challenge I can't neatly categorize or control. It's both disarming and thrilling, rattling the emotional fortress I've painstakingly built over the years. As I confront this revelation, I'm pulled between the compelling urge to explore this uncertain terrain and my deep-seated aversion to vulnerability rooted in scars I dare not acknowledge.

We both step into the elevator and for a moment, her gaze meets mine—no games, no pretenses. It leaves me pondering whether she, like me, thinks about the strange relationship we've started to forge.

The elevator doors close us in, a microcosm away from the world, detached and intimate in its metallic embrace. "You ready?"

"Yes," she says. Direct and to the point. Nice. An

intriguing silence envelops us, a silence neither stifling nor liberating, just laden with a nebulous something neither of us can name.

As we settle into the car, the supple leather of the seats inhaling our presence, she buckles her seatbelt with a quiet click. Her eyes, those windows to untold worlds, find mine. The air thrums with her unspoken questions.

"Just drive, Captain Control," she eventually speaks, the edges of her mouth curling into a sly half-smile that threads a spark of something lighter into the tensile atmosphere.

It's strange how a title coined in a moment of friction could fit so comfortably. I forget for a moment how much I detest pet names. As I return her smile, something deep within me churns, like the first fluttering leaves heralding an oncoming storm. The ignition roars to life, syncing with the silent charge between us.

We head toward Harmony Hills Treatment Centre, each of us a study in contrasts. She's strong, no doubt about it, fully aware of who she is. As for me, there's something stir-ring, something I've managed to lock away under years of control and deliberate isolation. I brush it off as simple friendship, but a nagging thought tells me it might not be that simple.

The road stretches ahead, a blank canvas waiting for the first brushstroke. My grip tightens on the wheel as I consider how last night's events have changed something between us—what that means, I can't yet say. Every mile adds a layer of certainty to my unease, this tension between curiosity and caution.

There's a stir of emotion, one I'd smothered and forgot-ten, making me uneasy in a way I can't remember feeling in a long time. But there's something magnetic about that discomfort. As we cut through the air, I'm caught between wanting to dig deeper into whatever's happening between us and my instinctual fear of emotional messiness. It's a risky balance, threatening either a liberating breakthrough or a fall into vulnerability—maybe both. But for now, the road is open, and anything feels possible.

12

RAYNE

The countryside blurs into a sea of green, a fleeting backdrop to the real show going on inside this car. Jaden threads the Ferrari around curves like they're nothing, and that engine—its purr goes straight to my gut, a sound that's way too intimate for comfort. I tell myself it's just the car's horsepower making my heart race, not the guy holding the wheel. What a load of crap.

The way Jaden controls this beast of a car—it's magnetic. He doesn't just drive; he commands, steering not just metal and rubber but the atmosphere in the car, shaping it into something I can almost touch. I want to dive deeper, understand what makes him tick. Dammit, why can't I shake this pull toward him?

Fact: he's killed people. But, man, there's layers to him, shades of something softer glimpsed beneath that lethal surface. When he showed that flicker of care and compassion, it threw me. I know that kind of darkness— the kind that makes you put up walls so high you can't even see the sun. I shake my head. No, he's not some broken bird; the guy can clearly fend for himself. But those walls . . . I recognize them. They're built from the same material as my own. But not everyone's a victim. Not even him.

It messes with me, this attraction. Half of me is shouting to run from the ticking time bomb beside me, but the other half? That part wants to get to the hidden layers beneath the killer façade. It's like some twisted rom-com narrative is playing out in my head: he's the Neo to my Trinity. A Matrix-level mind fuck, but for keeps.

Our eyes lock again, and it's like I'm diving into some kind of messed-up ocean, a place where you can't tell where the danger really lies. I see a flicker of vulnerability in his eyes, like a flashing "proceed with caution" sign, but hell, I'm already in too deep to heed it. The landscape outside is a blur of pretty and peaceful, but it's just surface-level calm. Kind of like me, really.

I can't help but look his way, and every time I do, it's like getting pulled in by a magnet. Jaden's a killer, dark and dangerous, and the more he's around, the more conflicted I feel. He killed for *me*, and something messed up in me is loving it. A killer and a perv? Yeah, he's got it all, and my brain is screaming red flags. But my heart, that traitor, is pounding to a different beat, perfectly in sync with the hum of the engine—or is it his own heartbeat I'm feeling?

I want him, no point denying it. It's a new kind of craving that pisses me off, but it's also too strong to ignore. I felt that dark hole in him yesterday, and it's like staring into an abyss. It's got its own gravity, pulling everything in, especially me.

My gut is screaming at me not to jump into that black hole. I've tried to see into it, but it's a no-go. It's like trying to figure out the end of a maze in pitch darkness. Gollum's twisted face pops up in my mind, a warning about where obsession can lead. But I've got Summer to think about. She's my reason to stay out of the chaos.

I sniffle a sigh, not even sure what emotion it carries. The world outside is speeding by, just like my racing thoughts. And there's Jaden, too freaking complicated for his own good. But he saved me. He's offering me revenge and a way out. And maybe even a job, something more stable than my hit-or-miss gigs so far. The idea of taking control of my life? That's tempting enough to make this insane leap feel almost reasonable.

So here we are, driving into the unknown. I'm on the edge, teetering, thinking about jumping into this crazy new life. It's a risk, but isn't that what living is all about?

Tightening my grip on the seat, I shake off the wild thought—Jaden is dangerous, period. But damn, as the Ferrari's engine roars, a part of me wants to roar along with it. It's not just that I'm attracted to him; it's like he's this magnet I can't pull away from. And hell, I know it's a risky game.

I should be focusing on Summer, planning a life miles away from creeps like Viper. But my mind keeps tripping over Jaden. He speeds up my pulse and stirs up feelings I've never had to deal with. He might be my Neo—or my biggest mistake. It's messed up, but part of me is screaming, "Take the risk!"

Pulling myself together, I force my thoughts away from Jaden's gravitational pull. The guy's got layers, dark ones, and that's a no-go zone for now. I let out a deep breath, reminding myself I've got shit to do: Summer, a place to call home, safety. But keeping that focus? It's like trying to stand still in a windstorm.

As we zoom through the open countryside, I make a promise to myself: no more getting sidetracked by my stupid crush on Jaden. I've got to be the rock here, because my emotions are a total shit show.

"Tell me more about your mother?" Jaden suddenly blurts, snapping me out of my mental spiral. The shift from his brooding silence is so jarring, it's like a jump scare in a horror flick.

"My mom? Seriously?" I blink, thrown for a loop. "Wow, way to break character from your 'silent but deadly' act."

I catch his gaze and feel it—the weight, the depth, and yeah, the danger. But for a split second, I see something else, like maybe I'm not the only one wrestling with what the hell is going on between us.

"What do you want to know?" My voice is edged, a balance of caution and defiance. My eyes narrow, taking in Jaden as I gauge his next move. With him, questions are seldom just questions. They're probes, disguised hand grenades set to reveal truths. Yeah, he's got that physician's intrigue, sure, but something more hovers behind that poised facade. Could he be after something else, some deeper insight cloaked behind the guise of medical curiosity?

"When did your mother's schizophrenia first manifest? How was she diagnosed?" Ah, there's the doc. He's not treating me like I'm clueless, and that's a point in his favor.

I feel a gnawing tension, a sharp itch for a joint to calm the nerves. But I can't afford that comfort, not with hospital staff on the horizon. My mom's first break with reality? That's one tale that usually stays locked up tight. People either don't buy it, or they look at me like I'm a tragedy in motion. But Jaden, he's radiating something else—genuine curiosity masked as casual interest.

"I was eleven," I begin, my words careful but direct, "when she went off the deep end. She'd yell at me to pick up a phone that never rang. Arguing was pointless, so I'd pretend to answer the goddamn thing. She also accused me of hiding drugs, ripped through my clothes, and hit me while blaming me for her screwed-up life. Oh, and let's not forget the screaming matches with E.S., accusing him of cheating."

I press on, recounting the grim reality but sidestepping the frightened kid I was—am. That kid had to grow the hell up, fast. Like when I walked in to find Mom pointing a shotgun at E.S., his eyes pleading. "What was I supposed to do? I was just a kid, barely eleven."

"Scratch my arm." Jaden's voice is low, his forearm resting between us. I hardly think about it; I just start scratching. A trickle of warmth seeps through me, like an unspoken 'go ahead.' It's strange; I sense no judgment, only an earnest want to understand. And that, that's disarming as hell.

"So, what'd you do?"

"They were between me and the damn phone. It's not like we had a cell; we were broke as hell." I'm dumping way too much, but once the faucet's open, good luck turning it off.

"Summer's there, right? Just out of Mom's line of sight. She looked terrified, so there was no question—I had to shield her. And E.S., he was like a god to me back then. My heart's slamming against my ribcage, but screw it—I run up that steep-ass hill to the payphone and dial 911. And that's how I got tagged as the family rat." Can't keep the bile out of my voice, even if I tried.

"Rats are smart, you know. Crafty. But you? You're more of a dragon," Jaden says.

I shoot him a 'what-the-hell' look, my fingers still scratching his arm. "Explain."

"Easy." His voice wraps around me like good whiskey—smooth, burning, leaving a trace long after it's gone. "Don't scratch a hole in me. What's next?"

"Why the dragon?" I'm braced for an insult, always am.

"Because you're loyal, you're a question mark in human form, and you're brave as hell."

And just like that, there's this warm buzz that fills me up. No one ever says good shit like that to me. Jaden catches my eye, then quickly looks back at the road. "Don't read into it. I'm just saying you'd go to the ends of the earth for your sister."

I narrow my eyes at him, letting him know that I call bullshit. But that weird emotional vibe between us? It goes cold really quick. Still, I felt it. So I pocket that fleeting warmth. 'Cause let's be honest, warm and fuzzy moments are not on the menu with this guy. But I felt it, I know I did. And that's something.

"God forbid." Yanking my hand back from his arm, I cross my arms, sealing myself off like a bar's last call—no more service, no more niceties. His lifted eyebrow and those damned compelling eyes telegraph his thoughts: he thinks I'm being a brat. It only amps up my urge to bite back.

"What happened next?" He tones down his voice. It's one of those split-second moments when I just know—this is as close to 'sorry' as he'll get. The man's arm is back on the console, twitching in this silent demand for contact. His version of an olive branch? What a selfish prick.

"Yeah, I'm selfish and damn good at it. So spill, little dragon." His words hit me like a rogue wave, unexpected and disarming. The warmth that had started to crystallize in my veins melts, seeping into my core. I can't help it; the words tumble out.

13

JADEN

Rayne wraps her arms around herself like she's bracing for impact, and I can't help but feel that impact right along with her. "I ran back home and got there just as the police arrived, so in time to see them literally drag my mother out of the house, kicking and screaming, wig askew, like some deranged creature, which I guess she was. Fuck, I wish I had a joint."

Her story cuts through me, layer by layer—a horror show I can't look away from. She's flatlining emotionally, and damn if that doesn't ring a bell. Warning signs light up in my brain, but some other part of me can't help diving deeper into this minefield. An irresistible pull to expose more of my brave little dragon's inner world.

As our emotional borderlines stretch thin, her pain comes at me like a tidal wave. For a second, I'm drowning, not sure where her feelings end and mine kick in. Amidst the chaos, there's this spark in her, this undying grit. A fierce, unwavering determination that's reminiscent of Brienne of Tarth. It's like finding a nugget of gold in the mud.

My gut says to pull the plug on this connection; it's a powder keg waiting to blow. She's too young, not seasoned by life's ugly turns, and that alone should have me running for the hills. But there's something about her, a complex allure that pins me to the spot. Most people, I can read like an open book, but Rayne's a puzzle—a damn complicated one that I'm not ready to put down.

This link between us surges, like a sudden hit of adrenaline. It's like stepping into unknown territory, firing up parts of me I didn't even know existed. I'm at war with myself, caution butting heads with this raw urge to let things unfold. It's as if her struggle puts a magnifying glass on my own, spotlighting the internal tug-of-war we're both grappling with.

We linger in this fraught stillness, two souls dancing on the knife's edge of revelation and catastrophe. And all the while, I can't shake the notion that in this tumultuous space, I find something that feels—astonishingly, perilously—right.

Be careful, Jaden. This connection is a double-edged sword; it could shatter my defenses. But then Rayne cracks the code to my inner sanctum, and I can't help but be drawn in. She's a damn puzzle that I can't resist picking apart. She's fire and vulnerability all rolled into one, and it feels right, like a thrill I haven't felt in years. That dangerous comfort of being close, emotionally close—it's like some forbidden vice. Savannah's ghost tries to intrude, but I slam that door shut.

As we pull up to Harmony Hills, a mix of apprehension and curiosity knots inside me. Rayne leans in, eyeing the sprawling place. "It's massive." Her words are lost in the background as I wrestle with this inner turmoil.

We reach the reception desk, Anne looking up with a

smile that can melt glaciers. Rayne's eyes flicker between me and Anne, radar on high alert. I feel the pull to mess with her just a little, to keep this complex dance between us going.

"Afternoon, Anne." I crank up the charm. "You're looking as radiant as ever." I toss her a wink and soak up her reaction.

Anne grins, putting her assets on full display. "Oh, Jaden, it's been too long."

Rayne's feelings seep through our connection—impatience meets something darker, something I can't put a finger on. I decide to fan the flame. "You can say that again." I let that sit for a moment, locking eyes with Anne as Rayne's gaze burns into me. "We're here for Summer Turner. Dr. Patton's expecting us."

Anne's eyes are curious, but it's Rayne's spike of possessiveness that gives me a thrill. "Funny, we were just talking about you." Anne's grin widens.

"Only the good stuff, I trust." I wink at Anne but am very aware of the tension building between me and Rayne.

As we head toward Dr. Patton's office, I lean close to Rayne. "Feeling a little green-eyed, are we?" My voice is a low rumble, designed to stir the emotional pot even more. I can't deny the twisted satisfaction I feel from making the air between us just a bit thicker, more electric.

She shoots me a glare, her cheeks flush red. "Don't get cocky. You're a real piece of work, you know that?" Even with the sting in her words, I can sense a hint of vulnerability.

I chuckle. Got to admit, messing with her emotions feels like a victory. The bond we share, this intimate connection, adds an intensity to our interaction that I can't deny. There's something magnetic about Rayne, a force that draws me in despite my better judgment. It's time I face the truth . . . I'm captivated, entangled in a web of emotions that threaten to ensnare us both. *Friendship, that's all this is.*

Walking into Dr. Patton's office, I'm struck by how relaxed it feels. Big windows let in tons of light, and the whole room just has a chill vibe. This isn't like the stuffy psych offices I've seen at the hospital. This one's got books and artwork, and even a spot for meditation. It smells like lavender, calming the nerves.

Dr. Patton herself matches the vibe. Jeans, old T-shirt, running shoes—she looks like someone you'd want to talk to. And her eyes, man, they look like they can see right through you, already catching the storm that's brewing between me and Rayne.

Rayne's shout cuts through the calm. "Summer!" It's like a mix of relief and worry that echoes right into me. I look over at the young woman sitting in the chair. She looks clean but spaced out. She's got a different build than Rayne, shorter and not as fit. Though the Caucasian family features carry a distinctiveness that sets her apart, her eyes and hair—those say she's family. She doesn't have the same fire as Rayne, though. Dressed in a sweatshirt and pants, she looks like she's just going through the motions.

Rayne engulfs Summer in an embrace, her face a canvas of conflicting emotions—relief wrestling with worry. She sits next to her sister, clutching her hand as if she could infuse life through the very act of touch. I feel it—the storm inside Rayne. Anger, sorrow, a tempest of frustration, all of it a mirror to Summer's unspoken pain. Then something snaps—a burst of energy that prickles my skin and seizes my senses. It's as if a light bulb goes on in Rayne's mind, and I can almost hear the gears clicking into place.

B.J.'s touch settles on my shoulder—a tether in the

whirlpool of emotion swirling around me. "You must be Jaden." She speaks softly, each syllable imbued with genuine concern.

I manage a stiff nod, my gaze anchored to the emotional spectacle unfolding before me. "It's tough to see her like this." I coat my words with enough truth to mask the disquiet roiling beneath my surface. I sense B.J. picking up on it—her eyes showing a flicker of understanding. Yet, there's an extra layer, an inexplicable charge that sparks from my link with Rayne, binding us in a way that leaves me at once fascinated and unnerved.

Rayne, consumed by her own struggle, rises from her seat. "You're the doctor, right? I'm Rayne, Summer's older sister." The metamorphosis in her is startling—she's gone from vulnerable to indomitable in the span of a heartbeat.

"Hello, Rayne. Thank you for coming," B.J. greets, shaking her hand with a grip that's at once firm and comforting. "I'm Dr. B.J. Patton, I'll be working with your sister."

As we settle into our seats, a modicum of calm begins to settle over me. B.J. offers refreshments—tea for Rayne, coffee for me. The intercom buzzes as she orders, and then she joins us, exuding a calming vibe.

Rayne leans in, eyes locked on B.J., her body language screaming urgency. "Look, B.J., my sister and I have this psychic connection. She's not here; she's checked out." It's the sort of candor I've come to expect from Rayne, her forthright approach peeling away another layer of my skepticism, replacing it with growing respect.

Each word from her mouth not only conveys information but also twines itself around my own conflicted feelings. As much as I want to fend off what I'm beginning to feel for her, the electricity between us weaves its own narrative—a story neither of us seems able to halt. It's an unfolding script tinged with both beauty and trepidation. As I sit there, steeped in the intricacies of our linked emotions, it occurs to me: fighting this connection might be a futile battle, and love—the very thing I've convinced myself is a dangerous illusion—might just be the most real thing I've ever faced.

Terrifying—this proximity to raw emotion, to the complexities of the human mind. It's like standing on the edge of a cliff, teetering between reason and chaos. After a brief and rather awkward silence, the doctor says, "Rayne, I've been meticulously studying Summer's behavioral patterns, trying to crack the code of her consciousness. I think you might have just provided a clue, a pattern in her catatonia."

Rayne's eyes narrow with an urgent need for understanding. "Break it down. You're talking dissociative disorder?"

"It's as if Summer has cocooned herself in a separate reality, disconnecting from what's emotionally insurmountable," B.J. elaborates, a soft cadence to her voice that feels almost soothing.

Rayne nods, like she's clicking pieces of a puzzle into place. "She's shutting down, going dark inside her own mind to survive."

"Exactly." B.J.'s words are a comfort despite the weight they carry. She dives deeper into the psyche's architecture, discussing ways to coax Summer back from her psychological exile. It's like watching two generals strategizing for an impending battle.

Rayne's eyes blaze with a determination that could topple empires. "Whatever it takes to bring her back, count me in."

B.J. smiles, and there's an unspoken promise in that smile. "You won't be alone, Rayne. We've got an army to fight for Summer's soul."

Rayne stands, her hand gently coming to rest on Summer's head. Soft words are whispered like a lullaby or a prayer. "Hold on, Summer. I'll find a way to reach you. When I come back, I'll have some of your favorite music and I'll sing to you."

In the frayed tapestry of their interaction, threads of profound connection glisten. I can't help but be moved, the sensation churning through me—somewhere between awe and something far more precarious.

And then the world shifts on its axis. Voices rise in the hallway, an outburst punctuating the air. Emotion—shock, mortification—ricochets through the tether I share with Rayne. Summer, too, stirs, a minuscule twitch that feels monumental. B.J. barely has time to react when the door bursts open, revealing a woman who looks like she's walked straight out of a Dali painting. "I am Jesus Christ," she declares, "and I'm here to see my daughter."

Everything freezes in that heartbeat of absurdity, the moment stretching like molasses. A surreal twist that kicks up dust in the crossroads of sanity and disorder. What I do next, well, it's inexplicable even to me. Maybe it's this heightened exposure to emotional fragility. Maybe it's Rayne's unwavering resilience that's chipping away at my own fortified walls. But in that instant, I realize my carefully curated detachment might just be my own brand of dissociation—a way to avoid confronting my deepest fears.

And that, for reasons I can't yet articulate, scares the hell out of me.

14

RAYNE

y mother's voice slices through the air like a cold blade, extinguishing the fragile glimmer of hope that had dared to flicker within me. The usual surge of emotions floods through me—horror, despair, and something deeper that's difficult to put into words. But right now, it's abject horror that wins out, for my mother's current state is no less than a full-blown psychotic episode. And what's worse, she's proclaiming herself to be Jesus Christ, sending shockwaves of shame coursing through my veins. This is bad. Really, really bad. She'll ruin everything if she's here.

Her eyes lock onto mine, a sick triumph gleaming within them. In this chaotic mess, I find a small sliver of relief, an unexpected silver lining. The fact that E.S. sold us to settle his debts made it easier for us to slip under her radar. But now, the universe seems to be playing a cruel joke on me, introducing her back into our lives at this pivotal moment. I almost collapse at the irony. Calling the woman in front of us a "mother" feels like a twisted misnomer. Dressed in an outfit more befitting her role as a madam in a brothel, she's a far cry from the woman who once held a touch of beauty. Heavy makeup masks the past, and her surgically enhanced figure is on full display, complete with fishnet stockings and go-go boots. It's an image that haunts me, mocking any lingering sentiments of love I might still harbor for her. How could she have fallen so far?

My sister's flinch pulls me back to the urgency of the moment. I can't let my mother's presence derail us. I need to act, to protect Summer. Panic surges within me, my mind racing for a solution. And then, like a beacon in the darkness, Jaden moves. His motions are graceful, cat-like, as he slips beside my mother. His touch under her elbow guides her out the door, his voice adopting an intrigued tone. "That sounds fascinating, Jesus. Why don't you come with me and tell me all about it?" It's a simple gesture, but it's a lifeline thrown to us in the midst of chaos.

As my heart rate begins to steady, I realize something startling. Jaden's actions, his concern, his willingness to step into the fray—they all come through the connection that's formed between us. And in this moment, it's not disgust or avoidance that I sense, but genuine concern and compassion. It's an odd feeling, a thread of connection that weaves itself stronger between us, defying logic and reason. I find myself giving him a piece of my heart, a sliver of trust that I had sworn never to offer again.

But Summer needs me now. She sits there, a shell of her former self, lost in a world we can't reach. The connection between us remains murky, frustratingly incomplete. There's so much I want to ask, so much I need to know. I give Summer's limp hand a reassuring squeeze before focusing on the psychologist, Dr. B.J. Patton, who has been observing the chaos with a keen eye.

Our conversation takes a more focused turn, and I direct my attention to Dr. B.J. "Who gave our mother Summer's location? Isn't that a breach of privacy?" I can't help the hint of confrontation in my tone, but my mother's intrusion scares me to death.

Dr. B.J. studies me for a moment before responding. "In most cases, that would be true. However, Summer is a minor with a missing person alert. We have an obligation to cooperate with law enforcement in such cases."

Her explanation makes sense, and I nod in acknowledgment. "I see. What's the next step then? When can I bring Summer home?" Despite the whirlwind of emotions, the psychologist's office feels like a sanctuary, a haven where I can begin to make sense of the storm that rages within me. The softness of the armchair cradles my restless soul as I settle in, ready to delve into the journey of rescuing my sister. Dr. B.J.'s presence is both grounding and mysterious, a guiding light in the darkness that shrouds Summer.

Dr. B.J. leans forward, her voice a soothing melody that draws me in. "Rayne, given Summer's delicate condition, I propose an innovative treatment approach that could lead her back to herself. Our program typically spans six months to a year, depending on her progress."

Hope flares within me, mingling with a hint of anxiety. Dr. B.J.'s words carry the promise of salvation for Summer, a lifeline that might pull her from the depths of her catatonic state. It's almost too good to be true. I narrow my eyes, a skeptical thought surfacing. "Will this be covered by our universal healthcare plan?"

"All treatment is funded through research grants," Dr. B.J. assures me. "I've developed a pioneering program centered around abuse healing through role play. But let's focus on the first step: Eye Movement Desensitization and

Reprocessing therapy, or EMDR. This technique has shown remarkable success in treating trauma-related disorders, helping process distressing memories and emotions through guided eye movements."

A spark of hope ignites within me. EMDR could be the key to unlocking Summer's captive mind. Dr. B.J.'s unconventional approach resonates with me, igniting a sense of faith. I gaze at her intently, my mind racing with possibilities. "And then?" I prompt, eager to learn more. Maybe a program like this could help me.

Her eyes hold mine, steady and unwavering. "Additionally, we'll explore the therapeutic power of music. Music therapy has the potential to reach Summer on a profound level, even in her catatonic state. Melodies and rhythms can bridge the gap between her conscious and subconscious, allowing her to express and process emotions. Does Summer have an affinity for music?"

A smile tugs at my lips. "Yes, she does. She loves to dance. How can I assist with this?" The concept of music therapy resonates deeply with me. It feels like a way to break through the barriers that have kept Summer locked away from us. The thought of her finding solace through music fills me with a renewed sense of purpose, a determination to bring her back from the brink.

We both turn our attention to Summer, her stillness a haunting reminder of what Jaden had been like last night. I can sense her, just beyond reach, and I'm willing to do whatever it takes to bring her back. "Dr. B.J., I'm ready to help in any way I can. What's the next step?"

Dr. B.J. leans back, a warm smile on her face. "I'd like to meet with you to complete our intake forms and discuss your family history. Understanding Summer's journey will guide our approach. After that, we'll establish a schedule for music therapy sessions, based on your availability."

I extend my hand toward her, a gesture of commitment. "Count me in. I'll do whatever it takes to help my sister." Our hands clasp, and I feel a sense of partnership, a shared determination to bring Summer back from the depths of her own mind.

As I leave Dr. B.J.'s office, a wave of determination washes over me. I fight the urge to raise my fist in triumph. There's a path before us, a way to save Summer. My mind spins with the tasks ahead, the to-do list expanding rapidly. But for now, my focus is on finding Jaden and dealing with the aftermath of my mother's visit.

Jaden is perched on Anne's desk, his attention on her. Jealousy prickles within me, an emotion I have no right to feel. He glances at me briefly, a glint of something unspoken in his eyes. Yearning surges within me, mingled with a pang of shame. But this is no time for indulging in such feelings. "Ready to go?" he says, his tone curt, all business.

"Where's my mother?"

"She left. We came to an agreement. In exchange for leaving Summer alone at Harmony Hills, I invited her to visit us tomorrow night. She accepted." Jaden strides through the door letting it slam in my face. Rude much.

I scurry after him. "Why would you do that? She's crazy. There's no telling what she'll do." I suck in a breath and rush on. "She stabbed a person in Montreal for no reason. Just because she felt like it."

"Why wouldn't I? She's your mother and besides, the mentally ill have a lot of things to teach us if we're willing to listen."

No, they do not! We get in the car, the Grand Canyon-sized chasm gaping between us. The car ride is tense, the air thick with unsaid words. My mind churns, a tempest of conflicting emotions. And then, against all reason, my mouth runs ahead of me. "So, is she your girlfriend?" I blurt out, my voice laced with a hint of bitterness.

He gives me a look that's a mix of annoyance and something else I can't quite decipher. "No," he replies curtly, the word hanging heavy in the air. A moment later, he adds, "I told you, I don't do relationships."

His words send a jolt through me, a reminder of the chasm that separates us. But I can't stop now. "Actually, you said you don't do love," I retort, my tone defiant. "And just so we're clear, I'm not looking for a relationship." My voice hardens. "And if I were, it certainly wouldn't be with you."

He looks at me, his eyes holding a challenge that I can't fully grasp. The connection between us pulses, a mix of heat and tension. "Why not?" he asks, his curiosity a tangible force between us.

A surge of anger rises within me, mingling with hurt and resentment. "Because you're too much like E.S.," I snap, my words sharper than intended. "I'll never be with a father figure, and that's exactly what you are."

The atmosphere in the car shifts, his anger mirroring my own. "I am nothing like your stepfather," he seethes, his grip on the steering wheel tight enough to turn his knuckles white. "Don't you dare compare me to him."

The tension is thick, suffocating. My temper flares, my own anger taking control. "Fine," I retort, my voice cold and biting. "I take it back. You're nothing like him. Happy now?"

His gaze burns into mine, a storm of emotions raging within him. And then, with a sudden change of tone, he speaks again. "I won't tolerate lies." His words are laced with finality. "I'm nothing like him, and if that's what you think, then maybe we should end this right here."

My heart sinks, a mixture of regret and fear welling up within me. I can't let this unravel, not now. "Wait," I blurt out, desperation tinging my voice. "I take it back. I didn't mean it like that."

The tension between us eases slightly, but the rift remains. I'm left grappling with my own impulsiveness, my own inability to keep my emotions in check. As we continue the drive, silence stretches between us, the divide growing with each passing second.

As we arrive at our destination, Jaden's demeanor is all business. The ache within me intensifies as he steps out of the car, his presence a reminder of the growing chasm between us. I can't help but wonder if this is the beginning of the end, if the bond that seemed so promising will shatter under the weight of our own insecurities.

I follow him, my resolve firm. No matter what lies ahead, Summer's well-being is my priority. I may not have all the answers, and my relationship with Jaden may be as tumultuous as a storm at sea, but I can't deny the pull between us. But I have no fucking idea how to bridge the gap between me and Jaden before it's too late.

15

JADEN

I am seething. I usually do my absolute best to avoid any intense emotion, but I'm coming out of my cave to embrace this one. How dare this little shit compare me to an abuser like her fucking stepfather. I pour on a full head of righteous indignation. Yet there's a little voice in the back of my head that sounds a lot like Rayne's that makes me want to find out why she thinks I'm like her despised E.S. Maybe she has a point. I can be a real controlling asshole sometimes.

I slam the heel of my hand into the steering wheel as if it's at fault then press the button to engage my Ferrari Portofino's cruise control. Goddamn cars! I hate these fucking computerized cars these days and yearn for the satisfaction of throwing a stick into gear. Yes, indeed, I'm diving deep into displacement mode because redirecting my fury is a lot easier than addressing it. Never mind that I'd probably strip the gears in the mood I'm in, which is precisely one of the reasons I'm in the Portofino today. I push back the uncomfortable truth that I'd chosen the Ferrari because selfish bastard that I am, its console gives me easier access to get my arm scratched. I don't stop to question why I, who abhors physical contact that isn't sexual, crave this connection with Rayne.

"What is wrong with you?" Rayne's voice cuts through the noise this latest inferno of emotions brought on, although for a startled second, I realize that this time, she's the cause of the noise.

"Absolutely nothing." I keep my face impassive as I'm a master of doing and give her a look that would scare off even the strongest of my adversaries. Although I'd like nothing better than to drop into my cave for a few hours, I've no choice but to stay in the present for this meeting with the task force. But I'd be damned if I'll let her get to me.

"Oh no you don't, CC. I can feel the anger coming through whatever this strange link is that we have developing. And you're the one who said no lies." Rayne folds her arms across the enormous sweatshirt she's chosen. Little does she know hiding her body has the opposite effect to what she's trying to achieve.

I drop an extra ounce of steel into my voice. "About this Captain Control bullshit, another thing you should know about me is that I don't do pet names. This is not a relationship. Am I clear?"

Rayne's chestnut eyes practically shoot flames as she glares at me, and for a brief second, the image of steam streaming from her ears dashes through my head. I keep my eyes trained on the road as her hot glare burns the side of my face.

"Crystal clear. Now it's my turn. If there is one thing I've learned to be good at," she says hotly, "it's staying on topic. So answer the fucking question. Why are you so pissed off, Jaden?" This time she emphasizes my name as if it's a curse word, making me wish I hadn't opened my big mouth about her moniker . . . because I kind of liked it. That's the problem. But that's all the poke I need for the fuse to ignite the bomb. I pull the car over to the shoulder of the road, shut off the engine, and turn on her.

I bleed every part of my conflicting emotions into my fury at this young upstart. "Fine, you want to know why I'm pissed off? As if you couldn't figure it out. You compared me to a child abuser, the lowest of pond scum who should be neutralized. And anyone who would make such a comparison is no friend of mine."

It's not just the insult, though it's a jagged pill to swallow, slashing at my sense of honor and virtue. No, it's more. It's the way that comparison slices through my carefully constructed walls, tearing at my protective instincts that have always driven me to shield and safeguard. My veins pulse with a mixture of indignation and frustration, a tumultuous storm of emotions that I can barely contain. The mere thought that someone might associate me, even indirectly, with the kind of pain and suffering that E.S. inflicted ignites a searing rage within me. It's toxic, corrosive, a venom that surges through my veins, demanding release. And here, now, it has found its outlet in the firestorm of words that lash out, fueled by an internal tempest I can't fully control. I feel her shrink from me as my vitriol pours over her, and I don't give a damn. If she's going to know me, she's going to have to go through the ring of fire. She's just like all the others. But that thought no sooner crystallizes when a thread of steely determination seeps through our link.

This time a punch of fury equal to my own surges through our link. "There you go with the threats again. Well, you know what mister, I've lived with threats from asshole men like you my whole life, and I'm not going to do it anymore. And let's get one thing straight. I didn't compare you to E.S., I said you're too much like him. And that asshole, means that although you may have redeeming qualities, you make fucking threats like this to try and manipulate me and control my behavior. And I'm not buying it." She pokes me in the arm with her index finger and hauls in a huge lungful of air.

I'm trying to get you to submit to me. I bat that troubling thought into the stratosphere.

She straightens in her seat, and this time, her gaze is cold like the edge of a scalpel. "One thing is for fucking sure, I'm not continuing this conversation while you're behaving all aggressive and shit. God forbid I compare your assholish behavior to E.S. We'll talk about this when you're ready to actually converse instead of acting like a goddamn boorish asshole."

Something inside me tingles with excitement as she lobs my vitriol back at me. She's not like the rest of them! For a split second I let hope at finally finding someone who allows me to be without putting up with my bullshit open a channel to my libido. Desire bolts in as I acknowledge that in just a couple of days, I've done things with this young woman I haven't done in decades. *You let her touch you.* I push that thought and my traitorous libido back where it belongs as I put the car in gear and merge back into the traffic on the busy 400-series highway. Not long now before we're at the meeting.

Silence reigns as we burn away the next half hour navigating traffic, not comfortable but not uncomfortable either. More like unfinished business. When I feel her rage hit a low simmer through our bond, I threw out a peace bone.

"I should probably tell you what to expect at the meeting."

She gives me another of her penetrating glares and I wait as curiosity slowly displaces her anger. Finally, she nods. "That would be good." Her arm remains folded on her chest closing her off, but she keeps her gaze trained on my face. It's rather unnerving the way she stares, but now is not a good time to bring up that particular complaint.

"As I mentioned earlier, I'm part of an undercover operation called Pandemonium Eruptus. Our mission is to shut down the Ontario sex trafficking ring called The Game and to rescue and rehabilitate as many victims as possible. Right now, there are nine people on the team: Razor Ramirez, the special forces operative and de facto leader and link to law enforcement; Connor McClane, owner of the Masquerade Club and one of the rescue team along with Sasha and myself; his wife and partner, Katherine, who coordinates our activity with the Harmony Hills Center; Brian, the Masquerade's head of security and his wife, Asha, and Aleah, our newly appointed director of the international team." I don't mention that Aleah is my celestial contact on Earth who's bringing a team of celestials that will run an expanded intelligence arm for the operation in the recently confiscated headquarters used by The Game. For now, that intel is on a need-to-know basis only.

Rayne takes a moment to load her questions. "What jobs are available? What makes you think they'll hire me?"

Now is not the time to tell her that part of the bargain for making me an avenging angel was that I become part of this task force and that gave me a certain amount of clout. "Because we have an opening for someone who's been on the inside who can give us intel and you fit the bill.

Asshole." I lay on the horn as one of Toronto's signature aggressive drivers cuts me off in the usual traffic snarl.

Rayne wisely keeps her mouth shut while I navigate my way to the Amber Star hotel, home of The Masquerade Club and our residence during an active operation. I pull up in front and toss my keys to the valet who opens the car door. "Welcome back, Mr. Stone."

I barely acknowledge the man's existence, instead focusing my attention on Rayne as she beams a smile at the valet who opens her door. Grabbing her elbow, I usher her through the door forcing her to yell her "thank you" over her shoulder.

Rayne yanks her arm out of my grasp. "Rude much, CC? What's the rush?"

"We're late, and we've still got the security check to complete." I continue my relentless march to the bank of elevators. She's right, I'm being an asshole, but now is not the time for introspection.

We're already on the elevator before Rayne can muster any protest or launch into another round of her analytical questioning. I swiftly initiate the retinal scan, the only key to the penthouse's exclusive domain. As the doors slide open, revealing the understated opulence of the club's lobby, Rayne's gasp is a small, satisfying victory. I find myself intently watching her, silently cataloging each reaction. There's a part of me that's keen to see how she navigates this world—a world so familiar to me, yet so new and possibly intimidating to her. Good thing I've perfected the ability to watch someone without seeming to because Rayne seems to have radar where I'm concerned. Every time I look at her, her gaze tracks to me like a spotlight. Her eyes are like a fucking laser beam searing into my soul.

16

RAYNE

Stepping into the lobby of what looked like an ultra-luxurious hotel, I'm momentarily taken aback. The place is dripping with extravagance, each detail screaming wealth. I feel a pang of discomfort, like a stray thread in a tapestry of finery. Following Jaden across the busy lobby, a part of me wonders if I'm just another naive protagonist in a cliche romantic tale, about to make a monumental mistake. My rational side screams at me to blend into the crowd and disappear, but something deeper, a whisper in the back of my mind, urges me to stay. It's like my intuition and my skepticism are at war, with Jaden unknowingly playing referee.

Jaden leads the way to the elevator, his stride radiating confidence. I follow, my eyes scanning the surroundings, taking in the surreal perfection. It's like stepping into a painting where every brushstroke is calculated, yet I can't shake the feeling of being a misfit in this masterpiece.

The elevator doors slide open, and Jaden motions me inside. As the doors close behind us, the atmosphere shifts. It's more intimate, more intense. Jaden approaches a gold-toned panel, pressing a small dark pad beside the top button. My curiosity piques as I watch a small red light above it glow and then fade after completing a fingerprint and retinal scan. It's all so... James Bond-esque.

He hums a few bars of a song, and I can't help but raise an eyebrow. "What's with all the scanning?" I ask, my voice laced with a hint of suspicion.

"We're heading into a members-only area. Security's tight," he replies nonchalantly, but there's a hint of something more in his eyes, something that speaks of secrets and hidden depths.

"And the song?" I lean against the elevator wall, trying to sound casual even though my heart's racing. It's not just the situation; it's him. He's like a puzzle I can't quite solve, and damn it, I want to.

"'Spanked' by Van Halen," he answers, and there's a flicker of something like amusement in his eyes.

The elevator dings, and the doors slide open. We step out into a vestibule that's a stark contrast to the modern world we've left behind. Wide burnished walnut and alternating gold paneled walls, a cathedral ceiling crowned with a crystal chandelier, and gold- and black-veined marble flooring – it's like stepping into a historical romance novel. For a moment, I'm lost in the fantasy, imagining myself in a different time, a different life. But then reality snaps back, and I remember where I am – and who I'm with.

Jaden moves ahead, and I follow, my mind a whirlwind of thoughts and emotions. There's a part of me that's drawn to him, to this mystery, but another part that's screaming caution. It's a delicate dance, and I'm not sure which way the music's going to take us. But one thing's for sure—I'm in this dance till the end, wherever it leads.

In my sweats, I feel glaringly out of place amidst this

grandeur. A fleeting fantasy of me in an elegant gown, lace teasing at secrets best left hidden, flashes through my mind. I push it away, cheeks warming. *Not the time, Rayne.*

I sneak a glance at Jaden, searching for a crack in his stoic façade. Nothing. He's a fortress, walls high and impenetrable. But there's something about him, something that draws me in despite my better judgment. It's infuriating and intoxicating in equal measure.

The grandeur around us is overwhelming, yet it feels oddly fitting, like a backdrop to this surreal chapter of my life with the Pandemonium Eruptus team. It's all a game of shadows and whispers, and here I am, smack in the middle of it.

I square my shoulders, shaking off the awe and the unease. I'm not here to play damsel; I'm here to figure out the next steps for Summer and me. The gold and marble won't distract me from my purpose.

Following Jaden out of the vestibule, I steel myself for what's to come. Whatever game is being played, I'm ready for it. Bring it on.

"Wow!" My voice bounces off the walls. It's all so cinematic, like a set from a spy thriller. I half expect to bump into a secret agent around every corner.

Jaden's usual intensity ebbs slightly, replaced by a faint smile. "You haven't seen the half of it," he says, a note of pride or maybe challenge in his voice. "There's more to see, but first, you'll go through security."

I arch an eyebrow. "A body scan? What is this, a high-security prison?" I can't keep the skepticism out of my voice. The whole situation is like a puzzle I can't quite solve, and Jaden is the most perplexing piece.

His smile grows, genuine and disarming. "We're thorough. It's not about invasions; it's about the safety and privacy of everyone." His words add another layer to the mystery, one I'm both wary of and drawn to.

I shake my head and can't help but let a wry smile play on my lips. "Never been one to back down from a challenge." I keep my tone light, but inside, it's a whole different story. My mind's a whirlwind, and Jaden is at the center of it all. He's like a puzzle, a maze I can't resist exploring, even though every instinct screams it might be a trap. And, damn it, there's this nagging thought that whatever's causing the weird twists in my gut is tied up in whatever this place is. Sounds insane, but here we are.

Taking a deep breath, I brace myself for the security check. This isn't just stepping through a scanner. It's crossing into the unknown. And Jaden, with his cryptic smiles and guarded eyes, is a part of this problem. I'm drawn to him, and it's infuriating how much that scares and excites me.

"So, CC, you're playing tour guide now?" I mask the turmoil inside with a bit of sass. But the grandeur around me makes me very curious, and I'm dying to find out more about this operation.

Jaden's fleeting smile vanishes, replaced by his usual stoic mask. "First, security. Brian will handle it. Just follow his lead, and you'll be fine. It's to keep you safe from Viper and the likes."

I nod, trying to quell the butterflies in my stomach. New territory, new rules. I'm not usually one to get jittery, but this place, this whole situation, it's like walking into a spider's web – intricate and potentially dangerous.

Jaden nods and walks away, the very picture of poise and mystery. Watching him, I can't help but feel a tug of something—admiration, irritation, definitely more than a hint of desire. I shove those thoughts aside as I turn to face the security checkpoint. This is more than just a job or a mission; it's a test of who I am and, maybe, who I'm becoming.

I step up to the checkpoint, trying to steel myself for what's next. There's a sense of crossing a line, of entering a world that's far bigger and more complex than I ever imagined. And I know this is where I need to be.

"Good evening, Rayne. Brian Patrick Farrell. I'm in charge of security here at the Masquerade Clubs. Welcome." His voice is firm and professional, but there's an unexpected warmth to it. I nod, mustering up as much professionalism as I can manage. This is it, stepping into a world that's equal parts thrilling and terrifying. Ready or not, I'm in the thick of it.

Standing in front of me is a guy who's got looks that could easily make him a model for those rugged outdoor ads—not that he's my type, but I can appreciate the aesthetic. His piercing blue eyes scan me like I'm a puzzle to be solved. When he shakes my hand, it's with a grip that speaks of controlled strength.

Brian's got this vibe about him like he's made of steel, not just physically but on the inside. One glance from those icy eyes, and you know he's not someone you'd ever want as an enemy. He releases my hand and points to a full-body scanner. "Anything in your pockets?" He's all business.

"Nope." My reply is curt. I'm not here to chit-chat either.

"Step on the footprints, arms up." Classic security guy —all about the rules and procedures.

"Yes, sir." My tone drips with sarcasm. He either doesn't notice or doesn't care, focused on his monitor while the scanner does its thing. The door opens, and I step through.

"This way," Brian directs, leading me to these grand

wooden doors like something out of a period movie. He goes through his high-tech security ritual, and the doors glide open.

"Thanks," I mutter, my attention already drifting else-where. Jaden's there, leaning against the wall with a nonchalance that belies his allure. He's like a modern-day Adonis, magnetic without even trying. Right now, he's all charm, focused on a stunning brunette who embodies sensuality. Dressed in a blue silk number, Greek tunic style, she exudes a raw sexuality. Her dress, with a daring slit revealing much of her ample cleavage, hugs her body in all the right places. The skirt, scandalously short, suggests a boldness I can't help but envy. As I draw nearer, her head bows slightly, and a whiff of her expensive, floral perfume hits me, amplifying my insecurities.

Jealousy, sharp and unwelcome, twists in my stomach. He's not mine—never was. So why does this sting so much? I shove the thought aside, frustrated with myself for even caring. This surge of emotion is ridiculous, and I'm deter-mined to quash it. I'm Rayne, and I don't get rattled by the likes of this—least of all by Jaden's fleeting attention.

"...That depends on how things go with Rayne. Ah, here she is now." Jaden straightens as I walk up, a hint of amuse-ment playing on his face. It's as if he gets a kick out of stir-ring me up. Inside, I'm a mess of annoyance and reluctant amusement, jealousy nipping at the edges. But I'm not about to let that show. I'm Rayne, and I don't crack under pressure—or so I keep telling myself.

The woman he's been chatting with gives me a quick once-over before turning her nose up. "My name is O, mistress." Her voice is as cool as her attitude. I bristle inter-nally. 'Mistress' my ass. But I let it slide. "If you're ready, I'll take you to the meeting."

"Lead the way." Just then, Jaden's hand finds the back of my neck, guiding me forward. It's a move that leaves me torn. I like the closeness, hate that I like it, and despise the possessive edge to it. The plush carpet muffles our steps as we follow O down the hallway, passing under soft lights that highlight an array of nudes on the walls—artistic, yet bold.

"We call this the War Room." Jaden slips past O and pulls me into a room that's straight out of a high-tech thriller—panoramic views of the city, colossal curved screens, and a mix of modern furniture and tech that would make any geek salivate. The people around the table pause and look up as we enter.

"Ah, you're just in time," says a Latino man with a build that screams efficiency, his skin a warm olive-caramel tone. The snake tattoo winding down his arm adds to his edgy aura. He's clad in black, his presence commanding. "I'm Razor. Welcome, Rayne. Come join the party."

Swallowing down a wave of nerves, I slide into the seat next to Jaden. I can feel the weight of their gazes, sizing me up. Then, Jaden squeezes my neck gently, a silent message of support. *You've got this, little dragon.* His touch sends a ripple of warmth through me, a reminder of this bizarre connection we share.

Razor introduces the team, his voice carrying the weight of authority. "That's Connor," he says, nodding towards a man whose tailored suit screams power, his posture exuding a sense of control that doesn't need to be spoken. "And beside him is Kat." My eyes shift to the woman next to him. She's striking, with black curls cascading around a face that's both fierce and gentle. Something about her demeanor puts me slightly at ease, a rare feeling in this whirlwind I've stepped into.

"Next to Kat, we have Asha, our..." Razor's voice trails off in my head, drowned out by the rush of my own thoughts. Here I am, in the thick of it all, surrounded by people who are more than they appear, playing a game that's much larger than I'd ever imagined. And there's Jaden, right at the core, inexplicably entangling himself in my personal chaos.

I let my instincts take over for a moment, tuning into the room's energy. It's a cocktail of trust and respect, an atmosphere unfamiliar yet strangely comforting. All except for Jaden. There's a guardedness about him, a sense that he's showing the world only what he wants it to see. And then it hits me—I'm seeing Jaden from a perspective few have, from inside his protective shell, and it's both exhilarating and terrifying. I catch his eye, and there's a flash of something — recognition, maybe?

Jaden's expression darkens. *"Now's not the time, little dragon."* His voice invades my thoughts, a stark reminder of this bizarre connection we share. He's right; I need to focus. This is about my future, my shot at something more. But it's tough, splitting my attention when half of my mind is tangled up with thoughts of Jaden and this strange bond between us.

The silence in the room is broken only by the soft hum of computers. Every pair of eyes in the room is fixed on me, sizing me up. It's like being under a microscope, and I'm not a fan. Finally, I nod, my words terse but polite. "Pleased to meet you." It sounds lame even to my own ears, but formalities aren't exactly my strong suit.

"Jaden has filled us in on your logistics expertise," Razor continues, his grin disarming in its sincerity. Despite his bravado, there's something about him that's inherently likable. "We believe you'll adapt quickly. Feel free to jump in when you're ready." He points to a monitor, where a series of illuminated dots marks the Highway 401 corridor. "Our focus is on dismantling a bawdy house network linked to The Game. We need to strategize the best way to shut it down and save the victims."

I sink into my seat, the discussion swirling around me. They're talking raids and tactics, but my mind keeps drifting to Jaden. It's like there's a magnetic pull, an undercurrent of something unspoken between us. The way he's simultaneously a part of this and yet apart from it all—it's intriguing and infuriating.

As the team hashes out their plan, my attention snaps back to the task at hand. They're missing something crucial. Cutting in, I lean forward, my voice confident. "If you hit the houses one by one, they'll lock down after the first raid. And the guards? They're living on takeout. The simplest way to neutralize them with minimal collateral damage is to spike their food. They order in bulk post-night shift. We can figure out where they order from, and tamper with the order to sedate them. It's cleaner, safer, and you'll catch them off guard."

The room falls silent for a moment, processing my suggestion. I can feel Jaden's gaze on me, a mix of surprise and something else — respect? It's hard to tell with him. But right now, what matters is that I've contributed, shown my worth. This is more than proving myself; it's about making a difference, about being part of something bigger than any of us.

As everyone's eyes turn to me, I feel a flicker of discomfort but quickly shove it aside. Sometimes, you just have to trust your gut, so I dive in. "Did Viper's goon mention how long this circuit's been running? They usually switch locations every few months unless they smell a raid coming."

"Three weeks," Sasha chimes in, finally looking up from her phone. Her posture shifts, all business now. "That gives us a window for recon. What do you need?"

Truth is, I'm winging it here. But hey, winging it's gotten me this far. My instincts are sharp, and I've always had a knack for figuring out systems, for making sense of chaos. "Let me see what you've got in terms of resources, and I'll lay out my recommendations."

Connor speaks up, his gaze shifting between Jaden, Razor, and me. "We have everything money can buy," he declares with a confidence that only the truly wealthy possess. Then, with a side glance at me, he adds, "But she needs to get a grip on our lifestyle to really be useful." He stands, taking Kat's hand, signaling the end of the meeting.

Kat throws a parting smile over her shoulder. "Nice to meet you, Rayne. See you soon." Her voice is warm, a contrast to Connor's brisk, business-like tone.

Razor's grin is wide as he looks at me, a twinkle in his eye. "Brilliant. You're hired," he announces, as though he's just found a rare gem. "Aleah will sort out your contract. Once that's settled, we'll regroup and hash out the details."

A mix of hope and apprehension courses through me. It's the classic 'too good to be true' scenario, yet sometimes, against all odds, things do work out. Clinging to that hopeful thought, I follow Aleah and her trio of Adonis-like companions out of the room. Jaden marches at my side. This could be my big break, or it could be a dive into unknown waters. Either way, I'm about to find out.

17

JADEN

The meeting wraps up better than I'd dared to expect. I make it a rule not to harbor expectations, a self-imposed safeguard against disappointments. Yet, with Rayne, it seems my defenses are already fraying at the edges. I'm finding it increasingly challenging to reinforce the walls I've meticulously built around myself, especially around her.

The flicker of... something, an indefinable pull towards her, is unsettling. I quickly label it as lust, my cock jumping on board with the idea. But deep down, I sense it's a convenient facade for something more complex, something I'm not ready to dissect yet.

Time, that's what I need — a luxury that seems elusive at the moment. As we trail behind Aleah and her celestial entourage into one of Magnum's offices, overlooking Toronto's sprawling cityscape, I brace myself. I anticipate a barrage of probing questions from Rayne, her perceptiveness a challenge I'm not sure I'm prepared to face. I need to strategize, to plan my maneuvering around her incisive inquiries. But, before all that, there's the immediate task of seeing how she reacts to this job proposal.

A realization hits me like a jolt; I've been subconsciously ticking off boxes in my "ring of fire" checklist with Rayne, a list whose existence I hadn't acknowledged until now. Never again will I allow myself to be vulnerable to betrayal, to be hurt by someone I trust.

Aleah's presence in the office pulls me back to the present. She settles at the conference table, her celestial partners forming a protective semi-circle behind her. She motions to a chair, her voice smooth and inviting. "Have a seat. Can we get you anything before we start?"

Rayne declines and takes her seat, her nervousness is masked by a facade of calm. It's been ages since I last saw Aleah—not since the celestials pulled me back from death's brink and reshaped me into something more. My memories from that time are shrouded in shock and despair, bits and pieces I've stored away for later reflection.

Aleah, a celestial being born of a human and an angel, exudes a power that outshines most supernatural entities. Her mates, Cassiel, Atroyel, and Tristan, are of an even higher echelon, their blood angel status granting them formidable might.

The air in the room crackles with celestial currents, and Aleah's blue-white Nephilim grace unfurls like ethereal threads, interweaving with her mates' angelic essence. This display is unexpected—I'm still grappling with the intricacies of magic, but I'm certain Aleah has dropped the glamor that usually masks their power. Why expose their true nature now? It's a risk, especially with Rayne in the room, a human whose keen perception might catch more than intended.

Rayne's head tilts subtly, her eyes sharp and observant.

She's aware of the shift but chooses to wait, to watch. Her reaction, or lack thereof, piques my curiosity. What does she see? What does she know? Rayne continues to intrigue me, and I find myself reluctantly admiring her restraint, her ability to stand amid the unknown without faltering.

Aleah leans forward, and the magic in the room flows between her and her mates. The tattoo on her arm, a living testament to her power, moves subtly. Rayne, ever the curious one, reaches out hesitantly towards it. "May I?" Her voice is soft, almost in awe. "It's moving." She's speaking her thoughts aloud, probably without realizing it.

Aleah nods, a hint of amusement in her gesture. "You may touch it, and yes, it's real. What do you see?" She invites Rayne to explore the mystery.

Rayne's fingers brush against the tattoo, and then she quickly retracts her hand, as if burned by the magic itself. Aleah remains silent, her mates standing guard, their mute presence formidable. "Wow. It's pulsing," Rayne murmurs, her fascination clear in her voice. She traces the tattoo's intricate design, focusing entirely on the artwork.

Her next question catches me off guard. "How come there's pixie dust floating around all of you?" She locks eyes with Aleah, her gaze intense. Despite the absurdity of the question, Rayne's earnestness shines through. She's diving headfirst into the unknown, unafraid of appearing foolish in her quest for understanding. I feel an undeniable pull towards this bravery of hers, this relentless pursuit of truth. It's as if my angelic power recognizes something in her, a resonance that defies my logical resistance.

Aleah glances triumphantly at her mates. Their tattoos pulse, a silent conversation flowing between them.

"I want to. I've seen a lot of psychics looking for proof, but sadly, so far, nothing," Rayne admits, her voice tinged with a mix of skepticism and hope. It's a response that catches me off guard—she's been seeking, searching for something beyond the ordinary.

"Well, today you're in luck." Aleah's voice holds a tinge of pride. "All four of us are supernatural beings, though we prefer the term celestial." Her matter-of-factness stands in stark contrast to the way I've lived—hiding, masking. Her open nature throws me off balance, making me reconsider my own walls. The men beside her nod, their silence and deference to Aleah clear. It's a dynamic foreign to me, a reminder of a world I'm only beginning to comprehend.

Rayne's gaze shifts to the angels, her directness cutting through the air. "Can they talk?" she asks before being captivated by the angelic grace swirling around them. I'm struck by her blunt curiosity, so different from the cautious approach I would have taken.

Tristan's response, light and almost flirtatious, feels incongruent with the gravity of the revelation. "Hi there, I'm Tristan. Want to see my wings?" His approach doesn't faze Rayne; she's absorbed by the magic, not the man. It's a trait I find unexpectedly admirable.

"Maybe," Rayne says, still fixated on the grace. Her sudden shift to more pointed curiosity is intriguing. "Wait. Did you say you have wings?"

Tristan nods, playful yet earnest. "Indeed, I did. My offer still stands."

Troy cuts in, his voice booming yet melodious. "Cool it, Tris," he says. "Give the woman time to adjust."

Watching Rayne, I'm caught off guard by her unguarded reactions. She's delving into a world that would intimidate most, yet she does so with a rawness, an openness that's both refreshing and unsettling. It's a stark reminder of the barriers I've erected around myself, of the emotional detachment I've always viewed as necessary. Her bravery in the face of the unknown tugs at something deep within me, something I've long suppressed under layers of control and self-preservation.

Her willingness to delve into this newfound reality, to embrace what many would dismiss as fantasy, strikes a chord within me. My own initiation into the celestial realm wasn't a choice but a forceful thrust into a hidden world. And here she is, stepping into it with an open mind, a thirst for understanding that's both admirable and unnerving.

As I observe her, wrestling with the tangible reality of the supernatural, I can't help but feel an unexpected connection. Her path into this unearthly world mirrors my own tumultuous journey, yet she treads with a hunger for understanding I never had the chance to explore. This stark contrast between her openness and my inherent reserve draws me towards her, compelling in a way I can't quite articulate.

Rayne recoils slightly, a visible reaction to the angels' presence. "Oh my God. This is so happening. It's like my dream." Her eyes narrow as they find mine. "Jaden, is this a dream or proof that the supernatural exists?" Her direct approach, seeking clarity without pretense, impresses me. It's then I feel that undeniable surge again, a primal acknowledgment from within. *She's ours.*

Aleah and her partners turn their attention to me, seemingly passing the narrative baton. I hold Rayne's gaze, ensuring she understands the gravity of my words. "You're not dreaming. Aleah is a Nephilim, half angel." I gesture towards each of her mates. "Cassiel, Atroyel, and Tristan are angels." My voice trails off as I hesitate to speak of my own celestial nature, an admission that feels like standing at the edge of a vast chasm.

Aleah, perceptive as ever, fills the silence. "Jaden is being modest," she says, earning a sharp glance from me. But she doesn't falter. "He's an angel too, but of a different kind. My mates are blood angels from another realm. Jaden, however, was human, bestowed with the powers of an avenging and guardian angel."

Her words hang in the air, adding a new layer to my identity, one I'm still reconciling with. I raise an eyebrow, a silent acknowledgment of this revelation, yet choosing to remain mute. This new aspect of my being – a guardian angel – it's a mantle I'm still learning to wear.

"And your knowing simplifies our next steps. You, Rayne, are believed to be one of the last Luminaras, a lineage of white witches of ancient and rare origin. There are forces of darkness seeking to extinguish your power, forces tied to the sex trafficking ring we're dismantling," Aleah explains, her words carrying the weight of centuries.

"We'll provide a brief overview now, but uncovering the depths of your power is a journey you must embark on yourself. Jaden here," she nods in my direction, "is inexplicably linked to this path. And there are certain non-negotiables moving forward," Aleah continues, her gaze fixed on Rayne.

Without hesitation, Rayne asks, "And they are?"

"First, Jaden will be your constant companion. Consider him your guardian angel." Aleah glances at me, a silent challenge in her eyes. I remain silent, my thoughts a turbulent sea, unsure of what words, if any, would suffice in this moment.

Rayne's gaze locks onto mine, assessing, calculating. There's a deliberation in her eyes, a weighing of realities that I find both vexing and enthralling.

"Is he in charge of me?" Rayne's question catches me off

guard, and a laugh nearly escapes me. Her unpredictability is both a puzzle and an allure. *She's ours.* The power within me surges, acknowledging a connection I'm still grappling to comprehend.

Aleah's response is blunt. "Only in matters of your protection. In those instances, Jaden holds veto power, and he'll answer to the gods if he fucks up." Her casual use of profanity punctuates the seriousness of her statement.

Rayne processes this, a hint of acceptance in her tone. "I can work with that. What else?"

"Your sister will stay at Harmony Hills for the duration of our operation. You'll reside in one of our secure apartments." Aleah lifts a finger, and the papers float towards Rayne. "You'll find the terms of your employment more than favorable—a generous salary, accommodations, and provisions for severance if you decide to leave post-contract."

With another gesture, Aleah summons a leather briefcase through the air, no doubt showing off her magic. "Your immediate priority is the training program. It will be the key to unlocking your power. Inside this briefcase, you'll find everything to get started, including your new computer and phone."

As I observe this exchange, a sense of duty mingles with a nascent, inexplicable bond. Rayne, a woman of mystery and strength, is now my charge, my responsibility. The depth of this new connection, this uncharted territory, both daunts and intrigues me.

Rayne maintains her composure, her expression revealing only a flicker of surprise. Her next question is pointed. "Are you considered powerful among Nephilim?"

Aleah responds with a hint of a smile. "Quite possibly. However, you, as a Luminara, would be a formidable match. Let's stay on friendly terms, shall we?" Standing up, she exudes an aura of authority mixed with an undercurrent of camaraderie.

Rayne, undeterred by the shift in conversation, presses on. "And your tattoo? What's its story?" Her directness is refreshing, a trait that speaks to her fearless nature. Again, my power responds. *She's ours.*

Aleah's explanation is succinct. "It's more than just ink. It's a representation of the bond shared with my mates, a symbol that holds meaning for us. In our case, it's a black rose." She regards Rayne thoughtfully. "You, too, have been chosen by the Olympian gods for a soul bond with a celestial being. It's likely that the symbol for your bond has already been determined." Aleah holds out her hand and hands the small envelope that appears to me.

With those words, Aleah and her companions vanish. *What the fuck?*

I watch Rayne, her features betraying a whirlwind of thoughts as she grapples with the reality of her newfound identity and its implications. The weight of her celestial connection, her potential as a Luminara—it's a lot to digest. And in this complex web of fate, our paths intertwine, a connection that's becoming harder to dismiss or understand.

Before I can even process my next thought, she breaks the silence. "I'm starving. We need to find someplace to eat. I need some time to process all this." Her voice is steady, but there's an undercurrent of urgency—a need for space to think.

I feel the same, a pressing need to sort through the tumult of emotions and revelations swirling inside me. "As do I, little dragon," I murmur, almost to myself. My gaze falls on the small folder Aleah handed me, and I open it to find two key cards to the suite below. An idea forms—a private space, away from prying eyes and ears.

"We can order room service from our suite." My tone masks the turmoil beneath my calm exterior. I stride out of the room, exuding a dominance I'm not entirely comfortable with, yet it feels necessary. I hope she follows, avoiding the deeper question of why her presence has become so significant to me.

18

RAYNE

So, I've basically hit the jackpot of weird. Part of me's dancing inside, because, hello, I've got these crazy powers. But it's not all sci-fi and cool gadgets—it's real, and it's happening to me. Then there's all this talk about soul mates and these insane prophecies. And Jaden—Mr. Tall, Dark, and Broody – he's now officially my shadow. Like it or not, his awesome ass is stuck in my life.

I'm so lost in these revelations, I barely register our surroundings until Jaden flings open a door, his movements all precision and control. The thought hits me—maybe he's trapped in this mess too. Maybe he'd rather be anywhere but here, in this labyrinth of secrets and supernatural bonds.

"Hey, if this place is secure, maybe they'll let you go home." I keep my voice casual, but my heart's doing a weird dance at the idea of separation. It's for the best, right? I'm getting too caught up with this guy when I should be focusing on building a life for Summer and me.

Jaden shoots me a look, like I've missed the mark. "Where I am doesn't matter. I adapt," he says, but there's an edge there, a hint of something more beneath that composed exterior.

"Yeah, right. Like you'd last a day in the wild." Not one of the brightest things I've ever said, but I'm trying to lighten the mood. He's too polished, too put-together and in love with convenience. He belongs in a world of luxury, not rugged wilderness, regardless of what he thinks.

He dismisses my jab with a nonchalant, "I'd manage," before leading us into a lavish living room. He casually tosses the keys and hops onto the couch with an ease that belies the tension simmering just beneath his surface. He's like a coiled spring, all pent-up energy and hidden depths.

"Get us some food," he commands without a glance my way. The authority in his voice sends a shiver through my core, a mix of irritation and an unbidden, primal reaction.

I can't help but fire back, "What am I, your servant now?" It's a challenge, a push against his dominance.

His response is immediate, a hint of a smirk in his voice. "You're my first and last." It's a loaded statement, tinged with something that feels a lot like desire.

"Arrogant much?" I mutter under my breath, my pulse quickening.

He's unapologetic, "That's me. And I'm good at it. Keep in mind that I'm a meat and potatoes guy." He casually mentions his preference for simple food, but there's an undercurrent to his words, a subtle pull that's hard to ignore.

Fighting the urge to cater to his needs, I scan the room —all plush furnishings and understated opulence—until I find the room service menu. My fingers brush over the glossy pages as I read aloud the options, each word laced with a new, unsettling, and strangely exhilarating tension. "Fish and chips, chicken and roast potatoes, or steak frites?"

"Steak, medium. And throw in some fried mushrooms and onions," Jaden orders without even a glance in my direction.

"Last I checked, you weren't my boss," I snap back, but a twist in my gut says maybe I don't mind as much as I should.

He shoots me a look, half challenge, half amusement. "With me, you play by my rules, little dragon."

I'm about to protest, but he cuts me off with a finger in the air, his eyes never leaving the TV. "First, dinner. Then we can argue."

Grumbling about how I've apparently lost my mind, I call room service. Fish and chips for me and that steak he's so keen on. Part of me wonders why I'm not more upset about following his orders. But another part, the part that's always looking for a challenge, finds it strangely exhilarating.

I slam the phone down and let out a long breath. Time to dive into whatever this training package is. I haul the sleek black briefcase onto the desk, curiosity piqued despite myself. I've seen my share of corporate setups, but this? This is next level. I sift through the contents: welcome letter, contract, training plan, and iPhone that probably costs more than my rent and books to start a small library. I catch my breath at the six salary figure—I hit the jackpot twice in one day. Financial freedom? Check. No more relying on any man for me and Summer? Double check.

"Sweet," I murmur, thumbing through the contract. No legal jargon, just straightforward, everything tipping in my favor. Generous doesn't even start to cover it.

"You seem pretty cool with all this," Jaden comments, his tone more curious than critical. It's a fair point.

I shrug, my heart skipping a beat at his attention. "It's like another weird dream of mine just walked into real life."

"Daydreams, more like," he shoots back, but there's a hint of something in his voice as if he's trying to figure me out and see what makes me tick.

"Nope. Night dreams. I have a recurring dream that I've been put under a spell or some science experiment where my special abilities are hidden because I'm so powerful that I'm a threat to humanity." I pause, letting that sink in, half expecting Jaden to roll his eyes or something. But instead, here I am, all my secrets spilling out unfiltered.

"Go on. Maybe precognition is one of your gifts."

I blurt out before I can stop myself, "So you don't think I'm odd, a nut bar?" There's an edge to my voice, a mix of hope and a fierce need to not look like a complete idiot in front of him.

He gives me that almost-smile, the one that hints he's not as tough as he pretends. "If you asked me six months ago, my answer would've been different. But now, hell, we're walking proof that 'normal' got thrown out the window. Besides, I like odd." He turns my arm over gently, his touch igniting sparks along my skin. "We can deep dive into the whys later. Tonight, it's all about you." His focus is so intense it feels like a spotlight shining right on me. And there's something else in his gaze too—a kind of fiery interest that's new, unfamiliar, and sends my heart racing.

"Any idea how to start figuring out my powers? I should've asked Aleah more questions. Shit, there's so much to unpack." I pick up the training plan, trying to look like I've got my act together when inside I'm all fluttery and excited like a kid in a candy store.

Jaden's voice drops lower, a note of command that resonates deep inside me. "Put that down and come here." I set the papers aside, moving closer to him as he pours two drinks. The aroma of pineapple wafts over, soothing and sweet.

"What's this?" I take the glass he offers.

He watches me, his gaze analytical yet intense. "Stoli Doli, vodka with pineapple. Good, isn't it?"

"Yeah, it is," I admit, the drink warming me, smoothing out the edges of my excitement and nerves.

"You seem pretty stoked about all this." Jaden once again proves he's a master of understatement. But for once, I'm too caught up in this whirlwind of discovery and sheer joy to shoot him my usual are-you-kidding-me look.

"Oh my God, Jaden. How could I not be excited by all this? One minute, I'm this little Black woman who men seem to think is their plaything without a brain in my head because Black people have smaller brains and thicker skulls, don't you know. And the next minute, I'm some rare breed of witch with superpowers who nobody can call stupid anymore. And I've got a fabulous new job and have my own guardian angel." I stop the verbal vomit I seem compelled to make before I say something else I hadn't meant to reveal and because I run out of air. Jaden takes it all in and gives me another drink. "And now I've got a training program to get through in the next month. I probably should be figuring out what I'll be doing tomorrow since the letter says I'm on the payroll as of today." I take another swig of the drink.

"That's right, and your training starts tonight at the Masquerade Club. There's a kink event on tonight." Jaden takes a sip of his drink while he leaps right to the point, those wolfish eyes locked on my face, reading every muscle twitch.

I damn near jump out of my skin when a buzzer goes off on the far wall.

"Ah good, dinner's here. Let's eat." Jaden sets his glass on the dining table before opening the doors to a dumb waiter laden with steaming, dome-covered dishes. I barely have time to ogle Jaden's fine ass before he's laid out our meals and tucks into his fish and chips. Slowly, I follow him.

I have no idea what to do with this dark, intense man. I have no idea how to behave. Out of nowhere, I'm on the verge of hyperventilating as a panic attack bubbles to the surface. *I. Will. Not. Do. It.*

I will be the poster child for self-restraint. I drift off into one of my imaginary stories. Jaden has kidnapped me. He doesn't bend me to his will with violence; he uses silence. Each night, he dines with me. The finest dark brown silk shirt outlines each muscle . . .

I sigh. I suck on my bottom lip, then catch myself. *Stop that.* He might notice. I throw a quick glance in his direction. The tunnel lights dimly light the interior, giving me a startling glance at his chiseled silhouette.

"What's going on, Rayne?" Jaden's voice, a low rumble, drags me back to the present, away from the dangerous edges of my mind. I can't tell him about the PTSD, the scars that mark my psyche. That I'm not just complicated; I'm damaged. He'll want to dissect it all, understand every fragment, but I can't let him. *Not yet.*

I shut my eyes, barricading my thoughts from him, focusing on steadying the erratic dance of my pulse. My body's no stranger to pain, to reactions both fierce and frightening, but this, this electric current zinging through me is alien, unsettling. Jaden, ever the perceptive observer, grants me the space I so desperately need, his silence a balm. He refills my drink and, unexpectedly, places a joint and an ashtray within reach. It's an escape, a temporary reprieve I know I shouldn't take, but the urge to numb the chaos within is too potent to resist. I light up, inhaling deeply, letting the smoke curl through me, loosening the tight coil of tension.

After a few moments lost in the haze, I find my voice again. "Did you say the Masquerade Club is a sex club?" My words are slow, but curiosity pierces through the pleasant haze in my brain.

Jaden pauses mid-bite, a flicker of something unreadable crossing his face before he resumes his meal. He fixes his intense gaze on me. "Yes, the Masquerade is a sex club, and yes, I mentioned it earlier. What exactly do you want to know?" His question hangs in the air, thick with implication, a challenge I'm not sure I'm ready to meet.

"Earth to Rayne," Jaden's voice, tinged with a hint of amusement, pulls me from my spiraling thoughts. His eyes, those deep pools of mystery, lock onto mine, holding me captive without a touch.

I blink, snapping back to the here and now, my mind a whirlwind of questions and unspoken fears. "Sorry, just... thinking." It's an understatement, a feeble attempt to mask the torrent of emotions churning inside me, but I don't know what else to say. Too much interest will make me look like a brazen hussy.

Jaden leans back, a slow, knowing smile playing on his lips. "It's okay to be curious about the Masquerade. I like that you're curious." He pauses, the air between us crackling with unspoken words. "It's a place of exploration, Rayne. A place where fantasies come to life, where boundaries are tested, and desires are fulfilled."

My heart hammers against my ribs, each beat a drum of

anticipation and dread. The idea of such a place, with Jaden, stirs a dangerous mix of excitement and fear in me. His presence alone is enough to send my senses into overdrive; the thought of being with him in a *sex* club is both exhilarating and terrifying.

"And you?" My voice is barely above a whisper. "What do you do there?" The question hangs between us, heavy with implications.

Jaden's gaze darkens, a hint of something more primal flashing in his eyes. "I'm a participant, like everyone else. Exploring, experiencing, enjoying." He leans forward, closing the distance between us. "But tonight, I'm there for you. To guide you, to protect you. To show you a world you've never imagined."

Oh dear God. The air is so thick with tension that it's as if a magnetic force draws me towards him. I'm caught in the gravitational pull of his charisma, his power, his undeniable allure. It's a dance of desire, each step drawing me closer to the edge, to a precipice I'm both eager and hesitant to leap from.

His voice drops to a husky whisper, "Are you ready to explore the unknown, Rayne?"

His question lingers in the air, a challenge, an invitation, a promise of something wild and uncharted. My breath catches in my throat, my body and mind at war. I'm on the verge of a discovery, teetering on the brink of a revelation that could either break me or set me free.

I swallow hard, my heart pounding. There's a part of me, a reckless, daring part, that wants to dive headfirst into this new, mysterious world . . . with this man. To feel, to experience, to lose myself in something so completely foreign and yet strangely inviting.

"Enlightening, huh?" I manage to quip, trying to maintain a façade of nonchalance. But the truth is, I'm anything but indifferent. My body hums with a strange mix of excitement and anxiety like I'm on the cusp of something monumental. Maybe it's the Stoli or maybe it's the pot or maybe it's both, but for the first time in a long time, my rational brain can't control my emotions. It's as if something inside me is screaming, "hell yes. This Jaden is my Neo, and I'm going to enjoy the ride." And everything about his damned presence is sucking me in further—his scent, a mix of musk and something uniquely him, intoxicates me. The warmth of his skin radiates through the inches of space separating us, beckoning me closer. His features, so damned gorgeous, are like a siren's call I can't resist. I probably should try to resist him, but I won't.

Jaden glances at me, a flicker of something indecipherable in his eyes. "You might be surprised at what you discover about yourself," he says softly, almost a whisper. "And about us."

Us. The word lingers between us, heavy with unspoken promise and potential. We're playing a dangerous game, a dance on the edge of a precipice, and I'm not sure who's leading anymore. But one thing is clear: the tension between us is a living, breathing entity that consumes the space, igniting a fire that threatens to consume us both.

19
JADEN

Jaden,

You'll be staying in the Eros' Haven suite. Security has set up your biometric scan. We'll have Rayne set up as part of her induction. Included is your Ticket to Temptation. Keep this on you at all times. There will come a time very soon when Rayne will need what appears to be medical attention. Do not take her to a hospital. There's a Druid temple in a forest in New Jersey. This ticket and your power will guide you there. Ignore the call at your and Rayne's peril.

Aleah

That cryptic note, with its strange message and a carved wooden card etched with intricate symbols, are the contents of the envelope Aleah handed me. They come with the room number and WiFi for the secure suite Rayne and I will be sharing. There's a certain relief in this neutral ground, yet a part of me aches for the solitude of my sanctuary. But my newfound power, seemingly with its own consciousness, jolts me, calling out my self-deception. It's not just solitude I miss. It's Rayne's intriguing presence, her unguarded curiosity that seeps through our bond, stirring something in me.

I sense her fumbling with the connection, a curious blend of resistance and exploration. She prods and pokes, like a child with a new toy, all while maintaining a seemingly effortless conversation. It's an odd dance, and though I should be figuring out how to shield my thoughts, I find myself ensnared by her, this little dragon entrusted to my care.

Then, like a fool, I use the word "us," and her eyes spark to life, a clear interest kindling in their depths. My power and desire surge in unison, urging me on, while my rational mind screams for restraint. But tonight, the usual shadows that haunt me are drowned out by the buzz of the Stoli and the allure of Rayne's presence. For this moment, I'm allowing myself a reprieve from the usual self-imposed exile, as much as I'm capable of.

"You might be surprised at what you discover about yourself. And about us."

The simmering desire in Rayne, a whisper through our bond, surges as I speak. Despite the alcohol dulling my senses, her presence resonates with me, her tension interlaced with an unmistakable yearning. She eats with a restraint that's uncharacteristic, a faint smile playing on her lips, her posture stiff. It's clear she's grappling with more than just the electrifying atmosphere between us. My own desire for her, undeniable and growing, pulses within me.

I trace the path of my finger along her arm, eliciting a shiver from her, a thrill of anticipation echoing back to me. There's an art in drawing out a woman's response, a game I've mastered. But with Rayne, it's an entirely different game. Her guarded history, her complexity, challenges me to delve deeper, to discover the passionate, sensual being lurking beneath her cautious exterior.

"We're in the club right now." I gesture around the luxuriously appointed suite. Its design melds comfort with subtle eroticism. The high beams, the furniture—each piece functional yet designed for sexual activity, far from the garish displays in other clubs. This understated elegance, where pleasure intertwines with refinement, is what draws me in.

Rayne halts, her attention shifting from her meal to survey the room. "So, is this like a 'Fifty Shades' thing? Where's all the sex stuff?"

Laughter, genuine and rare, escapes me. "Each suite has a private playroom. The main events are in the penthouse. We have time," I say, hoping my words encourage her to relax and eat.

Her mention of 'Fifty Shades' grates on me. That narrative, with its flawed portrayal, trivializes the complexities of sexual dynamics. To me, sex is a profound exploration, a dance of power and vulnerability. It's not a frivolous game but a journey into the depths of desire and control. My experiences have shown that only music and the intensity of a scene can hold back the shroud of darkness that looms over me. Yet, the paradox remains—a scene is, in essence, a form of roleplay, a game that holds the potential for deep, meaningful connections.

And even as the thought forms, I can't escape the irony of it. The shroud, my ever-present nemesis, begins its encroachment, a suffocating tide of darkness. It provokes a reaction, stirs my power that lies dormant within. It's an insatiable need to release, a force that builds when I battle the darkness. The choice is stark—succumb to the shroud or find release in fucking or killing. The war within me, a tempest of conflicting desires, pushes me away from my safe havens—both the literal fortress Rayne mockingly calls my Batcave and the mental sanctuary I've built. Here I am, venturing down a path fraught with potential pain and rejection for reasons that elude even my rational mind. A surge of irrational annoyance wells up within me.

"First off, I haven't read that book. Can't believe you bought into that shit. "Fifty Shades" gets BDSM danger-ously wrong. You're too intelligent for that." My words are tinged with frustration, a hint of irritation seeping into my tone. If Rayne and I are to coexist, she must accept me as I am, in all my fucked-up glory.

I catch a fleeting glimpse of something in Rayne's eyes, a spark I can't quite define before she exhales a sigh and pushes her plate away. Our bond, while revealing, offers no clarity here.

"Yes, I bought into it. I'm stupid that way. Why didn't you read it?" Her gaze pierces me with its intensity, her mental shields rising. I brace myself; she's gearing up for a confrontation. Is this really her takeaway from my words? *We want her.* My power and libido are unconcerned with the future implications of our entanglement with Rayne. They crave the immediate, the here and now. And right now, they yearn for this woman who stands apart from anyone I've chosen to engage with before.

"Stop selling yourself short. I never implied you were unintelligent." My voice carries a rising tone of righteous indignation, my dominant nature surfacing in defense.

"Yes, you did. You said, and I quote, 'you're too smart to buy into that.' Implying if I did buy into it, I'm not smart. Just like everyone believes. So, yes, me and millions who read the books and watched the movies are idiots, right?" Rayne's retort comes in a rapid torrent. Before I can formulate a response, she's taken another swig of her drink. Our bond signals a shift in her mood a mere moment before she challenges, "So what's so dangerously wrong with it? Enlighten me."

I let out a long sigh, a performance of patience, while internally acknowledging my own asshole tendencies. But I justify it as a necessity—Rayne needs to understand this side of me if we're going to spend any significant time together. "First of all, that Grey guy is abusive. There's a zero-tolerance policy for abuse in the kink world, especially at the Masquerade Club. Connor and Kat ensure that what happens here is always pleasurable and consensual. But my real beef with it is the misrepresentation of BDSM. Like the absurd idea that nobody uses a safe word." I take a swig of my drink, letting the sharpness of the alcohol match my tone. "And Grey is definitely not a Dom, that much is clear even without reading the books."

"How do you know all this if you haven't read the books?" Rayne's curiosity pokes through her defiance.

"I listen, observe, and form my own opinions." My response is clipped, a contrast to the swirling emotions inside.

The intensity between us crackles, almost tangible.

"You don't strike me as someone who lets others shape your views."

She shifts gears, maybe sensing the heat of our exchange getting too intense. "What'd Aleah give you?" Rayne's question offers a momentary respite from our verbal sparring.

I hesitate, weighing how much to disclose. Aleah's selective sharing of information irks me. Another tick against those in power. Reluctantly, I retrieve the wooden tablet from my pocket and place it on the table. Its surface is adorned with detailed scrollwork and an explicit carving of a man and a woman, each embodying raw sexual power. "Ticket to Temptation" is inscribed on one side and "A Chosen One" on the other, words that hold more meaning than they let on.

Rayne picks up the tablet, examining it closely. "It's beautiful," she murmurs, her voice laced with wonder.

I brace myself for her questions, but she takes a different route. "Looks like sex is tied to my new powers. Maybe it's time I figure out why sex seems to complicate everything. So, what should I know about these scenes? What's expected of me?" Her question cuts through the room, sharp and demanding, yet laced with a hint of vulnerability.

Rayne's response, simple yet laden with unexpected conviction, catches me off guard. My power surges in response, almost reveling in her straightforwardness. She articulates the questions that I, shrouded in my own complexities and past traumas, find difficult to confront. It's a peculiar sensation, feeling this surge of hope, as if Rayne might be the key to unlocking parts of me long buried in darkness.

Launching into a discussion about our mission, I talk

about the clubs and their connection to the criminal under-world, but my thoughts are elsewhere. I focus on Rayne, peeling back the layers of her persona, and exploring the depth beyond her outwardly vanilla appearance. I want to discover her, understand her, delve into the intricacies that make her unique.

"So, what's lesson number one?" Curiosity tinges Rayne's voice.

I forcibly restrain my thoughts, pushing away the tantalizing images of Rayne in a state of vulnerability, bound in surrender. It's not the time for these fantasies, not when there's so much at stake. Yet, the conflict within me rages on, a battle between desire and the scars of my past.

"First, we need to understand if you're more of a submissive or a dominant," I say, surprised at my own boldness. My power, it seems, is steering the ship now, compelling me to engage in this dance of discovery with Rayne.

"Oh, I love stories about Subs and Doms. I'm a Sub." Rayne announces with a degree of finality, not that I doubt her. Her declaration of being a submissive is stated with such finality it feels like a confirmation of my own instincts. My power echoes her sentiment, urging me to reach out, to bridge the physical gap between us. Yet, the mere thought of contact stirs the darkness within me, a reminder of past traumas that still haunt my every move.

"But how can you be sure, given your limited experi-ences?" I challenge her, my voice laced with a harshness that I instantly regret. The link between us conveys her hurt, yet she remains poised, her bright demeanor dimming under the weight of my words. The realization that I've caused her discomfort, that I'm pushing her into a corner, fills me with self-loathing, yet I'm powerless to alter my course.

"I took a few surveys on the internet. They all say I'm a sub."

Her response, while seemingly trivial, strikes a chord within me. It's her way of navigating our complex world, a world where power, submission, and desire intertwine in an intricate dance. And in this moment, I'm both a participant and an observer, caught in the throes of my own internal struggle yet utterly captivated by Rayne.

The idea of introducing Rayne to the world of kink, albeit as a mere observer for now, sets my pulse racing. The distinction between being a Dom and a Top might be lost on her at this stage, but it's a lesson for another time. Right now, my main concern is not to overwhelm her or push her into realms she's not ready to explore. My role, as I see it, is to guide, to enlighten without casting any shadows of fear.

Rayne's admission that she's never even met a Dom is not surprising, yet it stirs something within me. Her hesitation, tinged with a hint of apprehension about my perception of her, only makes me more determined to be her guide in this uncharted territory. Her innate curiosity, that raw eagerness to learn, is like a beacon, drawing me in.

Refusing to dwell on the notion that I might be the one to give Rayne her first real taste of kink, I focus instead on the immediate plan. "We'll start with something simple, something easy to digest. Tonight, at the club, we'll observe a beginner flogging session. It'll give you a glimpse into the dynamics, the trust, the communication that's crucial in these interactions."

The words leave my lips with a blend of trepidation and anticipation. It's a fine line I'm walking, introducing her to a world that's second nature to me—albeit more as an observer than a player—yet so alien to her. I need to be cautious to ensure that her first experience is one of understanding and not intimidation.

In my mind, I'm already preparing for the evening, running through the possible scenarios, the questions she might have, and the reactions she might exhibit. It's a dance of discovery, not just for Rayne, but for me as well. For in guiding her, I'm also exploring new facets of my own being, peeling back layers of control to reveal the vulnerabilities hidden beneath.

And as I ponder this, I feel a surge of excitement, a recognition that this journey with Rayne might be the most exhilarating one I've ever embarked upon. A journey not just of physical exploration but of emotional and psychological revelation. It's a path fraught with potential pitfalls, yet the prospect of traversing it with Rayne by my side fills me with a sense of purpose and anticipation that I haven't felt in a long time.

20

RAYNE

Fire and Ice. One face for the show, another just for us. Jaden's a pro at this game, way better than I ever could be. I'm scratching my head trying to pin him down, but it's like trying to catch smoke with my bare hands. When I think I've got a read on him, he flips the script. Call him out, and he either blows a gasket or comes back with something slick like, "Predictable? Not my style."

Two things are crystal clear after seeing him with others: Mr. Charm is his go-to move, and the ladies? They eat it up. He's got a thing for curves, too. Thinks he's slick about it, but I'm not blind. I feel his eyes, his interest, even if he plays it cool.

Jaden's like those wild ice volcanoes I saw on a documentary once. To the world, he's like this impenetrable block of ice, all stoic and tough. Struts around, covered in this frosty armor, keeping everyone at arm's length. But underneath? There's this fiery storm brewing, a heated geyser ready to burst through that icy exterior. He's a bundle of contradictions—cold on the outside, but inside, there's a fiery core that's just simmering, waiting. And sometimes, he slips, shows a spark of that inner fire, and you realize Mr. Ice King's got more layers than you thought.

And there's me, caught between wanting to smack him for his arrogance and wanting ... something else. Something that's more than just physical, despite his constant reminders that it's all about sex. I can feel it, this pull between us. But now there's this weird urge to give in, to let him lead, and it freaks me out. I shove that thought away but know I can't hide from it for long.

"Rayne." Jaden's voice snaps me back to reality. "Focus. Before we hit the club, we need to lay down some rules. Any physical stuff between us? It's just sex. No strings attached. We're just friends, that's it."

"Got it, loud and clear." My voice is laced with sarcasm. I'm not blind to his physical attraction to me, this unspoken tension that he seems to despise as much as I do.

"If I'm going to teach you about kink, you'll have to be absolutely honest and open with me. No lies. That's one of the things I like about the BDSM community. The community is an accepting and judgment-free zone, at least when it comes to sex."

I glare right back at him as he gives me his best CC look. "I will if you will. What's good for the goose is good for the gander after all. Are you going to answer my questions?"

"We'll see." There he goes again with the damned cryptic answers. "Right now we're talking about you, not me."

That back and forth goes on for a while until Jaden decides it's time to go. Good thing, too, because I'm getting quite the buzz on from this damned Stoli. It goes down way too easily. Maybe that's why I'm not super embarrassed and mortified by the direction the conversation takes—the third-degree about my sex life. It dawns on me that Jaden has an inordinate amount of interest in my sex life . . as I do in his.

I almost choke when Jaden asks, "How often do you masturbate?"

"Um . . . Never." Now I cannot meet his eyes but I sure as hell feel something like displeasure or disappointment through our link.

"Why not?" His tone is more curious than judgmental, but it still stings.

"Because we learned at Bible school that it's a sin. My mother was very clear that she'd break a broom over my back if she ever caught me doing it and made sure we wore underwear and pajama pants to bed and it's just wrong." I force myself to meet Jaden's gaze as something compels me to choke out the answer.

'That will definitely have to change. Starting now.' Jaden says this with a finality that warns of all kinds of consequences if I don't obey. Dirty thoughts that I keep hidden from the entire world, including myself, start to surface. Jaden's giving me that non-blinking look of his, waiting for me to comply. For some reason, I know on an instinctual level exactly what he wants without him speaking a word, and I stare right back at him, trying to think of an excellent one-liner I can return.

Our stare-downs are becoming a staple in this non-relationship of ours. Then, just as the tension hits its peak, he cracks a grin. Damn him. He stands, offering his hand. " Time to go." He marches off muttering about religious people, and I obediently follow."

I try to play it cool as Jaden charms his way through the crowd, but I'm barely aware of our surroundings. The viewing room he leads us into is a study in seductive elegance—dim lighting casts an eerie glow, highlighting the deep burgundy walls and contrasting with the stark black drapes of both the viewing room and playroom. A large, clear window offers an unobstructed view of the scene unfolding before us. A polished mahogany St. Andrew's Cross dominates the far wall, accompanied by a spanking horse and strapping bench—all reminders of the power dynamics at play here.

I'm a bundle of nerves and excitement, my heart racing as I watch the flogging scene, grateful for the glass that separates us. My outfit, a silky number that clings to every curve, heightens my awareness of every movement. I've always been curious about sex, devouring every book and article I could find, but they never captured the raw, visceral reality of it. I'd never admit it out loud, but being able to watch without being part of the action is like a fantasy come to life.

Feeling awkward as hell, I stand near the one-way glass separating the viewing room from the playroom, I feel a magnetic pull drawing me to the intense scene unfolding. It's terrifying, yet thrilling, and I sense my heart racing to keep up with the pace. I stand in the dimly lit viewing room, my gaze fixated on the scene unfolding before me. I'm watching a woman tied to a St. Andrew's cross, her body arched and exposed, while a man holding a flogger stands just a few feet away from her.

"Are you ready?" he asks, his voice low and commanding.

"Y-yes," the woman stammers, her breaths shallow and uneven.

"Good," he says, drawing back the flogger and swinging it forward with expert precision. The sound of leather connecting with flesh echoes through the room, followed by a sharp intake of breath from the woman.

"Did that hurt?" he inquires, his tone almost teasing.

"Y-yes." Her voice quivers. *Then why the hell are you staying?*

"Good," he says again, and I can't help but feel a shiver run down my spine at his response.

My mind races, wondering what it would be like to be in her place, feeling the sting of the flogger on my own skin. I've never considered myself one for pain, in fact I hate it, but something about the raw vulnerability and intensity of the moment has me captivated.

Miss me with that bullshit. I try to push away the intrusive thoughts. But I can't deny the growing heat pooling between my legs, a sensation that both excites and unnerves me. It's a side of myself I've never felt, and I'm not sure if I'm ready to embrace it.

Jaden moves beside me, his presence stirring up a whirlwind of emotions within me. "Hi," I whisper, keeping my eyes trained on the playroom. Despite my fear and doubt, I can't help but be drawn to him. Do I really want this? Hell yes! Yells that naughty voice coming from my core.

"'Hi,' he responds, his voice smooth and confident. 'There's no need to whisper. The room is soundproof. They can't hear us.'

We watch the scene play out, our shared silence amplifying the tension between us.

"Submission is all about receiving direction," Jaden murmurs, moving closer to me, and I have to remind myself to breathe. 'Subs crave guidance and want to know the Dom's expectations, especially during sex play.'"

"Is it just during sex?" I ask, curiosity getting the better of me.

"Depends on the Sub and Dom, and whether it's about

psychological control or just play. There are Doms who want to take control of their Submissive's life, but many prefer the lifestyle of sex play. If it's purely for sex play, they're usually Tops or Bottoms."

I'm about to tell him I wouldn't like any man telling me what to do in the bedroom or anywhere else when I realize I have no fucking idea what I'd like in the bedroom because I'd never had a chance to find out.

As we continue watching the flogging scene, my curiosity grows stronger. It's intriguing and horrifying all at once, and I can't tear my eyes away. I feel Jaden's heated gaze on me, his desire clear through our bond.

"Chatty, isn't he?" I try to mask my nerves with sarcasm. But deep down, I'm searching for answers—permission to explore this unknown world further.

"Nothing turns me off faster than a woman who decides she's auditioning for a role in a porn movie while you fuck her," Jaden's voice is low and seductive. "You are not like other women."

His words wrap around me like velvet, sending shivers down my spine. The tension in the air thickens, crackling with unspoken promises and suppressed desires. Despite every bit of rational thought telling me I should run, I'm drawn to him like a moth to a flame.

He inches forward, closing the gap between us, and I force myself to keep my cool. No way I'm letting him see me sweat. It's like a high-stakes game, and I'm not about to show my hand first. The room's dim light can't mask the whirlwind of emotions crashing inside me. I try to chill out as Jaden edges closer, his warmth reaching me like an invisible force. His breath tickles my neck, bringing back a flood of thoughts and wild daydreams I've kept locked up tight. But he doesn't say anything.

We're just standing there, caught in this crazy, intense bubble, everything else fading out. It's like the whole world's boiled down to just him and me. I'm shaking inside, all tangled up in this crazy mix of nerves and excitement. This whole thing's like walking a tightrope, and I'm balancing really careful not to fall off.

We stand there, lost in a moment where the world blurs into nothingness. The sexual tension wraps around us, thick and tangible, making my heart race and my body tremble with a heady mix of fear and excitement. It's a dance on a knife's edge, and I'm teetering dangerously close to the blade.

As we watch, I can't help but be drawn into the world unfolding before us. It's like I'm peeking through a keyhole into a realm where all the rules I've ever known about love and desire are turned upside down. I've always felt like I was on the outside looking in, but in this place, where people chase their deepest passions without fear, I could fit in.

"Can I ask you something?" The words tumble out before I can stop them, and I face him, feeling my cheeks heat up. But I hold his gaze, not backing down.

"Sure."

"Have you . . . ever done this kind of thing?" I nod towards the playroom, my heart thudding hard against my chest as I wait for his answer. *Of course, he has, you twit.*

He pauses as if he's weighing his words. "Yeah, I have. It's intense, not everyone's cup of tea, but it can be mind-blowing."

"Mind-blowing, huh?" I echo, my curiosity buzzing like a live wire.

"Yeah. It's all about the give and take . . . and trust. It's freeing in a weird way.

"I mull over his words, grappling with the thought of surrendering that much control. For a split second, I'm hit with this gut feeling through our bond that he understands me in a way nobody else ever has. That maybe, just maybe, sex could be something good . . . especially with this guy."

"Maybe . . . I could give it a try." I throw the words out there, watching him for any sign of judgment. A flicker of something, maybe surprise or satisfaction, zips through our bond, but it's so quick I can't be sure.

"Only if you're sure." His voice is gentle, making me fall in love with him just a little bit. His hand lands softly on my shoulder, grounding me. "And only with someone you trust."

"Like you?" The words are barely a whisper, a question loaded with so much more. I know Jaden's like a switch—one wrong move, and he'll clam up.

His smile is a slow spread of warmth. "If that's what you want, Rayne. Really want."

"My heart's slamming against my ribs as I fix my eyes on the flogging scene playing out in the next room. What's Jaden trying to show me here? What's he think I need to learn from this? Or does he figure I'm some kind of freak? I shoot a look his way, trying to get a read on him, but his face is a closed book."

Jaden's all focused on the scene, but he edges closer till I can feel the heat radiating off his body against mine. He's silent, but his hand sneaks under my dress, his fingers skimming my skin and sparking shivers all over. My breath catches when he gives my nipple a gentle but firm pinch, and it's all I can do not to reach out to him. But I get the vibe he's not about that right now. I end up frozen, arms awkwardly pressed against my chest, not sure where to put them or what to do next.

I can't help but let out a soft moan, even as I struggle with the morality of what we're doing. My past abuse tugs at the edges of my mind, making me tense, but the pleasure Jaden offers is hard to resist. All the while, the sounds of the flogging echo through the room like a siren song, pulling me further into the darkness.

Without warning, he slides onto the couch like it's second nature and tugs me onto his lap, smooth as silk.

"Jaden," I whisper, my voice quivering. His hand glides down, nudging my dress aside with a thrilling and terrifying determination. He doesn't say a word, but there's a fleeting look—a silent command that flashes in his eyes before he's back to watching the scene. "No talking," he murmurs, barely audible yet laden with an authority that sends another shiver through me.

His fingers tease the edge of my panties, making my pulse race with anticipation. As he pushes them aside and begins to masturbate me, I can't help but watch the flogging intensify in the next room. The woman tied up seems to take pleasure in her pain, and I find myself wondering if I could ever feel the same.

The scene unfolding before me is like a car crash—you can't look away. There's this woman, tied to a St. Andrew's cross, all exposed and stuff, and this Dom, right out of some BDSM poster, with his leather pants and harness, looking all commanding. He's got two floggers, and man, the way he uses them—it's like he's painting with pain and pleasure. Each crack of the floggers sends this jolt through me, like electricity snapping in the air.

But then, this weird chill crawls up my spine, and my reality comes crashing in. The Dom . . . he reminds me of those creeps who jumped me that night on the street. It's a flicker of a memory, dark and twisted, nothing like the clean-cut, smells-like-heaven Jaden beside me. Thank God for Jaden's pristine hygiene and that trim body. They're like a lifeline right now, pulling me back from the edge of that nasty flashback. I focus on him, on his presence, letting it anchor me in the here and now, away from those shadows.

Yet, there's something undeniably captivating about the scene. The woman's reactions, her moans and gasps, they're real. They're raw. And I can't help but wonder, what's it like to surrender that much? To trust someone to take you to the edge and back? My body's reacting, all tense and alert, and part of me is intrigued, caught up in the strange dance of dominance and submission playing out before my eyes.

The tension inside me ramps up, pushing me to the brink. I'm right there, teetering on the edge of something big. But then, my past traumas grip me tight, denying me the release I'm aching for. It's like being stuck in some twisted limbo, caught between wanting and fearing, not getting any relief from either. A frustrating reality that might be part of the deal with Jaden.

Watching the flogging scene wind down, I'm left hanging, all wound up with nowhere to go. Jaden finally pulls back, his expression giving nothing away. My heart's drumming a mad rhythm, full of pent-up energy and a ton of questions that hang there, unanswered.

"Rayne," Jaden's voice cuts through, soft but clear. "We should go." I can only nod, a mix of relief and regret washing over me as we step out of the viewing room. There's a wildness inside me that's still raging, unchecked. Maybe that's for the best. For now, I'll trail along with Jaden into whatever crazy is waiting for us, not sure what's coming but desperate to figure out this thing between us.

21

JADEN

One month has blurred past since that night watching the scene, the night my power seemed to stake its claim on Rayne. It's not just about want anymore; it's a need that pulses through me. She's become a light in the darkness I'm habitually cloaked in.

Rayne's adaptation to this new life was immediate and fiercely independent. With a brisk efficiency, she carved out her domain, establishing herself as a force to be reckoned with. Her "Sweet," was tinged with a self-assurance that was impossible not to admire, even as she detailed her daily routines with an enthusiasm that was as infectious as it was relentless.

Her days are a whirlwind of visits to Summer, training sessions, and shopping sprees—her acceptance of my fashion advice is both a surprise and a subtle thrill. The notion of caring for someone else used to be a foreign concept, mired in shadows and doubt, but with her, it's different. It's fulfilling in a way that doesn't chafe against my sense of self.

Together, we orchestrated a raid that was nothing short

of a masterstroke, thanks to Rayne's insights. Even Sasha, with her hard-earned skepticism, has been charmed by Rayne's tenacity. It's nothing short of miraculous.

Our evenings are spent at the club, observing, learning. Her innate inquisitiveness when watching scenes is captivating. I've always found solace in solitude, my pleasures strictly my own, without the complications of another's presence. But the fantasies of Rayne lost in her own pleasure have become an unexpected delight, a private theater of the mind that I hadn't visited in far too long.

The craving for her is intoxicating, an endorphin rush that I'm chasing with a hunger I haven't felt in ages. It's a slow burn, this game of anticipation and patience. Intercourse remains a boundary I've yet to cross, but the thoughts of her—the soft sounds she can't help but release as I play with her clit, the way she confronts me head-on yet never casts judgment—consume me. She's both a delicate paradox and a dauntless warrior, fearlessly charging ahead. I need to shut this down. *Enough.*

The gnawing in my gut twists tighter with each passing day. There's a strength to Rayne that's both admirable and a glaring beacon of my own shortcomings. Her assured denunciations, her certainty in confronting the vile and the weak, leave me in turmoil. I'm certain the day will come when her rose-tinted glasses will shatter, and she'll see the man behind the mask—the flawed soul I truly am.

In the War Room, her presence is commanding, her debates with Razor spirited and sharp. She's a force, bolstering my ego in ways I didn't know were vacant. Even the shroud that constantly berates me, that sardonic voice that whispers about my looks, my stature—"Look at you, all beautiful..."—it's less convincing when I watch her.

My power, if I can call it that, surges, bolstered by her

nearness, and the shroud retreats, if only slightly. She's candid about her preferences, unabashedly telling me, "You're damned lucky I even let you near me, CC. I don't like big men, and you're huge. Way over my maximum requirements." Her words should sting, but they don't. Not when she looks at me with that blend of defiance and curiosity . . . and reverence.

Her contradictions are baffling—she's wrapped in conviction, shining a light into my too-often darkened days. Yet with each day she's here, each day I allow her closer, she unwittingly sharpens the blade of betrayal I fear will one day slice through me. The echo of my mother's biting admonishments—"You should have fought harder."—clashes with the reality that Rayne is nothing like her. The adage rings hollow: trust no one. No matter how fervently I try to convince myself that Rayne's presence is inconsequential, deep down, I know it's not true.

She's a maelstrom of intelligence and adaptability, yet oblivious to the brilliance she exudes. And the only reason she tolerates me, I'm convinced, is because she hasn't yet seen me for the pitiful mess I am. The day will come, likely sooner rather than later, when she discerns the futility of her time with me and walks away. The mere thought is a punch to the gut, a visceral reaction I can't suppress. Regardless of the fear that grips me, this strange, burgeoning connection with Rayne—it matters more than I dare admit.

Struggling with the torrent within, I grapple with the riddle that is Rayne—and, by extension, the enigma that is myself. She's become an anomaly in my life, the first since childhood to stir something akin to positivity in my worn-out soul. She's defiant in ways that resonate deep within, seeing in me a hero, an idol, not just another handsome face. Her reverence is unsettling yet invigorating; my power revels in her adulation. And despite my protests, I find solace in her refusal to relent without cause.

The compliments she throws my way—meant to be kind—are double-edged swords, each word reopening old wounds that time has failed to heal. "You have to know how gorgeous you are," she insists, and every fiber of me wants to scream the truth—that her words are a torment, reminders of a beauty I cannot see and a curse I've borne all my life.

"I wish you would stop." My tone is sharper than I intend. She recoils only slightly, her resilience quick to bounce back. "You keep saying that, but you won't tell me why. I don't understand, Jaden. You are beautiful. Like Most GQ gorgeous. How can you not know that?"

Her confusion is genuine, but I can only offer a feeble response, "I don't see it, and I don't like it. That should be good enough." It's a dismissal, a weak defense against her probing.

I watch her now, aware that each day she becomes more entwined in my life, more vital to my existence. And as much as I dread the depth of my need for her, I can't deny it. I'm on the precipice, teetering on the edge of confessing the depths of my desire—how I long for her, fantasize about her, the way my thoughts of her become my nightly solace. Yet, I'm petrified. To admit such things would be to hand her the power to annihilate me.

In her presence, I'm torn between dread and an inexplicable joy. Each interaction with her, each time our bodies align in whatever game we play, I'm left wondering if maybe, just maybe, there's a chance for intimacy without the aftershocks of fear, guilt, or shame. A glimmer of hope flickers within, but it's a flame I must shield, hide deep within before the harsh winds of reality snuff it out.

Sex. That's the mantra I must cling to. It's the boundary I've set—a line drawn in the sand. Yet as I watch her, considering the 'what ifs,' I can't help but indulge in the fantasy for a fleeting second. Rayne's with me, under my tutelage, learning to navigate the intricacies of physical pleasure. And for now, I allow myself the luxury of enjoying the journey, however brief it might be. Because nothing lasts forever, especially not this.

Amidst this semblance of routine life Rayne has crafted so deftly, the woman's become a force in my world, one that my power seeks out like a beacon in the dark. It's a dangerous game, this blend of fear and fascination she stirs within me. She believes in me, sees something noble, a savior where I only recognize the facade. And despite my hesitations, I can't deny the draw I feel toward her—a magnetism that defies explanation.

The vibrancy she brings into every space, and every task, whether laying out plans for a mission or simply recounting her day, it's something that either lifts me or grates on me, dependent on the whims of my mood. Surprisingly, catering to her needs, this caretaking role has brought unexpected satisfaction, allowing me to step outside the chorus of critical voices I've come to associate with my own thoughts.

But it's not all about the mission or her ambitions; there's an allure to our evenings at the club, a curiosity that she can't help but exude. It's in these moments, watching her untamed interest, that I find myself indulging in thoughts better left unexplored. The thought of her, alone, lost in pleasure—it's a concept that has become a tantalizing addition to my solitary indulgences, a source of intense personal gratification.

Yet there's that persistent echo of doubt, the one that tells me I'm getting too close, letting her in too much. It's a battle within, a seesaw between longing and self-preservation. I'm caught in her orbit, yet every day that passes is a day closer to the inevitable—when she sees through the veneer and into the void that I am.

Her brightness, her intelligence, they're a balm, yet also a blinder. She doesn't see the truth yet, doesn't realize that a man like me can offer nothing but transient moments. The thought of her departure, it's a gut punch, a sensation that leaves me reeling, dreading the day she realizes her worth and turns away.

For now, the bond we share is a tightrope I walk with trepidation, feeling the push and pull of something that wants more, that dares to dream of a reality where the shadows are kept at bay. Yet deep down, I'm bracing for the fall. It's a familiar refrain, the knowledge that all good things come to an end.

Tonight, as she enters the room, the sight of her strikes me anew. The dress, the way it clings to her, it speaks of things unsaid, of desires unclaimed. Owner-ship, a possessiveness I've no right to feel, surges within me. Compliments sit on the tip of my tongue, yet they remain unspoken, buried beneath layers of defense mechanisms.

"Ready?" is all I can muster, a single word heavy with unvoiced emotions. The hurt that flickers through our bond is a blade to my gut, but she stands tall, the little dragon I both admire and fear.

"Sure, lead on."

With a resilience that I both envy and cherish, she

follows me out, leaving behind the sanctuary of our suite for the uncertainty that awaits

Rayne's curiosity, it's like a beacon, always hungry for knowledge, seeking to pierce the veil I've carefully constructed around my world. There's a certain pride in being the one to unravel the mysteries of desire for her, to channel her inquisitiveness into the dark alleys of pleasure and pain. Yet, there's a twinge of something else — a protective instinct that snarls within me every time I'm reminded of how she's been wronged.

"Tonight's agenda?" Rayne's voice, casual as she accepts the drink, belies the acute attentiveness I've come to expect. She lounges with a grace that's all her own, yet her posture subtly shifts, aligning with my unspoken cues. Despite her vehement assertions of autonomy, there's an unspoken dance between us, a give-and-take that edges closer to the domain of dominance and submission than either of us may openly acknowledge.

"We're observing an edge play scene." I watch as her expression morphs from relaxed to riveted. Her innocence in these matters is a stark reminder of the trust she's placed in my hands — a trust I'm determined not to betray.

Her brow arches, the spark of her spirit never far from the surface. "Edge play? Define it," she demands, her directness a challenge and a plea all in one.

I pause, choosing my words with care. "It's the art of flirting with limits, a dance on the knife-edge of desire and danger." My explanation is cryptic, an intentional prod to her ever-active mind.

Her eyes darken, the thrill of the unknown beckoning. "That sounds ... risky." Her voice a blend of trepidation and intrigue.

"Risk is part of the allure," I sip my drink, the fizz a stark contrast to the smoothness of her skin—skin I'm increasingly desperate to touch.

She's silent for a heartbeat, contemplating. "And what about you? Do you find pleasure in such extremes?" The question is tentative, probing the shadows I've fought to keep hidden.

"It's not about my preferences right now." My question lingers like smoke, a reminder of the murky depths I'm wary of revealing. "Tonight, we focus on the role of a submissive. That's your lesson."

Rayne's gaze flickers, the wheels of her mind turning. The weight of guiding her is both a privilege and a shackle, the intensity of my protective instincts warring with the raw need she ignites within me.

"I'm ready," she declares, her resolve clear in the set of her jaw. "Let's do this."

I nod, the facade of calm control firmly in place. "Finish up, then we'll proceed." The words are even, but beneath the surface, the turmoil rages—a tempest of doubt, desire, and the dawning realization that the line between teaching and yearning is blurring dangerously.

The flicker of uncertainty in Rayne's eyes doesn't escape me; it's a silent call for understanding. "What about edge play gets to you?" she asks, and I find myself in unfamiliar territory, uncharted waters where sharing personal inclinations isn't just clinical—it's personal.

"For me, it's the cerebral challenge." The truth spills out more freely than expected. "It's the dance of wits, the brinkmanship between power and yielding." My admission is a half-truth; the full spectrum of my desires, especially those concerning her, remain caged.

Rayne digests this, then probes deeper, "So, it's a

mental thing over the physical for you?" I nod, acknowledging her quick grasp of the dynamics at play.

"It's about trust," I elaborate, "the kind that's strong enough to endure the fire of our connection." I don't mention the rest, the unspoken yearning to traverse those realms with her.

Her cheeks bloom with a flush, but there's a spark of understanding in her gaze. She fumbles over her next words, voicing a concern that's been lurking in the shadows. "Is that why we haven't gone further? Is it a sort of . . . restraint?"

"Rayne," I hesitate, my explanation teetering on the edge of full disclosure. "It's not punishment. It's about building something that can withstand the storm of what we might become." I stand abruptly, tossing my napkin aside, a signal to move on.

As we settle into the viewing room, my guiding hand rests on Rayne's thigh, a silent testament to the charged air between us. Her reaction is instantaneous—a shiver that speaks volumes. Every fiber of me yearns to unravel her, to explore the depths of her soul just as she unwittingly delves into mine.

The warmth of Rayne's skin seeps through the thin fabric of her dress, her body subtly yielding to my touch. As my hand ventures beneath the hem, grazing the edge of her G-string, there's a collective tightening of breath and body —an unspoken dance of desire and restraint.

There's a raw need pulsing within me, a hunger that craves not just the carnal pleasure but the profound connection that's been weaving silently between us. Yet, I resist, my grip on control fraying but not yet broken.

"Do you enjoy the scene?" My voice is a low rumble against the charged silence.

Her response is a whisper, a confession of intrigue and understanding amidst the intensity of the act we've witnessed. The conclusion of the scene leaves a void, an empty stage where the echoes of our inner turmoil reverberate.

Our ritual continues, the one where I play with her clit until my balls are about to rupture. It's a familiar dance of desire that edges us both to the brink of something undefined. Tonight, though, there's a shift—a challenge in Rayne's eyes that's new, unyielding. Her frustration mirrors my own inner conflict.

"Bedtime." I signal our usual endgame, but tonight defiance replaces the compliance I expect. Her glare pierces through me, a silent accusation of the unfulfilled promises hanging in the air.

"Rayne." I keep a firm edge to my voice that's usually enough to steer us back to safe waters, "I'm serious about boundaries when it comes to intimacy."

Her glare doesn't waver, and she storms off, leaving a turbulent wake of anger and confusion. My power reacts, a visceral sensation acknowledging the inevitable crossroads we're approaching.

With a heavy sigh, I acknowledge the impasse. The smoldering embers of Rayne's yearning for me are now a bonfire, and I'm standing too close, feeling the heat lick at my resolve. It's a pivotal moment, one that demands a decision. Do I succumb to the desire that's been building within me, to embrace the risk of complete surrender? Or do I retreat, preserving the safety of solitude but forsaking the electric connection that's come to life between us?

The question hangs in the air, a specter of choices yet to be made. As I stand alone, the silent echoes of what could be are both a torment and a temptation. But one thing is for certain: the status quo can no longer hold. The next step is mine to take, and it's a leap that could either meld us together or rend us apart. For now, the night ends with a question, but the dawn will bring an answer—one way or another.

22

RAYNE

Late next morning. The nerve of him, standing there in my room like the king of the damn castle, poking me like I'm some snooze button on his personal alarm clock. I blink at the fuzzy outline of his figure, not bothering to reach for my glasses. He doesn't deserve my clear-eyed attention, not after leaving me strung up in knots of frustration the night before.

I sit bolt upright, yanking the blanket around me like armor, my hands flying out almost of their own accord. Fingers fumbling, I grab the sash of his robe and start knotting. Something completely juvenile but I'm in a hormonal freefall. He's pushed me to the brink, again and again, leaving me teetering on a precipice of desire without ever granting me the fall. What am I to him? A plaything? A tease? My mind shies away from the answers, anger bubbling up like a geyser.

With each twist of the fabric, I punctuate my rage and frustration with a word. "I. Hate. You." Each word is a knot, a binding of my fury. And what does he do? He grins. That rare and infuriatingly cocky grin that makes me want to wipe it off his face with the back of my hand.

But I don't. Because despite the volcanic rage within me, there's something else too—a twisted sort of pleasure in seeing that smirk, knowing I put it there, even if it's for all the wrong reasons. It's a dangerous game, this dance of anger and attraction, and he's playing his part with infuriating perfection.

Then, what's his next move? This infuriating man begins to untangle each knot, painfully slow, all the while fixing me with this steady gaze. Doesn't utter a single word. Just looks, his eyes doing all the talking. It's like he's trying to unravel more than just the knots on his robe, like he's peeling back layers, trying to get under my skin. Like I poked the bear one too many times and this time, I'm going to get what I asked for. Every slow, deliberate motion of his hands feels like a challenge, a silent dare that stops my breath.

I glare at him, the memory of last night replaying like a broken record. Close, he was so damn close to letting go, to admitting that he wanted me. I could feel it, almost taste the victory, the moment when he'd finally break.

But then came that guttural groan, a sound torn from the depths of his soul, as he pushed my hand away. His words, a mantra of restraint, echoed in my mind. "Not the right time," he'd said, shaking his head, his control a towering, unbreakable dam against the flood of desire flowing through our bond. He ordered me out, his eyes a turbulent sea of willpower and agony.

I almost had him. I'm no expert in sex, but I can sense when someone's about to crack. Or maybe I'm just fooling myself.

He methodically unties each knot as I turn these

thoughts over, his eyes burning into mine, a fierce inferno barely contained. I narrow my eyes in response. *No more fucking games, Jaden. You had your chance and you blew it.* My mind screams defiance, loud and clear.

But despite my resolve, my body betrays me, responding to his proximity, his touch. My heart races and my nipples are hard as stones. It's a battle between mind and body, and I'm caught in the crossfire. I'm determined to resist, to not give in to the temptation that's Jaden. But it's hard, so damn hard, when every fiber of me screams otherwise.

His eyes stay fixed on my body, but I can't help but notice that he's not looking at my face. My heart sinks for a moment, torn between desire and disappointment. But then I remember our bond, the connection that ties us together. I can feel his desire through it, hot and insistent, and it's impossible to deny the sheer intensity of his need. And yet, there's something else lurking in the background. His terror. It's like an ever-present shadow, creeping closer when we least expect it.

As he continues to undo the knots, the world around us seems to slow down. Time stretches out like taffy, each second lingering as if reluctant to let go. I watch with bated breath as the veins in his cock pulse, hard abs taut with anticipation. Every part of his body is in perfect proportion, sculpted by some divine artist with the sole intent to drive me wild. He's a living, breathing master-piece, one that I'm desperate to touch, taste, and claim as my own.

All thoughts blow from my brain as he undoes the last knot and lets his robe fall to the floor. God, his body is something else altogether. He's perfect. Every toned muscle and curve of him designed by the gods. Every hot and handsome man in the world pales in comparison. He's that perfect.

My eyes take in every inch of him as he stands before me, completely bare for the first time. Absolute perfection, he stands, the warrior angel about to make his conquest. His large cock commands my attention and a surge of fear and desire courses through me. *Dear god, please let this happen.* I send my frantic prayer to the heavens, all while my eyes remain glued on his cock, my heart about to punch its way out of my chest. For the first time, maybe ever, I want a man to enter my body. But I know there's a good chance I'll freeze up and be unable to take him inside me. But my frustration from weeks of Jaden teasing and playing with my clit without ever bringing me satisfaction has primed me, my body aching for release. I'm soaking wet and can smell my arousal but before my embarrassment registers, he moves.

His eyes never leave mine as he crosses the distance between us, climbing onto the bed and positioning himself above me. My brain doesn't have time to register the speed with which he's spread my legs and stabbed his hard length inside me leaving a trail of searing pain. Every muscle in my body clamps down hard but it's too late. He's already inside me.

Maybe it's the echo of his response through the bond that fuels me. But I can't focus on that right now because if he can be the master of control, then so can I. So, I focus hard on controlling my responses and matching mine to his. Then, he throws his head back and closes his eyes.

The entire time, he doesn't make one sound. Doesn't breathe hard. Doesn't break a sweat. Nothing.

Victory and agony pulse through me as he drills into me, but fuck, how it hurts. *Focus on something.* I move so I can hold him. But he pulls my arms above my head, taking away my control as he immobilizes me with his other hand on my hip. He gives me no choice but to lay back.

The pain intensifies with each thrust. My body is a battleground between pleasure and torment, and I don't know which will win. His fear and desire are noticeable through our bond, adding another layer to the war going on inside me. God, how it hurts. But as I close my eyes and slide into the pain, something changes. The searing fire in my belly turns to a pool of liquid heat. A strange sensation builds within me. It's like a storm brewing in my core, threatening to burst forth and sweep us both away.

I submit to the sensation, and I swear I feel a pulse of pleasure from inside him. But when I look up, his face still holds the same mask of control as if he has to think about being anywhere else but here. Closing my eyes, I block out the pain and focus on his smell—earthy, primal, intoxicating—and the heat emanating from his body as he takes me.

Slowly, the receding pain melts into pleasure that courses through my veins. My heartbeat quickens, my breaths shallow.

And then it's over, and he's pulling out of me. In an instant, he's off the bed, shrugging into his housecoat, and heading toward the door before I've caught my breath.

"Get dressed, and we'll grab something to eat." He keeps his tone nonchalant as if nothing just happened between us, but his back is ramrod straight with tension.

What the fuck? His turmoil surges through our bond. I know he's struggling, too, but why is he acting like this? I lay there, utterly confused, feeling something strange pulsing deep within me.

I liked being held down and fucked. Guilt and shame

course through me as I entertain such dirty thoughts. But there's no denying it now. Something inside me is awake, and I don't know if I can ever return to how things were before Jaden entered my world.

I hustle into a black long-sleeve crew-neck sweater, its asymmetrical cutaway a stark contrast to the wide-leg cream pants and black leather ankle boots. All pieces picked by Jaden, Mr. Fashion Guru himself. My mind rewinds to that day at the Toronto Eaton Centre. I've always been a practical shopper, mostly 'cause my wallet didn't allow for frills. My go-to? A no-fuss pants and T-shirt combo. So, marching into H & M, I'd started grabbing the usual suspects off the rack.

But Jaden, oh man, he had other ideas. He watched me for a bit, a scowl etching his face, before swiping the clothes from my arms. In a flash, he's got this whole new stack, pushing me towards the change room, playing sugar daddy or something.

That's when things got weirdly fun. He hands me stuff that's like, gigantic. I'm drowning in fabric, laughing my ass off as I shuffle out to him. "Jaden, seriously, this size?"

He's all dismissive, "Size, smize." And then, bam! He's Mr. Popular, surrounded by those walking billboards they hire. You know the type, the ones who look like they've never eaten a carb in their life. I shove down that twinge of jealousy as he flashes that killer smile – never at me, though. "Ladies, a little help here?"

I focus back on Jaden because, damn, he's actually looking at me. He's all in his element, circling me like I'm his canvas or something. He tweaks the sweater here and nods approvingly there.

And you know what? Despite my whole spiel about being Miss Independent, having my own personal stylist wasn't half bad. Around us, other shoppers start gathering, asking for his advice. Desperate husbands are practically begging him. But Jaden? He laughs it off, "Sorry folks, exclusive service for her only."

This guardian angel I'm stuck with, he's a whole different breed of weird. One minute, he's all eyes on me like I'm the last living soul on earth, and the next, he's shut down like a guillotine. What's up with him? I mean, what's really eating at Captain Control, who seems to have it all? But something deep down tells me it ain't all rainbows and sunshine in Jaden-land.

The way he just . . . unplugs from reality? That's not normal. I might not be a shrink, but even with my lowly psych degree, it's clear as day—Jaden's got this switch he flips, and poof, he's detached. Like he's somewhere else entirely. And the guy never smiles. Except, I've cracked that tough exterior a few times. Made him laugh, even got a grin or two. And yeah, despite his protests, I know I've got under his skin.

My heart's doing this crazy dance in my chest, and I can't figure if it's fear or excitement—or maybe a mix of both. That blend of dread and thrill whenever I think about what's next, or about Jaden. They both got my heart racing like crazy. But I know better than to get my hopes up. Good stuff never lasts in my world.

I catch him standing there, like some statue, just staring out the window with this impatient tap-tap-tap of his foot. Everything coming through our connection is suddenly murky, like peering through a thick fog. It's all blurry and mixed up. Is he tangled in a mess of emotions, or is he just hiding in his cave? As I come up behind him, he spins on his heel and strides out. "Car's waiting. Time to go." He snaps the words out, not even pausing to see if I'm following.

I almost ask where we're headed but clamp my mouth shut. Pointless. When Jaden's in this headspace, it's like talking to a brick wall. He says nothing as we get into the car and he pulls into the busy downtown traffic. His face is a mask of stone-cold intensity, his gaze sharp enough to slice through steel. Fuck, he's focused. Like a laser beam. I study his profile, my mind bouncing between a million thoughts.

God, he's gorgeous. *Stop it, Rayne. Focus.* What's on the agenda for today? Don't think about him. *I want to touch his hair.* I bite my knuckle. Shit. I can't think about this. I squeeze my thighs together hard and try to bring order to the chaos in my mind.

"Put on some music." His voice slices through the silence like a razor slicing parchment.

I shake myself back to the present, exhaling a long breath. Music, right. I rummage in my new purse for my iPhone and tap into my Spotify app. "What kind of music do you like?"

"Anything. You choose." His abrupt tone puts a wall of distance in his voice.

I sync my phone to the car's system and select one of my favorite pop playlists. Beyonce's "Crazy in Love" starts to fill the car, but Jaden's hand shoots out, pressing the forward button. "Not that."

"For fuck's sake, Jaden. You said I could choose."

"And you can. Just not that song."

I roll my eyes. "Why not?"

"I just don't like it."

"So, what then?"

"I told you. You choose."

I grit my teeth, pissed that he's probably just messing with me. Classic rock becomes our weird middle ground in this crazy relationship minefield. He casually drops his arm on the console, a silent ask for a scratch, and I comply. It's these tiny moments, these damn tiny connections he lets slip through, that screw with my head. We settle into this tense, strangely cozy silence, like we're navigating some weird, twisted bond.

As the car devours miles towards Harmony Hills, I zone out to the rhythm of scratching his arm. It's better than letting my brain spin out with all the shit he stirs up inside me. He's like some messed-up Pandora's box—cracking open thoughts and desires that 'good girls' shouldn't even whisper about. He's a safety net and a fucking lucky charm rolled into one. Ever since he came into my life, stuff's been looking up—this kickass job, the whole 'special calling' deal. But I can't shake him—not from my head, not from under my skin. That massive body of his is like a frigging fortress and a danger zone all at once.

One second, I'm daydreaming of ways to make him pay for all the crap he puts me through. The next, I'm all swoony, thinking he's the one. And Jaden? Mr. Hot-and-Cold himself. Beams like a damn Christmas tree when I call him my hero, then turns around and slashes me with his words the next minute for saying the very same thing. He's a walking storm, always brooding, and half the time, I'm the one kicking up the winds. There's a truckload of reasons I should cut him off and sort out my own mess. But here I am, stuck in this crazy loop with him.

23

JADEN

I exhale sharply, the words tumbling out in the afterglow of our intimacy. "I've got a chromosome missing." It's a raw admission, an attempt to bridge the gap between us with something more profound than physical connection. Instantly, I regret it. Such disclosures crack open doors to dark places I've strived to keep sealed. Memories of childhood, tinged with shame and a day marked by betrayal, surge forward. *"Don't be a woose,"* my mother's voice echoes, a haunting refrain from a past that claws at the edges of my carefully constructed present. Rayne's response, though, had a surprising calm, devoid of judgment. "Well, since I'm incapable of loving or being loved, that makes us peas in the same pod. Or do you mean like Trisomy 21?"

Her brilliant mind pleases me as much as it terrifies me. It pisses me off that she's stuck in someone else's narrative of her. Unlike me. I've meticulously built a facade, a persona of control and invulnerability that had remained intact until Rayne happened onto the scene. Now, it teeters on the edge, threatening to crumble. The constant vigilance, the fear of being unmasked as the imposter I believe myself to be, is exhausting. Rayne's intelligence is piercing, her understanding unnervingly acute. It's a matter of time before she sees through the armor I've worn for so long.

What to do with Rayne? The question circles in my mind, a relentless vulture. I lean back in my office chair, lost in the memory of her touch, the silken texture of her skin that glows like burnished gold. Her skin, an addiction I can't, and don't want to, shake off.

But it's her scent that truly ensnares me. It's a melody of desire and mystery, each note weaving through me, leaving me spellbound. I can still feel her essence on my fingertips, a lingering promise of sensuality and secrets yet to be uncovered. I catch the faint taste of her on my tongue, and it's intoxicating. Her quick, nervous bite of the lip revealing layers of longing and restraint. A vulnerability laced with a hint of something darker, something deliciously kinky.

I drift into a daydream, her scent and taste dominating my senses, a siren song luring me deeper into uncharted waters.

My cell phone pings with a text from Razor.

Razor: Urgent: Sasha compromised.
Location: The Manor. Convene War Room
ASAP. ETA 10 mins.

Fuck! I tear out of the suite and join Brian and Connor in the War Room where they're searching through the surveillance videos for the last twenty-four hours. Rayne is off with Kat taking a BDSM class. We opt not to call them back. Time enough to update them later.

Adrenaline courses through my veins as I watch the footage, each frame etching deeper into my memory. The anger, the frustration, it's all there, bubbling beneath the surface, ready to explode. But it's not just anger. There's a cold, seething determination that settles in my gut. I've been in this game long enough to know when things are about to get ugly, and this is one of those times.

"Razor, any leads on why they took her?" I keep my voice level, but it's a struggle.

He shakes his head, his expression grim. "Not yet, but we're working on it."

I nod, my mind racing. This isn't just a random abduction. It's a message, a calculated move by Viper to throw us off balance. And it's working. Realizing that my personal distractions might have contributed to this situation gnaws at me, a relentless voice whispering accusations in my ear.

I glance at Brian and Connor. "We need to gear up. We're going into the field. Razor, keep working on those leads."

They nod, and we move into action, a well-oiled machine fueled by urgency and a shared resolve. But even as I slip into the familiar comfort of tactical planning, there's a part of me that's reeling. A part that's looking back at the last few weeks, wondering if I've been too careless, too distracted by my growing connection with Rayne.

It's a dangerous game, letting someone in. A game that can have dire consequences. I've always prided myself on my control, my ability to compartmentalize, to keep my focus sharp. But with Rayne, it's different. She's gotten under my skin in a way no one else has, and now Sasha is paying the price.

As I slide into the driver's seat of our armored vehicle, I can't shake the feeling that I'm teetering on the edge of a precipice. One wrong move, and everything could come crashing down. And in this line of work, a fall from grace is rarely a solo affair.

"We've tracked the car using CC TV and it looks like they're headed for the Pandemonium," Brian says referring to the pit of corruption masquerading as an adult entertainment club. The only people entertained at that club are the sadists. Their victims aren't so lucky.

Misery and fear obliterate all rational thought, and I pull on my martial arts training to anchor me amidst the chaos.

Crack! The sound is a vile interruption to the still air of The Pandemonium's basement, a place where shadows cling to corners like cobwebs. I stand at the door of a cell, the noise a grotesque symphony that sends shards of fear skewering through my guts. That low moan of pain's got Sasha's name written all over it, and it chafes against every nerve ending I possess. With practiced ease, I tuck my Glock into the back of my jeans—a cold, reassuring weight against my skin.

Then, with a thought as sharp as the blade itself, I conjure a knife using my avenging power. The obsidian blade materializes in my palm, its presence both an extension of my will and a testament to the rage simmering within. I balance its heft, fingers adjusting to its contours, ready to throw.

"Where is he, bitch? Tell me, and this all ends." The man's voice slices through the deathly silence behind the door, each word dripping with malice that curdles the stagnant air. He's unaware of the storm that's about to break upon him—my storm. His question hangs between us, a taunt that only fuels the fire in my chest.

The rage is there, a living entity writhing beneath my skin, but it's shackled by the knowledge of what needs to be done. My thoughts whirl, tempting me with visions of violence and retribution. Yet, I'm not some mindless beast driven solely by instinct. I am control. I am precision. Sasha needs more than blind vengeance; she needs salvation, and I am her deliverer.

Every fiber of my being screams to burst through that door and unleash hell. But hell can wait for a heartbeat longer. I need to be smart, keep my head clear and my movements silent. This isn't about me—it never was. It's about rescuing one of our own from the clutches of a sadistic monster who calls himself Viper.

The knife handle becomes slick with anticipation, my grip tightening just as my resolve does. There's no room for error—not now, not ever. And as I prepare to infiltrate the depths of depravity, I know this is where I belong. On this edge, where darkness meets dark, where my demons serve a purpose greater than their own existence.

I am Jaden, and this is my dichotomy: the man who keeps everyone at arm's length while yearning for a touch that doesn't bring destruction; the protector whose very essence is intertwined with death. It's a precarious balance, one that Rayne has unwittingly tipped. Her presence in my life stirs something primal that threatens to consume the carefully erected barriers around my heart.

But that's for later. Right now, there's only the mission, only Sasha, only the vengeance that courses through my veins like a promise. And when I look into the eyes of the man who dared harm her, he'll see nothing but the abyss staring back at him. For now, though, I focus on the task at hand, steeling myself for what comes next. It's time to move.

"Viper," I whisper to myself with all the venom his name deserves. "Your reckoning awaits."

My nod to Brian and Connor is almost imperceptible, a mere tightening of the skin around my jawline. They recognize the signal instantaneously—years of silent communication in the shadows have honed our instincts to near perfection. Brian's eyes narrow, a glint of resolve flashing within; Connor's posture shifts, muscles tensing like a coiled spring.

The guard by the dungeon door is oblivious to his fate. One moment, he's a breathing monument to Viper's cruelty; the next, he's a crumpled heap on the cold stone floor. My hand moves with lethal precision—an open-hand strike to the nape of his neck—and now he lies motionless, the sound of his spine cracking still echoing off the walls.

A red haze descends over me, filtering the world into stark contrasts of blood and shadow. I'm in automatic pilot now, the well-worn path of vengeance as familiar as the back of my hand. The dam within me strains against the surge of emotions, but I reinforce it with iron will. There'll be time for reckoning later.

"Crack!" The bullwhip's report shatters the hush. A guttural moan follows, muffled and strained, and my heart clenches. "What was that? I don't hear you," taunts a voice from beyond the door, each syllable dripping with malice. God, let that be Viper. Let me end this.

"Compound. At the compound." Sasha's voice is a shadow of its former defiance, a strained whisper that barely climbs its way through the pain. The words hit me like a shot to the chest, and my grip on the knife tightens reflexively.

In that moment, I'm not just Jaden; I'm an avenger, a storm of retribution brewing with every heartbeat. There's no time for second-guessing, no space for doubt to take root. My soul bond with Rayne might be deepening, but

Sasha's agony carves through the fog of emotion, honing my focus to a razor's edge.

I grasp the door handle with my left hand, feeling the cold metal press against my skin, grounding me. I burst through the door with a surge of fury and fear. A split second—that's all it takes for my senses to absorb the scene, painting a picture in stark, brutal detail.

My eyes scan the room, taking in everything at once—the dim lighting, the stench of blood and sweat mingling in the stale air, the too-quiet murmur of malevolence hanging heavy around us. I don't need to see more; I know what I'll find. My pulse throbs in my throat, a drumbeat of impending violence.

Sasha's response echoes in my mind, "At the compound," her voice now woven into the fabric of this hellish tableau. It's a rallying cry, a call to arms that sends adrenaline through my veins, fueling the fire within. I can't let my guard down, not even for a second. Not with Sasha depending on me, not when every fiber of my being screams for vengeance.

The dam of emotion inside me swells, threatening to overflow, but I force it back. There will be time for rage and grief, but not yet. Now, I am precision incarnate, every move calculated, every breath measured. I am the eye of the storm—calm, collected, deadly.

Jaden, focus, I command myself as I prepare for what comes next. There's no turning back now. My power, darker than any abyss, rises to the surface, ready to be unleashed. And as I stand there, on the threshold of violence, I realize that this—this is where I belong. In the maelstrom, where darkness collides and where my demons dance to the tune of justice.

"I've got you," I say, though it's unclear whether those

words are for her benefit or mine. A part of me, a shadow lurking in the recesses of my soul, knows this is a turning point. This is where the façade cracks, where the doubts seep in. Rayne's image flickers in my mind—her warmth, her light—and for a moment, it anchors me amidst the chaos. But then the darkness surges back, stronger, reminding me that nothing good comes from letting people in.

The door bursts open under the force of my shoulder, a silent explosion in the dimly lit chamber. I take it all in—the stench of copper and sweat hits me like a punch to the gut. Sasha, her naked body suspended from the ceiling by chains that dig cruelly into her wrists. Her head is thrown back by Viper's grip, an inch away from snapping.

"Viper!" I growl his name like a curse, the sound cutting through the thick tension of the room.

He turns, shock splashing across his face as he registers my presence. "What the—"

I don't give him time to finish. My hand moves with superhero speed, the conjured blade spinning from my fingers. It's a dance of death we perform, him with his whip, me with my knife. The blade arcs through the air, whistling its deadly tune, and finds its mark below his right ribs. He crumples, the bullwhip slipping from his grasp, his blood adding to the macabre painting on the dungeon floor.

"Should've known..." His voice is a wet gurgle as he gasps out his last words. "...you'd come for her."

"Always." My answer is more a promise to myself than a reply to his taunt. I step over his writhing form, my focus shifting to Sasha, whose breaths come in ragged gasps. Every instinct screams to tend to her wounds, but there's a cold fire burning through my veins, urging me to finish what I started.

"Jaden. . . no. . ." she whispers, the effort costing her.

"Quiet, Sasha. Save your strength." I kneel beside her, my hand finding the chain and snapping it with a flex of dark power I barely recognize as my own. The metal clinks to the ground, a mournful bell tolling for the fallen.

"Let him bleed out," I hear Connor's voice behind me, steady as ever. But there's no satisfaction in those words, not when Sasha's life hangs by a thread and every second counts.

"Connor, get the med kit." I order the command with a tone born from countless battles and countless losses.

"Got it," he says, his footsteps retreating.

Sasha's body hangs limp, a marionette whose strings have been cut one brutal slice at a time. My hand recoils from the chains, slick with her blood, before I force myself to grip them again and release the metal cuffs binding her wrists. It's a tableau of horror, the kind that leaves a permanent scar on your retinas, a stain you can never scrub clean.

"Connor." I spare him a glance as he steps closer, silent as death itself. "She's in shock. Pulse weak." I strip off my jacket, wrapping it around her trembling form. The fabric soaks up the crimson that spills from her, a grotesque inkblot test challenging my sanity. I freeze as images of Savannah on my operating table dance through my head. Not again. After a beat of hesitation, I shake off the fear gripping me and get to work.

My hands are gentle yet swift as I use magic to free Sasha from the remaining restraints. She's so light in my arms, too light for someone her size. The scene feels eerily familiar, a reflection of a past I'd rather forget. The memories claw at me, desperate for attention, but I shove them down. Now is not the time.

"Stay with me, Sasha," I whisper, though I'm not sure if it's for her benefit or mine. "I've got you."

There's a part of me, a shadow lurking in the recesses of my soul, that knows this is a turning point. This is where the façade cracks, where the doubts seep in. Rayne's image flickers in my mind—her warmth, her light—and for a moment, it anchors me amidst the chaos. But then the darkness surges back, stronger, reminding me that nothing good comes from letting people in.

"Medevac's inbound," Connor's voice brings me back, and I nod, my hands still pressed against Sasha's wounds, willing her to hold on. But there's not much I can do. She needs an OR.

"Good." My voice remains strong but hollow. The doubt is there, worming its way deeper. Can I really afford these distractions? Can I let myself feel when feeling leads to this?

But even as I question it, I know. I can't shut it off—not the concern for Sasha, not the bond with Rayne. They're a part of me now, for better or worse. And as I wait for the medevac, holding onto the life bleeding out in my arms, I realize the truth. The battle isn't just out here; it's inside me, a war between desire and duty, connection and solitude.

And right now, despite everything, desire is winning.

It's two in the morning, the world around me eerily quiet except for the distant murmurs of the city's nightlife. I stumble into the suite, my body aching, feeling several notches below my best. Sasha's now safe, under the care of the skilled team at Women's College Hospital. They'd sprung into action the moment we'd brought her in, her state more dire than I'd care to admit.

Exhausted, I slump into a chair in the private dining area, where Kat's already ordered a pitcher of my usual—Stoli Doli. It's not often I drink, but tonight, the sharp tang of pineapple-infused vodka seems like the only thing that might ease the raw edges of my soul.

Each sip is a small reprieve, but it can't stop the flood of memories from tonight and long-buried. We'd found Sasha just in time, but the physical and psychological scars will take longer to heal. Viper spouting excuses as his life bled out, was a reminder of the depravity we were up against. Viper's end was a small victory, but it's just the tip of the iceberg. There's more abuse to unearth, more to fight against.

But Sasha's image haunts me—broken, yet resilient. I grimace, trying to shake off the image and the pain that comes with it. The hospital reassures us of her recovery, but at what cost? I down another shot, the burn of the alcohol a welcome distraction.

My thoughts uncontrollably drift to Rayne. Inexplicably, I feel she's the only one who can understand and can ease this burden. I stagger to my feet, navigating the room with a focus I can barely muster. I need to find her . . . now.

I track down Connor in his office, the man lost in his own thoughts over a glass of scotch. "Where's Rayne?" My voice is raspier and rougher than I intend.

He eyes me with a mix of concern and caution, his expression unreadable. "In your suite," he replies evenly. "Get some rest, Jaden. You're no good to anyone like this. Talk to her in the morning."

But waiting feels impossible. Every fiber of my being

screams for her presence, her understanding. It's a new, unnerving sensation—this dependency, this craving for someone else's solace. I nod slowly, accepting his advice while the turmoil inside me rages on, an unending storm of guilt, pain, and an undeniable longing for Rayne.

As I lean heavily against the door frame, the world tilts a little. "I gotta see her," I mumble, my words slurring just enough to betray the alcohol's grip.

Connor exhales a weary sigh, watching me shuffle towards our suite. My feet feel like lead, each step a laborious effort. I pound on the door, heart hammering, bracing for rejection or worse, indifference.

The door swings open and there's Rayne in a disheveled state, her hair wild, her eyes unguarded without her glasses. She peers at me, a frown creasing her forehead. The sight of her, so raw and real, cuts through the fog in my mind.

"What's happened? Where's Sasha?" Her voice is laced with worry as she surveys the hallway, then focuses back on me. The stench of alcohol must be overpowering, yet she doesn't recoil. Her eyes search mine, reading the unspoken turmoil.

"I. . . I can't," I stutter, pushing past the threshold into the familiar sanctuary of our suite.

Rayne trails after me, abandoning her glasses on the nightstand. There's a vulnerability in her gesture, an unspoken offering of trust. She stands defiant in her oversized shirt, a sight that stirs a deep, primal need within me.

"I should throw your ass out." Her voice is sharp. "You're drunk."

"I may be drunk, but I'm not out of control. I'm never out of control." I refuse to think about the thin thread I have holding said control as I collapse onto the bed, the weight of the world pressing down on me.

Her gaze softens, concern replacing anger. "Are you okay?" She steps closer, her innate empathy reaching out to me. Magical grace rises from her skin, shimmering in the air before surrounding me, enveloping us in an intangible yet evident aura. This unexpected display of her ethereal side adds a layer of complexity to the moment, heightening the emotional intensity. Her grounding and otherworldly presence offers a solace that I've longed for yet feared to embrace.

I can't bring myself to answer. Instead, I reach out, then hesitate. No matter how much I want her, I can't—won't—cross that line without her consent. My restraint hangs in the air between us, a silent testament to the respect I hold for her.

In a move that catches me off guard, Rayne peels off her shirt, her bare skin glowing in the dim light. She takes my hand, leading me without a word. In that moment, her actions speak louder than any reassurance she could offer. She understands, she accepts me—flaws, fears, and all. And that terrifies me as much as it draws me in.

I gaze up at her, a mix of awe and despair washing over me. She stands before me, a vision of beauty that transcends my wildest dreams. My body reacts instinctively, a raw, undeniable yearning coursing through me. At that moment, the barriers I've so carefully constructed begin to crumble under the weight of my need for her. Despite the screaming protests of my mind, my heart surrenders to the magnetic pull of her presence. I'm a man adrift, caught in the tide of my own weaknesses, and as I fall into her embrace, I'm painfully aware of the fragility of the walls I've built around me.

24
RAYNE

There's something unmistakably altered in Jaden now, standing there with a tempest of raw vulnerability clashing against his habitual urge to dominate, to control. It's a side of him I've never witnessed, and it sends shivers down my spine, a mix of caution and unbidden desire. Every instinct I possess screams at me to back off, to guard my heart against this unpredictable storm. But, damn it, I can't. The link between us, usually so clear, now whispers of fractures in the fortress Jaden has constructed around his soul. My own resolve wavers, torn between self-preservation and the magnetic pull of his brokenness. There's a part of me that wants to delve deeper, to understand and perhaps mend both of us. Yet another part fears the chaos that might unleash within me. I stand there, a war raging inside me, as I try to decipher Jaden. And I let him in.

I have no idea what possesses me or why I have such a need to care for Jaden, but now isn't the time to explore it. A flicker of doubt sparks within me, questioning if this growing connection will last. But I push it away, focusing on the moment.

"Little Dragon," he whispers, his voice hoarse with emotion. He takes a step closer, the air between us crackling with intensity as our eyes lock.

The defiant part of me considers turning away, refusing him the satisfaction of my surrender. But curiosity overwhelms me, and I find myself captivated by the vulnerability he's exposed. The raw emotion radiating from him tugs at something deep within me, something I've long kept hidden.

With a shaky breath, I peel off my nightshirt, my bare skin glowing in the dim light. The cool air caresses me, raising goosebumps along my arms, but I don't flinch. Instead, I hold out my hand, challenging Jaden to accept or reject me.

Without a word, he places his hand in mine. His touch is warm and electric as if he carries otherworldly energy beneath his fingertips. As we stand at the edge of the bed, I can feel Jaden's heart pounding in sync with mine, the rhythm echoing through our intertwined hands.

"Show me what you need." Although I have no idea how, I try to send a message through our mate bond urging him to reveal his true self, whatever that may be. I'm not just asking for the physical act but for the emotional connection as well. I want to understand the man he is, the darkness and hidden light that make up his essence.

"Rayne." Despite being intoxicated, his eyes search mine for any hint of hesitation. But all he will find is determination and an unquenchable curiosity.

"Show me."

"Rayne. . ." His tone is heavy with emotion, and I see his struggle to utter my name. He seems to be at a loss for words, his fingers tightening unconsciously around mine. I know what I have to do.

"Command me." I show my trust through our locked gazes. "Show me your darkness, and I'll show you mine."

He hesitates for another moment, then exhales slowly, letting his walls waver just enough for me to glimpse the tumultuous storm within him. As I watch, his aura shifts, becoming an ethereal tapestry of shadows and light. It's beautiful and terrifying in equal measure, a stark reminder of the power that lies dormant beneath his skin.

Jaden's gaze is unwavering as he motions with his head for me to lie on the bed. I don't hesitate, my heart pounding in anticipation of the unknown territory we'll explore together.

As I settle onto the bed, my eyes never leave his. The vulnerability he's shown me ignites a hunger within me that I can't quite understand. I lie back, arms crossed over my chest and thighs pressed together, as if I'm ashamed of my body, but really, it's a challenge—a dare for him to take control.

Jaden approaches the bed with purposeful strides, his eyes darkening with every step. He takes a moment to study me, then reaches for a strip of fabric on the nightstand. My heart races as he binds my hands to the headboard, ensuring I'm secure but not too tight. Being restrained sends a shiver down my spine, an odd mix of fear and exhilaration coursing through me.

"Ready?" His voice is low and controlled. I nod, biting my lip in anticipation.

His fingers slip between my legs, and I see surprise flash across his face as he finds me slick with lust. He doesn't say anything but watches my reaction closely, gauging my response to his touch.

A moan escapes my lips as Jaden works his magic, teasing

and taunting me with each deliberate stroke. He knows exactly what buttons to push and how far to take me before pulling back. But there's something different now, a desperation underlying his movements that wasn't there before.

"Take what you need."

He gives me a curt nod, signaling the beginning of our rough and desperate dance.

"Make us forget." My voice is barely audible as the weight of my conflicting emotions bears down on me. As if in response, I feel a surge of gratitude flood through our mating bond, warming me from within and momentarily soothing my inner turmoil.

Jaden doesn't hesitate any longer. He positions himself between my legs and drives into me, buried to the hilt. His arms brace him above me, taking care not to press against my injuries. "Gods, you feel good." His hot breath whispers against my ear.

I make a small sound, a mix of pleasure and pain, as my vagina burns and stretches around his big cock. Jaden pauses, ensuring I'm all right before continuing. In that moment, my defiance fades, replaced by a vulnerability I can't ignore. I can take the pain. I will give him what he needs. I wrap my legs tightly around his buttocks and arch into him, silently urging him on. That's all the sign he needs.

Jaden loses himself in me, and each thrust sends shockwaves of ecstasy through both of us. Each thrust is hard and fast, his control slipping as he loses himself in the rhythm of our bodies. We move together, seeking release from the chaos of our lives. Nothing exists but the pulsing, surging sensations radiating through his body . . . and mine. Our connection deepens with every desperate, rough movement, fueled by a desire to escape our own demons, if only for a little while.

My mind races, unable to focus on anything but the intensity of the act itself. Yet, beneath it all, a seed of doubt continues to sprout. How long before Jaden trades me in for a better model? Can we truly trust one another when so much remains hidden? Jaden's face is a mask of lust and concentration. He keeps his eyes closed tightly, blocking the world and focusing solely on our bodies moving together.

As Jaden continues to move inside me, I feel a rush of emotional pain through our bond. It's there, just beneath the surface, a wellspring of torment he's been holding back for far too long. My heart aches for him, even as I struggle to maintain my own fragile balance.

But now isn't the time for introspection. Right now, all that matters is the raw, primal connection between us, the blurring of boundaries and the merging of two fractured souls. For a brief moment in time, we find solace in one another's embrace, escaping the darkness that threatens to consume us both.

I try to push away my conflicted thoughts and focus on the pleasure that Jaden's touch brings me. But it's not just the physical sensations that are driving me wild. It's the way he takes control, dominating and possessing my body in a way I've never experienced before.

His movements are primal, as if he's trying to claim me as his own. And as much as it goes against every independent bone in my body, I can't help but crave more of it.

Jaden's hand travels down my stomach and between my legs, teasing and tormenting me until I'm begging for release. But Jaden is relentless, pushing me closer and closer to the edge I've never tipped over.

And as Jaden drives himself to climax, I cling to the hope that maybe, just maybe, we can weather this storm together.

My breath catches in my throat as Jaden's pace quickens. Each thrust becomes more frenzied and urgent. The intensity of our coupling reaches a fever pitch, blurring the line between pleasure and pain. I can't help but cry out, my voice ragged and broken, as we lose ourselves in this carnal dance.

"Rayne. . . gods. . ." Jaden groans, his grip on me tightening as he nears the edge. I feel his need, his desperation, mirrored by my own—two souls seeking refuge in the storm.

But then, as if struck by lightning, I become aware of something deeper, something simmering beneath the surface. Through the haze of passion, I see the shadows lurking within him, a darkness that claws at my heart. It's his pain, his torment, seeping through our bond like poison. And I realize that, despite the raw intimacy of our union, there are secrets he keeps locked away, barriers he won't allow me to breach.

"Jaden," I whisper, barely audible over our pounding hearts. "Let me in."

He doesn't respond, too consumed by the onslaught of sensation to hear my plea. But even without words, I know the truth: I'm not enough to save him—not yet, anyway. And that thought cuts deeper than any wound, stirring up doubt and fear where love should dwell.

It isn't long before Jaden reaches his breaking point, shuddering violently as his climax crashes over him like a tidal wave. For one brief, shining moment, we're connected on a level beyond the physical, bound by threads of desire, pain, and something that might almost be hope.

And then it's gone, as quickly as it came. Jaden pulls out, rolls onto his back, and falls into an alcoholic stupor. I can't help but wonder what the future holds for Jaden and me. Is this newfound connection enough to withstand the tests that lie ahead? Can I live with someone as emotionally detached as he is? Or will we crumble beneath the weight of our own secrets?

Only time will tell. I snuggle in beside him, careful not to touch him, watching him toss and turn until sleep drags me into its inky depths.

The darkness of unconsciousness wraps around me like a familiar embrace, and as always, my dreams come to life in vibrant motion pictures. My heart races with anticipation, but tonight isn't the same as the others. Instead of the sterile walls and menacing machines of my recurring nightmare, Jaden stands before me, his eyes filled with a mixture of confidence and vulnerability I can't quite place.

I'm an unseen spectator, watching as he walks into a locker room, steam from the showers clouding the air. The smell of sweat and soap fills my nostrils, and I can almost feel the damp tiles beneath my feet. Three large teenagers follow him into the room, their bulky frames casting ominous shadows on the walls. Jaden doesn't seem fazed by their presence; if anything, his chest puffs out a little more.

"Good practice," he says, turning to one of the guys who towers over him. "Great goal, Bruce."

Bruce's laugh sends a chill down my spine, something sinister lurking beneath his words. "Oh, it's only getting better, Jaden."

My stomach clenches, an uneasy feeling settling deep within me. I recognize the predators and know what's coming next. *It's just a dream, Rayne. You're not really here.*

But somehow, this feels different from my other dreams—more vivid and real. And I can't shake the fear that Jaden's in danger.

Before me, the scene rips open like a raw wound. Jaden, usually a pillar of strength, is now torn down, his confidence shattered. Each blow, each mocking jeer the boys hurl at him, hits me too. It's like I'm there, feeling every punch of pain, every sting of humiliation that racks his body. My throat burns with the scream I can't release. My fists clench in helpless rage. I'm forced to watch, to endure his torment as if it's my own. It's a brutal, gut-wrenching connection, and it's tearing me apart.

"Is that all you got?" one of the boys sneers, his voice dripping with disdain. "You're such a pussy."

"Pathetic," another adds, his eyes cold and unfeeling.

Despite the pain, Jaden's eyes remain defiant, a flicker of fire burning within them that refuses to be extinguished. But his gaze also has a deep sadness, as if he's losing something irreplaceable.

My heart races as the dream shifts, morphing into something far darker and more sinister. I can feel it in my gut—that twisting, sickening sensation of dread that tells me something terrible is about to happen. I watch helplessly as Jaden struggles against the larger boys, his face twisted in a combination of pain and defiance.

"Aw, isn't he beautiful?" One of the boys taunts Jaden, grabbing his chin and forcing him to look at him. "Come on, let's see those pretty lips of yours."

Jaden tries to pull away. Bruce grabs a handful of hair and viciously slams Jaden's head against the metal taps. Blood sprays from his mouth as his front teeth shatter upon impact. The sound of the running water from the shower muffles his cries, and although I know it's just a dream, I feel a burning rage building inside me.

"Keep him still," one boy orders, and another grips Jaden tightly, pinning him in place. The first boy slides his hand down Jaden's back, positioning himself against Jaden's crack. He moans with perverse satisfaction as he begins to force himself inside Jaden, who sobs uncontrollably.

"Pathetic," one of them sneers. "You're such a pussy."

As abruptly as it began, the scene shifts again. Jaden stumbles into a kitchen, injured and bleeding, his face a mask of raw anguish. A woman appears, her eyes narrowing in suspicion as she takes in his disheveled state.

"Look at you," she says coldly. "What happened this time?"

"Mom. . . I. . .." Jaden hesitates, tears streaming down his battered face. "I was raped. . . ."

My heart positively ruptures at the agony consuming this broken boy. She hands him a towel, her voice dripping with cold disdain. "Don't get blood on the floor. You mean you were beat up in the locker room." Her dismissive words slash through the air, echoing with cruel indifference. Her arms fold across her chest, a barrier of unyielding indifference to her son's pain. I want to scream at her, shake her for her callousness. What kind of mother does this to her child?

"Mom, please. . ." Jaden's voice breaks, quivering with the unbearable weight of pain and betrayal. Tears streak his battered face, pleading for compassion that won't come.

'Enough!' Her voice is a whip, snapping with finality. "Maybe now you'll start acting like a man. You will never speak of this again, do you understand me?" The harshness in her tone is like a death knell to any hope of empathy.

Jaden nods, a silent, defeated acceptance as his mother

coldly orders him around. The heavy burden of shame and despair that settles on his shoulders seeps into my own being, the seed of doubt burrowing deeper.

I watch, my heart pounding, as he struggles to regain composure, his hands shaking as he showers away the blood and tears. His reflection in the mirror transforms, the broken boy morphing into a hardened shell. "Never again," he whispers, a vow of self-preservation, a fortress built against the world.

In this dream space, I drift towards him, wrapping ethereal arms around his pain-wracked form. "I've got you, Jaden," I chant, though I know it's just a dream. But it feels profoundly right to offer solace, to share his burden. Agony laces through me, his rage and shame becoming my own as they course through my veins.

"I've got you, Jaden." Pain laces through me as the vision dissolves, sliding me into a dark, encompassing void. I shudder, the icy fingers of this newfound darkness clutching at my heart. I'm in an abyss and sinking deeper into its shadows, compelled by a force beyond my understanding."

25

JADEN

I savor that fleeting moment of perfection each morning, the brief reprieve in the hypnagogic state where reality hasn't yet infiltrated my mind. It's a blissful ignorance, a sanctuary from the suffocating anxiety that lurks just beneath the surface. But then reality hits with the soft scent of Rayne, a reminder of last night. She saved me, pulled me back from the edge. That realization freezes me. She's infiltrating my thoughts, my defenses. It has to stop.

I watch her sleep, her vulnerability laid bare, stripped of the protective armor she usually wears. The remnants of our encounter linger, and a part of me yearns to claim her again, to lose myself in that insatiable need she ignites within me.

But then, a chilling stillness in her form jolts me from my daze. The physician in me takes over as panic and fear claw at my heart. She's pale, unnaturally so, her skin a ghostly shadow of its vibrant self. *Coma.* The word echoes in my mind as terror grips me, but I push it aside. Rayne needs me.

I methodically check her vitals, my hands moving with

practiced precision even as my mind races. She has no response to pain, and a vacant stare when I check her pupillary reflex. The grim results of the Glasgow Coma Scale confirm my fears. Guilt and terror surge, threatening to overwhelm me. Did I cause this? I lay my hands on her, willing my power to heal her. Nothing happens except my shroud looms, its presence more menacing than ever, but I can't succumb to it. Not now. *Rayne needs me.*

I dress mechanically, my actions automatic as I clamp down on the chaos within. There's no time for my own breakdown. Not when Rayne lies comatose, her fate uncertain. I have to be strong for her, even as doubts and fears assail me. This is not the time for weakness.

Frantically, I dash to my room, grabbing my phone with trembling hands. Next to it lies Aleah's wooden "ticket," its engraved words almost taunting me with their ominous promise:

> *. . . Included is your Ticket to Temptation. Keep this on you at all times. There will come a time very soon when Rayne will need what appears to be medical attention. Do not take her to a hospital. There's a Druid temple in a forest in New Jersey. This ticket and your power will guide you there. Ignore the call at your and Rayne's peril.*

"Fuck!" My mind races as I fire off a text to Elijah, our standby driver.

> Have the medivac copter on the helipad in
> ten minutes.

I'm about to alert the PE team, but my finger hovers over the send button, the desire for privacy wrestling with the need to inform.

> Rayne and I are offline dealing with some
> personal business.

I debate dressing Rayne, but every second counts. Wrapping her in a blanket, I carry her to the helipad. The harsh morning sunlight stabs at my already pounding head. Gently, I place her on the medivac litter, securing her with Elijah's help.

As the helicopter lifts off, bound for a mysterious forest in New Jersey, I'm left to confront the echoing void inside me. The universe is screaming a message loud and clear: attachments bring nothing but pain and loss. And now, I'm teetering on the brink of losing the two people who matter most.

In desperation, I strike a silent bargain with the shroud. *"Bring her back to me and I'll surrender. You can have me, just save her."*

The helicopter descends onto a grassy knoll, surrounded by an expansive circular driveway. Before us stands a majestic mansion, its grandeur hinted at by the large wooden door adorned with intricate scrollwork. Engraved above the knocker, the words "Please knock" catch my eye just as the door silently swings open. I barely have time to register the odd shape of the solid brass plate with a hinged ring overlay with a life-sized phallus, curving down to meet the pouting lips of inviting labia.

Greeting us is an elderly gentleman, his attire a throwback to a bygone era. His gray suit, reminiscent of the early 1930s, speaks of a timeless elegance. His age is a mystery, a paradox of graying hair and youthful posture, strength radiating from his stance. His warm, welcoming smile feels like a reunion with a long-lost friend. "Welcome to our home, Jaden," he says, a twinkle of mischief in his eyes.

Then, as if from another world, a spectral figure materializes. She bears a striking resemblance to the woman carved on the wooden Ticket to Temptation. "Welcome to Blackstone Manor." Even her voice is ethereal. "I am Anais Blackstone but you can call me Nye or Lady B. You are now protected by the Druid gods within our sacred grounds. As the high priestess, I will guide you in harnessing your power." She motions towards the suited man. "Raphael, the manor's magic keeper, will attend to your earthly needs while I care for our young witch. Give us a few hours, then decide your next steps." With a flourish of her ornate stick, she and Rayne vanish into thin air, leaving me alone with my dilemma and this strange old man.

In stunned silence, I watch Elijah's helicopter disappear into the distance. Resigned, I follow Raphael, the house's silent guardian, deeper into its heart, my mind a whirlwind of apprehension centering on Rayne. I'm relieved when Raphael leads me into a grand library, gesturing towards a plush armchair beside a table laden with books.

With a respectful bow, Raphael steps back, his open palms an emblem of deference. The dimly lit hallway we traverse is adorned with sconces and oil paintings, some depicting the spectral Anais in various states of undress. The house reveals its secrets slowly, each room a testament to an era long passed.

In a vast living room, my gaze is drawn to the erotic sculptures populating every corner, their exaggerated forms a dance of sexuality and artistry. Raphael guides us next into a retro kitchen, then into a study. The room, lined with floor-to-ceiling bookcases, exudes a charm of its own. The scents of paper, ink, and leather, tinged with the ghost of a fine cigar, fills the air.

Raphael presents a cup of tea, prepared to my liking. As I reach for it, my attention is captured by the tray. For a moment, I'm convinced I'm seeing things. The woman painted on it—is she winking at me? I blink hard, questioning the reality of my senses. I open my eyes, and sure enough, there Nye is, sketched in perfect graphic and very explicit detail—naked, groping herself, her head thrown back in the throes of orgasm. Looking directly at me. She doesn't find sex humiliating, degrading, or just plain dull. For this woman, sex is pure pleasure and joy.

Raphael rises to his full height, hands clasped, his posture the epitome of rigid decorum. I take a cautious sip of the tea, finding it to my liking, and offer him a nod of appreciation. In response, he executes a formal bow, an anachronistic gesture that somehow fits this surreal environment. "Lady B advises you to settle in comfortably while she tends to the young lady's needs," he states in a measured tone. His eyes briefly flicker to a thickly braided rope dangling from the ceiling, a silent indication of how to summon him. "Should you require anything further, please do not hesitate to pull the cord." His voice carries a subtle, unspoken promise of unwavering service.

Raphael's departure leaves me in silent solitude, the library's ornate door sealing my temporary sanctuary. Enclosed in this space, my thoughts spiral, a tempest of guilt and fear. I've bartered with my shroud, pledged to embrace its dark clutches if it spares Rayne. The price is letting her go for both her safety and mine. Despite the haziness of last night, a nagging certainty gnaws at me: I am the catalyst for her comatose state.

Images of Sasha's battered form invade my memory, unbidden and relentless. I force them back, focusing instead on the sequence of last night's events. Viper's gone, but his henchmen will be hunting for blood. The alcohol, the intense, raw encounter with Rayne, the dangerous vulnerability of sleep beside her—it's a sequence fraught with peril. I recall fragments of a nightmare, a sinister echo of my darkest moments. Had I turned on her in my sleep? The thought sends a jolt of panic through me. Fuck! I bang my forehead with my fist, a mix of frustration and self-reproach. I never sleep with anyone for this very reason—to avoid the risk of my nightmares spilling over and hurting someone close to me. One lapse, one momentary slip of control, and now my nightmare, a haunting mirror of my past, has bled into our reality."

But what exactly transpired? How did my demons reach out and ensnare Rayne? The weight of potential culpability is crushing. Could my own tortured psyche have reached out in the night, weaving its shadows around her? The thought is unbearable.

And there lies the crux of my torment. My feelings for Rayne are a double-edged sword—a source of unexpected warmth and an avenue for unforeseen peril. Is my mere presence a danger to her? The irony isn't lost on me; the one person who's managed to breach my walls could be the one I harm the most. This internal conflict, the battle between longing and the instinct to protect, is a war I never anticipated.

In this library, amidst ancient tomes and relics of a bygone era, I'm forced to confront a truth I've long evaded —my past, no matter how deeply buried, shapes my present. And now, it threatens my future with Rayne. The realization is a bitter pill, a reminder of the chains I cannot break.

But the thought of never seeing her again sends me spiraling toward despair. And she sees past the image I've crafted to perfection, the one where I'm the man who meets society's expectations of all I should be. All the things that keep me tied in knots, which basically means I hardened all my soft edges replacing them with an aloofness and rough rudeness that most described with approval versus the scathing condemnation given my authentic self. But Rayne's reaction is the polar opposite, making her a threat and a treasure. But more than anything, she makes me forget.

Engulfed in the library's hush, a question hammers in my mind: How do I keep Rayne close yet at a distance, now that her need for my protection seems diminished?

Drawn as if by an unseen force, my gaze lands on the stack of books. I reach for the topmost volume, its leather cover etched with intricate calligraphy that beckons my curiosity. Flipping it open to a random page, I find myself engrossed in the words, soon realizing it's an entry from Nye's diary.

"...and then I met Edward Carrington. What a magnificent specimen of a man. All broad shoulders, thin hips, and a prick of such magnificence it made even a tart like me blush. A gentleman of refined tastes, he made it clear quite quickly he had different appetites in the bedroom. He had no use for my virtue...]

The words pull me into a foreign and intriguing world, a window into a past that seems to mirror the complexities of my emotions. The strange cadence of her ancient narrative pulls me deeper into her story while the beginnings of a plan dance at the corners of my mind.

...he spread me on the settee, threw up my skirts, and inhaled the delicate aroma he loved so much. Then, he made me frig myself for his enjoyment and mine. My quim drenched with longing. I set to work with my fingers, plunging them in and out of my cunt. Just the way he liked it. I was eager to have him bogg me but knew he wouldn't relent until I climaxed. I raced on to the finish.

It doesn't take me long to realize I'm reading about a Sub and her Dom and I realize something I should have thought of before. Setting aside all the nonsense about a mating bond, there's a perfect way for Rayne and me to have a friendship without emotional attachment—friends with benefits. I can bring her into the lifestyle I've managed to explore as a voyeur and occasional participant. We can both explore. Like the Edward in the journals, I can be her mentor, the catalyst who helps her recover from the trauma she's suffered. I'm so engrossed in inhaling every detail from the many journals I startle when Raphael's hand touches my shoulder. "She's ready for you."

Raphael leads us through the forest, at length stopping before a cave. He opens a portal, and we step into the large cave with a wall reflecting the blue-green waters of a deep pool before us. Rayne lies draped on a stone slab, still unconscious, and Nye hovers above her. I can't help but think of her large chest heaving in the throes of passion as I look up at her. The smile she gives me tells me she knows exactly what I'm thinking. Embarrassment floods me, and I cover it by kneeling at Rayne's side and checking her vitals, pretending I don't see Nye.

"Welcome to our temple," Nye says, her Scottish brogue turning the words into a warm invitation. I remain silent, observing. She drifts closer and gives me a sharp rap on the shoulder. "Och, ye big dafty. I ken fine well ye can see me, and I'm no fond o' bein' ignored. Let's try this again. Welcome to our temple." Her tone, while not unkind, carries an edge that signals she's not one to trifle with. It's a demeanor I recognize and respect. To most, they were dubbed 'auld battle-axes,' but I resonated with the resilient and determined spirit beneath their stern exteriors.

I sit back on my haunches and look up at the spectral figure. Rayne may take all of this in stride if her nonchalant attitude is any indication, but it's on the strange side for me. Everything is happening much too quickly and I need time to get a grip. Seemingly, that will have to wait. I open my mouth to thank her for her hospitality, but panic makes my power take over. "What the hell is wrong with her? Why isn't she healed? Aleah said this is where she'd be healed."

"Ah, he speaks," Nye says. "I have healed your little dragon of her physical wounds but can't purge her of the darkness. Only the two of you can do that."

How the fuck does she know I think of Rayne as my little dragon? I shake the thought off. Time to go into the weeds later. Right now, taking care of Rayne is what matters. The lack of connection that's been humming between us twenty-four-seven since we met remains a shadow in the background that I can't connect with. I frown and give her my full attention. "What are you talking about? What darkness?"

Nye studies me so intensely that I feel like fire ants are crawling through me, and I force myself not to fidget. I slip into the carefully constructed façade I've perfected over the years and patiently hold my ground, waiting for her to continue.

Eventually, she sighs and floats over to perch beside Rayne, looking at me. "There's only so much I can tell you. We believe Rayne comes from an almost extinct line of very powerful seers and healers called the Luminaras, white witch human descendants of ancient Druids. They've long been a beacon of light, warding off dark forces. But it's a double-edged sword, laddie. The brighter the light, the deeper the shadows it casts."

"And you think Rayne's one of them? A Luminara?" Skepticism laces my tone.

"Aye, that she is. Born with a gift of intuition so sharp, it cuts through the veils of reality. But it's more than that. The Luminaras were once guardians, protectors using their magic for good, fighting against the darkest of evils.

"Guardians? Protectors?" I echo, trying to wrap my head around it.

Nye nods, her expression turning grave. "Indeed. But with great power comes great vulnerability. They often attracted malevolence that sought to snuff out their light. They had to be strong, resilient. Yet, despite their struggles, they remained committed to safeguarding the balance of the world."

Her words hit me like a punch in the gut. Rayne, with all her strength and defiance, could be part of this ancient lineage? It explained so much yet raised a hundred more questions. "So what does this mean for Rayne?"

Nye's gaze softens as she looks at Rayne. "It means she's more than just a simple witch or a healer. She's a beacon, a focal point in the cosmic struggle between light and darkness. And right now, she's fighting a battle within herself, a battle only she can win, with a bit of help from her soulmate. That would be you."

Soulmate. The word echoes in my mind, igniting a deep, unsettled feeling. I try to shake it off. "And what am I supposed to do to help her?"

Nye's eyes sparkle with a hint of mischief. "Ah, laddie, that's a journey you'll need to embark on yourself. Just know that the bond between a Luminara and her soulmate is no trifling matter. It's got the power to break curses, mend hurts, and might even alter fate itself." She twirls her stick through the air, her expression turning serious. "Here's a wee bit of advice for ye."

I didn't ask for any advice, and my face must give away my thoughts. Nye, perceptive as ever, continues. "I ken you didn't seek my counsel, but I'm offering it nonetheless. If facing your own demons is too daunting, try seeing them through Rayne's eyes. Healing's a two-way street for souls like yours. There's no 'strong' or 'weak' between you, only equilibrium."

She starts to fade away, but I can't let her go without one last question. "Hold on. What about waking Rayne?" I motion towards her still form, anxiety gnawing at me.

Nye lets out a sigh, her tone patient yet imbued with a firm resolve. "I've patched up her bodily hurts, but the drain of her power can only be set right by her soulmate.

The key to replenishing her magical well, so to speak, lies with you." Her figure becomes translucent, her presence diminishing as if melting into the air.

Left alone with her words, I'm forced to contemplate the weight of this newfound knowledge. The bond, the magic, our intertwined destinies—it's overwhelming. Yet one thing stands clear amidst the chaos: Rayne is more than just a woman in need of protection, and perhaps, I am also more.

26

RAYNE

I'm in this bizarre limbo, straddling the line between consciousness and something else entirely. It's like I'm watching myself from outside, a surreal out-of-body experience. And then, there's the trio that's right out of a Dickens novel, except it's Jaden, a younger Brad Pitt with wings—seriously?—and an old lady who could star in her own Victorian painting. Jaden's pacing, worry etched all over his face. I wish I could feel our connection, but he's been cut off from me.

As I scrutinize the room, my eyes keep darting back to my own motionless form on that grandiose bed. Jaden's the only one seemingly attached to the ground, the rest just floating around. Does he even notice them?

Brad Pitt with wings glides over to me, and despite the craziness, I can't help but take him in—black leather jacket, grey shirt, those jeans, and those wings. Indeed, he's got wings.

"Hey, there." He's all casual as if we're in a coffee shop. "Bet you've got a bunch of questions about your Jaden. I'm here to fill in some blanks while Anais handles him."

I almost trip over the 'Jaden's mine' thought but push it aside. Focus. "Who are you?" I ask. Blunt, maybe, but hey, that's me.

He grins, and it's a panty-melter for sure. "Name's Bob." He extends a hand. "Bob the Angel. Angel of Death, to be precise."

I automatically reach out, expecting air but finding a firm grip. I shoot a quick glance back at my body. Still there. Back to Bob, I raise an eyebrow. "Angel of death? Really?"

Bob's laughter is warm, echoing around the void. "Yeah, really. You're in Bardo, kind of a waiting room between life and what comes next. I help with the transition."

His words sink in. Bardo. Transition. This is way bigger than any drama I've faced before. Standing—well, floating—here with Bob, the angel of death, it dawns on me that this is serious business. But a fire in me is not ready to call it quits. Not even close.

"So, I'm dead?" As the words come out of my mouth, I wonder why the idea that I may be dead and gone doesn't bother me. Maybe it's because I don't think I'm dead. Maybe it's because for the first time I'm certain I'm on this earth for a purpose. I might not know what the purpose is, but I know I haven't fulfilled it yet.

Bob gives me that wicked grin, and I must admit it gives Jaden's rare flashes of sunlight a stunner run. Bob's grin widens as he says, "I'm taken, but thanks for the compliment. And I agree, your Jaden is a looker."

"He's not my Jaden." I respond too quickly and hotly so am not surprised at the raised eyebrow I get in return. What is it with these guys and their eyebrows...

His clear blue eyes fasten on mine for what seems an eternity, and I'm about to cave when he says, "I understand you're feeling a bit overwhelmed and confused. It's perfectly normal in your situation. Let's start with the basics. You're currently in a state of transition, a place where souls often find themselves when they're not quite ready to move on. It's a place of reflection, understanding, and sometimes, healing."

He pauses, letting the words sink in. "You've been through quite an ordeal, and it's important to process it all. I'm here to help you with that. To answer your questions, offer guidance, and maybe provide a bit of perspective. So, to answer your first question, you're not dead, but you're suffering a power drain so drastic it's tricked the universe into thinking you're dying. You won't remember all this when you wake."

I cross my spectral arms, still skeptical. "And you do this often? Help lost souls or whatever?"

Bob nods. "It's part of the job description. Helping souls transition, understand their journey, and sometimes, find their way back. Each case is unique, but the goal is always the same—to help and to heal."

I take a deep, unnecessary breath. "Alright, Bob the Angel, let's hear it. What's the deal with Jaden and me? Why all this drama?"

Bob's expression turns serious. "Your story is unique, Rayne. You and Jaden share something rare—a soul bond. It's a connection that transcends the usual boundaries of human relationships. It's more than just emotional or physical; it's a deep, spiritual link that can be both a source of great strength and, at times, profound challenges."

His words hit me like a freight train. *Soul bond.* That's why I feel so drawn to him, why I can't seem to shake him off even when he's being an absolute ass. But it also scares the hell out of me. What does this bond mean for us? For our future?

Bob continues, "This bond you share, it's powerful. It has the potential to heal, to bring out the best in both of you. But it also requires understanding, patience, and a willingness to face some hard truths about yourselves and each other."

I frown, processing his words. Understanding and patience aren't exactly my strong suits and Jaden . . . well, he's a whole different story. But something in me knows Bob's right. This bond, this connection with Jaden, it's not something I can ignore or walk away from. It's part of who I am now, part of my journey.

"And before you ask," Bob gives me a hint of a smile, "yes, you can find your way back to him. But it's going to take more than just wanting it. You'll need to confront your own fears, your own shadows. And so will he. It's a journey you'll need to take together."

Together. The word resonates within me, filling me with a mix of dread and hope. Jaden and I taking on this crazy, mixed-up world together. It's a daunting thought, but deep down, I know it's the only way forward. The only way to truly understand this bond and what it means for both of us.

"I was just inside one of Jaden's nightmares, except I think it was a flashback. Is that possible?"

Bob looks pleased as he nods. "You are very perceptive. Intuition is one of your many gifts. A defining trait of Luminara descendants is their heightened intuition. They possess an uncanny ability to sense energies and emotions, making them incredibly perceptive and empathetic towards others. This gift grants them an innate understanding of the world around them, which they use to navigate through life."

"So, my powers have something to do with dreams?"

"Yes, but only with your soul mate. You have the power to slip into his dreams where your souls intertwine. Your link creates a bridge between your subconscious minds.

I guess that confirms what I know in my gut: Jaden is my soul mate because I was most definitely in his dream. "What else do I need to know?"

"White witches use music and movement as channels for their magic as a way to tap into their full magical potential and strengthen the bond with their celestial counterparts," Bob says.

"This is a lot to unpack. Can you spill more about this soul bond thing? Am I stuck with it?" I can't help the edge in my voice, a mix of curiosity and fear.

Bob studies me, his gaze unnerving yet kind. "Do you really want to break it?" he counters, and damn, he's good at this.

A hot flush creeps up my neck, but there's no bullshitting an angel. "Maybe. He's . . . broken. And I'm not exactly whole myself." I swallow hard, the words tasting like acid. "What if I can't give him what he needs? Can you tell me more about our soul bond? Will I be able to dive into his nightmares again? I've only got a piece of the puzzle."

Bob's eyes hold a world of wisdom. "You might never have the full picture. Can you live with that uncertainty?"

That hits me hard. My instinct screams to drag every dark secret out of Jaden, to force him to face his ghosts head-on. But what if that breaks him even more?

"We've got to find a way to beat this shame thing. He can't keep drowning in it." I'm trying to convince myself more than anything.

Bob's wings flutter gently. "Sometimes, it's about learning from each other's scars. Are you ready to lay bare your own demons to him?" He pauses, letting the weight of his words sink in. "Now, let your knight in tarnished armor care for you before he loses himself in his own abyss. You both can heal each other. Work through the shame books Aleah gave you and trust your gut. When you're ready, Anais will guide you to embrace your full potential." He stands, a picture of otherworldly grace.

"Oh, and one final tip. Listen to what Jaden does, not what he says. And that's your cue for today. Remember, Rayne, the path to healing is never easy, but it's always worth it. Trust in yourself and in the bond you share with Jaden. You're stronger than you know. Those with extraordinary gifts rarely fit neatly into society's boxes." His smile is slow, almost seductive. "Meeting you has been a treat, Rayne. I suspect it'll be a long while before our paths cross again." He steps through a portal that materializes out of nowhere, leaving me alone with a whirlwind of thoughts and fears while I wait to see what happens next. It's strange being in this kind of limbo, but oddly, I'm not reacting to it with my usual fear and anxiety. Maybe it's because I feel safe.

When I look at my sleeping form, Jaden's sitting on the rock ledge and has my head in his lap. He's staring down at my face with a mixture of love and loathing, or at least that's how I read it. I miss our link, that connection that let me know how he was feeling. Or is Bob right . . . Maybe it was my gift telling me. I have all kinds of time to ponder that. Jaden's started murmuring in a low voice, and I drifted nearer so I can hear. Seems supersonic hearing is not one of my gifts.

"What am I going to do with you?" Jaden strokes the side of my face while I roll that very question around in my head. What is it that draws me to this man anyway?

His temper is like a storm brewing on the horizon, fierce

and wild. But it's his withdrawal that really chills me to the bone. Seeing him so fragmented is like watching someone try to piece together a shattered mirror, knowing some pieces are too small to find. The jagged edges of Jaden's complexities are not just random anymore. It's like a puzzle slowly coming together, revealing a picture that's both heart-wrenching and awe-inspiring.

There's a resilience in him, something unyielding and stubborn that clashes with any logic. For some reason, he doesn't see it, but it's there. It's like watching a tree stand tall in the middle of a tempest, bending but never breaking. And then there's this unexpected tenderness he cloaks under his guise of apathy. I've seen the way he lights up around those kids at Harmony Hills, like a beacon in their stormy lives. Maybe that's what hooked me, this unspoken understanding between us. The world's expectations are twisted, punishing us for being what we're not. I'm branded as too tough, too blunt, and there's Jaden, always dodging bullets for being too 'sensitive.' Screw that.

Sensitive! I despise that word. It boxes you in and tags you as something fragile or in my case, not delicate enough. But there's nothing fragile about Jaden. He's like a fortress with walls too high for most to climb. But those kids, they see something in him. A safe haven, maybe. And I get it, I really do. Because underneath all that bravado, there's an innate kindness in Jaden that he suppresses but is as real as the scars we both carry. That rare glimpse of gentleness, hidden beneath layers of self-defense, draws people to him. It's what drew me to him.

In Jaden, I see a mirror of my own struggles—a reflection of what it means to be misunderstood and misjudged. We're like two puzzle pieces, fitting together in our misfit way. I can't help but wonder, though. Is this connection, this inexplicable pull towards each other, going to be our salvation or our undoing? The thought scares me more than I care to admit.

But one thing's crystal clear—walking away isn't an option. Not now. Not when I've started peeling back the layers of Jaden's enigma. I'm drawn into this emotional maze he's crafted, and damn it, I'm determined to see it through. Jaden's complexities are a challenge I can't resist.

He tenderly brushes my curls aside, his vulnerability laid bare in that simple gesture. "What am I going to do with you?" His voice echoes in the cavernous space. "You see me as this valiant hero, but the truth is, my armor's corroded, flawed." His touch contradicts his often harsh exterior, a truth spoken without words. I realize Bob is bang on—with Jaden actions scream louder than any words he spits out. *Listen to what he does, not what he says.*

"I don't know all the ropes of this soul bond thing, but I know you need to come back to me. You're like an escape for me, a break from the nightmares. From that cloying feeling of powerlessness. But damn, I can't even admit how fucking scared I am. Scared of losing whatever semblance of control I have . . . and hell, scared of losing you."

His head drops to his chest and the words are so faint I second-guess whether I heard him. "I'm terrified." Two words spoken so softly they're only an echo in my mind.

"Well, then haul my ass back from wherever this is so we can sort this mess out," I shout, but my words dissolve into the ether, unheard by anyone but the ghostly Druid priestesses.

Jaden rests against the cold wall, his hand still cradling my head. "You're tearing down the walls I've built, brick by brick, invading my every thought. It's a chaos I've never known, but somehow, it feels right." He sinks into a silence that tests my already thin patience.

Then, his face lights up. "I have an idea, a way for us to figure this out. But you need to come back first."

That perks up my spectral ears. We're on the same wavelength, even in this bizarre situation. *"I want to, Jaden! But how? We're supposed to figure out this magic crap ourselves, right?"*

Just as I'm about to explode with spectral frustration, Jaden makes a move. He lifts my limp form and strides into the shimmering water. His clothes cling to him, but he doesn't care. This raw, vulnerable side of him, which he guards fiercely, is now mine to witness.

He submerges us, and the water comes alive with a swirl of colors. Magic encircles us, an intimate dance of light and shadow. He kisses me gently, sending a jolt through my being.

"Come back, Rayne. We're not done yet."

That pull, that undeniable force, yanks me back into my body, and the connection between us resurges. I cling to him, whispering, "You kissed me."

"More like CPR," he deflects, carrying me towards the edge. "You need rest. Let's get out of here."

I rest against him, surrendering to his care. Physically spent but internally buzzing with a newfound energy. Details of our magical reunion begin to blur as exhaustion takes over. But one thing is clear—I'll navigate this path with Jaden, guarding my heart yet daring to hope. Tomorrow, I'll piece it all together.

27

JADEN

Two nights later, the scene is set with meticulous precision in my private dining room. Low lighting casts soft shadows, enhancing the intimate atmosphere. The table is elegantly laid out, a blend of refinement and subtle sensuality. Understanding the terms that suit me, we can proceed. A plan to protect myself while confronting my demons with Rayne at the forefront. Yes, I'm using her, and the absence of guilt about it is a shadow I deliberately ignore. To stay with me, it's my way or no way.

Rayne enters the room, halting momentarily at the threshold. She looks every bit the scared child trying to behave like a sophisticated woman. Her attire—a dark navy sheath, cut on the bias with a Mandarin collar—clings to her form, accentuating her delicate curves. The dress sways gently with each step, hinting at the garter beneath. My breath halts at the sight; she's stunning.

I pour two glasses of wine and move toward her. I rarely drink the stuff, but it gives me something to do with my hands. She steps slowly, weaving slightly in black heels, giving me time to study her. My cock pokes his head out of his cave. I keep my breathing steady, something I pride myself on. Only my unexpected hard-on can give me away, but this little one doesn't seem to notice.

I almost laugh as I see the pad and pen she holds at her side. Placing my wineglass on the table, I pluck the paper and pen from her hand and set them next to my glass then turn back to Rayne with her glass of wine. Her hand shakes a little as she wraps a tiny hand around the bowl of the glass. The intensity of those dark eyes is a little disconcerting. This woman makes me feel self-aware . . . and aware of my shortcomings . . . like no one else ever has.

I hold my glass by the stem and examine the color and legs of the Ornellaia Archivio Storico wine, watching Rayne surreptitiously through my peripheral vision. She watches intently and mimics my every move. There will be enough time later for a wine tasting and many other lessons.

Tonight, we are here for one purpose. To cement our agreement. Much as I won't admit it, the thought that nothing is holding her to me unsettles me. People make commitments like throwing confetti at weddings, with just as much intention of cleaning up after themselves. Somehow, I know with her it's different. Somehow, I know her integrity is her bond.

Our server delivers something called love dumplings. I pause for an inward smile as I remember the discussion Kat and I had about the menu. As always, Kat won the day. According to her, Rayne loves shrimp and would get a kick out of the name. Sure enough, she oohs and aahs over the smell, an instant saliva trigger, then pops one in her mouth.

"Will there be more wine?" she asks, breaking me out of my thoughts.

"No one will bother us unless I give a signal."

Well then, give the damn signal. Her inner voice snaps through our connection.

"I actually have to use the can." She stands up.

Without thinking, I grab her hand and pull her towards me. Our bodies are so close that I can feel her warmth radiating off her. I brush my lips against hers again, savoring the slight heat that builds between us. But even as she moans softly, a nagging thought creeps into my mind—is this all she wants from me? Just physical pleasure? I immediately chide myself for the thought. **Why do you care, asshole?** This is about sex, that's all this is pure and simple.

"I want you to be relaxed, not drunk," I whisper against her lips. "Maybe a little high, but not completely out of it."

Her response is barely audible, but I hear it loud and clear. My grip on her tightens as I fight off my own insecurities. How can someone like her possibly want someone like me? But for now, all I can do is hold onto her and hope that these moments together mean something more than just fleeting passion.

In a few weeks, Rayne's managed to put cracks in the impenetrable walls I've built around myself. After the "event," I spent years in a state of unbearable sexual need but was rarely able to satisfy it. I learned quickly to act like the arrogant playboy society expected me to be. The ruder and more offensive I behaved within limits, the happier everyone seemed to be.

I'd gotten to a point where my PTSD was at bay, which was a fucking miracle. Because despite my best attempts to avoid the truth, the physician in me knows I'm suffering from a severe case. Then Rayne came along, and I fantasized about a life where I could have sex like a normal person and have my version of the white picket fence. But

Sasha's attack is a wake-up call that puts things in perspective. Yet I want Rayne with every fiber of my being. I'm fifty-eight degrees of fucked up.

I've ignored her since the night I took her without her explicit consent, something I'd sworn never to do. Consumed by guilt, I hadn't known just how to approach her and I'd waited for her reproach. I thanked the gods when our connection went live after the coma or whatever we're calling the state she fell into. Through it, I can tell that she's confused, but I get no sense that she's ready to leave . . . yet.

While she's in the washroom, staff replaces the dining table and chairs with a luxurious Tantra sofa. A wine glass and a joint are beckoning to her on the coffee table. With no other option for seating, she cautiously sits beside me, perching on the very edge of the cushion as if trying to distance herself from me. She lights the joint and inhales deeply, holding the smoke in before exhaling in an attempt to create fanciful designs. Then she reaches for the wine glass, taking it by its stem and examining it just as I had done moments before. Taking a sip, she lets out a contented sigh.

I clear my throat and take the plunge. "Where do you see this thing happening between us going?"

She leans against my chest, seeking stability in our physical closeness. We sit there together for several minutes, enveloped in silence before she finally speaks.

"I haven't really thought about it," she says quietly.

Using the nickname I've given her, I say, "Little Dragon." My tone holds a hint of warning, conveying my refusal to be played with. Emotions flicker across our bond as Rayne flips through a Rolodex of emotion, finally settling on determination. I brace myself. Here it comes. The moment I've been hoping to avoid for the last two days. The moment she kicks me to the curb for being a drunken asshole taking her without her consent.

Her words are hesitant but determined as she continues, "Okay, that's not entirely true. We'll be friends." She stops. I hold my breath but don't break the silence. She has to be the one to take the first step. I try to read the myriad of emotions flickering through our bond, but nothing lands long enough for me to identify it. When she speaks, it's a whisper of need and apprehension. "You'll teach me how to have amazing sex."

Delight thrums through me. This is exactly what I'd hoped to hear. Maybe she intrinsically understands that through sex, we can communicate on a level beyond words, a realm where our true selves can connect without barriers. I press her further, eager to hear her thoughts on the matter. "I'll show you how to have exceptional sex. Where would you like to begin?"

A hint of confusion laces her voice as she asks, "What do you mean, where?"

The air between us crackles with electric energy and desire, creating a continuous circuit from my body to hers. I force myself to remain still, fighting against the urge to act on our mutual attraction. *Patience, Jaden.*

"I liked what you did the other night. How you took control." A deep blush suffuses the warm brown of her cheeks and makes her already beautiful skin seem to glow. Her words speak to my own desires.

With a gentle tug, I pull her closer against me, feeling the heat radiating from her body. My hand slides further up her smooth thigh, and she jumps slightly as my fingers brush against her G-string, igniting a spark of heat within her. Heat radiates off her body as I continue to explore, slipping my finger into the dampness pooling at the entrance of her vagina.

"Next time, no thong." My low, husky voice is almost unrecognizable to my ears. "Do you orgasm when we have sex?"

She's quiet for so long I wonder if she heard me. "I don't think so," she says, taking another hit from her joint and sipping on her wine. "I guess that means no."

I pause for a moment, letting her words sink in before diving deeper. "Have you ever truly experienced pleasure?" I keep my voice low and seductive. I've perfected the lover-boy persona.

Her cheeks flush with embarrassment, the heat spreading through our connection. "I don't think so."

With those four words, I am consumed by an intense desire to fulfill her every fantasy and craving. As a voyeur, I have observed and fantasized about satisfying a woman's every need, but now I can make it a reality with Rayne. And she sees me as some sexual hero, so there is no need for me to reveal my lack of experience or any potential dysfunction.

She rambles on nervously, her words tumbling out in that endearing yet frustrating way she has when she's nervous. "I mean our sex is great and all . . . don't get me wrong, I feel a level of excitement with you that I've never felt with anyone else. But it's like I reach a certain point and can't go any further."

I have found my mission. Without hesitation, I slip my finger under her thong and delve into her warm, wet folds. A surge of electricity courses through my body as her heat engulfs my finger. She gasps as I locate her G-spot and expertly massage it.

With a devilish grin, I lock eyes with her as my finger

continues its rhythm inside her. She traces the laugh lines around my eye with her index finger, sending waves of desire coursing through me.

"What can I do to help you over the edge?" Every other thought except that I can be the one to bring this strange and mysterious woman her first pleasure blew from my mind. I focus every neuron on the pulses coming through our connection trying to read her confusion and desire as she sifts through thoughts. Finally, she says so quietly I wonder if I hear her, "I think you'll have to force me."

Excitement blasts through me, replacing my need to kill with my need to pleasure her. But the bond tells me she's turning her embarrassment into a litany of reasons why this won't work. I need to shut that down before it takes root.

"How old are you?" Her breathless question breaks the intensity between us.

"Thirty-three," I reply without missing a beat. I'm well aware of the age gap, but I am not going to discuss why our relationship may not work tonight. "Let's focus on the task at hand." I emphasize the word 'hand'. My digit continues its pulsing rhythm, evoking moans of pleasure from her lips.

She clears her throat awkwardly. "Shouldn't we have a contract or something if we're going to do this? And what about a safe word?" Her words trail off, but I know that deep down, my little dragon craves submission and control in the bedroom. And it speaks directly to my own desire for dominance.

"What arouses you, makes you excited?" I take us back to the book she has been studying.

"You are what excites me." Her voice is low and husky.

A rare chuckle escapes me, surprising even myself. I

quickly mask it by playfully nipping at Rayne's neck. "Oh no, you don't get off that easily." My usually lurking power surges, mixing pleasure with triumph. The thought of being her first in true fulfillment excites me. She's a kink virgin. Hell, since losing a hymen to rape doesn't count in my book, she's a virgin. Despite the risks, my heart swells with cautious optimism.

My power, sensing the shift, leaps into overdrive. A primal part of me awakens, affirming her as ours. The admission from Rayne sends a thrill through me, igniting a fervor to explore and discover every facet of her being. I find myself drawn irresistibly to the challenge of unraveling her secrets while guarding my own heart.

With her uncharted depths and myriad secrets, Rayne presents a challenge I can't resist. My guarded walls, formidable as they are, seem less daunting as I contemplate exploring this enigmatic woman who defies my every expectation.

28

RAYNE

Two whole days, that bastard's given me the cold shoulder. Two days since he took me, and here I am, internally chastising myself for being melodramatic. But it's not just me. This new power inside me isn't letting me off easy either, forcing me to confront truths I'd rather ignore. It's a relentless reality check.

I stretch, comfortably wrapped up in a blanket and settled into a wonderfully comfortable armchair. The last few days, I've mainly rotated between this chair and my bed. The events following Jaden's drunken visit are somewhat hazy, a phenomenon I'm accustomed to after experiencing trauma. Not that letting Jaden take me was all that traumatic. I push away the guilty thought that I'd liked it rough.

My head does this nifty trick where it turns trauma into scenes I watch, stripping the sting right out of the memories. Strangely, shortly after an abusive event, details seem to slip from my grasp, along with the overwhelming shame and fear typically associated with such attacks. It's as if I have Edward Cullen's mind-reading skills from "Twilight," allowing me to observe events without feeling their impact, my own personal shield of detachment. It's a concerning pattern I've quietly observed in myself, one I've hidden away. ES certainly didn't need more ammunition to claim I was on the path to mental illness, much like my mother.

I sigh, wishing I had more energy. Whatever's happening in this strange rendition of my science fiction dream took a turn the other night. Vague, very vague, memories of a ghost with a Scottish or Welsh accent, an angel named Bob who looked like Brad Pitt in his Joe Black role, and a warm cave. Whispers from Jaden's voice talking to me float through my mind, making me happy and sad all at the same time. "You're like an escape for me, a break from the nightmares." "I'm terrified."

My heart breaks for him because of something that happened as a teen, but I can't grasp the details. It's all so confusing. This is one time when my ability to emotionally distance myself from an incident isn't serving me well. I heave out yet another sigh as I push that thought aside for now. Because there are times when I have absolute certainty that I know something is right although I can't explain why, and this is one of those cases. My gut, and maybe something that happened last night, tells me that figuring out my magic is something I can't force. But for some reason, just knowing it's there and that I'm not a loser is enough for now. Or maybe it's because I'm obsessed and consumed by the strange man who rescued me.

Once again, I let my mind roll around the last two days. Jaden's been strangely distant—either out early or holed up in his room. He's insisting I stay put, declaring it's for my own protection now that Viper is no longer a threat. He's convinced there's a contract on my head, which I find hard to swallow—I'm hardly a priority target. Part of me rebels against the idea of being confined, but if I'm being honest, a larger part is strangely at peace with it. This growing impulse to please him is unsettling and throwing me for a loop. I've got enough on my plate, what with my new role on the Pandemonium Eruptus team and all the tech toys I get to play with. My life's a well-oiled machine now, except for the Jaden-shaped wrench thrown in.

He's not too keen on my packed schedule and makes snide remarks about wanting me at his beck and call. I blast them apart as fast as he shoots them at me—I'm nobody's plaything. But still, there's this pull, this infuriating attraction that I can't shake off.

I rummage through my closet, seeking the perfect outfit for tonight's dinner. This bizarre connection we have, it's whispering that he's been doing some soul-searching too, come to some crossroads about me. With Viper gone, I'm half expecting Jaden to show me the door. But then there's the other half—the unknown, the unpredictable.

I can't figure him out. He's a puzzle and my usually reliable instincts are at a loss with him. It's like trying to grasp a shadow—whenever I think I've got a hold of something solid, it slips right through my fingers. The vagueness of details is maddening, yet I've learned that digging deeper only makes them slip further away. He exudes this overpowering Edward Cullen vibe—overprotective, controlling, yet ridiculously better-looking. I pause to muse on the absurdity of comparing a flesh-and-angel to a fictional vampire, but then again, what part of my life isn't bordering on the bizarre now?

Part of me wants to scream at Jaden for his Edward Cullen-like high-handedness, but I'm inexplicably drawn to him, like some character in a twisted fairy tale. Beneath his cool exterior, I sense layers of damage. I've dreamt about it, even dropped into his dreams, I'm sure of it. He's become an all-consuming presence in my thoughts, a tapestry I can't unravel.

We're both observers of life, yet he does it with such subtlety, constantly suggesting I could learn a thing or two from him. One moment, I'm seething, ready to lash out at him, the next, his intensity and command have me dissolving into a puddle of desire and confusion. *Grrr*, it's as if he holds some mysterious power over my emotions, flipping them on and off at will.

I choose a sleek navy blue kimono dress that flatters my athletic build. I've always been proud of my lean, agile body —perfect for track and dance. But around guys, my confidence wavers. I remember the cruel jibes in high school, the 'Twiggy' taunts, and worse, the derogatory remarks about how much I looked and acted like a boy. They were a warm-up for what would follow as I entered young adulthood when men labeled me a 'dead fish' or an 'ice queen.' But Jaden's different. He doesn't want me to move, to touch. Just to be still while he plays. It leaves me tense and unsure. Does he even like me? Our link offers more riddles than answers. *Grrr*, why can't he just be straightforward?

I slide into the dress, appreciating how it gives the illusion of curves. I tug on black silk stockings, glancing at my slender legs. I allow myself a brief moment of self-pity, wishing nature had been more generous in certain areas. But then, I shrug it off. Can't change what I am. Jaden claims he doesn't have a 'type,' but I suspect he's a boob man. Yet, when I called him out, he just brushed it off. "I don't have a type." Typical Jaden, always keeping me guessing. When I call him out on that particular behavior pattern, he grins like he's just won an Oscar.

I let out another sigh, examining myself with a mix of

reluctant acceptance and growing confidence. The reflection shows a woman who's not a conventional beauty, but there's a unique allure in the symmetry of her features, something my therapist drilled into me until I believed it. Reflecting on Jaden's words, I recall our conversations about my self-image. He's consistently challenging the negative narrative I've internalized over the years.

Jaden, in his uniquely cryptic way, insists that I'm far from ugly, pushing against the detrimental beliefs I've held about myself. It's a rare moment when he steps out of his usual guarded demeanor to offer genuine reassurance. It's not a direct compliment, but the clinical analysis coming from Jaden is as close as it gets. His words linger in my mind, a contrast to the usual silence and mystery that shroud his interactions. This acknowledgment from him, subtle as it may be, is a significant departure from the indifference he often projects.

My gaze lingers on my reflection. Curly black hair falls around an ambiguous oval or round face, set with wide, expressive chestnut brown eyes filled with a blend of anxiety and excitement. Everything's proportionate, right down to my cute nose. But it's my full lips that deviate from conventional beauty standards, setting me apart. Lips that led to more jeering in high school about "flapper" lips.

I trace a finger down my arm, mimicking Jaden's touch, acknowledging my skin's rich brown tone. It's a part of me Jaden seems fascinated with, a stark contrast to the societal biases I've encountered. Angel Bob's advice resonates in my head, reminding me to focus on Jaden's actions rather than his words. Despite the struggles of accepting my skin color in a world that often favors lighter shades, I'm learning to see its beauty, thanks to Jaden's unspoken admiration.

I shake off the introspection. I have to hurry. Jaden's

impatience is evident through our connection. He's summoned me for dinner, mentioning that we have important matters to discuss. His usual impatience is evident, and I can almost feel him on the brink of coming to fetch me himself.

As I enter the dining room, Jaden's mouth quirks up slightly—the only clue I have that he's either happy to see me or approves of what I'm wearing. It's a subtle expression, easy to miss if I weren't so attuned to his every move. These little things, these rare glimpses into his guarded persona, keep me intrigued and tethered to him despite the whirlwind of emotions he stirs within me.

I stride into the private dining room, heart pounding with anticipation and dread. Jaden's presence dominates the space. He offers me a glass of wine, and I take it, my hand trembling slightly.

Every single signal coming through our link screams of being uptight, laced with desire. His gaze is intense and unyielding as he studies me. "Let's discuss how we will make our time together work." No small talk. He leaps directly to the point. His voice is steady, but there's an undercurrent of something more, a depth I can't quite discern through our bond.

I take a deep breath, steadying myself. "Where do you see this thing happening between us going?" His question catches me off guard, and for a moment, I'm lost in the depth of his bronze eyes. Is he talking about the other night?

"I . . . I haven't really thought about it." My voice is barely above a whisper, uncharacteristically. Something about this man, in these moments, hinders my ability to articulate.

He leans in closer, his breath warm against my skin.

"Little Dragon." A warning edge to his voice sends shivers down my spine.

The silence stretches between us, heavy and charged. I can feel his eyes on me, searching, probing. "Okay, that's not entirely true." I finally concede and meet his gaze head-on. "I think we can be friends."

Jaden's expression shifts, a flicker of something like hope crossing his face. "Friends," he echoes, and for a moment, I see a vulnerability in his eyes that he quickly masks.

The tension in the room is apparent, and I'm drawn to him despite my better judgment. "You'll teach me how to have amazing sex." The words drop from my mouth, surprising me with their boldness.

Jaden's eyes light up, a spark of excitement igniting within him. "I'll show you how to have exceptional sex." He corrects me, his voice laced with a promise that sends a thrill through my body. "Where do you want to start?" No hesitation. He's been thinking about this.

I bite my lip, unsure of what comes next. Wishing like hell I had more experience with men. "What do you mean, where?" More words tumble out before I can stop them.

He leans in, his gaze intense and unwavering. "I mean, where do you want to begin exploring?" His question hangs in the air, loaded with possibilities. "Physically, emotionally, the places you've always wanted to go but never dared. I can take you there, but only if you're willing to trust me."

My heart races at his proposition, a mix of fear and curiosity. "I . . . I don't know. I've never thought about it like that." I hate it when his questions show my lack of experience but stutter the words out. My gaze drifts momentarily to "Cuffed, Tied and Satisfied," a book on BDSM that I've been studying, trying to understand this world I'm working in.

His smile is a challenge and an invitation all in one. "We'll start wherever you're comfortable," he says. I can't help but feel a surge of excitement at the prospect of discovering this new side of myself with him. Letting go and exploring the unknown with Jaden terrifies and exhilarates me. It's one thing to read about it in a book, quite another to live it.

Jaden's approach to sex is like navigating the maze in the movie "The Shining," each turn revealing a new layer of complexity. I've read enough to know that his behavior deviates from the typical male bravado. He's cautious, needs time to prepare, and dislikes surprises in the bedroom. But what's more perplexing is the sense of a deeper wound in him, a shadow lurking in his past. I'm haunted by dreams that hint at his trauma, yet the details elude me. Maybe it's a mercy that I can't remember; Jaden is nowhere near ready to confront his demons. He's like a fortress, resilient in his own way, but unlike me—who dives in once I find solid ground—he treads carefully, always testing the waters.

His throat-clearing snaps me back to the present. I realize how important it is for Jaden to feel seen, to know that I'm here with him, even when he pushes me away. "Well, I suppose we can start with some bondage and light flogging. Sort of dip my toe in the water." I try to gauge his reaction. His expression shifts, so I quickly add, "After signing the contract and all that."

"There won't be a contract, and we'll use the stoplight safe words recommended by the club. Keeps things simple." His tone is edged with steel, leaving no room for argument.

Internally, I roll my eyes, but outwardly, I nod, trying to

appear submissive. "Yes, boss."

"I prefer sir or master."

His words catch me off guard. "Sir, maybe, but I'm not calling any white guy my master. That's a trigger word for me." I'm surprised at my bluntness, but I need to make my boundaries clear.

"How so?" Jaden fires back, his question sharp.

"It reminds me of slavery and racism and takes my mind away from what we're doing." I meet his intense gaze.

He considers my words for a moment before nodding. "Fair enough. Do you have any questions before we begin?"

"Yes, actually. Explain the stoplights." I recall the club's safe word guidelines, but I want more clarity from Jaden.

"If either of us says red, all activity ceases, and the scene is done. We say yellow if you want to continue but need to adjust an activity. And if you're comfortable and want to proceed when I check in, you'll say green. Do you understand?" Jaden adds a new touch to the stoplight system I read about with his green light, but I keep my mouth shut. Because what he doesn't vocalize but screams through our bond is the unspoken ultimatum: if I say red or reject him, we're done. Despite the urge to address this, I remain silent on instinct.

So I nod. I've learned to tread lightly when discussing sex with him. He can be relentless in extracting details, prying into every nook and cranny, much like a miner relentlessly chipping away, seeking that hidden vein of gold deep within the earth's crust. However, like said miner, he keeps his information nuggets to himself. Jaden's a master of giving obscure answers that never answer the question asked.

And now, his hot hand rests on my thigh, sending a flood of heat through my body. "I wish I had skin your color." Jaden's index finger traces a path up my forearm, leaving goosebumps and a trail of fiery sensation.

His comment on my skin color catches me off guard, stirring a mix of warmth and anger. Here it comes, the conversation about race. Is this where I see Jaden's true colors? My mind races with doubts. "You don't need to pretend to like my skin color just to sleep with me," I blurt out, fixing him with a searching gaze, bracing for his response.

He keeps his eyes on my arm, his touch light yet maddening. I'm on edge, irritation and desire battling within me. "Well?" I snap, impatience laced with fear.

Jaden pauses, his voice calm, but our link is pulsing with restrained anger. "Under normal circumstances, I'd take offense to that assumption. But considering your past, I'll let it slide. Just know, it's unfair to accuse me like that. Have I ever given you a reason to believe your skin color matters to me in any negative way? If anything, it adds to your appeal, and I'm pissed you'd think so poorly of me."

His words strike a chord of guilt and realization within me. The truth is, Jaden's never shown any sign of caring about my race or color. His issues are all about intimacy, not skin. "I'm sorry." Embarrassment flushes through me. "I didn't mean to offend you."

He sighs, and just like that, his anger softens into understanding. "No need for apologies. In fact, I owe you one."

His admission surprises me, snapping my attention back to him. An apology from Jaden? Now that's something new.

"Want to talk about the other night?" His voice is low, almost hesitant. There's an underlying note of concern that I'm not used to hearing from him.

My head snaps up, matching his intensity with my own fiery response. "What about the other night?" My words come out sharper than I intend, fueled by a mix of defensiveness and curiosity.

Jaden pauses, his expression unreadable for a moment. "Are you okay with what happened?" There's a flicker of something in his eyes, a hint of guilt maybe, that mirrors my own internal turmoil.

Turning to face him fully, I can't help the slow smile that lights up my face. It feels like a rare moment of clarity breaking through the confusion. I scoot closer, yet there's still a careful distance between us, a dance of proximity we both seem to be navigating. "It was consensual if that's what you're asking." A bit of boldness creeps into my voice. "Are you okay with it?"

His response surprises me. "Yes," he says, and there's an unspoken weight behind that single word. I can tell he's holding back, but I don't push it. Instead, I lean back, lost in thought, analyzing my feelings and trying to make sense of them. "I'm surprised, really. I usually can't stand the smell of liquor on guys, but you . . . you weren't an asshole like they are." I stop, surprised at my own admission.

Jaden's expression shifts, a brief flash of something like surprise or realization crossing his face. It's gone as quickly as it appeared, replaced by that familiar guarded look.

I gather my courage for my final ask. "I don't mind it rough, but don't take me in anger again." I hold my breath, hoping I haven't crossed a line.

Jaden meets my gaze, a quirk of his eyebrow conveying more than words could. It's a silent acknowledgment, an unspoken agreement that hangs between us. I sit back, waiting, wondering what this means for us from now on.

29
JADEN

"I think you'll have to force me." Rayne's words echo in my mind, a siren call that pushes back the ever-present shadows. She keeps me anchored, here and now, away from the dark recesses where I hide the remnants of who I really am.

I ponder our earlier conversation, each word a piece of the puzzle that is my new identity. I'm usually shrouded in doubt, a truth I've concealed from the world, but this time, I'm certain. I've devised the perfect plan to keep my defenses intact while keeping Rayne close. Her responses to my probing questions send a thrill through me, a sensation that's becoming increasingly familiar.

My power thrums with excitement, reveling in this newfound shortcut to intimacy. The long preparations, a legacy of past trauma, seem less daunting now. Rayne's submissive demeanor, contrasting with her fierce independence, ensnares me. Her willingness to let me choose her attire, to shield her from what she perceives as flaws, strikes a chord in me. She's internalized society's shame, a burden unfairly placed upon her by the very gender I belong to. *Just like the ones put on me!*

I want to tell her how beautiful she is, to break through the walls we've both built, but I've learned the hard way the cost of vulnerability. Every action must be calculated and guarded. Yet, with Rayne, it's different. She mirrors my hidden tenderness, reflecting the pain we've both endured at the hands of a judgmental world.

There's a freedom in her presence, a release from the constant need to conform or seek approval. She draws out the dominant side of me, a part I've kept hidden. Her wide, desire-filled eyes are a window to her soul—open, honest, unguarded with me. I'm eager to explore this uncharted territory with her, to communicate in ways words cannot.

And yes, I can't deny the thrill of being her first in this realm of dominance and submission. She sees me as an expert, a role I relish. Rayne, my kink virgin, is a blank canvas, and I'm eager to leave my mark.

"Let's begin, shall we? Tonight, I want to explore a blindfold and light bondage. It's time I truly learn your body, understand how you react to my touch."

Rayne's snort catches me off guard, her eyebrow arching in playful defiance. "CC, you've been 'exploring' me since day one. Don't play coy with me now. You must have figured me out by now." Her candidness is both refreshing and challenging.

Despite the grin tugging at my lips, I can't help but push back a little, still struggling with the nickname she's bestowed upon me. "I've asked you not to use pet names," I reply, even as Captain Control starts to grow on me.

She gives me a sly look, taking a sip of her wine before setting it down with a deliberate motion. Her hand finds my thigh, her touch firm and provocative. "Well, CC, I believe in equal treatment. No double standards between us." Her determination both irks and intrigues me.

Just as deliberately, I remove her hand and place it under mine on her thigh. "Obey my instructions or be punished. No touching."

"I will never simply 'obey' you." Her defiance is loud and clear. "That word's another trigger for me. You'll need to find another way to get your point across." She quickly adds, "Clarity is kindness, according to the book I'm reading," as if worried she's offended me.

Her mix of strength and vulnerability mirrors my own inner battle, making her even more fascinating. I clear my throat, adopting the authoritative tone I've honed through observation at the Masquerade. "Understood. But if we're going to proceed, you need to follow my rules."

She throws me another challenging look before bowing her head.

I lead Rayne down the private elevator to one of the playrooms, each step heightening the sense of anticipation coursing through me. The room is a carefully crafted blend of stark functionality and intimate coziness designed to cater to a myriad of fantasies. It's a space where every detail is meticulously thought out, from the placement of restraints to the selection of toys that lie in wait.

As we enter the playroom, the large bed at its center immediately commands attention, its black sheets and plush pillows set against the pale wood floor—a striking visual that promises untold pleasures. But it's not the bed alone that sets the tone for tonight. The tools for our exploration lie on a sleek, dark wood side table: a silky blindfold and leather padded cuffs. These items, symbolizing sensory deprivation and restrained freedom, are deliberately placed, hinting at the readiness and intent for the evening.

The room, like all others in the Masquerade Club, is meticulously crafted, blending stark elegance with sensual anticipation. It sets the perfect stage for the dance of dominance and submission we're about to undertake.

Rayne's sharp intake of breath propels me forward. Now that the moment's upon us, I want to push her, to see how far she'll go to please me. "Undress. Now."

She startles but recovers quickly, deftly pulling her dress over her head. I stop her as she bends to undo the garters holding up silk stockings and lightly slap away her hand. "Leave them." I hand her the blindfold, a silent command she obeys without question. I circle her, drinking in her lithe form. Her curves beg to be explored, marked as mine.

I run a finger along her collarbone and down between her beautiful breasts. As I trace my fingers along her skin, I notice the subtle shiver that runs through her, sending a thrill of satisfaction through me. "On your knees."

She kneels immediately, back straight in a show of obedience that stirs my arousal. I caress her cheek, trailing my hand to her full lips. "Open."

Her mouth opens, and I slide two fingers inside, stroking her tongue. She sucks greedily, and I close my eyes, imagining her warm mouth on my cock, giving me exquisite pleasure.

Rayne's mouth feels warm and wet like a velvet glove around my fingers. I can feel her eagerness, her need to please me, and it sends a thrill through me. But I want more. I remove my fingers. Her soft whine of disappointment turns into a gasp of pleasure as I wipe her saliva on her large, swollen nipple before pulling it into my mouth. She tries desperately to control her breath as I pinch the sensitive nub, her hips shifting restlessly.

"So eager, yet you'll take what I give you. I'm going to learn every inch of you, Rayne, until you're writhing and begging for release." The words tumble from me, surprising me with their mixture of promise and power.

A whimper escapes her, a symphony of arousal and trepidation in each rapid breath. It echoes in the hollows of my own desire, amplifying the urgency that courses through me.

For the first time in forever, my desire surges as a vibrant, insistent force, battling against my inclination for a slow and deliberate exploration. I yearn to claim every aspect of her—her heart, her body, her very essence. Yet, the shadows within me loom large, reminding me of the parts I cannot offer. Some pieces of me are irrevocably cloaked in the abyss, segments of my soul I cannot bear to face.

Shaking off the shadows, I focus on Rayne's soft cries, each sound a brushstroke painting a picture of our temporary union. Tonight, she's mine, and I'm determined to etch myself into her memory. It's the only place I can truly belong to her.

Her body responds to my every touch, a canvas of sensitivity and yearning. I explore her with a reverence that surprises even me, my fingertips tracing paths that elicit shivers and sighs. In these fleeting moments, I allow myself a glimpse into what could be, even though I know it's a dream that can't last.

As I navigate the contours of her body, I'm acutely aware of the dichotomy within me—the burning need to connect, coupled with the ironclad resolve to hide my deepest self. It's a dance of shadows and light, where each caress is an offering and a barrier.

This night is a fragile thing, a bubble of time and sensation that I know will burst at dawn. Yet, I can't help but immerse myself in it, in her. She's a mystery that compels me, a challenge that I can't resist, even as I'm haunted by the knowledge that I can only ever offer her a fraction of who I truly am.

I secure the blindfold over Rayne's eyes, effectively plunging her into darkness. The act heightens her other senses, a fact betrayed by the subtle quickening of her breath. It's a surrender—not just to the darkness but to me, to the uncharted journey we're embarking upon together.

I trace a finger down her jawline, sliding over the delicate skin to the pulse point fluttering at her neck. The shiver that courses through her, a visceral response to my touch, sends a thrill of satisfaction through me. "So beautiful. So mine." The words are a possessive claim, slipping out unbidden but steeped in an undeniable truth. In this moment, Rayne belongs to me, a fact that stirs a fierce sense of protectiveness and ownership within me.

Yet, as I utter those words, a part of me recoils at the raw honesty they reveal. I'm not used to such open declarations acknowledging the depth of my needs and desires. Rayne has become an unexpected buffer in my tumultuous world, a beacon in the darkness I so often find myself engulfed in. The admission that she is 'mine' is both exhilarating and terrifying—a glimpse into a vulnerability I rarely allow myself to acknowledge.

Her trust in me, her willingness to let go and be guided by my hand, is a responsibility I don't take lightly. In her blindfolded state, Rayne is more than just a submissive partner; she's a mirror reflecting back my own need for connection, for something real and tangible amidst the shadows that I navigate daily.

I'm loath to share her, to expose this private world

we've created to the harsh light of reality. If I had my way, I'd take her to the deepest bowels of my cave and never let her free. Tonight, this playroom is my cave and it will have to do. Here, in this secluded space, Rayne and I exist in a bubble of intimacy and exploration—a place where I can be both the master and the student, learning the contours of her desires even as I confront the complexities of my own heart.

It's a delicate balance, a dance of power and surrender, and with every whispered word and lingering touch, I'm drawn deeper into its spell. Rayne, blindfolded and trusting, is both my canvas and my muse, inspiring a tenderness and passion I didn't know I was capable of.

Pulling her to her feet, I cup her breasts, kneading the soft flesh and rolling her nipples between my fingers until they pebble. She arches into my touch with a soft moan, her hips rocking in a silent plea for more.

Patience, I remind myself, even as my erection strains against my jeans. I want to drive into her and claim what's mine in the most primal way, but I restrain my baser urges.

There's pleasure to be found in the journey, not just the destination. My power notes that every movement, both hers and mine, takes me further away from the horror that usually consumes my libido and tucks that nugget away for future consideration.

I trail kisses down her torso, circling her navel with my tongue before moving lower. Her scent intensifies, a mix of arousal and anticipation tinged with a hint of trepidation. She shudders, a silent admission that she's never been explored with such care. A surge of satisfaction ripples through me, my power resonating with this newfound connection.

My fingers trace her folds, swollen and slick with need. "So wet for me already. I've barely touched you."

A flush creeps over her chest and neck, deepening the richness of her gorgeous tawny skin. Her teeth nip at her lower lip again, drawing my attention back and amplifying her allure.

"No hiding from me. I want to witness every shudder of pleasure, hear each cry I elicit from you." A sudden insight strikes me—her vocal expressions help silence the relentless horrors in my mind. The discordant emotions roiling through our connection scream that Rayne is still holding back. "I need to hear you." I give my voice a commanding edge, demanding her complete surrender.

Her breath catches as I expose her further, laying her bare to my intense scrutiny. I blow softly against her clit, and she jerks in reaction, a strangled moan that resonates deep within me tears from her throat. It's a revelation of how deeply in sync we are, how her body instinctively responds to my touch. A sharp jerk, a strangled moan rips from her throat—a sound that resonates within me, obliterating all else.

"Please, I need—"

I silence her plea with a firm nip to her inner thigh. "You'll take what I choose to give." A resolute thought fortifies my resolve: *Tonight, I make you irrevocably mine.*

30
RAYNE

The silk of the blindfold caresses my skin, plunging me into darkness. I'm at his mercy, the world reduced to sensation and sound. My heart thunders in my ears, a mix of excitement and nerves. This is new territory, and every part of me is alert, waiting for his next move.

His finger traces my jawline, sending shivers down my spine. "So beautiful. So mine." His words are possessive, and a part of me rebels against them. But another part, the part that's drawn to Jaden in ways I can't explain, finds comfort in them. It's confusing and thrilling all at once.

I'm not used to letting go like this, to surrendering control. My whole life has been about self-reliance, about building walls to keep people out. But here, with Jaden, those walls seem less important, more transparent. His touch and voice are dismantling my defenses, and I'm not sure how I feel about that.

I want to push back, to assert my independence, but his touch ignites something within me that craves more. I feel vulnerable and exposed, yet a part of me revels in it. The

power dynamic between us is shifting, and it's both terrifying and exhilarating.

I can't see him, but I can feel his presence, a
commanding force that demands my attention. We're
dancing on the edge of something profound, a precipice of
emotion and desire. I'm teetering, caught between fear and
longing, and I don't know which way I'll fall.

I'm aware of every breath, every heartbeat. My heightened senses are attuned to his every movement. The anticipation is maddening, a delicious torture that has me
yearning for release. But I know he won't give it to me, not
yet. He's in control, and I'm his to command.

And that's when it hits me—this is more than just
physical. Jaden's speaking to me with his body, and I'm
responding in kind. It's a conversation without words, a
dialogue of touch and sensation. In this moment, in this
darkness, I'm not just surrendering my body. I'm opening
up parts of myself I didn't even know existed.

The realization is both terrifying and liberating. I'm
exposed in a way I've never been before, not just physically,
but emotionally. I push away the negative thoughts, the
fears and doubts, and allow myself to sink into the passion.
For now, I'm his, and that's all that matters.

The shift between us is pronounced, like a current
charging the air. Anticipation and dread are a knotted mess
inside me, making it hard to relax. I'm strung tight with the
fear that I might freeze up. But deep down, it's not just fear;
there's this craving too, a hunger for something more,
something Jaden keeps pushing me towards.

Tonight, he's set his sights on hearing me. It's weird,
considering he's usually Captain Silent Control. His quiet-
ness has two sides to it. On one hand, it's a relief—he
doesn't make those gross, grunting noises like the scum

from my past. But on the other, it's like a spotlight on me, making me hyper-aware of every little sound I make.

I worry that I'll sound like the women in those porn movies Jaden watches late at night, trying to empty his mind. Totally fake. Yet the trepidation pulsing through our link suggests he needs to hear me. His entire focus is on my pleasure, a dedication I've never experienced before. It's more intoxicating than any high I've chased, a profound realization that leaves me reeling.

These thoughts whirl through my mind, a maelstrom of confusion and curiosity. But deep down, I know this is more than just about making noise; it's about breaking down barriers, about connecting on a level we haven't yet explored. It's a challenge I'm both eager and hesitant to accept.

I gasp as my body arches off the bed, Jaden's mouth capturing my clit, a tiny growl escaping him as his tongue sweeps through my juices. The surge of desire that bolts through me at this new experience is overpowering. No one has ever taken the time to explore my body like this. The sensations his tongue and lips elicit drown out the faint traces of embarrassment and shame. Pleasure builds, teetering on the edge of a peak I've never reached before. Jaden is relentless, his skilled ministrations leaving me breathless with anticipation.

"Jaden." I pant his name as if it's a plea, a prayer. My mind races, conflicting emotions surging through me. A part of me wonders if I'm insane for trusting this man—a killer. But there's a magnetic pull between us that defies logic, and I can't deny it any longer.

"Relax, Rayne." His quiet voice is both commanding and soothing. "Give in to it."

It's terrifying and thrilling all at once. With a few deft

movements, he lifts me from the floor and carries me to the bed. Before I have time to process what's happening, he secures the wrist cuffs to the bed, pulling my arms above my head. Restrained and blindfolded, I'm entirely at his mercy.

Is this really happening? Have I lost my fucking mind? My thoughts race, but they're soon drowned out by the sensation of his hands exploring my body. He seems to know just where to touch me, how much pressure to apply. It's an intimate knowledge that stirs up a fierce desire, even as fear prickles at the back of my mind.

His fingers trail down my sides, tracing patterns that send shivers up my spine. He spends what feels like hours playing with my body, teasing me into a state of unbearable longing. But he rarely kisses me, as though that act is too intimate for this dance we're engaged in.

My heart races, anticipation and fear warring inside of me as we push boundaries together. And even though I'm restrained and vulnerable in a way I've never been before, I can't help but trust Jaden.

"Wait for my command to come." Jaden whispers, yet his voice is authoritative and laced with a raw, protective intensity . . . and a whole lot of wishful thinking. His fingers deftly slide between my legs, teasing my clit with a feather-light touch that has me squirming against the restraints. I need it rougher. My breathing grows shallow as he slips one finger inside of me, seeking out that sweet spot that tips me closer to the edge.

"Focus on your pleasure, Rayne." The silent message from Jaden pulses through our bond, a mix of warmth, encouragement, and raw desire for me. It's a novel sensation, feeling desired for me, not just my body. I try to push down the ingrained thoughts about pleasing him, the things I've

read and heard that say I should be doing more. With bound hands, it's a frustrating tug-of-war, yet there's an undeniable thrill in this surrender.

"Give yourself to me." Jaden's unspoken command reverberates through our bond, a blend of gentleness and insistence. Despite the fear gnawing at me, there's a deep-seated urge to obey, to trust him completely. I'm teetering on the edge, torn between my need for control and the alluring freedom of letting go. Can I truly allow myself to experience the full depth of pleasure he's offering without losing a part of myself?

Tension builds inside me, a mix of excitement and a bit of fear, as Jaden works his magic on me. He knows exactly how to drive me crazy, slowly ramping up the heat. I feel this crazy pressure building up as if my body's about to burst into flames with his every touch. Through our bond, his mental voice gets stronger, like he's right there in my head, guiding me toward letting go.

"Just let go, Rayne." He's in my mind, urging me on. *"I need you."* And damn, it hits me that this isn't just about getting off. It's about trust and letting myself fall into this thing with him.

That thought hits me hard. It's a little bit scary and a whole lot amazing. I need to stop overthinking and dive into this moment with Jaden. And then, just like that, something inside me lets go. We're flying together on this wild ride, just him and me. Every part of me is buzzing, wound up tight, but at the same time, I feel like I've just let out a breath I've held for several beats. I'm giving into this guy who's pulling me in, body and soul.

"Wait for my command." Jaden's voice pierces the charged atmosphere, authoritative yet laced with sensuality. His words anchor me, promising guidance through this unknown journey.

A wave of reassurance and encouragement floods our bond from Jaden, answering my unspoken fears. He's with me every step of the way.

"Focus on your pleasure, Rayne." Although his urging comes through our connection, his voice is so tangible it's as though he speaks aloud. My mind is a whirlwind of BDSM theories and the need to please him. Yet, here I am, bound and at his mercy, my only option to surrender.

"Trust me, Rayne." His silent command resonates within me, drawing me back toward the deep relaxation necessary for release. His fingers orchestrate my responses, each touch pushing me closer to the brink as his clever fingers work my clit and G-spot simultaneously. *Oh my God.* Something inside me shifts as Jaden's silent commands continue to weave through our connection. My usual barrage of thoughts and analyses starts to fade, replaced by an all-consuming need to give myself over to him. It's as if my mind, usually so active and questioning, goes blank with the urgency of this singular desire. In this moment, there's only Jaden, his touch, and the growing trust between us. The complexity of our bond simplifies into this clear, intense focus, where surrendering to him feels not just right but necessary.

"Give yourself to me." His mental insistence hits with an undeniable force. His presence—both physical and mental—envelops me, urging me to let go of all control. This level of vulnerability is terrifying, but the realization that I'm safe, even cherished, in his hands begins to break down my walls. As I inch toward surrender, I sense a new kind of strength emerging—one born from trust and the intense connection we share.

Sensation pulses through me, drowning out any lingering thoughts. Deep within my core, something dormant stirs to life, unfurling like a tendril coiling tighter, winding into a spring of intense pressure. It's a crescendo of sensation, halting my breath, as if a powerful force within is straining to break free, waiting to detonate. The tightly wound coil of orgasm sits precariously on the brink of exploding.

This moment feels like fleeing a relentless demon, my heart pounding in a desperate race, only to come to a sudden, jarring halt at a precipice. Suspended on this edge, there's a terrifying yet exhilarating realization of no turning back—a moment of profound transformation and surrender. It's as if I'm about to leap into the unknown, trusting in a plunge into depths of pleasure and connection I've never experienced.

"Come for me." At Jaden's command, something within me shatters. An explosive release courses through my body, tearing down walls and unlocking a power I never knew I possessed. Teetering on the cusp of a momentous awakening, a potent force radiates from my core.

But he doesn't stop there. Instead, he anchors me in place, and I feel the heat of his gaze, a steady presence amidst the tempest of sensation. Wave after wave, each contraction more intense than the last, cascades through my body in a relentless, surging tide. It's an almost unbearable crescendo, a tumultuous peak that overwhelms my senses.

I hit the crest of the wave I've never reached. Before I have time to think or catch my breath, Jaden pushes my legs farther apart and buries himself to the hilt. The inevitable burning pain sears through the walls of my pussy as he enters me, but this time, pain carries the promise of pleasure. More waves of pulsing pleasure crash through me as Jaden drives his need into me. A whirlpool of sensations bursts like fireworks through my core as I release to Jaden, and a mystical feeling of power, like an ancient force awakening, washes through every cell in my body.

As everything hits its peak and I'm riding the biggest wave ever, each pulse of pleasure overwhelms me, one after the other. The feeling is so strong it's overwhelming. I'm still soaring high, teetering on the edge of something even more intense. Before I can catch my breath or make sense of this wild ride, Jaden's relentless thrusting drives me deeper into this vortex of raw sensation. I'm caught in this torrent, each move from him reigniting that blaze within me, sustaining the surge. A low, guttural moan escapes me as my body arches to meet his, and in that moment, my power bursts free.

31
JADEN

I cradle my coffee, the afternoon sunshine and the cacophony of Toronto's busy streets a distant backdrop to my thoughts. Rayne's slumber grants me a rare moment of solitude, a state I once sought relentlessly but now, since Rayne's arrival, find myself needing less. The transition in my life's markers—from 'After Savannah' to 'Before Rayne'—is a testament to the profound impact she has had on me. The taste of Rayne still lingers on my tongue, her scent envelops my senses, and the memory of her power awakening is vivid in my mind. She has become a liberating force, challenging the persona I've meticulously crafted to meet the world's expectations. My moments with Rayne are increasingly essential, not just for the solace they offer but for the acceptance and understanding I find in her presence. The question of who I am, hidden beneath layers of pretense, becomes more pressing with each day spent by her side.

As I savor the quiet, I can't help but let my mind wander to the possibilities that lie ahead for us. Optimism, a feeling I've long kept at bay, begins to take root. The thought that

Rayne might truly see me, accept me, and perhaps even need me, fills me with a cautious hope. Yet, as I envision our future, a familiar shadow of doubt creeps in. Can she truly accept the man behind the mask, the one haunted by shadows and marred by the past? My hand tightens around the coffee mug, the warmth a fleeting comfort against the chill of uncertainty.

Just as I'm about to sink deeper into these reflections, the sound of footsteps delivers a one-two punch to my heart. Rayne bursts into the kitchen, her energy and excitement a stark contrast to my introspective mood. Without hesitation, she flings herself at me, a spontaneous display of affection that, under normal circumstances, would bring me joy. Rayne's sudden embrace triggers an immediate, visceral response. My heart freezes mid-beat, a cold vise gripping it tightly. Muscles coil like springs, primed for confrontation.

In the blink of an eye, the world narrows to a tunnel of fight-or-flight instincts. I'm yanked violently back to a time and place where vulnerability meant danger, where every touch brought pain and degradation. Panic floods my system, adrenaline surging like wildfire through my veins. My body reacts on pure instinct, hard and fast, my arm shooting out in defense. It's not Rayne in my grasp but a specter from my past, a ghost I've battled in the shadows of my mind. The room spins, reality blurring with memories, each breath a struggle as I fight to regain control, to remember where—and when—I am.

The pleas for mercy become a distant echo as my grip tightens, a primal satisfaction coursing through me with each labored breath of my adversary. *Not this time, you bastard.* My avenging angel power surges forward, coalescing within me, transforming the shadows of PTSD into a sharp blade of vengeance. I'm no longer a victim but a warrior, exacting retribution. The dark energy swirls, amplifying my strength, feeding the righteous fury that's been smoldering within.

Suddenly, a different force collides with mine—a commanding, unequivocal demand from Rayne. *Let go!* Her power, a torrent of pure, unbridled energy, crashes into me with the force of a tempest, hurling me across the room. I land with a thud, the impact jarring me to my core, a stark reminder of the line I had nearly crossed. *Fuck! Fuck! Fuck!*

Scrambling to my feet, the room spins as I steady myself against the wall. My breathing is ragged, my heart racing as if I've just gone ten rounds in the ring. Every muscle ache is a physical testament to the turmoil churning inside. I need to get out of here, to put distance between me and the chaos, to find a semblance of control in the eye of the storm that is my life. *I have to get out!* Shoving Rayne away, I rush from the room, my steps quick and desperate as I put space between us.

My mind is a whirlwind of shame and self-loathing as I haul ass to one of the War Room offices. But the stillness offers no solace, only amplifying the turmoil within me. As I pretend to focus on work, the door bursts open. "What part of Do Not Disturb don't you get?" That sounds just like Rayne. Looking up from the computer screen I've been blindly staring at for the last however long, I groan as I look into the sharp blue eyes of Superintendent Tempest Cross. Her entry is like a storm breaking the oppressive silence, her sharp movements and undeniable presence impossible to ignore.

Tempest is all confidence and calculated appeal, a stark contrast to the chaos churning inside me. Today, she's clad in a navy-blue designer suit that clings to her curves, the fabric barely containing her ample cleavage. The suit, cut to accentuate her hourglass figure, leaves little to the imagination, with just a hint of black lace peeking out from under the jacket, a deliberate tease. Her blonde hair falls in soft waves around her shoulders, framing a face that's as striking as it is calculating. Despite my efforts to remain indifferent, the sight of her, so assured and blatantly sensual, unnerves me more than usual. And makes me want Rayne. I slam shut the thought.

The familiarity of Tempest's seductive charm, which once could easily draw me out of my darkest moods, now feels unsettlingly hollow. The woman has the personality of an iceberg, but her glacial calculation without whatever filter blinded me to it no longer appeals. Rayne's vibrant presence in my life has filled me with a depth of emotion I hadn't anticipated, leaving little room for the emptiness Tempest represents.

The stark realization that what once satisfied me now leaves me cold, serves as a stark mirror to the changes within me. Rayne's influence, her undeniable warmth and complexity, has begun to thaw the ice I didn't realize had encased my heart. Next to her genuine brightness, Tempest's allure dims, a reminder of a path I no longer wish to walk. This shift, unsettling as it is, forces me to confront the depth of my feelings for Rayne, recognizing that what I crave now is not the distraction of the flesh, but the connection of souls. A connection with Rayne I just fucked up.

"Jaden, let's grab a drink and talk strategy." Tempest's voice, dripping with a promise of familiar distractions, sends a ripple of unease through me. Indulging in her allure, once a refuge, now feels like a stark betrayal of the connection I've unexpectedly found with Rayne. And yet, such thoughts are dangerous, forbidden. I need to quash them—immediately. Rayne and I . . . whatever we had, I've likely destroyed. Choking a woman will do that. It's not the first time my PTSD has hijacked a moment, turning a potential connection into wreckage. And it likely won't be the last. Each time, it's as though I'm a bystander to my own life, watching helplessly as the darkness within lashes out, destroying what I dare to care for. With Rayne, it feels like I've not just crossed a line—I've obliterated it, leaving a chasm between who I want to be for her and who I am.

"Tempest, now's not a good time." The words come out icier than I meant, a reflexive barrier against her seduction. The thought of her touch, once a balm, now feels like it would erase the last traces of Rayne from my skin, from my soul. The shudder that runs through me isn't from desire— it's from the cold realization of what I stand to lose, what I may have already lost.

Undeterred, she smirks, misunderstanding my reluctance for reticence. "A 'good time' is exactly what you need." She air quotes the two words before stepping closer, the challenge in her eyes clear.

I'm torn between the ease of falling back into old patterns and the newfound resolve Rayne has inspired within me. "Not today, Tempest. I've got too much on my mind." I hope like hell to convey the finality of my decision.

She pauses, then leans in closer, her calculated movements ensuring her cleavage is nearly impossible to ignore, a deliberate tease that sends a wave of her seductive scent my way. It momentarily slices through the guilt, a siren call to my basest instincts. "Alright, if not a drink, then let's at least talk strategy. No strings attached." Her voice purrs a soft caress that knows just how to stir my desire. Maybe this is exactly what I need to distract myself. My power surges in protest, a silent sentinel loyal to Rayne, I forcibly shut it down. Not now, not when I'm teetering on the edge of losing myself.

The offer tempts me as much as her attitude annoys. She'll be a momentary escape from the weight of my actions, a way to stop the noise for awhile. Yet, as Tempest encroaches upon my personal space, a part of me recoils. Being with Rayne has sparked a change, one that I'm still grappling with. I crave peace, time to think. Maybe a session with Tempest *is* just what I need—a familiar routine of Stoli to numb the demons and empty my mind enough for my libido to take over, or until oblivion claims me. With the alcohol as with life, I meticulously control the descent into numbness, making the shadows recede, if only for a while.

"She's got you pussy whipped, Jaden." The sneer in my mother's voice slices through my thoughts, a reminder of the standards I need to uphold. This thing with Rayne, it's clouding my judgment, challenging the very essence of my autonomy.

I feel a tension grip my jaw, a turmoil swirling within. Flashbacks of Rayne, vibrant and unfiltered, clash starkly with the facade I've upheld for what feels like eternity. It's a jarring reminder. I've laid my cards on the table with Rayne, never sugarcoating the reality of my views on love, commitment, and the walls I've built around my heart. My hands clench, not out of anger, but as an emblem of the resolutions I've made, the solitary path I've steadfastly walked. A deep breath steadies me, less about bracing for impact and more a reaffirmation of the autonomy I've prized above all. We're both free agents. It's time to remind me and my power about just that.

I glance towards the door, half expecting, half hoping

Rayne might burst in at any moment, an interruption I'd welcome. But the doorway remains empty. I nod in reluctant agreement to Tempest's proposition. "Alright, let's talk strategy. But only a drink." As I speak them, the reluctant words taste like defeat. Tempest's eyes light up, a predator sensing the weakening resolve of her prey. She moves closer, invading my personal space with a familiarity that once comforted but now feels intrusive.

Her hand finds its way to my shoulder, her touch igniting a familiar trail of warmth that once would have led me down the path of least resistance. "That's all I'm asking for, Jaden. A drink, a chat, nothing you haven't done before." Her breath is a mixture of temptation and challenge. Her closeness, once a beacon, now serves as a stark reminder of the crossroads at which I stand, the choice between the fleeting solace of old habits and the daunting, uncharted territory that Rayne represents.

I manage a stiff nod, the action more automatic than intentional. As Tempest smiles, satisfied with her victory, a part of me recoils, mourning the loss of the progress I thought I'd made. But I've made up my mind, and as we head towards the Amber Star hotel's bar, I steel myself for the evening ahead, a temporary escape from the turmoil that Rayne's presence has stirred within me.

The bar is quiet as staff get ready for the Happy Hour crowd. Tempest leads us to a dim corner set up with plush armchairs around a low table. Settling into one, she signals the server and orders two Stoli and two shots of tequila with a Sangria chaser. Irritation needles through me at her refusal to respect my boundaries, but I say nothing. Just down one of the drinks before settling back in my chair.

Tempest intersperses inconsequential aspects of our next mission with cutesy seductive behavior—a finger trailed up my arm here, a burst of cleavage in my face there as she leans forward to brush a nonexistent something from my cheek, but my thoughts are elsewhere as the hours drift by. With Rayne. Her laughter, her energy, her cute ass, the way she's turned my world upside down. I let more Stoli wash through me. Tempest's words fade into background noise, a dull hum compared to the vividness of my fantasies] about Rayne. I let one of them play through my mind until I can feel the softness of her warm flesh under my hands.

And then, as if summoned by my thoughts, I feel a surge of emotion through our bond—curiosity, happiness, a bright spark that momentarily dispels the darkness enveloping me. It's Rayne, her essence reaching out to me, a balm to the tumult inside. I look around the crowded bar, startled. I'm loaded and Tempest sits in my lap. Fuck. It happened again. Another blackout. *Fuck!*

That thought has barely formed when the mood shifts. A wave of jealousy, sharp and sudden, cuts through me. Rayne sees us. Sees me. Sees Tempest draping her arms around my neck and shoving her tongue down my throat.

The bond between Rayne and me flares with more jealousy, hurt, a sense of betrayal so profound it feels like a physical blow. And in that moment, I make a choice, one born of panic, of a desperate need to sever the connection that's become too intense, too real.

I shut down the bond, a deliberate act that leaves me feeling cold, empty. And as Tempest leans in, her lips seeking mine, I respond, not out of desire, but out of a misguided attempt to escape the intensity of what I feel for Rayne. It's a hollow act, a poor imitation of connection, and it leaves me feeling more alone than ever.

As I kiss Tempest, the confusion and conflict within me

grow. Part of me knows this is a mistake, a betrayal of the connection I share with Rayne, yet another part clings to the illusion of control it offers. It's a momentary escape, a way to prove I'm still my own person, not entirely consumed by my feelings for Rayne.

But even as I try to lose myself in the act, the hollowness of the connection strikes me with a jarring clarity. Mindless sex, the physical act devoid of emotional depth, leaves me feeling emptier than ever before. Rayne has irrevocably altered my perception, illustrating the profound difference between mere physicality and genuine connection. And here I am, ensnared with Tempest, engulfed in a desolation so profound it's suffocating.

The realization slices through me with the sharpness of a knife, a bitter acknowledgment of the emotional depths I've plunged with Rayne and the stark void I now find myself in with Tempest. It's a pivotal moment, a dark night of the soul where I'm forced to confront the harsh truth of my desires and fears. The clarity that emerges is piercing—I yearn for Rayne, not for the fleeting escape she offers, but for the tangible, visceral connection we share.

Yet, the bitter irony is that I've pushed her away, perhaps irrevocably so. The act of pushing Tempest away now seems an insurmountable task, a betrayal of the bond I've so carelessly fractured with Rayne. Each kiss, each touch, drives home the realization that I've never felt more alienated, more adrift.

As Tempest's seduction escalates, my participation becomes rote, an automaton going through the motions. The bar's laughter and chatter, once a backdrop to my escapades, now underscore my isolation, my divergence from the path I truly desire. Catching a glimpse of Rayne at the bar, surrounded yet alone, her defiant gaze locks with mine—a silent challenge, a mirror of the tumult raging within me.

Her eyes, a tempest of emotions, convey betrayal and defiance, a clear message that she won't be sidelined. The acknowledgment is a gut punch, a visceral acknowledgment of the schism I've caused. And as I mechanically select floggers, preparing for a scene devoid of desire, the facade crumbles. Tempest, once a symbol of escape, now epitomizes the chasm between me and Rayne—a chasm my actions have only widened.

It's Rayne. It's always been Rayne. Her laughter, her resilience, her unerring ability to peer through the masks I wear—she's the one I've been searching for, the one I need. Yet, in a moment of folly, I've betrayed her trust, and by extension, my own heart.

The realization is both a torment and a revelation. As I stand on the precipice of action, the clarity of my need for Rayne clashes with the immediacy of my mistake. The path forward is murky, laden with the debris of my actions. Yet, the undeniable truth remains—I want Rayne, for all she is, for the connection that transcends the superficial. In the act of betrayal, I've only illuminated the depth of my feelings for her, a paradox that leaves me reeling and uncertain of the way forward.

32
RAYNE

In the Manor's library's quiet, I curl up in an armchair that seems soaked in Jaden's presence. Maybe he's never been here, but it feels like he has. So, here I am, doing mental gymnastics over what to do next.

I replay that heart-ripping moment with Jaden, but deep down, I know I played myself. He was upfront about not doing love or commitment. His reputation and those overheard conversations had warned me. Yet, seeing him with someone else was like a punch to the gut, reigniting jealousy and betrayal.

Being away from him let me see things clearer. It wasn't just about him nearly choking me; it's how he made me feel overall. After bolting from that scene, I found strength I didn't know I had. As I lay there, this new power inside whispered, "Heal yourself." So, I did, tapping into something amazing that's part of me now.

I realized too late why Jaden flipped out—I'd startled him, breaking one of his cardinal rules. After calming down, I did some Googling and, yep, classic PTSD behavior. I had been setting off alarms left and right with him.

Fueled by my newfound knowledge and power, I went to make things right, only to slam into the harsh truth of where I stood with him. Him with that blonde on his lap crushed me. He'd said he was saving kisses for someone he loved, which clearly wasn't her, but it didn't matter. I felt invisible.

I had to shut him out, cut the bond right then. My first instinct was revenge—show him two can play this game. But even as I flirted with the idea, following him out with her made my decision. Our eyes locked, and I saw his pain before he hid it. I wanted to hurt him back, but I couldn't. I fled, wishing tears could wash away the pain.

Clutching the carved tablet from the coffee table in our suite, I called out for help and suddenly, I was in this mysterious house. The ghost, Nye, from those vivid dreams of mine, welcomed me, suggesting I make myself at home. So, here I am, diving into diaries, dodging reality, while this cool old dude, Raphael, keeps me fed.

After days lost in the sanctuary Nye and Raphael provided, immersing myself in the past through the diaries of strangers, I can't ignore the nagging feeling that Jaden's in trouble. Another wave of nausea hits, and I force myself to breathe through it. "He's in deep, and that witch Tempest is circling. You've gotta see him," Nye's voice breaks through my thoughts. I study her, my head and heart swimming with questions I can't focus on right now. She's right and I can't avoid the inevitable. There's some force in me that's pulling me to him, at least until I understand why he's trying so desperately to push me away.

With heavy reluctance, I return to our suite. The suite's tension is a sharp contrast to the library's quiet as I step through the portal. Jaden's on the floor, curled up and looking so lost and small, a complete mess. And Tempest is just . . . there, watching like she's at some weird show at the zoo. I ignore her, focusing on Jaden. The shock of his pain hits me hard, but I breathe through it, sitting down to face him and his demons head-on.

My heart does this weird flip-flop seeing him like this, and all I want is to be by his side, to try and fix whatever's tearing him up inside. I barely notice Tempest as I make my way to Jaden, feeling more determined with every step. As I get closer, I see just how much he's hurting, and it makes my resolve even stronger. I sit down in front of him, ready to face whatever comes my way.

I don't say anything at first, just focus on making our connection stronger, letting him feel that I'm here for him, no matter what. This whole superpower thing is still new to me, but figuring that out can wait. Right now, Jaden needs to know I'm all in, ready to listen and not judge. He has to feel that my heart's wide open for him.

As our eyes finally meet, the depth of his pain nearly overwhelms me, a vivid testament to the turmoil within. "You came," he whispers, his voice a mix of surprise and something akin to hope.

"I'm here." I let the weight of those words carrying more than just my physical presence. I yearn to reach out, to comfort through touch, but restraint holds me back. The air between us thickens with his silent struggle, and I can almost taste his remorse.

"What do you want from me?" When he finally manages to speak again, the words are strained, as if each one costs him.

What do I want? The question echoes within me, finding answers ready and waiting. "I want to know how you feel about me. Not as something transient for your bed, but as me, Rayne." My words hang in the air, heavy with the need for his honesty. I draw in a breath, shutting out Tempest's invasive energy, focusing solely on Jaden. "I want to understand us."

Silence stretches, a test of patience and nerve. Just as doubt creeps in, he speaks, "I can't define or even identify my feelings for you . . . or even for myself." His admission cuts deep, a raw, unguarded moment. "You're not a play-thing to me." His gaze lifts to mine, haunted yet sincere. "I thought . . . perhaps we were friends."

My next words catch in my throat, "But you kissed her. You said..." My heart hangs as I replay the betrayal I felt so keenly.

He hesitates, then, "I lied. Kissing . . . it's different when it's meaningless. With you, it can never be just that." His confession is a whisper, barely audible, followed by an even softer plea, one that might not have been meant for me but resonates all the same, *"Please come back."*

His silent plea hangs between us, a fragile bridge over the chasm of his turmoil. The bond pulses, a lifeline that vibrates with his pain and silent request for forgiveness, for another chance. And that's all it takes to soften my weak and wimpy heart where this man is concerned. The nasty little voice inside my head screams that I'm being a goddamned idiot by coming back to this man. But some-thing else even deeper and more forceful lets me know I'm doing the right thing.

I shift my focus to Tempest with a penetrating glare that makes her sit straight. "Do you need a ride some-where?" Not that I'm about to give her one but I need to get her the hell out of here. The wash of relief through our bond tells me I'm doing the right thing. Tempest gathers her bag and I walk her to the front door more to make sure she gets the hell out than to stretch my legs.

As I pointedly open the door and wait for her to slip into her fuck-me boots, she looks at me and says, "What on earth did he say that would make you come back to him?" She seems flabbergasted by my decision. I stifle the first words that want to burst free—none of your fucking business, and settle on the truth. "He was honest with me."

Shaking her head, she strolls out the door and I resist the urge to slam it after her.

Jaden hasn't moved and inch. The silence in the room feels charged, an electric current of unsaid words and unshed tears. I pour two drinks from the pitcher of Stoli on the sideboard, the clear liquid casting warm reflections in the dim light, and place one in front of him. His eyes, when he finally raises them to mine, hold a world of regret, a silent plea for understanding that goes beyond words. The bond between us thrums with a new intensity.

Sitting across from him, I take a deep breath, our eyes locked. "I'm here," I say simply, my voice steady despite the storm of emotions inside me. "But I'm not the same person who left this room. Nor are you." The truth of my words hangs heavy between us, a recognition of the pain we've both caused and suffered.

He nods, a gesture heavy with meaning. We sit in silence, the drinks untouched, as we communicate through the bond. It's a silent acknowledgment of the hurt, the betrayal, but also of the undeniable connection that refuses to be severed by anger or fear. My heart, though guarded behind a newly erected barrier, still beats for this man. But I'm cautious now, aware of the fragility of what we're trying to rebuild.

"You understand, don't you?" I telepathically send the question, not needing to voice it aloud. *"That I can't just forget what happened. That we can't go back to how things were."*

His response is a slow exhale, a resignation mixed with hope. *"I know. And I don't expect you to. But I also can't imagine moving forward without you in my life, in some way."* Raw pain slices through every word as he forces them through the bond.

The honesty in his admission, the raw vulnerability, shifts something within me. The understanding that we can't erase what's happened hits me hard, but we still have a shot at figuring things out from here. We don't have all the answers about this crazy pull between us, but one thing's for sure—we're not ready to walk away from whatever this is.

"Friends," I finally say, the word feeling both like a concession and a promise. "With an understanding." The drink in my hand suddenly seems more appealing, a tangible symbol of the tentative truce we're forging and I stare at it as if it's a lifeline as I choke out the next words. "And maybe a few benefits." Because suddenly I know with absolute certainty that sex will be the only way to pull Jaden from the bowels of the cave he's buried himself in.

He reaches for his glass, a silent toast to our new understanding. Our eyes meet over the rim of our glasses, and in that gaze, I see a glimmer of the man I'm falling for. The man I'm willing to stand beside, even if it means keeping my heart shielded behind armor.

As we drink, the room feels less like a battlefield and more like a sanctuary, a place where two wounded souls can find solace in the company of one another. The path forward is uncertain, fraught with potential pain and betrayal, but for the first time, I feel equipped to navigate it. Not alone, but together, as friends who share a bond deeper than mere attraction. A bond that, despite everything, offers a glimmer of hope for something more.

33
JADEN

The solarium at Harmony Hills is bathed in a gentle sunlight, casting a warm glow over everything it touches, including Rayne. She's there with Summer, the two of them lost in a world of music and shared silence. I'm on the outskirts, watching, waiting for Sasha's intake process to wrap up. It's a moment of quiet before the storm, a brief respite that allows me to confront the turmoil swirling within me.

Seeing Sasha today, for the first time since the attack, feels like stepping into a ring I've been avoiding, one where the opponent is my own guilt and remorse. Despite Rayne's logical arguments—that we fight against the darkness, and risk is part of our calling—my heart refuses to listen. It's burdened with the weight of what-ifs, haunted by the thought that if only my focus hadn't been so divided, I might have prevented Sasha's suffering. And though she's never voiced it, my distraction, my preoccupation with Rayne, almost cost Sasha her life.

Now, Sasha's journey, one she's been thrust into without choice, gnaws at me. The path she's on, the gender confirmation surgery that was more a necessity than a choice, strikes a chord deep within. We've never delved into the depths of such personal matters, but I've always known, always been aware of her contemplation of this step. The forced acceleration of her decision, the invasive transformation she's had to undergo, it's a pain I can only imagine, and it bites and bites hard. I have no idea how to be there for her, support her. Something that comes naturally to Rayne.

My gaze drifts back to her. There she is, a vision of comfort and support, her presence a stark contrast to the coldness of the world. My gaze lingers on her, and I'm struck by a realization that shakes me to my core. My desire for her, it's different—it's more potent, more consuming than anything I've felt since that defining event that shattered my world. It's as if she's become the center of my universe, the pivot on which my desires turn. Each day with her I need less time to retreat into the recesses of my mind, to images and fantasies, to find release. Rayne, in her very essence, has become my solace, my escape from the shadows that haunt me.

In the solarium's warm light, unease wraps around me like a shroud. Tonight, more than ever, I'm drawn to Rayne, compelled by a need to sift through the chaos that's been our lives of late. Observing her, I'm struck by the ephemeral grace that dances around her as she works her magic on Summer. It's like watching fairy dust in motion, a visible sign of her growing powers that she's only beginning to master.

Music is a catalyst for her as it is for me, connection to whatever mystical force she channels . . . And to me. This dual-edged gift, though, has its toll. Each session leaves her diminished, drained of the vibrancy that so defines her.

Usually, I welcome the quiet that follows, a selfish respite from the emotional tempest our visits to Harmony Hills stir within me. The stories of pain and survival we encounter here wage war on my senses, a relentless siege that leaves me craving silence and solitude to regroup.

But now, Rayne's the eye of my storm, the center of a chaos I've let swirl too long. I need that voice.

After the shitshow with Tempest and witnessing Rayne's fling with Nick, I'm staggered by the depth of my fuck-up. Our confrontation, raw and searing, left no illusions between us. Rayne had no problem leaning into the discomfort of taking me on no matter how fucking intimidating. One of the very best things about her is that she holds nothing in, needs to purge and clear the air. It's a breath of fresh air and I always know where I stand with her. Her declaration, that we're merely friends with benefits free to pursue others, felt like a gut punch. Her words, sharp and final, echoed with a strength I'd forced her to muster. Behind her armor, I'd sensed her pain, a sharp sting across our bond before she slammed it shut.

"You sound as if you're saying you're going to fuck someone just to get even. Well, that's just juvenile." I'd spat the words out, desperate and defensive.

Rayne's retort was a slap, her defiance clear. "Oh, I won't fuck him out of revenge for you, you asshole. I'll fuck him because you just opened the door for me to see just how cute he is and how much better he treats me. He likes me and has absolutely no problem showing it." Her fire, her unyielding spirit, was and is both infuriating and intoxicating.

Fuck, she's right. In my quest to keep her at arm's length, to maintain this facade of detachment, I've only succeeded in pushing her towards what I fear most—her finding someone who can give her what I convinced myself I couldn't. Or wouldn't.

As I watch her, a resolve solidifies within me. A resolve to face the fears that have kept me caged, to confront the feelings I've denied for too long. Rayne isn't just someone I can push away with harsh words or cowardly actions. She's become the linchpin of my existence, the challenge and the comfort I didn't know I needed.

Stripping away the layers of defense around my heart feels like standing on the edge of a precipice, the drop below both terrifying and inevitable. As I watch Rayne, her generosity of spirit shining as she gives herself over to the healing, I'm confronted with a truth I can no longer ignore. The thought of a life without her, without the light she infuses into my darkest corners, is more frightening than any demon I've faced. Imagining my existence, confined within the shadows of my own making, without Rayne's spark to guide me, is a future too bleak to contemplate.

Calling myself an idiot doesn't begin to cover it. Instead of owning up to my mistakes, of letting her believe I sought comfort in another's arms, I pushed her towards someone else in a moment of pique. The truth is, I hadn't been with Tempest, not really. No amount of alcohol could dull the sharp sting of jealousy that lanced through me when Rayne saw us together. And the realization hits hard—I didn't want Tempest. Not then, not ever. Especially not when Rayne has shown me what being with someone could truly feel like.

This realization tears at me, a painful acknowledgment of my own failings. Yet, it's also the jolt I needed, a sign that it's time for change. I can't keep fleeing from what I feel for Rayne, from the intimacy that terrifies yet calls to me. I'm the architect of the barriers between us, barriers that seem to be nudging her further away with each passing day.

Her willingness, her openness with me, it's something I've begun to rely on more than I care to admit. I suspect our intimacy does more than just satisfy a physical need—it seems to rejuvenate her, to bolster her abilities. And it does the same for me, binding our powers together, granting us a strength that's as intoxicating as it is bewildering. Or maybe, I've just found a convenient excuse to keep her close, to claim that I bring something of value to this... whatever it is between us.

Closing my eyes, I take a moment and bring Rayne's lithe body to mind. Her warmth seeps into me when our bodies meld together, her small curves fitting perfectly against my hard lines. I'm an average size, but Rayne's insistence that I'm "huge" speaks to my sagging ego and delights my power. Our breaths mingle, hot and heavy, when we fuck, the mingling of our lust tangible in the air. It's a dance, one of passion and power, as we explore each other without reservation or constraint.

Her responsiveness is like a drug, addicting and all-consuming, blurring the boundary between where she ends and I begin. The way her body arches into me, her soft moans a symphony to my ears, it's a balm to my soul, blotting out the horror of my past. She possesses an uncanny ability to put aside her feelings no matter how pissed at me she may be, allowing our bodies to speak the language only they understand.

Then there's the way she scratches my arm, a simple gesture she offers tirelessly, understanding my needs without judgment or disdain. Her touch, light yet electric, sends a warmth coursing through me, igniting a desire that's become synonymous with her presence. This connection, this silent exchange of need and fulfillment, has become our unspoken language.

Sasha's entrance, guided by a young attendant whose patience seems as boundless as her kindness, snaps me back to the present. Sasha's essence, once a beacon of strength and defiance, now flickers softly, dimmed but not extinguished. She navigates the room with a deliberate, measured grace, her attire—a testament to her recent journey—loose and forgiving, yet another marker of the battles fought and still to face.

Once Sasha is comfortably settled, her characteristic grumbling met with an attendant's practiced ease, she seeks me out with a gaze that cuts through the residual awkwardness of our prolonged separation. "Did you get him? Rayne says you did."

The weight of her question, the things left unsaid between us, hangs heavy in the air. There's an apology in my silence, a regret for the distance my own turmoil has imposed. "That poison's thoroughly purged." My words are more a promise to myself than to her. "As for not visiting..." The sentence trails off, unfinished, but loaded with the weight of unsaid apologies and explanations.

Sasha's response, a simple acknowledgment in her glacial blue eyes, bridges the gap my words cannot fill. "Yeah, I know," she says, an understanding that transcends our spoken language.

In the quiet that follows, a silent agreement passes between us, a mutual recognition of the new ground we're navigating. Sasha breaks the silence, her voice rough with emotion as she touches the tender scar along her neck. "You know, I wouldn't have made it without her."

Her admission, raw and unguarded, leaves me grappling for a response. "How so?"

"I wanted to die," she confesses, her gaze drifting to where Rayne continues her work beyond the glass. "She showed me a future without me in it, and suddenly, I found a reason to fight."

As Sasha's focus shifts back to me, there's a hesitance before she shares something unexpected, "You know, she's stepped in since I've been out of commission."

"Stepped in how?" My curiosity piqued, I probe further. Sasha has always been the keystone of our operations, her absence a void I've been ignoring. Anything to do with money stresses me right out.

"She wanted to know how she could help me focus on healing, so she took the reins of your empire. Just like that."

I can't hide my skepticism. "She's what, twenty-five? And a psychology major, not a business mogul. What's left of my empire?"

Her laugh is sharp, a clear rebuke to my doubts. "You'd be surprised. She's not just kept it afloat; she's expanded it. Her approach to problem-solving, to turning chaos into strategy, is something to watch, Jay. And she's doing it all behind the scenes, content to let me take the credit."

I'm momentarily speechless, my brain scrambling to align this revelation with the image of Rayne I hold. "Huh," is all I manage, the implications swirling in my mind.

Sasha leans forward, her tone serious, "Think about what she means to you, buddy, before you push her away for good."

I bristle, ready to defend myself, but she cuts me off, "Just think about it. And Jaden, it's time she met Gloria. Isn't one of her command-performance parties coming up?" The mere mention of my mother's name sends a chill down my spine. The hurricane that is my mother will chew Rayne up and spit her out under the guise of the perfect hostess and belittle me at every opportunity in the process.

The thought of exposing Rayne to that tempest, to see if she could weather it, terrifies and exhilarates me. If Rayne could stand tall against my mother's onslaught, then maybe, just maybe, there's a sliver of hope for something real between us. But the prospect feels like wishing for a miracle in a world where I've long since stopped believing in them.

34
RAYNE

Hovering in the chopper's hum back to Toronto, exhaustion wrestles with the buzz in my brain. Normally, it's Jaden I turn to for bouncing ideas—he's got this way of cutting through bullshit that I just can't. But, hell, even bone-tired and with our connection dialed down, his essence is a constant echo in my thoughts. His presence, it's like an anchor, especially when I'm tapping into my newfound healing magic. And yeah, I manage to shove aside this maddening pull toward him when the magic demands my all. Still, he's there, in every quiet moment.

Out the window, Ontario sweeps by in a green rush, and I'm thinking how this beats being jammed in traffic on highway 401. Not that I'd mind any jam with Jaden. Lately, we've slipped into this easy rhythm, me steering our daylight hours. The PE team's flexible—rescue ops call, we're there; otherwise, we chart our own course. My 'training' has been this wild ride of learning and adapting, trying not to trip over my own feet.

Although Jaden isn't at my side twenty-four-seven, he's always nearby. And any time I left the secure hotel building, he was glued to my side. I only grumbled a little, but Razor, our team lead and law enforcement guy, had made it quite clear that the bad guys are still looking for me. I love the job, and it comes easy for me. It didn't hurt that Razor had asked me to treat the work as a startup and to create my own job description. Sweet!

I'd put myself through university doing contract work with small startup businesses because I'm gifted at putting together systems. With some of them, I simply cleaned up a mess, put things in order, and left them to it. I loved startup work, and putting a system in place had been a no-brainer with these guys because they simply reacted to each rescue mission without a lot of forethought or planning. They'd like what I'd suggested, and Razor kept "picking my brain," and before long, I was finding the flaws in their rather rough plans and finding ways around them. Oh, we argued and debated, but nine times out of ten, we went with my plans. The last two rescues had gone off without a hitch. More and more, Jaden chimed in during our brainstorming sessions, showing an enthusiasm and energy that made me think of the boy he must have been.

I've often questioned my priorities, wondering if there's something wrong with me. Despite my ability to adapt easily, my focus should be on establishing a new life for Summer and me, not pining for an emotionally unavailable man who might never offer the love I yearn for. Yet, despite the sensible counsel from my rational mind, my heart rebels, continually drawn into Jaden's tumultuous orbit.

My anger towards Jaden reached its limit after he fucked Tempest, tempting me to seek revenge by flirting with Nick, the very cute bartender who claims to love me. His declarations might be absolute crap, but I can't deny the boost it gives my ego. Our drunken nights led to a lot of making out, all spurred by my spiteful urge to show Jaden just how it feels. However, Jaden's lack of reaction to my hookups with Nick only intensified my irritation. Far from being jealous, he probed into how I felt during those moments with Nick, analyzing every single detail with unnerving precision.

"Listen to his actions, not his words." Bob's advice echoes as a constant mantra in my mind. Time and again, whenever I spent time with Nick, he chose those nights to crawl into my bed, seeking reassurance. Was it to confirm my affection for him? His actions make me want to tear my hair out.

I can't keep letting my libido overrule my brain. According to Nick, my feelings for Jaden boil down to mere lust, a lust that isn't reciprocated. I had confided in Nick, and Jaden had exploded with anger when I mentioned it, infuriated by the breach of privacy.

He jabbed his finger into my chest with enough force to leave a mark, issuing his ultimatum. "Do not ever talk about me again, or—"

Surprise ripples through our bond, likely at how quickly I confronted him, showing we both had our triggers. "Don't you dare, Jaden. Sometimes I need someone to talk to, and it's clear you're not available for that. He's part of my life now, and by extension, so are you. I can't help that you're part of my story at the moment." I put extra bite into the last three words.

"Well, you'll stop including me in your stories to Nick." He'd towered over me, trying to intimidate me as he punctuated his demand with pointed jabs in my direction.

"No, I will not," I shot back with equal intensity until he stepped back, inhaling sharply as if to launch another verbal assault. But I wouldn't tolerate any more of his crap.

"Oh no, you don't. You said you wanted someone strong, someone who stands by their principles. Well, this is me being strong. You can't expect me not to talk to anyone. That's how I process. It's not fair." Then, we retreated to our metaphorical corners of the ring, each nursing our grievances.

We'd avoided each other for the rest of the day, our tempers smoldering in subdued exchanges through our bond. I let loose with my extensive repertoire of curses at him, and though perhaps it was just my imagination, I could swear he parried each jab with his usual, "Yeah, but I'm good at it." The audacity. Yet, beneath the surface anger, I find myself craving his intellect and my body yearning for his presence. Late into the night, he joined me in bed. My tension hung between us, but he simply rested his hand on my thigh and patiently waited. The atmosphere was charged, as if the heavy silence between us could have been cleaved with one of Jaden's ethereal daggers, our thoughts clashing silently. But as much as my mind resisted, my body gradually succumbed to the warmth of his touch. Eventually, I broke the silence, murmuring into the night, "I'm pissed at you, you know."

"I know," was his simple acknowledgment, his hand a constant weight on my leg, his body heat spreading through me like a mudslide—relentless, engulfing, and utterly consuming. Some switch in my head goes off with this man, and my body softens for him despite my resolve. My damned traitorous body seems to know what my mind won't admit. Every damned time I surrender to the inevitable and spread my legs for him.

Jaden dictates the evenings after six o'clock . . . at least when he's mentally present. When he retreats into his cave, I'm essentially free to do as I please, provided I stay within the secure confines of our facility. Initially, this meant I was left to my own devices for five or six nights a week . . . unless Jaden found himself in one of his more amorous moods. With him, sex is an all-or-nothing affair. Once he decides on intimacy, it becomes an intense series of encounters that last until he exhausts his desire. Afterwards, he often withdraws, but increasingly, he chooses to stay close, content to simply watch movies or listen to music with me. Nick might think I'm crazy, but I can't help feeling that Jaden is my 'Neo,' worth every moment of waiting.

Today, though, there's a new tension in Jaden, a swirl of emotions I can't quite pinpoint flowing through our bond. I'm itching to probe, to unearth whatever he's holding back, but with Jaden, patience is key; he opens up in his own time.

"Come on. Let's grab a bite." He abruptly leads me to a nearby café. We place our usual orders—his boring double-double and a caramel latte for me.

"My mother's throwing a party. Come with me?" His request is casual, his gaze averted, but an undercurrent of urgency vibrates through our connection, betraying a deep-seated need.

I hold off on responding until he fixes me with that imperious look I've grown accustomed to, the one he thinks will spur me into action. "Sure." I buy time drawing out the word while I try to figure out what the hell is behind his invitation. There's clearly more at play here, and I'm not in the frame of mind to navigate another of his crises. His escapes from reality can be downright terrifying, and chasing after him, regardless of my energy levels, is a given. But why do I get the feeling this isn't just any ordinary party?

He clears his throat and taps the edge of his coffee cup, avoiding my gaze. After a moment, he looks up. "My mom . . . she's intrusive and interfering. I'd rather keep her out of my business." He clears his throat again. "She can be very critical." He shudders, then seems to steel himself, his posture straightening as if bracing for what's next. "But nothing she says will change how I feel about you." But there's a layer of self-loathing beneath those words that scares me.

That's the closest he's ever come to admitting he feels anything at all for me. I mull over his curious words and an involuntary laugh escapes me. "Don't worry about me, CC. I've faced criticism all my life. I can handle your mom."

A blend of relief and desire flickers across his face. Jaden's fingers brush my forearm gently, signaling his easing tension, though our bond hints at more to come. I wait patiently, resisting the urge to either stare too deeply or make a move that might disrupt the fragile peace between us.

Suddenly, Jaden shatters the silence with an unexpected revelation. "I didn't fuck her, you know." His words jolt me from my thoughts, leaving me speechless. As the reality of his words settles, my reaction must resemble a fish gasping for air. Although I could pretend ignorance about who he's referring to, a triumphant inner voice—my power, perhaps—silently cheers, "I knew it." Yet, I can't get the image of Tempest's tongue down his throat out of my mind. . .

I'm not ready to let it slide. "But you were close, you almost did."

He gives a single, grave nod, leaving a thread of tension —or is it worry?—trickling through our bond. What is he leading up to? Time stretches, dragging moments into an eternity as I try to mask my growing impatience with a few too many glasses of wine. My thoughts meander through society's expectations, questioning whether Jaden can fulfill my deepest longing: to be loved and cherished. Despite his protests, I remain hopeful, albeit slightly inebriated. That warrants another glass.

All the while, Jaden seems lost in his own world, fixated on tracing patterns along my forearm until he finally meets my gaze. "And what about you with Nick? Did you fuck him?"

The wine emboldens me. "I thought it didn't matter to you?"

"It doesn't. I'm just curious." He's just a little too casual.

The urge to make him squirm is strong, but my resolve falters under his gaze, and honesty pours out. Perhaps I'm fated to follow in my mother's footsteps, drawn to a man destined to break my heart, despite his undeniable allure. I'm puzzled by his unease; he insists he's never been the jealous type. *"Listen to his actions,"* echoes in my mind.

So, mirroring his earlier gesture, I nod. Jaden's raised eyebrow demands more. After another sip of wine for courage, I say, "No, but we almost did."

He remains silent, leaving me braced for another interrogation. But instead, he surprises me, cutting to the core of my fears.

"I want you. Tonight." His words hang in the air, heavy with anticipation.

I nod, afraid that speaking might break the spell between us.

"You know you can say no, right?" His eyes search mine for an answer, a silent question about desire and consent. Our mate bond is probably screaming my answer back at him—I'm terrible at hiding my feelings, especially now, with alcohol loosening my inhibitions. A part of me wants to tease him—maybe 'no' should be my safe word? But I know Jaden doesn't joke about sex, so I bite my tongue and nod dutifully, attributing my newfound self-control to either my emerging powers or the extensive self-reflection I've been doing.

His desire hits me like a wave as he looks at me, the intensity in his gaze shifting from my skin to my eyes. The moment our server removes the dishes, Jaden's attention is entirely on me.

"So, what's this I hear about you asking Nick to flog you?" His question catches me off guard, wine nearly going down the wrong pipe. How did he find out?

"If anyone's going to flog you, it will be me. Seems like a good time to start." Without waiting for my response, he pulls me to my feet, his determination clear. We head for the door, his intent unmistakable.

Yes, please, sir.

35
JADEN

The dim light of the playroom washes over the lavish furnishings, casting an aura of gothic elegance that shrouds everything in a veil of mystery. The deep purple hues of the Victorian-style sofa beckon with the promise of opulent comfort, while the haunting relief of the barren tree in the oversized frame watches over the room with a solitary bird as its silent sentinel. My heart pounds in rhythm with the subtle flicker of the lantern-style wall sconces, as I arrange the floggers on the small round table beside the sofa. Each tool is a silent promise of the sensations I intend to draw from Rayne's skin, a cascade of experiences heightened by the luxurious and dramatic setting that envelops us.

I'm finally going to give Rayne what she wants, what she's been begging for. As I lay out each instrument, a wave of anxiety washes over me. The theories and techniques are etched in my mind, the product of intense study, but self-doubt whispers, questioning whether I'm in over my head. Rayne's perception of me is one of expertise, a master in the realm of control, yet I've barely dipped my toes into these waters. I've been an observer, a shadow at the periphery of countless flogging sessions, and I've absorbed the lessons of the Masquerade's Master training program. Yet my hands-on experience is scant. At the anticipation of this uncharted journey, my power stirs with a surge of eager anticipation, ready to make the leap from theory to thrilling reality.

When I hear her soft footsteps, my panic flares. I pause, my hand hovering over a leather flogger, and glance up to find Rayne in the doorway, a vision of feminine grace. She's wearing an asymmetrical black dress with a zipper running diagonally down the front from neckline to hem. Her eyes glow with eagerness, her lips curling into a shy smile, and a spike of fear lances through me. I want to give her a performance worthy of her, show the dance between pleasure and pain executed with flawless skill. If I falter, the illusion shatters, my inadequacy laid bare. I can't fail her. I won't.

Summoning my control, I tamp down the nerves and greet her with a steady gaze. "Are you ready?" My voice betrays none of the turmoil within. She nods, approaching with slow, deliberate steps until she stands before me. I reach out, tracing the line of her jaw with a knuckle. "Safe words?"

"Green for go, yellow to slow down the action, red to stop." Her breath hesitates as I slide my hand into her hair and tighten my grip.

"Good." The praise is as much for myself as it is for her. I can do this. I will.

Tonight, I prove I'm the master she believes me to be.

My heart thunders in my chest, a raging storm contained behind a veil of calm. With a slow exhale, I steady my nerves and draw upon the power coiled inside, letting it seep into my limbs. No room for doubt, no space for fear. I am in control.

I meet her gaze, my own simmering with purpose. "On your knees."

The game begins.

She sinks to her knees, head bowed in submission. I circle her, boots clicking on the polished hardwood floor, examining my prize. Mine to shape. Mine to break. A surge of possessiveness rises within, dark and primal, silenced only by the rapid beat of my heart.

I crouch before her, tilting her chin up with my fingers. 'Look at me, little dragon.' Despite her attempts to control her breath, her chest rises and falls rapidly as her gaze locks onto mine, eyes dark with longing, lips parted in anticipation. My chest tightens at the sight, a blend of anticipation and anxiety. I want nothing more than to give her everything she craves, to be the man she sees when she looks at me with such raw need.

With a slow breath, I temper the riot of emotion and slip into the role I was born to play. My fingers curl at my side, power crackling over my knuckles, as I peer down at her. "Who do you belong to?"

"You," she breathes. "I belong to you."

A fierce surge of possessiveness rises in my chest at her words. Mine. She could be mine, now and always, bound to me in body and soul. I fight the urge to claim her, to lose myself in the heady ecstasy of taking what is mine. Not yet. We have only just begun.

"Stand up and undress for me. Slowly." My voice emerges as a low growl, rough with desire and the effort of restraint.

She rises in a fluid motion, fingers playing with the zipper running down her dress. Inch by inch, she bares herself to me, revealing her gorgeous tawny skin and supple curves. I watch, motionless and silent, as her dress pools at her feet, desire warring with the need to maintain control. As I instructed, she's wearing nothing underneath.

When at last she stands bare before me, I close the distance between us in two swift strides. My hand finds her throat, tilting her head to the side to expose the vulnerable line of her neck. She shivers under my touch but remains still, trusting in my lead.

"You are exquisite," I whisper against her ear. *"And you are mine."* I want to kiss her, seal my claim with a bruising kiss but my fear holds me back. Instead, I pull back to admire her once more. Her chest rises and falls rapidly, flushed skin and parted lips betraying her arousal.

Mine.

The word echoes through my mind, a mantra I cling to as I grapple for control. I want nothing more than to lose myself in her, to drown in sweet surrender, but I can't afford such weakness. Not now, when she needs my strength and composure. I must be the anchor to tether her to this world, the shelter in which she can take refuge.

"On your knees," I command, my voice steady despite the riot going on inside me.

She obeys without hesitation, gaze locked on mine as she sinks gracefully to her knees. Trust. It resonates between us, a silent promise that steadies my resolve. I can do this. For her, I can do anything.

With slow, deliberate movements, I remove my shirt, watching her eyes widen in appreciation. Her tongue darts out to wet her lips, and a spark of heat ignites low in my abdomen. Soon, I tell myself. Patience.

I step closer, tilting her chin up to meet my gaze. "What is your color?"

"Green, Sir. So green." Her smile is radiant transforming her beautiful face, all traces of doubt banished from her expression. Those four words ground me.

Reassured, I card my fingers through her short hair, fisting strands to pull her head back. A gasp escapes her, morphing into a soft moan as I place open-mouthed kisses along the column of her throat. Her pulse flutters rapidly under my lips, a staccato beat that matches my own.

"Please," she whispers, tilting her head to grant further access. "Please, Jade…"

"Who?" A low growl rumbles in my chest at the plea. Not yet. We have only just begun. Tonight, I will lay claim to every inch of her, draw from her a symphony of sounds to echo the melody within me. And when at last I grant release, she will know to whom she belongs.

"Please sir."

The dim light in the playroom casts elongated shadows on the walls, giving life to an eerie, yet seductive atmosphere. As I arrange the floggers by size and material, the dark, ornate furnishings surrounding me seem to whisper promises of uncharted pleasure. My fingers brush over the suede and leather, each tool a promise of the sensations I plan to draw from Rayne's skin.

I start with a light touch, a caress that's as much a test for myself as it is for her. The first stroke lands delicately on her skin, and she lets out a faint sigh. The second follows, a little firmer, and her body shifts slightly, leaning into the sensation. A thrill of excitement courses through me at her responsiveness; this early in the session, her reaction is to sensation rather than pain, a discovery that sends an even deeper thrill through me. The rhythm builds, each stroke growing more assured, feeding off her reactions.

By the tenth stroke, I've honed in on her desires, reading

the subtle cues of her body as if it were a map unfolded before me. I pause to look into her eyes, asking softly, 'Where are we at?' Her full lips part, and she responds with a breathless 'Green.' Her eagerness, her trust, and her responsiveness ignite a wave of desire within me, making me hard and fueling my resolve to explore this uncharted territory together.

My heart races as we proceed, our connection deepening with each stroke of the flogger, with every gasp and moan that escapes her lips. Through our bond, a surge of admiration and vulnerability washes over me, her silent testament to the strength she perceives in me, speaking volumes in a way words never could. As we navigate this new world together, my confidence swells, bolstered by the bond we share and the trust that binds us. What Rayne needs from me isn't about achieving perfection or living up to any ideal; it's about the journey we're undertaking together, discovering the secrets of our desires hand in hand.

The room transforms into a symphony of sensations, with candlelight casting flickering shadows against the haunting artwork on the walls, our breaths syncing to the rhythm Rayne craves. My internal monologue falls silent, giving way to the symphony unfolding between us.

"Ah . . . Jaden." Rayne moans, her voice a tender melody of surrender that encourages me to delve deeper into this uncharted territory. The arch of her back speaks volumes, her muscles tensing and relaxing in tandem with each precise strike of the flogger. She's a canvas, and I'm the artist painting our desires with each expertly landed stroke.

Rayne lets out a deep moan as she thrusts her reddening ass at me. Her juices run down her inner thighs as she spits out one guttural word, "More." That word soothes my insecurities and stokes the fire within me. Her fingers grip the velvet fabric of the chaise lounge, signaling the intensity of her pleasure. Every neuron in my body thrums as my power surges through our mate bond. Something indescribable happens: my power meets Rayne's, using our sex to say the things neither one of us can—"*I want you. I need you. Just you. For you.*" As I watch her body respond to my touch, my power surges, humming with pleasure that mirrors the crescendo of our experience. My control, a gift I've long harbored, seems to work in perfect harmony with the energy we share in this intimate space.

"Jaden, please... More." Rayne's plea reaches me, her gaze locked with mine, radiating trust and a raw hunger. My heart expands, touched by the depth of her surrender. This moment feels like a breakthrough, a rare gift I'm compelled to cherish.

"Are you sure?" My voice is thick with a mix of concern and yearning as I pause for her consent. "Remember, yellow or red if it becomes too much."

"Green." Her voice is solid, unwavering, sparking something in me that steadies my nerves. In this instant, all doubts evaporate, replaced by an overwhelming clarity. I enter a realm of pure focus, known to some as Dom space, where sensation intensifies and my consciousness shifts. It's as though I step from the shadows of my own baggage into the radiant warmth of Rayne's light, fully present and powerfully connected to the moment.

I switch floggers and watch in awe as my little dragon succumbs to deep subspace, her euphoric state echoing through our bond. I intensify the rhythm of my strokes, each one affirming our deep connection. The room resonates with the sound of leather against skin, Rayne's cries of pure pleasure cutting through the silence. In these moments, there's nothing but the two of us, lost in our own world, with the night around us fading into oblivion. Just as a flicker of concern grazes my mind, I pause to gently explore her warmth, her skin a canvas of our night. Her response is a deep, primal groan, and our powers converse silently, a primal plea in the space between us. *"Take me,"* her essence calls out. Carefully setting aside the flogger, I shed my own barriers along with my clothes, savoring the anticipation.

"What did you say, little dragon?" My power prepares to leap, ready for whatever comes next.

And there she lies, spread out, legs wide, dripping wet and all for me. I need to be in her. Now. Spreading her hot ass cheeks, I drive into her, meeting no resistance. I moan and almost lose my shit as her warm heat envelopes me. I thrust into her again, harder, deeper, setting something free within me. Our bond keeps me tethered to the present, to her, to this moment. *"Mine."* The word echoes through our connection and she answers in kind.

"Mine."

There is no sound but our ragged breathing, the slap of skin, her loud cries that are music to my ears. I drive into her relentlessly, bent over the chaise, my fingers biting into her hips. Taking a fistful of short curls in one hand, I grab and pull, hard. Her answering groan resonates deeply, a symphony to the essence of my power.

My power strains against its bonds, clawing to break free, to claim her as only it can. I hold it back through sheer force of will, giving her only what she can handle, what will bring her pleasure laced with a hint of pain.

She leans into me, craving more, every part of her responding to my thoughts, to the slightest changes in my mood and what I want next. I'm amazed at how perfectly we fit together, body and soul. It's as if I become one with her, part of her, no longer able to tell where I stop and she begins. Her deep moans draw out sounds from me that have long been buried in silence.

I pound into her, harder, deeper, the cords in my neck standing out as I push back the orgasm tightening my balls. She gasps, trembling, so close, and through our connection I feel the first sparks of her release.

Mine. My power rears up, snarling inside my mind, and at last I let go.

The orgasm hits us both like a bolt from the blue, sharp and hot, searing away all thought, all boundaries, all sense of self. There is only sensation, power, connection, as our individual selves dissolve into the whole.

In that moment, something ignites between us, a flame to light our way through the dark. And I am free.

36
RAYNE

Two weeks later, we're en route to Jaden's mom's party in Smalltown, Ontario, immersed in the sounds of my latest playlist while Jaden skillfully navigates the traffic. He had mentioned the town's name, but to me, all these rural places start to blur together. I sigh, glancing at the folder on my lap. We have a couple of hours' drive ahead, and I know I should be productive. Yet, my thoughts are preoccupied with Jaden, trying to piece together the final part of the puzzle that's been bothering me for two weeks. I've been eager to question him about his mother, careful not to provoke him, cherishing the fragile sensation of belonging to him. It seems as if our recent intimate experience unlocked something in him, allowing a brief period where our mate bond felt liberatingly free. I had dared to hope he might finally verbalize his feelings for me, not during our sex but in sober daylight. Though the bond shows me his desire and need, hearing it from him directly matters to me . . . a lot. Yet, I recognize my insecurity, or perhaps it's Jaden's voice echoing in my mind, fueling my doubts with fragments of our conversations.

"Why do you like living with me?"

"I'm here, isn't that enough?"

I long for him to affirm his feelings outside the influence of liquor or desire. But as Jaden points out, I can't compel someone's affection.

"Scratch my arm," Jaden requests, his tone edged, as he extends his forearm across the console, signaling his need for physical connection yet also a measure of privacy. Instinctively, I place my hand on his arm, offering a surge of my healing energy before starting to rake my nails over a small section of his forearm. He finds comfort in this numbness that results, though it drove me nearly mad when he tried it on me.

Our connection is profoundly in sync, yet there are aspects of Jaden I might never fully grasp. I've learned to curb my curiosity when my insistent questions start to irritate him, a reminder that not all questions about human behavior are welcome or easily answered. My studies in psychology, initially a quest to understand myself, have become a broader exploration of what drives individuals like ES to inflict harm on their own kids. While my building bank of knowledge has helped me identify some of Jaden's issues, there's a hell of a lot more to learn.

So, I scratch, allowing my thoughts to drift as I sing along to a new song that's quickly become a favorite. Song lyrics often resonate with me, clarifying confusions, some more so than others. This particular track, "Hearts Not Here" by the Red Dirt Skinners, sheds light on Jaden in a way that's uncannily accurate. While the song's narrative of a woman suffering from dementia diverges in detail, the theme of emotional unavailability mirrors Jaden perfectly, as if the song were a suit tailored just for him—a look he'd undoubtedly pull off with ease. I begin to belt out the lyrics, finding the song's register and harmonies a perfect fit for my voice.

> *By the time that I had met you, you had one foot*
>   *out the door.*
> *This world just didn't captivate your passion*
>   *anymore.*
> *At times I caught a glimpse of who I heard you*
>   *used to be.*
> *But now I see your empty stare helplessly*
>   *through me.*
> *Your heart's not here, your spirits gone but your*
>   *body carries on.*
> *It's not quite clear what went wrong, but your*
>   *body carries on.*

I'm deep into the second chorus when Jaden abruptly changes the song. "Hey, I was into that."

"Yeah, well, I'm not." His determination mixes with a hint of frustration through our bond. He exhales deeply. "Listen, there's something important you need to know before we get there."

His sudden urgency halts the retort on the tip of my tongue, his tone signaling more than just a dislike for the song. It reminds me of the careful dance we've perfected over time, avoiding steps that tread too close to his shadows. I'm learning to read the silent signals he sends, the ones that scream louder than his words ever could.

As I maintain the gentle scratch on his arm, a gesture that's become our unspoken language of comfort, an insistent voice inside, perhaps from the new power, reminds me to focus on the light, not the dark. "You've come a long way, baby," it seems to say. I recall the first time I navigated this minefield of avoiding sending Jaden into his cave, how clumsy I felt. Now, it's second nature, but the fear of misstepping, of triggering those dark memories for him, always lurks.

"We can't share a room at her house." Layers of unspoken tension stream through our link. This isn't just about room arrangements. Before I have time to formulate any theories on what might lie beneath Jaden's reaction to any mention of his mother, he pulls up in front of a slightly worn but sturdy wartime home. A small, well-tended garden blooms at the front, a splash of color against the drab brown of the brick, with a large blooming bush dominating the small front yard. Without a word, he gets out of the car and strides to the front door. "Coming?"

I guess I am. I grab my bag, quickly take in the gravel drive and a house that could use some work, and file away another nugget about Jaden to ponder later—why hasn't he fixed up his mom's home or bought her a new one?

We step into the happy chaos of a family gathering, a scene I've only dreamed of until now. The large farm kitchen buzzes with people, surrounding a dining table set with fine china and a tablecloth. Happy laughter and welcoming slaps on the back greet Jaden. "Hey Jaden, so good to see you," says his Uncle Clancy, "short for Clarence," he informs me with a jolly laugh and sparkling eyes. He's well on his way to being shit-faced, but there's something about him I like. It reminds me of glimpses I see of the Jaden that he works so hard to hide from the world.

A small, older woman with a radiant smile makes her way through, gently pushing Clancy aside. "My turn. We were beginning to think you wouldn't come again."

Jaden's body tenses at her words, but before I can delve into his reaction, another woman, imposing in stature with the largest rack I've ever seen, steps forward and gives Jaden a hearty slap on the back. "Jaden, dear, we almost sent out a search party for you." She laughs, but her tone carries an undercurrent of criticism. I wince, feeling the sting of her *affection* through our bond.

Her gaze then turns to me, appraising. "And who have we here?" A woman with an aura of authority walks through the gathering as if she commands it with mere presence. Despite her friendly facade, I sense her disapproval. Guilt washes over me for my uncharitable thoughts, quickly countered by Nye's advice echoing in my mind: "Follow your instincts. They're one of your gifts."

"Mom," Jaden's harsh tone hides something softer, more vulnerable than I'm used to coming from him. "This is my friend, Rayne."

His mother's eyes flicker to me, sharp and assessing, before a polite smile graces her lips. "Pleasure to meet you, Rayne. Jaden hasn't mentioned you."

Her words, laced with an edge of surprise—or is it suspicion?—send a wave of discomfort through me. Jaden's hand finds its way to the small of my back, a silent reassurance that's more for him than me. The complexity of their relationship unfolds in that brief exchange, a story told in the silence between words.

He leads me through the den to a small, secluded room, dropping our bags on a single bed. "This was my room," he says, the past tense hanging in the air.

Before I can absorb the room's details, his mother's voice calls us back to the kitchen, where we join the family around the massive table for dinner. Jaden's hand wraps around the back of my neck as we leave his bedroom, only dropping it when he pulls me into a seat at the other end of the table from his mother.

For the most part, we manage to blend into the background amid the turkey dinner hustle, surrounded by family, friends, and neighbors gathered for Gloria's birthday—a detail Jaden omitted. Gloria's attention pivots to me only once, pushing lima beans towards me with a zeal that's unmistakably personal. "Leave the girl be, Gloria," Uncle Clancy chuckles as he passes the bowl.

"No thanks," I say, giving the beans the vomit-worthy look they deserve.

"You've not tasted mine. Give them a try. You'll change your mind." Gloria's tone turns the moment into a challenge that silences the room. The collective anticipation feels almost tangible, a bizarre spotlight on me over something as silly as beans.

Feeling Jaden's tension spike, I relent, sampling the beans with exaggerated care, only to confirm, "Nope, still not a fan, but thank you." Uncle Clancy barks out a laugh and the room's tension breaks. Gloria, momentarily taken aback, disguises her surprise with a huff, pondering aloud to the universe how anyone could dislike lima beans. Jaden's brief squeeze on my thigh sends his silent approval of how I handled his mother, and I send a silent prayer of relief to the universe. Whatever the hell is going on between him and his mother, one thing is clear: he needs me.

I'm safe until dessert, which offers a choice between damned good pumpkin or apple pie. Jaden leans in, the warmth of his whisper tickling my neck and igniting a familiar heat within me. "My mother can't cook worth a damn, but she makes a great pie."

As if on cue, Gloria presents a plate of tarts with a flourish, declaring, "And of course, I made your favorite, mincemeat tarts." She places one on my plate with a definitive defiant gesture. "Have one."

I instinctively move the tart onto Jaden's plate, murmuring a polite "no thanks." The very thought of mincemeat—far worse in my book than lima beans—makes my stomach turn. The room's reaction is immediate, a collective gasp that cements Gloria's role as the undisputed matriarch.

The ensuing "try one" dance feels painfully familiar, yet I manage to keep my composure, barely suppressing an eye roll. A part of me yearns for his family's approval, but another, more defiant part, whispers that my gut instincts about this evening were spot on. Yet, I can't pinpoint the source of my unease, only that the subtle undercurrents of disapproval and superiority from the older generation feel almost palpable. Jaden's three siblings seem more curious than judgmental, hinting that Jaden rarely brings guests around.

As the dinner winds down and the neighbors depart, the atmosphere shifts. The din subsides to a comfortable hum, but Jaden's growing tension is apparent. His mother's announcement of "our usual celebratory drink" seems to heighten it further. Aunt Mary and Gloria fixate on me with an intensity that feels like scrutiny, while Rowan, with her striking red hair, appears more interested in her wine than the family dynamics at play.

Jaden's agitation is evident, his foot tapping a silent rhythm of anxiety. I admire his restraint, the way he holds himself with a quiet strength that speaks of battles fought and inner demons wrestled into submission. I telegraph my admiration, my pride in his resilience through our bond, but Gloria's voice slices through the moment, demanding attention with a sweetness that doesn't quite reach her eyes.

"So, Rayne, where are you from, dear?" Gloria's question, cloaked in the guise of casual conversation, reminds me eerily of Lady Portia Featherington from Bridgerton—politeness veiling a manipulative and controlling core.

"She doesn't need the third degree." Jaden's voice is laced with a dry belligerence.

Gloria's response is a theatrical display of indignation, her huge bosom heaving dramatically. "We're just trying to get to know your little friend, son. It's not every day you bring someone home." The unsaid hangs heavily in the air, implying a trespass on her domain without her permission.

"Yes, Jaden, we just want to get to know your little friend better," Aunt Mary chimes in, mirroring Gloria's tone, a condescension thinly veiled as interest. Their generation's tone is all too familiar, but it doesn't unsettle me; it's an echo of attitudes I've encountered before, a reflection of a bygone era's mindset.

I intervene, aiming to steer the conversation away from escalating further. "I'm from Toronto."

"But where were you born, dear?" Gloria persists.

"Toronto—"

"For fuck's sake. I'm out of here." Jaden reaches the end of his patience and abruptly stands, the scrape of his chair cutting through the tension. His departure is swift, leaving a silence punctuated only by the door slamming behind him.

"What's wrong with him? Where is he going? When is he coming back?" The collective gaze shifts to me along with the barrage of questions.

I shrug to cover my surprise at his departure. "I have no idea. Your guess is as good as mine."

The brief standoff, charged with tension and unspoken truths, momentarily silences the room. "Leave her alone, ma. It's not like this is the first time he's taken off. I bet he doesn't like your insinuations about Rayne's color." Rowan's assessment, laced with the same dry wit as her brother's, pierces through the mask of politeness.

Her words catch me off guard, a stark reminder of a reality I seldom have to confront. In the predominantly white, middle-class neighborhood of my upbringing, within the sprawling diversity of a large metropolitan city, I have very little experience with racism. So, when I'm faced with such an overt reminder, I find myself momentarily speechless, the sting of the insinuation catching me unprepared.

"We haven't said a word about her color." Gloria's gaze locks on mine as if seeking an ally.

"Of course, we don't see your color," Aunt Mary chimes in, echoing Gloria's denial with practiced ease. Once upon a time, I might have found her words reassuring, but the undertone is clear—they don't see me.

"Of course not." Gloria's assertion of obliviousness to racial differences spews forth in a tale of camaraderie with "your kind" during her service days.

I seize the opportunity to divert the conversation. "So, you were in the army?"

"Navy," Gloria corrects, launching into her story, allowing me a moment's respite from the scrutiny and the thinly veiled digs at my background. The evening drags on, Gloria and Mary holding court with war stories as I find solace in the bottom of my glass, the alcohol a temporary escape from the evening's undercurrents of tension and judgment.

Later, as Gloria shows me to a modest room across from

hers—a strategic placement, no doubt, to keep a watchful eye—I review the night's events. Despite Jaden's abrupt exit, my feelings are surprisingly unbruised by his behavior. Maybe that's because of the complexity of our bond or the numbing effect of the wine. As sleep claims me, I put together another piece of Jaden's motivations, his silent battles, and the intricate dance of our relationship that continues to unfold in unexpected ways.

37
JADEN

I'm almost suffocating with fear as I stumble out of my mother's house. Yes, I'm fleeing, leaving Rayne amidst the vultures of my past. But it's not without cause; the thought of my mother's manipulation tearing at the fragile connection between Rayne and me is unbearable. That disappointment from her, a piercing through our bond, was unexpected yet painfully revealing.

Driving aimlessly, I find myself at Sasha's, seeking comfort in the solitude of her lakefront property. It's here, in the quiet, that I confront the chaos within me. Rayne, she's woven herself into the fabric of my life in ways I hadn't imagined possible. She's not just filling the gaps; she's restructuring the entire foundation.

Her presence in my business covering for Sasha started as a convenience, a relief from the burdens I carry. But it's evolved into something more—recognition of her worth and an acknowledgment of my own limitations. My aversion to dealing with financial aspects isn't just a quirk; it's a scar from past battles, ones she's unknowingly helping to heal.

The decision to give her half of my holdings isn't a whim. It's a testament to her impact, a gesture of trust I've never afforded anyone. And it's hers whether she chooses to stay or not. Yet, how do I convey this without implying a debt or diminishing her independence? She's fiercely self-sufficient, a quality I admire and do not wish to cage.

Tonight, her resilience against my mother's thinly veiled barbs solidified my decision. She's my equal, not a liability to be protected or an asset to be managed. This partnership, offering her a stake in my world, is perhaps the most genuine expression of my feelings—a leap towards vulnerability I never thought I'd take.

Taking the next step terrifies me. Sharing my feelings about her and my past makes every cell in my body scream. If she hasn't seen through me yet, confessing my love might just reveal the fraud I am. The thought makes me cringe, imagining her reaction when she discovers she's not getting the man everyone admires but rather someone who loves art, sex, and rock and roll. *But does she care?* Suddenly, my unique ability—my power—chimes in with its perspective.

Can I hope for her to see and accept me as I truly am? Doubts linger because she seemed to embrace my mother's idealized portrayal of a "Full House" TV family life. Does she really see me?

She's appeared in our dreams, a place where our minds and souls intertwine. It's happened too often to be my imagination . . . Hasn't it? Is it too much to hope? Sometimes, I awaken, convinced Rayne has visited my dreams, suggesting my power is urging me to share my pain with her. Even if that's just wishful thinking, Rayne's boundless energy and enthusiasm envelop me like a warm hug, offering an escape from my nightmares.

Our connection transcends mere physical intimacy; it's a profound communion of spirits. Voicing such sentiments aloud could easily become a subject of ridicule, not the kind of laughter I'd welcome. The mere thought of Rayne laughing derisively at what she might deem my 'sissy ass thoughts' nearly strangles me with fear. *No, she won't. She's not like that.* I reassure myself, bolstered by the confidence my power lends me, ever her champion. My power overrode my difficulty in expressing my feelings, claiming her and ensuring Rayne knows she belongs to me. Our union the other night was more than mere physicality; it was a profound sharing that led her to expose her vulnerabilities, thereby deepening our bond and underscoring my yearning for her healing presence.

Memories of Rayne's challenging behavior bring unexpected smiles. Protecting her feels like an instinctive duty, yet I question if this drive stems solely from the celestial beings' mandate or my own deep-seated need. Her fearless intervention in a recent altercation at the Manor involving two teens and a knife, oblivious to danger, tested my nerves. Her puzzled reaction to my concern, those wide, chestnut eyes igniting my heart and desire, left me speechless. "I wasn't in any danger. I can sense it." Such a stubborn, fascinating woman.

Revealing my true nature as an asshole, I've left her with my mother, abandoning Rayne to navigate my mother's tempest of righteousness and morality alone. Unlike Savannah, who had aligned with my mother's vision for me, I'd left Rayne standing her ground, her loyalty shining through her defiance. Yet here I am, hiding in the dark, the rhythmic crash of Lake Huron's waves attempting to cleanse my mind of turmoil.

As I stand here, swallowed by darkness, I realize fleeing

to the lake's edge was more than escape; it was a retreat into my own fears, away from the one battle I'm terrified of losing—not with my mother, but with Rayne's perception of me. But I no longer want to keep running or hiding, not when I've had a glimpse of what might be.

I head back to my mother's house in the wee hours, no closer to a decision but acutely aware that my next steps must include Rayne . . . if she's still willing to speak to me after last night's cowardice.

Waking to the agricultural report blaring, a brief terror grips me, reminiscent of the months following my attack. Back then, mom had rejected me, and dad, too ill to intervene, passed away in my arms from a major heart attack. I lost my confidant, the one who accepted my sensitive nature. I'd been utterly alone. Now, I fear my mother might have spent the evening painting me as that sensitive little boy to Rayne, potentially altering how she sees me.

"Good morning. What on earth are you listening to?" Rayne's smoky voice cuts through my thoughts, her presence in the next room like a beacon. The sound of the kettle fills the silence, a mundane yet comforting ritual. Could she be making morning tea for us both, or is she about to demand I take her away from this place?

"You slept late." Mom's chiding ignites a flicker of hope within me. Perhaps Rayne did confront her. "It's the agriculture report. The only thing that gets Jaden up." She seems to have forgotten I grew up.

The kettle lands on the burner with a definitive clunk. "A hog report to wake Jaden? Now that's funny." Rayne's incredulity brings a smile to my face, rare moments of light piercing the habitual chaos. "I'll tell you one thing, he's a nicer son than I would be. Teenage me would have killed you by now if you'd tortured me with that thing every morning." The smell of coffee fills the air. Bless her. She found my mother's secret treasure. "Where's the sugar, please?" Rayne asks.

My face isn't used to this much grinning, yet here I am, smiling broadly as I picture Rayne flashing one of her 'reserved-for-morons' smiles at my mother. *Not that you'd say such things to their face, of course.* My smile widens to the breaking point as her words reverb through my head. *That would be shameful and politically incorrect.* Rayne's intolerance for stupidity is just one of the many traits we share. As my grin widens, I can almost see the look on my mother's face, utterly clueless about the force of nature she's up against.

The next sounds are of cups clinking, the door opening, and Rayne sashays in, bringing the light with her. She sets the cups on the bedside table and plops her pert ass on the bed, nudging into my groin as she settles on the small mattress beside me. "Jesus, Jaden. It smells like a distillery in here. Are you awake?" I swear I hear laughter, not condemnation, and crack an eyelid. The damn woman bounces beside me and croons in a wheedling voice, "Wakey, wakey." Her grin widens. "Looks like someone could use some of my healing touch."

My mother's probably having a seizure as she eavesdrops. Rayne's warmth seeps into me, blowing away most of the cobwebs, but the asshole in me still has to put on a show for my mother. "Could you be any louder?" There's a fifty-fifty chance this will trigger a bad reaction from Rayne. I lean around her and sigh relief into my mug as she wiggles her ass against my growing hard-on. "I could, actually. Want me to try?"

That's the moment when my power and I merge with one common goal . . . To get Rayne home, my home, and let the warmth of her body tell me once again that she's mine. She's blown through the test of standing up to my mother. *I am hers. "We're hers already."* My power punches me in the gut. This has to stop.

After a quick breakfast of pancakes with my sister, my mother makes one more valiant attempt to wrestle Rayne under her control. Rayne's chattering away with Rowan about clothes. I open the door of the fridge looking for juice. Mom's strident voice cuts through the friendly chatter.

"Jaden, what are you doing?"

My sigh is automatic. Here we go. I'm transported back to my late teens. "Looking for something to drink."

"Rayne, get up and help Jaden figure out what he wants to drink." Just like that, she belittles me and cuts me down to size.

I can't help it. Those thirteen words bring the shroud crowding in, eager to smother my brief glimpse of light. Three pairs of eyes swivel to me, and I hold my breath, waiting, teetering on the edge of a very high cliff as if Rayne's reaction is life or death. I can almost hear the death knell as my shroud closes in.

"Jaden." Rayne's voice isn't loud, but it's penetrating and insistent. "Do you want help?" Only when her words cut through the shroud do I hear the undertone of sarcasm. Rowan doesn't help matters when she takes that moment to practice some of her passive aggression on our mother. "Yeah, Jaden, do you need help figuring out what to drink?" she parrots.

"What I want is to be left alone," I say, deliberately adding an edge to my tone.

"That's what I thought," Rayne says.

I can feel the volcano simmering inside Mom as Rayne dismisses her, turning back to her discussion with a force that makes my heart sing. The moment I signal I'm ready to leave, a flurry of activity ensues. Rayne quickly gathers our belongings, gives effusive thanks and we make our way out the door.

Driving through the serene backroads, surrounded by miles of untouched nature and farmland, usually brings me peace. Yet, at this moment, I find myself wishing for the speed of a helicopter. My only desire is to be alone with Rayne, to connect through our bond and bodies so I can decipher the true extent of the damage my mother might have caused.

"Well, that was an experience," Rayne exhales sharply as we merge onto the road, settling in for the three-hour journey home. I sense a storm of thoughts and emotions churning through our link, indicating Rayne is on the verge of unleashing a torrent of words. Normally, I might tune out, letting her voice blend into the background noise of my own turmoil. But not today. Today, I'm desperate to shield myself from any reminders of my past that could draw forth the shadows.

"I don't want to talk about my mother right now. I need to think." I plead silently for quiet.

Rayne fixes me with a deep, searching gaze, but evidently, my expression conveys enough because she nods, understanding flashing in her eyes. "Okay. Do you mind if I listen to music instead?"

I nod, grateful for the reprieve, and retreat into the whirlwind of my thoughts as the landscape rushes by.

Rayne belts out a Beyoncé song, her voice filling the car. Yet, the lyrics from a song she played earlier haunt me, echoing a sentiment that's all too familiar:

> *Your heart's not here, your spirit's gone, but*
> *your body carries on.*
> *It's not quite clear what went wrong, but your*
> *body carries on.*

Trust Rayne to find a way to get through to me. In those lines lies the essence of my existence, and listening to her belt out the words is a reality punch to the gut. I've been merely existing, not truly living, since . . . For once, I push the past aside, daring to contemplate a future. What am I striving for? The Impossible Dream?

For so long, I've mastered the art of concealment, hiding behind walls built from pain and betrayal. But with Rayne, it's as if those walls aren't just crumbling; they're being willingly dismantled, brick by brick. Can I truly allow myself this vulnerability, to hope for a future where I'm not defined by my shadows?"

The thought of change is both exhilarating and terrifying. I've been defined by my past for so long, it's become my identity. Yet, here I am, daring to dream of a life where my past doesn't dictate my future. Is it possible to redefine oneself, to build a future on new foundations of trust and healing?"

Every moment with Rayne feels like a stolen piece of time, too precious and fragile. The fear of losing this, of reverting back to the darkness that once consumed me, is overwhelming. How do I hold onto this sliver of light without smothering it with my insecurities?"

In my darkest hours, I never allowed myself the luxury

of hope. It was a distant beacon, too far out of reach. Yet now, hope is not just a distant dream but a tangible possibility. Like the star in the east, guiding me toward home, not any kind of external structure but where the heart is. The battle between this newfound hope and the reality of my past is a constant struggle. Can hope truly outshine the darkness?

I've always measured my worth by my past failures and the shadows that follow me. The possibility of being seen, truly seen beyond those shadows, is both a deep-seated desire and my greatest fear. What if she judges me? Finds me lacking? Can I accept myself enough to believe in a future where I'm worthy of love, happiness, and a sense of belonging?

I briefly flash back on all those hours I've spent locked up in my own mind. Just as Golem treasured his precious above all, I've guarded my true self, keeping it hidden deep within the shadows of my cave. But Rayne, with her unwavering gaze, seeks it out, not to possess but to understand. She shows me that my most guarded treasure, my authenticity, is not to be feared but shared.

Exposing my "precious," my true self, feels like standing on the edge of a precipice with Rayne holding my hand. She asks for my trust, to step into the light and reveal the parts of me shrouded in darkness. It's a terrifying leap, fearing that once she sees the real me, she might turn away. Yet, her presence, her unwavering need for authenticity, beckons me forward."

Our bond, deeper than mere words, acts as a mirror reflecting my hidden facets. Rayne's insistence on seeing my authentic self isn't just about understanding; it's about trust. She needs to know the person she's entrusting her heart to is real, not a facade. This bond, it doesn't just tell me; it shows me that hiding isn't living.

I've clung to my "precious," my true self, like a lifeline in a sea of pretense. But Rayne, she's the beacon guiding me out of the darkness. With her, the struggle isn't about holding on to my precious but about the fear of what happens when it's seen. Yet, she assures me, without words, that it's safe to emerge, to be authentically me.

Trusting someone with your most prized possession, your authentic self, is a journey fraught with fear and uncertainty. Rayne's persistence, her need to see the real me, challenges every instinct to hide. Yet, it's in this challenge that I find strength. Her determination to unveil my "precious" shows me that true connection lies in vulnerability and trust.

I don't bother to park; I just pull up in front of my house, thankful for the isolation that will guarantee no interruptions. I'd texted my butler Steve advising that we'd be back, and that I'd want the house to myself for the next three days.

I drag Rayne through the house to my bedroom, a threshold no woman has ever crossed before. She follows, seeming compliant yet deeply attuned to my unspoken needs—a testament to her intuitive understanding of me. She has a knack for that, one of her gifts. She's always said she has a special intuition about me, mirroring my own understanding of her—a unique gift we've shared since we met.

I sit on the edge of the bed, pulling her to stand in front of me . . . And stop. I want this moment to be perfect, to be special.

As I watch Rayne in the golden light of the afternoon, I

find myself captivated in a way that feels both familiar and startlingly new. It's as if I'm seeing her for the first time again, but through a lens polished by the depth of our shared experiences. Her strength and resilience, so often displayed in her fierce determination and indomitable spirit, now seem to enhance her physical presence, lending her an ethereal quality that I hadn't fully appreciated before.

Her hair, a cascade of short black curls, frames her face not just as a feature but as a halo of her inner fire, reflecting her tenacity and warmth. The way she moves, with purpose and grace, reminds me of the first time I noticed her—not just as a physical being but as a force of nature. Her eyes, once windows to her soul's tumultuous weather, now hold a steadiness that speaks of our shared journey, mirroring the calm and the storm of our intertwined lives.

The curve of her smile on those gorgeous full lips, a rare gift that she bestows with genuine emotion, now strikes me as a revelation of her vulnerability and strength. It's a beacon that has guided me through many dark hours, a reminder of the light we've found in each other. Her hands, often in motion, weaving spells of comfort and defiance, now seem to me as instruments of healing, their touch a testament to our bond, capable of bridging worlds and mending the rifts in my own soul.

Standing there, amidst the chaos and calm of our existence, Rayne embodies a paradox—a warrior and a healer, fierce yet tender. The contours of her body, each line and curve, now tell a story of survival and triumph, a narrative in which I've become irrevocably entwined. In this moment, I realize that her beauty transcends the physical. It's a reflection of her essence, a mirror of the strength and the vulnerability that has drawn me to her time and again.

Seeing her now, through these new eyes, I understand

that my attraction to Rayne is more than skin deep. It's rooted in the profound connection we share, a fusion of spirit and heart that has transformed the way I see her, the world, and myself. In Rayne, I've found not just a partner but a reflection of my deepest hopes and fears, a companion in the truest sense of the word. And in her presence, I'm reminded of the preciousness of the journey we're on, a journey of discovery, healing, and, ultimately, love.

38
RAYNE

Anticipation coils in my stomach, a delicate tremor that echoes the depth of my journey with Jaden. His fingers graze the small of my back, sending shards of desire that shatter the shields I've meticulously built around my heart. In this moment, something fundamental shifts within him, a flame so fragile that what happens next could either smother it or allow it to ignite into a bonfire, illuminating the darkest corners of our souls. The magnetic connection of our mate bond, more electric and primal than ever, pulls me closer, binding me to him with an intensity that transcends the physical realm. With Jaden, the world narrows to this singular moment, where the pulse of his breath and the warmth of his skin become my entire universe.

As he touches me, it's not just my body that responds but my very essence, stirring in recognition of the trust we've built and the barriers we're dismantling together. His touch, a language of its own, communicates more than words ever could—promises made, battles fought, and the shared vulnerability that has become the cornerstone of our connection. This is the moment in time when he decides whether he can overcome his fear and let me in, which in turn will release me to love him openly and wholeheartedly. If he can just let me in.

In Jaden's eyes, I see not just the man I love but the journey we've embarked on together—a journey that promises to teach us the true meaning of strength in vulnerability. Each caress speaks of our shared struggles, a testament to the resilience and understanding that have come to define us. Yet, there lingers the question, the pivotal uncertainty: Will he let himself see it, truly see it? The room around us fades, leaving only the sound of our synchronized breathing and the scent of his skin, a heady mix of earth and something indefinably his. Wrapped in the cocoon of our connection, I find a profound sense of belonging and peace, even as I sense the war within him— the shroud battling the light, teetering on the edge of surrender.

His lips find my neck, soft yet searing, tracing a path of fire across my skin. I gasp, my fingers curling in the silk of his hair, an instinctive pull to bring him closer. He resists, gently but firmly, guiding my hands with his to rest against the small of my back. The elusive emotion that's been fluttering through our bond crystallizes into a wave of longing —a longing he's terrified to acknowledge.

Within me, a strange sensation unfurls, not merely in my core but deeper, in the very magma chamber of my essence, where the most fundamental parts of my being simmer. It's as though a dormant volcano has stirred to life; its awakening churns the molten essence of who I am, reshaping the landscape of my soul with a newfound understanding. He needs me—perhaps as desperately as he needs air—not only as a shield from a world that can be cruel but to accept him, flaws and all.

I answer with the reassurance he seeks, tilting my head to expose my neck further, a gesture of vulnerability and trust. His breath, a whisper of relief and desire, grazes the shell of my ear as his tongue traces its outline. I shiver involuntarily, melting as his mouth explores every inch, arching toward him, speaking volumes in the only language he hears.

Blinding heat blazes from his bronze eyes as our gazes lock, and I let him see the raw truth of me. In my shadows and scars, he sees beauty no one else does. In my vulnerabilities, he finds an unexpected strength. His hands tenderly cradle my face, and I lean into the warmth of his touch, tears threatening at the intimacy of the moment.

His lips crash against mine, showing me how much I mean to him with an intensity that sweeps away every last bit of hesitation. In this moment of complete surrender, my entire being focuses on the here and now—on him, on us. Jaden's kiss, both fierce and insistent, dismantles my remaining barriers. In the wake of this surrender, a remarkable shift occurs, illuminating the depth of his fear and desire. Lowering my defenses makes me a beacon through the darkness, guiding him toward my light. A profound connection erupts between us as he fully opens up for the first time, his essence—raw and potent—pouring into me. His complex emotions and untamed power intertwine with mine, forging a bond beyond the reach of mere words. As we kiss, that fragile flame he shelters brightens exposing his hope and resilience. I grasp it eagerly, recognizing its significance—a beacon of our shared struggle and triumph.

I drown in the taste of him, the feel of his body pressed against mine. Each caress of his hand along my skin ignites trails of fire, branding me as his. Lost in a sea of sensation, I am anchored only by the ferocity of his need. When we break apart, breathless, I find myself trembling, over-whelmed by the intensity of our connection. It strips away the last vestiges of my defenses, leaving me bare before him —every secret longing and unspoken fear exposed, with nowhere left to hide. My doubt dragons choose that moment to come knocking, but the acceptance in his stormy gaze sends them packing. Love, fierce and all-consuming, radiates from him, enveloping me in its warmth.

I realize then that the absence of barriers between us transcends the need for words; his silence doesn't diminish the depth of his emotions. With time as my ally, there is no part of him beyond my reach. We are two halves of one soul, shattered and strewn across lifetimes, only to be fused whole once more.

He trails kisses along my jaw, hands sliding the zipper and slipping my dress off my shoulders to explore the smooth skin he adores. As he takes a moment to imprint the image of my body in his mind, I give him what he needs, straightening to the submissive display position with legs apart and hands behind my head. A soft grunt of satisfaction is the only outward sign he gives that I'm kindling a slow-burning fire in his veins. I arch into him with a soft moan, craving more. Needing to be closer still.

With another quick shake of his head, he leads me to the large bed and gestures for me to lie down. With one smooth gesture, he pulls my G-string off and spreads my legs. After another long moment, when he looks with fasci-nated awe at my body spread open in invitation to him, he captures one pert nipple between his teeth. As his teeth tease the aching bud, a jolt of pleasure ricochets through me. I gasp, tangling my fingers in his hair to hold him there. He lavishes equal attention on its twin before continuing his descent, blazing a trail of fire in his wake.

My body is molten for him, thrumming with need. Anticipation builds as his clever fingers work their magic on my clit. I can't help but whimper his name, my hips arching into his touch. Jaden's response is to tease me even more, circling my swollen bud before he abruptly pulls away. "Shh," he whispers, his lips grazing my ear. "I want to hear every sound you make, little dragon."

His words send a shiver down my spine, and I bite my lip to stifle a moan. I can feel his pleasure even though I can't see it. He knows how much his dominance gives me what I need, the way it makes my core clench with desire. Slowly, sensually, his tongue begins to trace the slick lines of my folds, teasing my aching entrance before zeroing in on my throbbing clit. He laps at me like I'm the sweetest nectar he's ever tasted, his tongue painting electric circles that make my clit so hard it hurts. Each flick and suckle sends shockwaves of pleasure coursing through me, and I fist the sheets, trying to anchor myself in this dizzying whirlwind of sensation.

Jaden's hands press my thighs, pushing them wider apart. His tongue delves deeper, plunging inside my hungry depths. I cry out as the coil in my core winds so tight it's almost too much to bear. Heat pools low in my belly, my climax building with every flick of his skilled tongue. "Please." I pant and moan, my voice hoarse with need. "Please. Please." I'm not sure what I'm begging for.

He doesn't stop, doesn't slow down. Instead, he redoubles his efforts, sucking harder, faster, as if he's determined to unravel me completely. And unravel I do, my entire body tense as the orgasm builds, coiling tighter and tighter until it threatens to explode from my very core. "Let go for me, Rayne. I want to feel you come apart in my mouth." His words vibrate against my sensitive skin.

That's all it takes. With his words ringing in my ears, my climax crashes over me like a tidal wave, and I cry out his name, my body shuddering uncontrollably. Jaden doesn't relent, lapping at me until the last tremor subsides, his fingers stroking my soaking entrance, prolonging the most exquisite aftershocks I've ever known.

Gasping for air, my heart pounding in my chest, I reach for him. But he's not done with me yet.

"Hands over your head." Jaden's eyes smolder with something indescribable as he pulls off his clothes. Bronze eyes drink in the sight of me, reflecting hunger, reverence, and a tenderness that steals my breath. "You're exquisite," Awe threads the rough timbre of his voice.

No words pass between us as he thrusts into me, yet I hear his voice in my soul: you are mine, as I am yours. When he enters me, the world fractures into light and sensation. He pins me down, making my body an extension of his, making us move as one in a rhythm as old and eternal as the tides. I close my eyes and become one with the feel of him, anchored in the cadence of his breaths and the beat of his heart against my chest.

The climax hits like a breaking wave, scattering my senses and dissolving the boundaries of self. In those breathless seconds, I glimpse the joy we can share if he lets me in. With a roar, he comes apart with an orgasm that shatters through the thick walls of his cave releasing him to the light.

In the quiet aftermath, he holds me close. No promises need to be made as we drift off to sleep.

Awakening early with a pressing need to pee, I glance

over at Jaden's peacefully resting form, his gentle snores a contrast to the quiet of dawn. His tranquility brings a smile to my face, making me want to explore more of his world now that our relationship has evolved. Silently, I slip away to the bathroom, starting the shower on the way to the throne. The sound of the shower water cascading down coincides with unexpected terror floods through our bond.

The connection between us slams shut, a door closing with a rush of fear. I quickly turn off the shower and rush back to him, finding Jaden curled in the fetal position, the image of vulnerability. Approaching cautiously, mindful of the last time I startled him yet driven by an urge to comfort, I hesitate, not from fear—my power assures my safety— but from a desire to not exacerbate his pain.

"Jaden." The urgency in my voice must penetrate because his moaning turns to a few whimpers then stops but his body remains rigid with tension. "Jaden, what's wrong? I need you to tell me what's wrong."

At those words, "I need," my power rises, compelling Jaden to answer me, to let me in.

"I can't. . ." I think those are the tortured words that come next. His response is fragmented, a whisper of pain, as a faint trickle of connection flickers between us, fragile but unbroken. I have no idea how to help him. All I can do is absorb some of his agony. So, I gently lay a hand on his shoulder and pull pain from him until his body curls around mine. Then he turns onto his back, forearm thrown over his eyes. We sit like that for what seems an eternity of pain and indecision before his hand slowly crawls across the top of the sheet, seeking mine, a silent plea for connection. I take the hand in mine and pull it into my lap. And wait. I grasp it, anchoring us both in the moment.

Fear and indecision swirl intertwine through our bond,

fuse into a solid shard urging him to take the risk. Finally, he lets out a deep, shuddering moan.

"I love you." Tears leak from beneath the arm shielding his pain. With those three words, I realize the moment is confirmation of something I've known. "I know," I whisper back. "I love you." Recognizing the extreme power Jaden just dropped into my hands, I vow never to misuse it.

He holds my hand with a death grip as we cling to each other, navigating the storm of his PTSD, Jaden's forearm remains thrown over his eyes, a shield against the world, even as tears escape from beneath it, a silent testimony to the depth of his vulnerability. I fold over him, my hand gently scratching his arm, a soothing rhythm against the backdrop of his internal battle.

"I have to go to the bathroom. I'll be right back," I whisper, the urgency clear in my voice yet tempered by the gravity of the moment. His grip tightens around mine, a desperate clasp that bridges our soul bond, flooding it with a torrent of emotion. In that instant, a profound realization hits me: I'm privy to the most vulnerable, unguarded part of him, a part that no one else has ever glimpsed. The enormity of the power I wield over him is sobering. It's a precarious edge we're on, with two divergent paths unfolding before us—one shrouded yet promising a future bathed in light and love, the other a darker road paved with manipulation, where people are mere steppingstones to success. And there, in my hands, lies a man more precious than any conceivable treasure.

Gently, I lift his arm from his eyes, meeting his gaze, those tortured eyes brimming with a silent plea not to be broken. In that look, I make my choice: light and love.

"I've got you, Jaden," I assure him, a smile tugging at

my lips despite the tension. "But I really need to use the bathroom, so it seems you're coming with me."

With a strength born of desperation, he tightens his hold, allowing me to lead him, his trust in me a tangible force. Gratitude and hope surge between us, so potent it nearly overwhelms me.

Once back in bed, the intimacy of our connection deepens. I trace the contours of his scars with a touch as light as a breath, each one a testament to his resilience. He shudders under my caress, a silent acknowledgment of the pain and triumph each mark represents. To me, they're not just scars; they're the story of his survival, a narrative of enduring strength that I honor with every kiss, every touch.

His hands explore my own scars tentatively, a reminder of our shared vulnerabilities and the trust that has flourished between us. In this moment, every fear, every shadow we've both fought so hard to overcome, is laid bare, yet it's in this exposure that we find our greatest strength.

I take his hand and guide it lower, forcing myself to remain present in this moment. The past cannot touch us here. He enters me slowly, eyes locked on my face needing the physical and spiritual connection. I draw him closer in answer, wrapping myself around him. His fear recedes, washed away by waves of longing and trust.

"Look at me." His voice is rough with restraint. I meet his gaze and lose myself in fathomless depths, where I find only love and acceptance. He moves within me, and I move with him, beyond thought or pretense. No walls remain between our souls. In this place of perfect understanding, I am known—and knowing. Our pleasure builds, a swelling tide that carries us higher. I cling to him, breathless and trembling, overcome by the beauty of two hearts laid bare.

When our orgasm comes, it is a surrender. I fall into

light, shattering into a thousand pieces, only to be made whole in his embrace. We lie together, limbs entwined, and listen to the silence. No words are needed here. The promises made in this bed are carved into our souls, as lasting as the ties that bind two lives forever changed.

I open my eyes to find Jaden gazing at me with a softness that steals my breath. His hand cups my cheek, thumb tracing the line of my jaw. I lean into his touch, struck anew by how this man can reduce me to trembling with a single caress.

"You are the most beautiful thing I've ever known," he says. The reverence in his tone brings tears to my eyes.

"As are you," I whisper. "You are my heart, my home. And I'm yours."

He kisses me then, a sweet and lingering press of lips. I can taste the depths of his devotion, feel the devotion etched into the scars on his soul. Scars I will explore and claim as my own. When we part, I rest my head over his heart, listening to the steady beat that has become my refuge. His arms tighten around me, a silent promise to shield me from the darkness. A shield that will give me the strength and courage to explore the light.

In this place of sanctuary, the place in our souls, the world beyond these walls ceases to exist. It doesn't matter that he's older and emotionally crippled. There are no more battles to fight or demons to face. No more shadows to haunt our past. Here we are only Jaden and Rayne, two souls who have walked through fire together. Two hearts entwined. A love that transcends all earthly bounds, eternal as the dawn.

As I drift to sleep in his embrace, a single thought echoes through my mind. Our path may not be easy, but we will walk it side by side. Always.

EPILOGUE
JADEN

O ne year later, I find myself lying in a suite at the Hazelton Hotel in Toronto, with Rayne sleeping beside me, not touching but snugly fit in the spoon position. My hand rests firmly over one of her ass cheeks, her smaller hand placed over mine, seeking contact. This is yet another way we're perfectly matched, as neither of us can stand close contact during sleep. A burst of happiness fireworks through me as I drowse next to her, marveling at how fucking lucky I am, without the usual dread of waiting for the other shoe to drop.

When I'd told Rayne that I had transferred half of my company's ownership to her she'd nearly had a shit hemorrhage. Following a series of what we euphemistically call "intense discussions"—since neither of us believes in arguing, viewing it as a sign of dysfunction—she surrendered to my decision, albeit with a fierce declaration of financial independence.

"Fine. But I'm not spending one goddamned cent of yours." Yet, in a twist that's quintessentially Rayne, she's made her peace with using the resources now at her disposal to generate her own wealth. This compromise, like so many aspects of our relationship, is a delicate dance of give and take that somehow, miraculously, works for us.

Yesterday marked our "love you" anniversary—a date Rayne insists is an occasion worth making a big deal of, whether I'm inclined to or not.

"I've set this day aside just for you, Jaden. It's been the best year of my life." For once, in what I considered my previously worthless existence, I did the actual work of making the reservations myself. Rayne, as she always does, inspired me to be a better person.

"You've set the day aside for me... Now, I truly feel special. I hope I can live up to it.
Happy Anniversary!!
I know exactly how I want to celebrate. Since the day is also mine, I get to love you... My way! ...But of course, just for you.
Check out the fridge! J."

Rayne reciprocated the sentiment with a note that snapped another tangled strand in the web of my existence, forging another solid link in the chain of love that anchors me to her. Whenever I'm hit with insecurity about what she possibly sees in me, Rayne is more than happy to elaborate on how I anchor her, ground her. Yet, the truth is, she's my anchor and my buffer against the horrors of this world. She has reclaimed my heart, making it forever hers. Her short note offers me the reassurance that brightens each day to the extent that, some days, the shroud of darkness is completely absent.

"You are more than special, CC. You are my one. My only until death do us part.

And the cheesecake—how lovely. I adore your card!

Spending time with you, in any way life allows, is all I wish for! You have nothing to 'live up' to. That I know for sure.

Happy Anniversary!"

The realization that Rayne sometimes fears I might leave her for someone "better" stings. It's a thread of insecurity that occasionally pulses through our soul bond, stubborn and persistent. No amount of reassurances or grand gestures seems to fully convince her otherwise. And yet, she's the one who completes me. On some days, I'm still floored by the fact that she actually needs me as much as I need her.

But with time, we're learning to settle into the comfort of 'us.' It's like we're shedding layers of armor, finding that vulnerability isn't so frightening when it's shared. Our time together has become a sanctuary, a retreat from the world where we can be our true selves.

We're finding that 'together' isn't just a physical space —it's a state of being where we're safest and strongest. It's funny how love works, how it can make a shield and a refuge out of something as intangible as the space between two people.

Then she'd given me the best present possible right there in black and white so I can't deny they exist. I hold the piece of notepaper close to the heart she just freed with just five words—until death do us part. Words that give me all the time I need to show her I'm hers forever. That she's my one.

Last night was a celebration of the only anniversary that truly belongs to me, to us. She had instructed me to keep my day open without divulging any details. Anticipating she had something special planned, I surprised her by taking her to the Hazelton Hotel and booking a suite. The hotel holds a special place in Rayne's heart, not for its price but for its quality. "I don't give a shit how much it costs, CC. It has the best bathroom, and you love the bed," she'd say. That's my Rayne—although she appreciates the finer things, money is never the priority. Our comfort is. My comfort is. That's what I love about her.

After a delightful afternoon where Rayne led me through several of her favorite boutiques, we returned to the hotel. I sent Rayne off to prepare for our evening. Hearing her sing in the bath, I called the front desk to arrange a dinner spread of ribeye steak with all the trimmings, king crab legs, twice-baked potatoes, queso mac and cheese, truffle fries, and spinach salad, accompanied by several house sauces—a feast fit for my little dragon before a night of debauchery.

And that's precisely what we indulged in: over two hours of nonstop passionate fuckery. I had witnessed Rayne slip into subspace once before, yet I was still amazed at how quickly, a few minutes into light flogging, she descended into deep subspace. I felt the euphoric rush and followed her, disconnecting from everything but our shared reality, entering Dom space myself.

The hours flew by, filled with assorted fucking and sucking—lovemaking as we basked in our mutual ecstasy, surrendering ourselves to each other, body and soul.

I'd drawn orgasm after orgasm from my insatiable little

dragon before allowing my release to combine our power. Pulling her into a one-armed embrace after I joined her in a mind-blowing, earth-shattering climax. Never have I experienced something so powerful, so all-consuming, as what I share with this woman. She understands and accepts the effort it takes for me to maintain even this limited contact after we make love. But the more I opened up, the more I realized she has similar, if not identical, issues. She often breaks contact first, excusing herself to clean up.

Yet, she always returns minutes later, curling up beside me, sometimes, like tonight, with one small hand scratching my arm as she drifts to sleep.

"That was the best," she whispered. "You were simply marvelous, CC!"

Her smile infused our bond, making me swell with pride while I feigned nonchalance.

"Only because you are the best!" I replied, my hand finding its home on her ass. Peace, and gratitude wash over me as my power nudges me toward sleep.

Lingering in that peculiar state between sleep and wakefulness, the hypnagogic state as they called it in medical school, where we experience and remember sensory perceptions vividly, I was just about to drop into sleep when Rayne starts to moan and writhe beside me. As my consciousness bends to vault into wakefulness, something yanks me hard. For several seconds, disorientation envelopes me, but find myself in a strange theatre, sitting beside Rayne, both of us staring intently at the stage below.

Teenage Rayne is being dragged through the woods by a man whose arm is clenched around her neck. Her terror, so raw, nearly slices through me as sharply as the knife he's brandishing at her throat. A torrent of tears threatens to break free, yet her indomitable will clamps them back. *No fucking way will he see me break.* As he shoves her onto the tracks, commanding her to undress, the internal battle rages within her—to fight or to yield.

"Fight the bastard," Rayne's ethereal form whispers beside me, her gaze piercing into mine. "She needs to fight. How do I make her understand?" Her voice, laden with years of unshed tears, lowers even further. "If I'd fought, nobody could blame me. But they did. ES said I asked for it, even made me apologize to that monster." Her eyes flicker back to her younger self. "Fight him. Aim for his balls."

The anguish in Rayne's ethereal voice nearly shatters me, yet a stark clarity emerges amidst the pain. I reach out to her with the full force of my will, drawing her attention. "No, she can't fight him, little dragon. Look closely." I gesture towards the man, his figure wavering between drunkenness and madness, knife gleaming ominously. I'd seen that look too many times in the ER and it meant one thing.

"He's on the brink. Any resistance and he might have done something catastrophic." Stress makes me slip into doctor-speak.

As we continue to watch, her younger self's mind recoils so strongly it clamps shut her vagina making it impossible for him to penetrate her. So, he cuts her, doing his own version of an episiotomy. The dream blurs into a maelstrom of pain, terror and violence as he tries to enter her again and again. Her fury and self-disgust threaten to eject us from the dreamscape.

"I'm glad you didn't fight." My voice is barely a whisper. "I might have lost you."

"Easy for you to say, avenging angel." Rayne's ethereal form shimmers with a mix of sarcasm and pain.

A moment of stark realization crystallizes between us.

"Fighting him could have led to worse, possibly even death. Your choice saved you, preserved your beautiful spirit for a future—our future."

Rayne's ethereal form sniffs, her gaze softening as it meets mine again. "If you truly believed that, CC, maybe I'd accept it. But I've seen your dreams. You don't follow your own advice."

Suddenly, a familiar jolt wrenches us into another nightmare—mine. We're spectators to my own futile resistance and its brutal consequences, a narrative I've never managed to escape, indoctrinated by my mother and my rapists.

Forgiveness—of ourselves—is the beacon we both need to navigate through this darkness. As this truth settles between us, a wave of shame engulfs my ethereal form. "I wish I could. But I'm not strong like you," I say, the weight of my self-doubt pressing heavily upon me.

"So, you've embraced the narrative that you're weak, too." Her voice is a blend of sadness and resolve.

I nod slowly, bracing for the moment of revelation when she sees me for what I truly believe myself to be—a useless piece of shit. "I always liked who I was, but I never knew who that was." I reveal the depth of my identity crisis.

Yet, instead of disdain or disappointment, she gazes at me with a compassion that pierces the veil of my self-loathing. "I'm pretty sure I can use my healing magic to blur the memories, make it safe for you to figure out just who you really are, love," she says softly, her words imbued with a powerful blend of love and conviction.

In the quiet aftermath of a profound realization—that we could indeed save each other—a sense of hope pierces the darkness, illuminating the bond we share. This thought, both luminous and promising, cradles my mind until the world fades away and sleep claims me.

Jerking awake at the sound of a shower, a spike of terror rips through me—the bed beside me is empty. Panic tightens its grip as the thought of her absence becomes unbearable. I force my eyes shut, taking a deep breath, trying to anchor myself in the present. My hand, seeking her warmth, finds only the cold indent of her pillow. But as I brush against something, hope flickers to life, dispelling the shadows of fear.

> Jade—because I think of you as my most precious gem and I wish you could see why. You're the epitome of strength and integrity, qualities I not only admire but aspire to embody. You are my guiding light, offering a vision of life and love free from the shadows that once held me captive. Your care shields me from the chaos, just as jade wards off negativity. In return, I hope to offer you the same sanctuary, a haven from the storm. Your love has been my salvation. Thank you for freeing my spirit.
>
> Gone to get coffee and those hot donuts you love.

The note, a testament to her understanding of my deepest fears and insecurities, offers a balm to my soul. Whether these are the words she cannot speak aloud or a prelude to the reassurance she knew I'd crave upon waking, it doesn't matter. Clarity washes over me, guiding my next steps. With a resolve strengthened by her love, I make a quick trip to the bathroom before seizing the hotel pad and pen. It's my turn to convey the inexpressible.

Little dragon, you ignite a fire within me. In your presence, I've discovered the true essence of unconditional love—a gift I never thought I'd possess. Your spirit, a blend of fierce courage and boundless affection, sets the standard by which I measure all beauty and worth.

It is your love that inspires growth, allowing me to transcend my past and embrace the boundless potential of our future together. You are the mirror reflecting the best parts of me, encouraging me to explore the depths of our connection—emotionally, spiritually, and physically—free from the constraints of judgment or societal expectations. Your essence is permanently etched into the very core of my being, a constant reminder that I am home. How fortunate I am to have you, to experience the world through our shared lens of love and acceptance. You, my little dragon, are my everything.

A smile, born of countless shared moments and the recognition of our intertwined fates, plays upon my lips. My Brienne of Tarth, my indomitable little dragon, has indeed inked herself into the fabric of my soul. Together, we've embarked on a journey of discovery, shedding the weight of past fears and societal chains to revel in the purity of our love. In her, I've found not just a partner but a reflection of my deepest desires and highest aspirations. How did I get so lucky? The answer lies in the magic of our bond, a connection that transcends the ordinary and invites us into a realm of extraordinary love and understanding. It's a rare gift an asshole like me doesn't deserve, but I'll take it.

~

Thank you for reading *Dark Angel*!

Join Lilith's Smutty Readers Email List and get a free copy of *Mick's Mission*, a paranormal reverse harem romance!

lilithdarville.com/newsletter

Chapter One: Aleah

Every cell in my body screams for his touch, a touch that will never come. My Troy is gone. I'm so very alone without him, but life must march on. So, I wall off my shock and swim in a moat of numbness. But every Saturday night, our date night, I sit here for hours and bleed my sorrow into a bottle.

I'm perfectly content . . . That's a lie, but we won't go there right now . . . having my weekly vigil in our favorite private dining room at Maison Raul. Well, it was *ours*. Now it's just mine. Troy died. And for the six months since, I've been coming here, trying to recapture the feel of his oh-so-clever hands on my thighs and between my legs. They were some of our happiest moments, and many were in this very room. We were best friends, and there were not enough words to describe the depth of our love, so we'd used our bodies to speak the truth instead.

Even during the pandemic, while everything had been shut down, Raul, the owner and maître d', had graciously met me at the restaurant and let me occupy the space until it was time to pour me into an Uber.

Earlier in the week, my editor called, begging me to return to work, enticing me with an assignment. Now I have to make up my mind: resume some semblance of life or continue to wallow in my grief. But it's more than that. Whether I'm ready to return to work or not, I'm just not sure about this assignment. My confused thoughts have a firm hold as I try to make sense of what's bothering me about it. As a journalist, not every assignment turns my crank, but I don't usually feel any emotional connection with the client even when one does. This time I have.

I'd agreed to a video conference call with the mysterious Cyrus Stone, and something about him nags at me. While I could put part of it down to my grief, there's something more—something dark and possibly dangerous. Or I'm letting my overactive reporter's imagination run away with me. Let's face it, I haven't been able to think past the crushing pain in my chest that started when Troy died.

"Greetings, my dear, it's time for Name This Wine," Raul says as he places a large glass of wine in front of me. He straightens and waits for me to do the swish-see-smell-sip thing with the rich red wine. I've come to know the restaurant owner pretty well during the past six months. He prides himself on his "psychic" ability to match the right wine with a patron's mood, and it's become a weekly game with us. I look up at him and force a smile. "Baco Noir?"

"You got it in one." Raul's voice is filled with a warmth I can't help responding to. "Glass or bottle?"

"Bottle." My answer is his cue that he'll need to load me

into an Uber in an hour or two. Since Troy died, I've genuinely come to know the meaning of "drowning my sorrows."

"Chef has whipped up a beef stroganoff with your name written all over it, or would you prefer to see a menu?" Raul smiles as he wraps a napkin around the neck of the wine bottle before placing it in front of me.

"That sounds awesome. Beef stroganoff it is. Thank you, Raul." I give him another smile that doesn't reach my eyes. Eating, like everything else since Troy died, is no longer a pleasure; it's a necessity. Without food, I'd die, which might not be a bad idea, but I'm not the suicidal type. As if he can read my mind, Raul pats my hand before leaving my private dining room. Before the pocket door slides closed, I catch a glimpse of golden eyes that seem to glow. Warmth floods my body as the light reaches me, and I'm hit in the gut with memories of Troy. But then again, I see Troy everywhere.

I take another sip of my wine as I let my mind wander down memory lane to when Troy had given me an explosive orgasm while I sat on this very spot. I let my head rest against the wall while closing my eyes, letting the memories flood in. The feel of Troy's hands as they pushed apart my thighs and his fingers found my clit. I know I'll only have those experiences in my mind from now on, and I'm having trouble embracing my future as a celibate.

My cell phone rings before I get too far down Pity Party Lane and into the pit of pain that makes up my life these days. My editor Daisy's brilliant smile appears on the screen.

"Hey!" I try to force some cheer in my voice as I pick up.

"Hey, you. Is everything okay? How'd it go?" I can

almost feel Daisy crossing her fingers as she waits for my response.

"It went great." A lie. "I was just about to call you." Semi-truth. I *was* going to call her once I figured out just what to do about this contract offer.

Daisy breathes a massive sigh of what is no doubt relief. "This calls for a drink."

I can't help but smile at her enthusiasm. "Don't get too excited. I'm not sure I'm the best person for this job, hon."

My headphones pick up rustling sounds, and I imagine Daisy settling back on her leather sofa, crossing those shapely legs and taking a sip of wine. "Spill, girlfriend, and don't leave out one tiny detail." Daisy is one of those beautiful women you'd love to hate, except she's so damned nice, you can't help but love her.

I close my eyes again and think about Cy Stone, for once thankful I don't think in pictures. Tall, dark, and very French, the billionaire's presence had overwhelmed me from the moment he filled my computer screen. A presence so imposing, it was almost as if he were in the room with me.

"I look forward to developing a close working relationship with you." Cy's voice had been deep with an undertone of sinister that matched his brooding looks.

I sink deeper into the well-padded booth. Cy's words keep playing in my head, along with the heat from eyes that held mine far too long to mistake his meaning . . . and the flicker of interest it sparked in me.

"There's not much to tell that you don't know, Daise. He said the call confirmed that he wants me to do the series, and he'd contact you with the details, including a list of reading materials for research and a list of the places where I'll conduct his interviews. I told him I'd look over his proposal and let you know my answer. He gave me twenty-four hours."

"Let me add a little incentive. Cy's offering the magazine five million dollars to run a series of five articles on his clubs and lifestyle. His contract will keep us in the black for several years, never mind the hefty portion that comes to you." Daisy sighs. "Not that you care about the money, I know. But we sure could use it." The wistful tone in her voice tugs at my heart. And I can't hate her for that, either, because, with Daisy, there's no subtext to the message. She's not trying to manipulate me at all. If I say no, she'll accept it without malice. But her sigh and tone let me know just how important this is to her.

So I refrain from telling her that I was more than a little put-out at his controlling attitude. *Or that his penetrating gaze made me aware there's still life in my lady bits.* He'd made it clear he'd be calling the shots, and that just isn't how I work . . . Assuming I want to go back to work at all.

"I'll think about it, Daise. I know how important this is to you. I'm just not sure I'm ready to go back to work yet." I slowly rotate my head, trying to ease some of the perpetual tension I carry in my neck and shoulders.

"Ali." Daisy's voice is warm and gentle. "You're going to have to join the land of the living sometime. You'd be the first one to kick my butt if you saw me hurting myself. You know you would. So consider this your kick in the ass. I think you need this. Let me know what you decide."

"I'll text you tomorrow. Be good." I ring off before we can do our usual "but bad is better" exchange.

I squeeze my eyes shut as I let grief, my constant companion, wash over me. Since the day the doctor and I told Troy he only had four to six months to live, I haven't cried. Not even at his funeral. Oh, I started to. Two tears rolled, one down each cheek. Then the funeral director hauled my ass off to sign more papers.

I wish I could cry. Maybe that would relieve some of the weight from the mountain of grief sitting on my chest. The grief makes it very difficult to think past the deep sense of loss that consumes me. But think I must. If I'm to give Cy Stone my answer, I have a lot of research to do, not to mention figuring out the physical reaction I had to this man —I refuse to acknowledge it's a spark of physical attraction.

My nerve endings start simmering when two of the most exquisite-looking men I've ever seen invade my space and jolt me out of my alcohol-induced reverie.

"May I help you?" I squint at the two hunks staring down at me.

"We have a message for you from your Troy. May we sit?" Tall, dark, and very handsome asks.

My adrenaline surges into overdrive at the mention of my deceased husband. The love of my life. Message? It would be just like him to find a way to send me a message from the great beyond, the one he was sure didn't exist. That thought barely has time to form when my rational mind reaches through the alcohol fog. Shit like this just doesn't happen. Not in real life, anyway. This kind of thing only happens in the Netflix shows Troy and I binged on as we coasted through his last months. There had been two requirements when choosing the shows: there had to be magic, and either good had to triumph over evil, or there had to be a happily ever after.

No, you cannot sit, asshole. Have you lost your mind? I give them both the once-over while I get my racing pulse back under control. How dare they invade my privacy? My heart continues to hammer although I have no idea why.

I should be afraid. Lord knows with my history of abuse, being confronted by two strange guys should have vaulted me into protection mode. But I feel nothing but the weird hum, that simmering feeling. I'm perfectly safe, and I'll have to get used to talking to strange men if I take this assignment. Besides, all I have to do is yell, and Raul will throw their asses out posthaste. And there's something familiar about them. I wave my hand as if I'm a frigging princess allowing them a royal audience. It won't hurt to hear them out.

The two men sit, and a hum starts warming every cell in my body and intensifies as a breath of air caresses my cheek, drawing my attention to the men. The one sitting to my left is the epitome of tall, dark, and handsome but in a very different way from Cyrus Stone. While Cy reeks of European nobility, this man reminds me of an Israeli prince. Thick, curly black hair frames a sculpted face holding molten gold eyes. On my right sits a drop-dead gorgeous blond god. Certainly, someone so perfect must be Apollo or even Zeus himself. I rack my brains for the names of other gods while I examine them. Both have smooth olive skin and look at me with undisguised attraction.

"Okay, let's hear it." Not my most polite welcome, but these guys have a lot of explaining to do.

Gorgeous blond gives me a wicked grin and holds out his hand. "Forgive our intrusion. I'm Tristan Adams, and this is my brother, Cassiel." Magnetic blue eyes capture and hold my gaze, making me feel more than a tad as if I'm slowly being reeled in. The instant our hands meet, a jolt of electricity zings through me. Those are the closest words I can find to describe the strange sensation—one I haven't felt since the moment I met Troy.

Cassiel's hand replaces Tristan's, and a similar bolt strikes. I can't conceal the shudder that rolls through me.

"What's the message?"

End of Sample
To continue reading, be sure to pick up *Atroyel* at your favorite retailer.

ALSO BY LILITH DARVILLE

Wicked Angels Series

Dark Urban Fantasy Romance

Interconnected Standalones

Follow a team of fallen angels as they fight against human trafficking and navigate the blurred lines between good and evil. Set in Pandemonium, a notorious club where they blend in with humans, this heart-pounding series will leave you breathless. Don't miss out on this intense and spicy journey of redemption and second chances.

.

Rogue Angels Series

Dark Urban Fantasy Romance

Completed Series

Rogue Angels is a twist retelling of the Snow White fairytale. Enjoy an adventure with fated mates, midlife crisis, and evil demons. This story includes themes of love, sacrifice, and self-discovery.

.

Sexy Sins Afterlife Retreat Series

Paranormal Reverse Harem Romance

Completed Series

Warning: This series has one strong woman and four dangerously sexy immortal men. She's been their fated mate in every life they've lived and they refuse to live one without her. Read this series if you like why choose romance with a paranormal twist and hunky guys times four!

.

Masquerade Club Series

Dark Contemporary Romance

Completed Series

A contemporary saga with a side dish of spice and a second chance romance for two people you'll never forget. The Masquerade Club is exclusive and available only for the ultra-rich where all your dreams and fantasies come true. Join the party and fall in love with Connor and Katherine in this angst-ridden suspense-filled series.

.

ABOUT THE AUTHOR

Lilith Darville is a *USA Today* bestselling author of dangerously delicious romance, including sizzling paranormal reverse harem, urban fantasy and contemporary stories. Her books are guaranteed to make readers flush and blush. She lives in Ontario with the memories of her beloved Hubster and their somewhat challenged cat.

lilithdarville.com

www.ingramcontent.com/pod-product-compliance
Lightning Source LLC
Chambersburg PA
CBHW022303310726

48973CB00001B/190